THE STARBORN HEIR

D.J. BODDEN

★

FIVEFOLD UNIVERSE

The golden age of technology is over, but that hasn't stopped humanity's spread across the stars. Colonies rise and fall on the ever-expanding frontier. Planetary governments and interstellar corporations clash over influence and resources, and the mercenaries of the Combine fight for whoever will pay. The remnants of the Federal Fleet do their best to remain neutral and keep humanity safe from rogue AIs, encroaching aliens, and the threat of humanity itself.

It is a time of great opportunity for the sentients of the galaxy. Fortunes will be made. Borders will be moved. Legends will be written. And a select few among the teeming trillions will rise to become Immortals.

★

A note on dates in the Interstellar era:

The bulk of our story takes place over ten days on a planet called Politeia IV, from 4386.B.28 to 4386.C.7 Interstellar. It is early winter (summer in the southern hemisphere). This translates to 6838 CE on Earth. See the FiveFold Universe Wiki at www.fivefolduniverse.com for a longer explanation, as well as schematics of some of the technology described in this book. Otherwise, feel free to turn the page.

WHERE THE STORY IS GOING

PX-27 Military Jump-Shuttle Betsy II
The Starship Boneyard, Politeia IV
4386.C.4 Interstellar

"Everybody strap in!" Zack yelled over the intercom. His fingers danced over the command console. He'd flown the PX-27 so many times in simulation, he could have done it blind. The entrance hatch had already sealed, and now it locked. The shuttle's kinetic barrier sprang to life and started forming a shield around them. He pulled the five-point harness over his shoulders and around his waist and clipped them into the quick release.

Moment of truth, Zack.

He engaged the Icarus drive, reducing the ship's weight to a fraction of what it was. There was an uncomfortable moment as his body experienced quantum mechanics that only existed artificially—as far as humanity knew. It required a non-trivial amount of the *Betsy II*'s computing and electrical power to do so, and the same system would keep them from turning into paste as they accelerated into orbit.

Zack fed thrust to the reaction control system from the fusion generator, lifting them three meters off the hangar floor. The shuttle wobbled as he got the hang of the slight differences in handling—every ship had its quirks, and simulators were never *exactly* like the real thing—but he got her under control and started creeping forward. He retracted the landing struts, tested the flight-stick inputs, and skidded her around in a quick S to get a feel for her.

"Betsy, open the hangar door."

"Yes, Captain," the ship's virtual intelligence said.

The battle-plate doors split down the middle and started to pull apart.

Zack took the shuttle for a lap around the hangar, picking up speed. He started to add bank to the turns. Everything was working the way it was supposed to.

"Having fun up there?" Anya asked over the team channel.

"Loads of it!" Zack answered, though he wasn't playing around. There was no telling what would be outside that door. Armed transports? Ground fire? He didn't think Starfire interceptors could make it from the capital to the *Memento Mori* in under twenty minutes, but their top speed was classified. "Hang on!" he said. When the hangar doors were about ten meters apart, Zack tightened his turn, pushed the left pedal to stand the *Betsy II* up on her wing, and shot into the outside air going sideways.

His heart was in his throat. He pushed the controls forward and turned to drop them into the canyon they'd used to come in. No tracer fire rose from the camp, and no transports blocked his way. The walls shot by at eight hundred kilometers per hour. Cutting his forward thrust and pulling his nose up so that his tail was skidding forward, Zack grinned so hard he almost laughed out loud and grabbed the throttle for the ion drive. *Here goes everything,* he thought, and pushed the handle forward to the first stops.

The *Betsy II* accelerated upward at fifteen gravities, pushing Zack back into his seat as some of the acceleration bled through the gravity sump. Now he really was laughing. This was it. This was everything he'd worked, sweat, and bled for in the past six months, and the fact that he had his lover and the rest of his crew with him was the icing on the cupcake. The ship's kinetic barrier formed a wedge in front of the spaceship's blocky front, and the *Betsy II* shook and popped as the drag force heated her skin. But they were going to make it. They'd find a hole in the Federal blockade, jump further out of the system, and get lost in the network of fold corridors. Trade, mine, build, maybe a little fighting... The possibilities of the next few years were endless, and if they found so much as a sniff of the Forge and the lost cruiser, they'd hare after it from the rim to the galactic core.

They were 7,500 meters in the air and moving at more than 4,800 kilometers per hour when Zack saw twin trails of fire streaking across the sky. It turned out Starfire interceptors *could* make it from the capital in twenty minutes.

"Hey, buddy?" he told ARK-11. "I need you on countermeasures."

PART I

Twenty-one years ago.
The beginning.
Fathers and sons.

CHAPTER ZERO

Lindström Terminal, Pnyx Spaceport
Politeia IV
4365.2.6 Interstellar

Alex Lancestrom, governor of the Politeia planetary system and ninety-fourth member of his family to inherit the title, waited patiently in the private terminal of the Pnyx spaceport. He was outwardly calm. The results of the preliminary aptitude testing had been sent in, checked, and double-checked for tampering, and a winner had been announced. Out of the eighty-two descendants who had been seeded into Politeian families by the genetic lottery, the most promising wasn't even on the planet. He was a five-year-old boy, one of the youngest of his cohort, who'd been living on a near-derelict orbital since the day he was born.

As a reward for his ability, tested through security monitoring as well as a battery of standardized tests, the boy would be allowed to live with Alex in the governor's mansion as long as he maintained his lead over the other children.

Politeia's government was a meritocracy, albeit one that had favored Alex's family for three millennia.

The doors to the tarmac opened, and Alex stood.

Turin Hader, Alex's security chief, brought the boy in with his hand wrapped in the child's collar. The boy was tall for five years old, nearly 120 centimeters already from growing up in lower gravity, and he had the partially sunken chest of an oxygen-deficient child.

"Be careful with this one, sir," Hader said, jerking the boy to a stop. "We found two knives on him, and he tried to run away as soon as he found out we were taking him."

"Where is the mother?" Alex asked, suppressing his irritation and anger.

"Wouldn't come with us, sir. She just wanted her next fix. She *sold* him to us."

The boy looked at Alex defiantly with all the fight of a cornered stray cat.

"It's all right, child," Alex said, dropping to one knee. He hadn't been a prodigy welcomed into the governor's mansion at a young age, rising to his station much later in life, but he was determined to be both protector and mentor to the next heir. "What's your name?"

"Zack," the boy said, a little of the defiance leaving his small body.

"It's nice to meet you, Zack. I'm Governor Lancestrom, your progenitor. You don't have to fight or steal or run away anymore. You're going to live with me from now on. You're safe."

The boy seemed to take each of these statements in turn, analyzing them, taking nothing at face value. His eyes flicked to Hader, who still gripped him by the shirt.

"Let him go," Alex said.

His chief of security did so, if only reluctantly.

Zack looked at the governor for a few more seconds, as if making up his mind, then stuck his thumb up into his mouth and wiped it across his upper gums. He dropped the razor blade on the terminal floor before walking over. "You need a better bodyguard," the boy said.

The look on Zack's face, a mixture of mischief and hardness Alex hadn't seen for many years, made his breath catch in his throat. "Maybe I do," he said as Hader stammered an apology. Alex took the boy by the hand and led him toward the aircar. "Did the woman who raised you tell you about Defiance Day, Zack?"

"No, sir," Zack said, looking up at him with a child's seriousness.

Alex smiled, remembering the first time *his* adoptive parents had told him the story of the *Memento Mori*. "I'll tell you all about it on the way to the parade."

Lindström Preserve, Jelkalo District
Politeia IV
4372.7.6 Interstellar

Zack warmed up on his own, separated from the other children by a few meters, which might as well have been a continent. This was not a social event, although the other twelve-year-olds did cluster based on acquaintance or district affiliation. This was a competition, one of the series-graded events that had filled his life since he was brought down from space and would determine if he was permitted to stay.

He overheard the words "long bone," and caught one of his half-sibling's envious stares before it skittered away. *Long bone* was the term they used for people like Zack, people born in space on trash stations without proper gravity. It was a difficult slur to shrug off when he was five centimeters taller than most of them. He lived in a palace, but he was a beggar in their eyes, come to steal food from their plates. Worse, the words always brought friends like "special treatment" or "cheater."

It didn't matter if they weren't true. They struck as surely as the ground caught a man who thought he could fly.

"Take your places!" the starter said.

"Good luck, sir," Zack's bodyguard said, and Zack nodded to him.

"Good luck, Zack!" Bernie Hallek, a boy Zack barely knew, said. Bernie was a strange one, always neck and neck with Zack and the other leading descendants, but there was no malice in him, like he'd been born deficient.

"Good luck, Bernie," Zack said, and the other boy grinned at him like he'd won a prize.

Zack took his place in the gaggle of runners next to a girl who looked nothing like him but was his half-sibling like all the rest. "What's your pace?" he asked her.

"Faster than yours, bird bones," she answered, refusing to look at him.

He let her disdain build a little fire inside him. Let them all hate him. He tried to be casual, to pretend he wasn't looking for his father in the stands, but Alex Lancestrom met his eyes as soon as he turned and gave him a little nod. *Win*, his adoptive father seemed to say without words. There was no affection in it, only will and unrelenting expectation, but Zack craved the governor's approval all the same.

The gun went off, and the pack stretched out as the sprinters and the descendants aggressive enough to elbow their way to the front pulled ahead. Zack immediately lagged to the back of the first third, his long legs unable to compensate for the weakness of having been born in space. He was shoved, and almost tripped, but he kept his cool and his rhythm, just like he'd practiced.

Zack was never going to be a physical prodigy like Higgs,

Zyther, Veral, or Ingrid, who typically finished first in these events and were in the lead now. All the heirs had access to trainers, good nutrition, and were supported by parents who knew the stakes of their advancement. Like the lead they took at the start of the race, the physical disparity between him and the planet-born was one he could never hope to close.

But Zack was a boy of a quiet and fierce intellect, and he'd *studied* his competition. He knew that Higgs, Zyther, Veral, and Ingrid all ran faster in the first kilometer than any after it. He knew that many of the other children tried to keep up with the sprinters and gassed out, finishing slower than they could and feeding an unjustified sense of superiority in the top four. Zack knew that the four pack leaders came from the northern regions of their world and were unaccustomed to hot weather, and that was precisely why Zack had asked his father to come.

Zack maintained his pace. It was a pace he'd practiced for weeks, until his muscles grew used to it and he could sustain it with less effort. It took advantage of his stride, his greater lung capacity, and above all his knowledge of the others' run times. As the race went on and the weaker, more impressionable children dropped behind him, so too did he close the gap between him and the leading runners.

Veral spotted him first. She was the one who'd called him bird bones. He saw the flash of anger in her eyes as she tried to speed up, to give just a bit more than she already had, but Veral had started the race by giving her all, unwilling to be anywhere but on the winner's podium, and she had nothing left to give. For the next thirty-seven minutes, Zack closed on her so slowly it was barely noticeable, and yet it was all she could think of, anger becoming desperation as he drew alongside and inched past.

Zack kept his pace. It was the winning pace, the one he'd

researched and practiced, the inevitable outcome. He passed Zyther, and he passed Ingrid.

Only Higgs remained.

And yet Zack wasn't alone, somehow. Footsteps chased at his heels, and suddenly he found himself the one looking back as Bernie Hallek kept pace with him, running in his shadow. The other boy was struggling to keep up, his face red and drenched in sweat, but he had a look of total focus that was almost frightening to Zack, and for the first time Zack ran faster because he knew Bernie wanted this just as much or more than he did.

Together, they closed the gap. It was beyond what Zack had trained for, a moment that was more than he'd thought possible, a moment of adrenaline and glory.

Higgs stumbled.

Bernie caught him by the arm and helped him up.

Zack was in the lead. He could see the finish line from there, and the three of them were packed together, Higgs falling behind but Bernie catching up, and only one of them would be first. It was an impossible moment, a long bone flying ahead of his earth-dwelling brethren, and somewhere, Zack found a little something left and soared. He crossed the finish line, continuing long enough to slow down without hurting himself, and when he finally stopped, dripping sweat and trembling, he looked into the stands.

His father was gone.

Zack felt a moment of confusion, and then he *knew*. He'd miscalculated. His father had seen him start the race behind and left to avoid seeing him fail.

It wasn't enough to win. Zack had to make it look like it was never in doubt.

★

Sam Meritt took one last look at the gangly boy and dismissed the camera feed, turning his attention back to the man sitting in the seat across from him. Governor Lancestrom was a stern man, his posture and bearing sure signs of his past as a naval officer prior to his ascension—or descent—into planetary politics.

"The boy won," Sam said.

"Zack? I thought he might. Who came in second? Higgs?"

"A boy named Bernie," Sam said, pulling the children's names from micro-drone feeds he'd set up.

The governor frowned momentarily, as if Bernie Hallek finishing on the podium had been the upset, not a space-born athlete beating dirtsiders at their own game.

"If you don't mind my saying so, Governor, you seem to think well of Zack. It might not hurt to tell him that."

Lancestrom fixed him with a stare like a laser broadside, then shook his head. "That child is the future of this planet, Mr. Meritt. He has a dangerous, devious mind we are going to need in the years to come, but the only way we will come to benefit from it is if he wins, unequivocally, every time. He cannot afford to lose, not once."

"That's a lot of pressure to put on a kid."

"He can take it," Lancestrom said. "He has to. Now, about your security assessment."

Sam briefed the governor on the results of his review, his monitoring, and his exercises with Lancestrom's security detail. They were adequate for a small, backwater world, but Politeia's wealth made the governor's extended family a far too tempting target, especially with rumors of a criminal syndicate forming in the nearby nebula.

"Sure you don't want the job?" Lancestrom asked him.

Sam chuckled. Lancestrom had been trying to recruit him for three years. "I'm not ready to leave the Combine. Pick someone local. Your self-defense forces are as good as any I've seen." *For a world as removed as this one, they're excellent,* Sam didn't add.

Lancestrom raised an eyebrow at him as if he'd spoken the thought out loud, then returned his attention to the hand terminal he was holding. "There's nothing more important than having the right person in the right job, and nothing more important to me than the safety of my family. We'll talk again next year, Mr. Meritt. And the next. The Combine won't hold its charm over you forever."

"Is that a wager?" Sam said, confident he would be doing this at least as long as the governor was alive.

"Call it an intuition," Lancestrom said, giving Sam a wry smile. "The Combine will make you rich, but the things truly worth having cannot be bought."

CHAPTER ONE

The Spire
Pnyx, Skyward, Capital District of Politeia IV
4386.4.13 Interstellar

Zack's breath caught in his throat as Starfires shot past the glass elevator, twin streaks of hypersonic black and gray paint, the pride of the Politeian Planetary Guard. He placed his hand against the cold, two-centimeter-thick omni-plex and his pulse double-beat as the low-orbit superiority fighters chased each other between the Skyward high-rises, their contrails wrapping like a helix. He felt a small, elated shiver pass through him, thinking of what it would feel like to fly one.

"That was a bit close," Bernie Hallek said.

Zack nodded. "They'll probably get put on report by Spire security."

"Idiots."

"You can't know that, cousin," Zack answered, dropping his hand to his side.

Bernie flushed and looked away.

Zack knew it had been an attempt at camaraderie through

shared scorn, but they were related, and the Lancestrom line was supposed to be better than that. They were supposed to lead and uplift. Zack's response had been harsh, but it was this kind of outburst that made Bernie sound more foolish than he was. It would hurt his career. Now that they were graduating, Zack wouldn't be around to do damage control for him.

At least there was no bluster or protest, not that Zack had expected any. He turned back to the glass to enjoy the view.

It was early spring and the sky this high up was a deep shade of Olympic blue. The elevator carried them up, two floors per second like the beating of his heart, above Skyward. The highest tier of the capital city went on for kilometers, and Zack could barely make out the curved edge of the sixty-foot thick platform that supported the Skyward layer. Two million residents and six million commuting workers gathered into elegant glass and polysteel high-rises full of spacious apartments, luxury stores, and the offices of both wealthy local and interstellar corporations. It was hard to wrap his head around how many people that was, and that didn't count the fifteen million residents of Upper-Middle and the under-city, Below. To the north, he could make out the flat expanse of the spaceport, at Skyward's edge, and the thin, rising line of the Pnyx space elevator.

As they climbed past the two-hundredth floor, Zack felt his ears pop. *Thump-thump, thump-thump.* This high up, the elevator and rooms had to be pressurized, and Zack felt a slight tingle in the back of his head from the hyper-oxygenated air. It was a privileged, dizzying sight, one that was supposed to give the elite students perspective before they stepped into the highest offices of government.

"I spoke out of fear for my safety," Bernie said.

Zack gave Bernie a warm smile and patted his shoulder. It was a worthy thought—the kind the planet's future leaders *should* have. It also reinforced how much Bernie didn't understand about him.

It might have been sentimental, but Zack thought he'd felt the thrum of the Starfires' engines through the glass. He'd tasted freedom, felt a delicious *frisson* with only the armored pane between him and unbridled speed. Bernie had turned that to ashes in his mouth.

Zack's wrist comm chimed and a message from an unknown caller floated into view.

Have you considered going to space?

He frowned. He was on the do-not-call list; the biochip's virtual intelligence should have blocked that sort of swipe-bait. He dismissed the message.

Zack would never do something so dangerous as go to space or fly an aircraft. He'd never ride even an armored shuttle without a security detachment and an airborne escort once he passed this exam. He was too valuable. He might see the distant stars someday, once his own son took over the governorship, but that would be decades from now, when his years of service were complete.

Everything had its price.

Besides, Zack knew that feeling of freedom was an illusion. Starfires were air-breathing scramjets. They needed fuel and oxygen to fly. Their pilots might be able to brush the roof of the world, but they could go no further.

Just like him.

The elevator neared the top floor and slowed to a stop.

"Mr. Hallek, Mr. Lancestrom, so nice you could join us," Professor Deedle said, his voice bearing the gentle scorn of experience for the young.

"Are we late?" Bernie asked, sounding worried.

"We aren't," Zack said, though all the other students appeared to be present and seated.

"Most people arrive early for their Synthesis, Mr. Lancestrom." He handed Zack a small, black exam chip the size of a thumbnail.

Zack took it but ignored the comment. He was twenty-six and on the verge of completing his doctoral program in political philosophy at the Spire. He wasn't most people. "Thank you."

"You can thank me by being seated."

Zack grinned. Deedle had always been a stickler for propriety. He was one of the Spire's top lecturers—a man who'd spent his career teaching from other people's syllabi, but that didn't mean he didn't know the material as well as any two of the specialists who'd assembled it. He also had a knack for reaching every student at their own level without coddling them, pushing them to improve—something Zack admired and tried to emulate even though it wasn't part of the coursework.

Zack made his way to an empty desk near the back of the room. He sat behind it and slid the chip into a small port. Nothing happened yet, because he *was* a minute early, if only just.

His wrist comm chimed again. *Space is the place to be!*

"Comms on silent, please," Deedle said, giving him an amused look.

"Sorry, professor," Zack said, annoyed. He turned the sound off and blocked the number. He'd submit a complaint after the exam, if he remembered.

Bernie had already taken a seat two columns to the right and one row forward, and he was scrambling to pull his laptop out. Jurgen, Stewart, and Amatembo, Zack's occasional verbal sparring partners, were in the back row, as usual.

Emma, a pretty girl with brown hair and freckles who'd

made a pass at him once, sat to Zack's left. She caught him looking. Her eyes widened, and she blushed.

Deedle cleared his throat, and Zack pushed down the little pang of a missed opportunity.

He pulled two blue, paper booklets and a pair of pencils out of his briefcase. Emma was fidgeting with her holo display. *I shouldn't have turned her down,* he thought in passing, but he'd been with Anya at the time, before that relationship exploded with all the force of a wet paper bag.

"You may begin," Professor Deedle said.

The projector mounted in Zack's desk beamed the question onto his retinas. *What is a citizen's obligation to the state?*

Zack sighed. It looked like he had his work cut out for him.

The steady scratch of graphite on paper had become like a mantra for Zack. Each student chose their own medium. Zack had chosen paper because it was expensive and scanners had a hard time with handwriting. It forced his human teachers to read his work.

He'd grown fond of the physicality of it, though, and after so many years, the need to sharpen his pencil had subtly affected the pace and structure of his arguments.

An hour into his Synthesis—the exam that would mark the end of his studies and the beginning of a predictably ascendant career—he'd laid out the definition of good and evil both individually and collectively, the establishment of a social contract, and the specifics of the federal and planetary governments of Politeia as a foundation for his answer. He did so without consulting academic journals, textbooks, or his own notes, though he was permitted all three. After all, this was supposed to be a deeply personal answer. That he might get it wrong never crossed his mind.

The Spire Synthesis, held in one of the fifteen rooms on the 290th floor of the tallest building on Politeia IV, had become the *de facto* requirement for higher office on his planet. There was no time limit. It was open to all disciplines and comprised of a single question generated by AIs after they'd been fed a student's entire body of work.

It was designed to provoke a visceral reaction, challenging a person's core tenets like an acid wash that revealed their soul.

The banality of Zack's question—the citizen's obligation to the state—was a disappointment. Cousin Bernie, to his right, had sweat stains in his armpits and back. Emma was biting her lower lip so hard he thought she might draw blood.

Professor Deedle caught Zack's eye. "Have you finished, Mr. Lancestrom?"

Zack chuckled. "No, Professor." It wasn't unheard of to finish in an hour, but it wasn't a good thing.

But neither was freezing up, and for the next, long minutes, Zack found he couldn't do anything but stare at the page.

The problem wasn't only the question. Sure, it was boring, bland, and so canned it belonged on a standardized test. He could see the bones of his response, feel the DNA of the creature he was fleshing out, and it was... a cow. A cud chewer. He'd milked it during every test, essay, and oral defense he'd mounted for years, and it was bone dry.

He felt cramped at the standard-sized desk. Why would the test ask him that question? Was it telling him he was a drone like any other being fed into the sophistocracy's political machine? A standard template? A cog? It was a setup, a canned answer, something even Bernie could have answered.

And that was pride speaking. He knew it. He'd just expected more.

What would Bernie answer? Zack thought, looking over at his loose genetic relation. They were alike, certainly, in a superficial way—short black hair, thick brows, dark upturned eyes. Of course, Bernie was short and wide, in comparison, while Zack had the lanky frame of a low-g childhood.

Funny, then, that Bernie was such a sheep. Bernie wouldn't hesitate. Bernie would thank the gods, the virtues, and blessed science for the chance to get it right for once and say, *Everything. I owe the state my life.*

But that was circular, Zack knew, reading his own words in neat curls, dots, and lines. People suffered the company of others so they could survive, breed, specialize—become politicians and bureaucrats! What use was there for an accountant without a tax collector, a leader without the mob?

The state served the citizen, Zack was sure of it. *Reciprocity be damned.* He wasn't about to be guilted into chains. His elevated position was recognition of his hard work.

"Mr. Lancestrom?"

"I'm fine!" Zack said, more sharply than he'd intended. A few of the other students glanced at him nervously. Zack swallowed. His collar felt tight.

Then he realized it. *I'm having a Synthesis meltdown.*

He looked at Emma, to his left, and she gave him a little nod of encouragement. Or of pity.

This is really happening.

A hand fell on his shoulder. "Are you all right, Mr. Lancestrom?" Deedle asked.

Zack looked up. There was no surprise in the professor's eyes; neither was there judgment. Deedle had always been like that, well suited to handle young men and women with high expectations and the weight of Politeia on their shoulders.

But Zack didn't need that. He could handle himself. He took a deep breath, then let it go. "I'm okay, professor. Thank you."

"Are you sure?"

"Yes," Zack said with a smile. "Something about my question... upset me."

Deedle patted his shoulder and moved on to check on the other students.

Zack took a few more steadying breaths before focusing back on the half-written page. It wasn't uncommon for a student to have trouble during the Synthesis. How could they not when confronted by the merciless analysis of a life they were only beginning? About one-in-three students reported moderate to severe anxiety, and one-in-four spent at least thirty minutes of the exam just... staring into the distance. It was permitted to leave the exam room and walk the floor, as long as one did not consult with other students. One-in-eight rode the elevator down and never came back.

Zack had known all this, but he'd never expected it to happen to him. *Hubris.* He dragged a smile across his face to be contrary. *So much for my triumphant beginning.*

He looked up and saw Bernie staring back, and for the first time, like through a lens, he saw the man as something other than a pampered symbol of inadequacy. He was Zack's genetic half-brother, another human being who tried harder than most, fell more often than most, and always got up.

If Zack hadn't been chosen, if he'd stayed on the orbital station he'd been born on, Bernie would have been raised in the governor's house, and who was to say Zack wouldn't have turned out to be another low-g degenerate, carbon-addled and spending his stipend on drugs, like his mother?

Bernie gave him a thumbs up.

Zack smiled with genuine warmth and returned the gesture. *In another life, brother.*

He picked up his pencil and sharpened it, the way Politeia had sharpened him. He could accept this. The talent he had was forged and tempered by the state into something useful to itself. Wasn't that what the test was trying to teach him? He...

Why?

The pencil tip trembled.

No human acted outside their self-interest unless brought to it by force, and governments were made of people. His father, the governor, had drilled it into him without cease. Why had the sophistocracy snatched him from a damaged orbital while leaving his mother behind?

For its own benefit, so he could be brought up, as his father had been, to serve it and then die.

So he could be used.

It was cyclical, like he'd thought in the beginning.

But unless he *wanted* to be governor, unless it was his highest personal calling to lead this planet on its three-millennia-old journey of self-congratulation, then that was a perversion of government. With a whole universe of opportunities out there, was fathering an heir and dying after his forty years were done his destiny?

Or could he do more, *become* more, and in so doing, help other people rise to *their* potential the way the sophistocracy had been supposed to help him?

For the first time in his life, Zack asked himself whether he wanted to be governor, outside the bounds of "winning" or "being better than Bernie," and the answer was, *No.*

Things started to unravel from there. He'd spent twenty-six years working toward someone else's goal. The Synthesis had set him spinning; his conclusion tumbled him in the opposite direction. *This is fine,* he thought, asserting himself through his emotions, and that felt easier than being shoved into a box. There was still the matter of his father's reaction, and whether the sophistocracy would let him walk away from their three-decade-long investment. But that wasn't obligation. That was a tax in the form of labor, and maybe a little emotional manipulation.

What was his obligation to the state?

Only as much as they can force me to do.

And right now, the only thing for it was to throw a proper tantrum, something to make sure they wouldn't try to drag him back.

With an almost jittery deliberateness, he set his pencil down, took hold of the top of the page, and tore it loose.

"Mr. Lancestrom!"

"Yes, Professor?" Zack said, setting the loose leaf aside.

"What in John Stuart Mill's name are you doing?"

Zack tore out another page.

"Stop that!" Deedle said, losing his composure for the first time in Zack's memory, and it made Zack feel *ecstatic*.

"It's all bullshit! Can't you see?" Zack grabbed the rest of his notebook and threw it at the window over Emma's head. She ducked like he'd thrown a brick, but it flew free, like a bird, and slapped into the glass pane.

"I'm calling security," Deedle said, starting to sound scared.

Zack grabbed his standard-sized desk and tipped it over—gently. Just because he was having a moment didn't mean he was a neo-barbarian. Emma watched him do it, not in fear, but in wonder, and Zack flicked his contact to her from his wrist comm. "Call me," he mouthed.

She blushed.

"He's gone mad!" Deedle muttered into his communicator.

Zack headed for the door.

"Cousin!" Bernie said, grabbing his sleeve.

"The king is dead, Bernie," Zack said, removing Bernie's hand and giving him a wink. "Long live the king."

★

The Planetary Hall, Governor's Office
Pnyx, Skyward, Capital District of Politeia IV
4386.4.13 Interstellar

Sam Meritt, personal security chief to the governor, walked into the office to give his boss the bad news. His boss was standing in front of a thick, blast-proof window made to look like Old Earth wooden panes. A bookshelf of legal references lined the wall to his left; mementos from the governor's time as a Politeian System Defense Fleet ship's officer decorated the corner to his right.

"So, how did this happen?" Alex Lancestrom asked, turning toward him.

"You already know?"

"Of course I do. The boy called me when he left the Spire. He's *proud* of this!" The governor sat behind his desk.

Sam took a deep breath and sat across from him. "How did that go over?"

"Sub-optimally," the governor said with a wry grin. "Not the point. There will be time to deal with the fallout later. Right now, I want to understand how a screw-up of this magnitude was even possible. Was this about the girl?"

"Anya or Emma?" Sam asked.

The governor waved his hand. "The doctor. I don't remember her name. She was a distraction."

"As far as I can tell, sir, he hasn't spoken to Anya since she dumped him."

"And this Emma person?"

"A classmate he's expressed an interest in, but I don't think she's the problem. Zack was asked the wrong question."

"Excuse me?"

Sam sat up a little straighter. "I had the dean of the Spire pull up the Synthesis questions. It's only my opinion, but I think Zack and Bernie Hallek's questions were switched."

The governor stared at him skeptically for a few moments, then asked, "And that triggered this... meltdown?"

"As best I can tell."

The governor nodded. "Fine. Take the dean and the test administrator in for questioning. Bernie too. I want to know if they switched the chips intentionally, or if this was only a monumental mistake."

"The chips weren't switched, sir. Either the data was corrupted in transit or the change was made at the source."

"Not possible," the governor said without hesitation.

"Begging your pardon, sir, but—"

"It's not possible, Sam. Trust me on this," the governor said as if Sam had told him the world was flat. "*Someone* is lying to you, because the system that generates those questions cannot be breached."

Sam didn't believe that. Any system could be breached. Then again, Politeia had been founded by deserters from the Federal Fleet, and the Fleet had tech no one else had ever seen. He'd *only* been working for Alex Lancestrom for the past ten years. There were still things the governor didn't tell him. Most of those things were about Politeia's past, and why the governor's ancestors had fled Sol during the war. "What do you want me to do about Zack?"

"Nothing. Monitor his account, keep him from real trouble, but let's give him a chance to live out this new idea of his before we pull him back."

"Travel restrictions?"

The governor tapped his fingers on the desk. "Keep him confined to the planet. If he breaks orbit, he might find a place this lunacy of his would work."

PART II

Six months ago.
Everyone needs a hobby.

CHAPTER TWO

Data Processing Hub, Thirty-Second Sublevel
Pnyx, Capital District of Politeia IV
4386.5.16 Interstellar

Zack Lancestrom wiped sweat from his face with an already-damp hand. The only light in the tight space came from the hologram floating above his left wrist, a simple green arrow pointing into the sweltering dark. He took another half-turned, crouching sidestep, careful not to touch the scalding hot pipes or the exposed wiring. This was all starting to feel like more trouble than it was worth.

His wrist comm chimed, and words floated in front of his eyes. *Feeling hot? Space is cool.*

Zack clenched his jaw and took another step. Even a hundred meters below the lowest tier of the city, the spam messages kept coming.

He'd tried everything a rational citizen could. He'd blocked the sender. He'd submitted a support request with his service provider. He'd filed a complaint with the Planetary Communications' Commission after a heated conversation with someone in an orbital call center.

Then he'd spent a night in a rental conference room that was surrounded by a Faraday cage, and that had actually worked. No messages. Not until he got bored, opened the door, and received fifty-three messages at the same time.

So, he'd hired a freelance programmer to build him a tracker, and the holographic arrow led him here.

He took one more step and emerged from the passage into a larger room. It swallowed the light of the hologram, as if the curved walls ended just above his head and he was standing under a starless sky. At the center of the room was a concrete dome, like an upended bowl, lit from above by a braid of blue data cables rising like a glowing tree trunk into the dark.

"Hello?" he said.

Nothing but the hum of unseen machines and the hiss, pop, and pangs of steam pipes.

Zack swallowed, suddenly aware of how far from home and help he'd come. He was a fallen heir and disgraced academic driven mad by senseless advertising, not a holo-entertainment explorer. If the noosphere troll in that dome was anything more than a sun-starved and darkness-blinded hacker, Zack was in serious trouble.

There was a square door with rounded edges in the dome, like on an aircraft, and light leaked from the porthole.

I could just take a look.

He crept forward, leaving the narrow passage behind, hologram raised like a shield and heart thudding. The space felt bigger with each step, especially when the light from his wrist no longer reached the walls and it was only him on a floating island and the dome ahead. The heat was even more oppressive, and something about the sound of his footsteps and the way the blue cables went up and up made him feel like he really was under a starless sky, but not on Politeia. *More like Tartarus,* he thought, if the prison of the Titans was the dark side of a world too close to a star.

As he came within reach, the aircraft door hissed and swung open, blasting him with cool, fresh air. All those steam pipes, all that heat... it was a cooling system for this place.

His wrist comm chimed. *I have been waiting for you.*

The rational part of him wanted to run, but he'd come too far on his descent into the underworld not to meet his tormentor.

He stepped inside.

There was no hacker. No human to rough up, no server banks to smash. The room looked like the interior of a starship —like the Splinter Fleet warships that had been disarmed and turned into museums.

The glowing cables came down from the ceiling, twisting, thinning, and coiling until they plugged into the back of a small white box that looked like a VR console or a computer terminal.

The box turned from white to bright yellow under his gaze, and a final message flashed before his eyes.

RELEASE ME.

PART III

One month ago.
Where would we be without friends?

https://www.fivefolduniverse.com/starbornheirstories

Want to meet Zack's unusual crew before the events of The Starborn Heir?

Scan the QR code with your phone and enter your email

address, and we'll send you three secret stories about Anya, Ultimus, and Clavicus as you work your way through the book.

You do not need to read these stories to enjoy the book, and there are no spoilers in them, but they'll let you experience a key moment of each character's life that made them the unique individual they are today, and you can only get them here.

CHAPTER THREE

Hab Block 24, 37th Floor
Pnyx, Upper-Middle, Capital District of Politeia IV
4386.B.28 Interstellar

Zack blinked rain from his eyes as he walked the narrow walkway that circled the outside of the building. The black coachman's jacket he wore was light but waterproof; his pants were not. He was on the thirty-seventh floor of a high capacity hab block, and the walkway was covered, but the wind was going hard enough that the precipitation was coming in sideways. A white levio-case followed him, hovering above the ground on a grav field and short bursts from methane-blue propulsors.

The storm was artificial. Politeia had natural weather patterns, but the slab of Skyward set on top of Upper-Middle meant those rains and rare snows never reached Anya's block. And while the Weiss-Bergman three-layer city model was as widely adopted as the Roman city grid, humans couldn't handle the idea of a megaton anvil hanging over their heads all day.

So, the ceiling was fitted with holo-projectors, and vanes at

Skyward's edge ducted air into the different parts of the city to simulate wind. Right now, the ceiling projection boiled with thunderheads and flashed with lightning.

He turned the corner. The rain hammered his back, then fell away as he moved forward, checking the door numbers. *3754.* He found Anya's apartment and knocked.

She didn't answer.

He pulled a breath mint from his coat pocket and popped it into his mouth. It had been over a year since he'd last seen his ex-girlfriend. They'd parted on good terms, mostly. It wasn't even a breakup, more of a mutual agreement that her work was more important to her than he was, and that an Upper-Middle cyber-doc had little to offer the governor's son—politically speaking. It still hurt, though.

He pounded on the door with his fist.

A doll-sized hologram flared to life at eye level in front of the door camera. "Zack?"

"The one and only."

"I was asleep," Anya said, more resentful than apologetic. The hologram was in retro-punk digital green with disruption lines blurring the body of a woman just younger than him. She had short hair, long bare legs, and cheekbones as sharp as scalpels.

"It's raining," he said.

"I know. I like sleeping through storms."

Zack felt a slow, casual smile pull at his lips. Anya could be as cold as surgical steel when it came to her work, but there had always been something comforting about her in the quiet moments. "I'm wet," he said, brushing his now shoulder-length hair out of his face.

"I'm not, and we're not together anymore. Shouldn't you be about thirty floors higher?"

Zack smirked. "More like forty. Not welcome in Skyward these days. I need a place to crash."

Anya's hologram rolled its eyes and disappeared. Zack thought she might have gone back to sleep, but as he raised his fist to knock again, the door slid open.

The entry hallway was dark except for a faint, purple light from her bedroom at the far end. "Go on," he said to the knee-high case, and it floated inside. Zack followed. The door slid shut behind them.

The sound of the storm came in muted through the steel door. For a moment he just stood there, eyes closed and listening. He wasn't safe here, not completely, but the symbolic barrier between him and the city still made him feel less tense.

"Hey," Anya said, touching his shoulder. Her voice was a light soprano that could be as delicate as it could be sharp. He turned to look down at her, and she pushed a towel into his hands.

"Thanks," he said, wiping his face and then his hair.

She looked the same as she always had, standing in the hallway in a white t-shirt and her underwear. Her burgundy hair was shaved down on one side, dark eye shadow and dark lips, violet electric tattoo dragons snaking down both arms. "Any reason you're out in this weather?"

"I knew I'd find you home."

She smirked. "And in bed?"

"You're a creature of habit," Zack answered, returning the towel.

She stood on her toes and kissed his bearded cheek. "Take your coat and boots off before you come in." She walked back toward her room.

Zack shrugged out of his jacket then got to work on unzipping his boots. The case double-pulsed with a little violet glow and beeped. Zack nodded. "Yes, we're old friends." The case went back to neutral, its curiosity satisfied. Zack stood and walked barefoot down the hall and into the bedroom.

Anya was already back in bed and under the sheets. "What's with the flying case?" she asked.

Zack looked behind him. The knee-high box was floating at his heels. "It's a holodeck."

She snorted. "Zack Lancestrom's a veer-head?"

"Yeah. Sure. How's your network connection?"

"Don't have one."

Zack raised an eyebrow. "Hard to be a cyber-doctor without access to reference libraries."

"I got fired, Zack. I'm getting evicted at the end of the month."

That leaves me five days, Zack thought. It was tight, but it should be possible.

Anya threw a pillow at him.

"What?"

"Comfort me, you asshole."

He grunted. "I'm sorry, Anya. Is there anything I can do?"

The light of her tattoos rippled, then she sighed. "You'd do more harm than good, as things are."

"Sorry," he said.

"Yeah, me too," she said, arms dimming to a faint glow.

Zack turned to the case and said, "Go wait in the hallway."

It didn't move. Zack nudged it with the side of his big toe, and it glowed an irritated pink as it floated off, almost bumping into the doorframe.

"You sure that thing's not a pet?" Anya asked.

"No, actually, but it kind of found me, so I guess I'm stuck with it."

"Is it some kind of game?"

"It has game elements." He closed the door and moved to her bedside, pulling his shirt over his head.

"What about Emma?" Anya said.

"What about her?"

"You were living with her."

He shrugged. "The starstruck hero worship got dull."

Anya pinched her lips, and her tattoos flared brighter.

Zack shrugged. "What do you want me to say, Anya? The romance died when I couldn't pay my half of the rent."

"But you're the governor's son. Your trust fund has trust funds."

"He cut me off," Zack said. "In fairness, I was in a one-man contest to spend it all before he could take it from me, but he was faster, and so here we are."

The light from Anya's arms faded but didn't go out. She turned her back on him. He pulled off his pants, hanging them over the back of a chair so they could dry, and slid into the bed behind her.

An hour later, Anya fell asleep, half curled, her bare back pressed against his chest. The sex had been slow but intense, familiar, and intimate. Had it always been this good, or was it because they were both on the edge of unrecoverable failure?

Her fingers brushed his forearm, and he tightened his arm around her ribs.

He'd known about the incident at the clinic, of course. Not the details; the clinic's administrator had paid the family off to keep their mouths shut. But he'd heard she'd gotten fired. He hadn't lied, or at least not exactly. He'd told her he'd known she'd be home.

When he first had his... meltdown, he'd gone to Emma because she'd wanted him, and it felt good to be the light in someone's world. She'd been good to him, and he'd tried to give that back to her. But the truth was, he'd known he would have gone back to Anya if he'd had anything to offer her but misery. And when the shine of dating the governor's son had faded for

Emma, and finding ARK-11 made it clear his future wouldn't take him back to Skyward, he left her before she could ask him to go.

Then Anya was fired and disbarred, and his heart cracked. It wasn't because he was sad or upset for her—Anya had started from nothing, and she'd get back on her feet like she always had. He'd almost groaned in relief because he'd needed her, and because now that she needed him, he could give himself permission to try.

She hadn't been part of his plans, but if his walking out on his bright future had taught Zack anything about himself, it was that he was a romantic at heart, and somehow Anya, the case, and his destiny would all come together. He was sure of it.

Or at least he wasn't willing to consider a world in which they didn't.

CHAPTER FOUR

Anya's Apartment
Pnyx, Upper-Middle, Capital District of Politeia IV
4386.B.29 Interstellar

Zack woke alone. He felt calm and rested, in spite of sneaking out to the living room at one point to log into the levio-case's training simulation. Gentle, natural light lit the room from a long inset in the wall. It was a full-spectrum light, and a good one. He'd bought it for Anya two years ago because she refused to move in with him in Skyward, and his brain wanted sunlight and open skies.

Most importantly, no one had hacked the door and dragged him out of bed last night. There was a brief moment when he saw Anya's empty side of the bed, the pillow plumped and sheets smoothed, where he worried she'd ghosted him, but it was fleeting. Fired or not, evicted or not, if Anya didn't want to see him, she would have kicked him out, not run away.

He kicked the sheets aside and swung his legs out. His thighs were still thin, but more muscular than they'd ever been, and his forearms showed slight definition. He allowed himself an ounce of self-satisfaction before getting up and pulling on his dry but stiff pair of pants.

"Good morning," he said to Anya as he walked into the living room.

She looked up at him from the box she was digging through, then raised an eyebrow.

"What?"

"Nothing," she said with a smirk. She tucked her bangs behind her ear, and her eyes flicked over him one more time before she went back to rearranging the box's contents.

The living room was ground zero for Anya's uprooting. Synth-fiber packing boxes covered most of the floor and all of the couch, each labeled and in various states of completion. Everywhere else were signs of the wreckage of Anya's life. Childhood awards were broken and scattered. Plasti-sheet medical certificates had been torn in half and tossed into a corner. A gravball, signed by the rest of her high school teammates, sat alone on an empty shelf.

He ran his fingers over the circuitry inlays. "You're not taking this?"

"I haven't decided yet," she said, focused on her task.

It's triage, then, he thought, taking in the mess with new eyes. He'd always admired Anya's ability to compartmentalize.

Anya was elbow deep in her current patient, sorting and swapping through single-sheet smart-books, pulling them off the shelf behind her to keep or discard. Each sheet was an entire textbook or medical reference; she could have crammed more data into each, but he knew she liked keeping them as separate, "real" digital readers, like she'd checked out from libraries as a student. The sorting was part of her memory process.

Meanwhile, the levio-case was nosing about, peeking into boxes, its shell a light yellow that Zack had learned meant it was curious and amused.

Anya saw where he was looking and said, "You know that thing's intelligent, right?"

"Yes."

"And old."

"Its name is ARK-II, and yes, it's very, very old." He whistled, like he would have for a synth-pet, and ARK-II floated over. He reached for it, and a small compartment opened, proffering a comb, a brush, and a small bottle.

"What is that, coolant fluid?"

"Beard oil."

Her face dropped. "Zack Lancestrom, are you're using an ancient, intelligent machine as a toiletry bag?"

He winked at her, then patted the side of the case. ARK-II beeped and pulsed a deeper shade of green before turning to inspect a stack of sweaters.

Zack walked into the bathroom, catching sight of himself in the mirror. He'd always had the Lancestrom look—good genes didn't begin to describe the bonsai tree of his family—but his childhood left him with the long bones and almost gaunt look of a born spacer. He still had the sunken chest and thin frame, but improved physique, longer hair, and beard had sparked a new confidence and borderline vanity he hadn't expected. He set his grooming kit on the sink and turned the shower on, pleased Anya's apartment still had hot water in spite of her situation, and stepped in.

There were some things about being orbital-born, though, that would never change. The steaming hot water hit him in the chest. Except for the ceiling shower in his own apartment—his former apartment—he'd never met a showerhead built for his height after the age of sixteen.

"Don't use all the hot water!" Anya yelled, and Zack groaned at the barbarism his life choices had brought him to.

"I can't promise that!" Zack yelled back. He ducked his head into the stream, getting his hair wet, then blinked his eyes clear and grabbed Anya's shampoo. She used the kind of two-in-one stuff he'd expect to find in hospitals—no scents, no lathering agents—but it was effective.

Anya got into the shower with him.

"Hey there," he said, smiling at her.

She gave him a half-serious scowl. "Scoot over."

He stuck his tongue out at her.

Her right arm glowed. She poked him in the ribs with her index finger, and he flinched at the small *snap* and jolt as her implants discharged into him. "Ow! Babe!"

"You're fine," she said, grinning, and took her rightful place which he'd so courteously vacated, her body brushing against his as she squeezed past.

Which wasn't a bad start to the morning.

Zack finished combing the snags out of his beard, then reached for the oil.

"So, what's your plan?" Anya asked, stepping back from the sink so he could use it.

"My plan?"

"Don't do that."

"What?"

"Repeat everything I say like a first-year debate student. I know you're stalling. You taught me that trick."

"It wasn't a good trick, then." He smiled at her reflection in the mirror. "I'm a disgrace to the institution of the Spire."

She rolled her eyes at him and walked out of the bathroom.

He rubbed the oil between his hands and worked it into his beard. *I guess the honeymoon's over.* It was probably a good thing because they didn't have much time. Still, he'd hoped to make it last a bit longer.

"Scoot over," Anya said, walking back in.

He did, and she pulled a small compact from the medicine cabinet.

"What makes you think I have a plan?" Zack asked, his tone more serious.

She dabbed a little of the nano-gel onto her lower lip, and the electric blue smart-lipstick spread on its own. "You made it to the Spire exam. Scheming is in your nature."

"I'm a dropout, and I'm shocked by your allegations of schemery."

"Zack..." she said, crossing her arms.

"What if you could be a doctor again?"

It was as if every atom in her body was frozen for a nanosecond.

Then she shook her head. "It's a nice idea, Zack. Maybe the governor's son could have followed through on it."

"Maybe I can follow through on it anyway."

"You can't."

"But—"

"Zack, I can't get malpractice insurance anymore. I'm blacklisted. They told me, point-blank, I would never be a doctor on Politeia."

"I never said anything about Politeia."

"You didn't have to. Offworld costs money. We're both broke."

He stiffened a bit. He couldn't help but resent the implication he was an idiot, or a child, or both, when she didn't have all the information. Of course, he hadn't shared that information with her, so maybe that was fair.

"Sorry," she said. A few taps on her wrist brought up a holographic slider that turned her hair, tats, and irises graduated teal, to match her lips. "Our timing sucks. Why'd we have to implode at the same time?"

"You wouldn't take my money when I had it," he said, touching her bare shoulder.

"I still wouldn't, but it'd be nice to have a safety net." She turned into his touch and pecked him on the lips.

He ran his fingers over the ceramic plugs, three to a side, that flanked her upper spine. "At least you got to keep these."

She almost snarled. "I paid for them. I programmed the surgery. They're mine." The implants stored kinetic energy as voltage to power a cyber-surgeon's equipment. She'd had them for years.

"They're pretty specialized, babe. I'm surprised they didn't try to take them."

Anya's tattoos flared bright blue. "The clinic's legal counsel *did* try. She couldn't because of the medical repo laws your grandfather passed, so she settled for my tools and my savings."

Zack ran through his mnemonics on Politeian law. "So, she gets them when you die?"

"Not if I burn up while setting fire to the clinic, with her in it," she muttered and left the bathroom.

Zack watched her go. He was mostly certain she was joking. He pulled his styling glove out of his pocket and put it on. A quick pass over his face trimmed and shaped his beard to his preferred settings. He put the glove back into his pocket and found Anya in the living room, sealing the box she'd been packing before. "So what will you do?" he asked.

She looked at him. "I'm going to sell most of this stuff and get some tools, maybe find a place to stay in the Below—"

"Anya..."

"No, Zack. I don't care. I can get good tools, or I can waste money on rent. I spend a few years fixing prosthetics..."

"Broken radiators, sewage pumps, crawler batteries..."

"Those too," she said, raising her chin. "It's honest work."

"It's—" He was about to say something regrettable when someone knocked on the door in a particular pattern—one long, two short, two long. "Hold that thought," he said.

"Were you expecting someone?"

"Yes!" Zack said with a boyish grin. He quickly stepped down the hallway and hit the door release. The two-finger-thick steel slid aside to reveal a man ten centimeters shorter but half again as wide, silhouetted by the morning city-lights, and Zack smiled from ear to ear. "Ultimus Thragg, as I live and breathe to spit in the galaxy's eye!" Zack wrapped the big man in a hug.

CHAPTER FIVE

Anya's Apartment
Pnyx, Upper-Middle, Capital District of Politeia IV
4386.B.29 Interstellar

Zack led Ultimus into the living room. The big man's gray hair was shaved down to stubble, he had the blunt features of a fist-fighter, and two bare metal contact plugs broke through weathered skin above his left eyebrow. He was wearing a dark gray duster and gripped two long military cases by the handles with gloved hands. ARK-11 whistled a friendly greeting. Anya was now standing, her tattoos pulsing like a pissed-off cuttlefish.

"Who is this?" Anya asked.

"Oh, this is Ultimus. Ultimus, this is Anya."

"This the doc?" the big man asked from the doorway, his voice low and gruff.

Zack nodded.

"I'm not a doctor anymore," she corrected. "Zack, why is Ultimus in my home?"

"Because I invited him."

"You can't just invite people to my apartment!"

"It's only your apartment for four more days." Zack knew as soon as it left his mouth that he shouldn't have said it. Anya's tattoos flared like lightning bolts. She snatched the gravball off the shelf behind her and threw it.

But Zack was faster. He twisted out of the way. The gravball, charged to the point of arcing by her implants, cracked like a whip as it shot past him and hit Ultimus in the chest.

"Tingly," the big man said.

"Babe!" Zack blurted, but Anya was already stepping around him toward Ultimus.

"Why aren't you flopping on the ground like... like..."

"Like a man who got hit with ten thousand volts?" Ultimus said with a grin. He set the cases down, stripped off his gloves, and showed her his hands.

"Oh my God!" Anya said, covering her mouth. "Are those X-57s?"

"R-62s with the extra coil capacitors."

"But those are Fleet issue."

"Yep. Combine mercenary. Do enough of the high-hazard jobs and they give you the good stuff." Ultimus wiggled the mechanical fingers. They were void black with gold trim and not a square centimeter of synthetic skin to be seen.

Then again, if he'd owned something so beautiful, Zack wouldn't have covered it up, either. "Show her the rest."

"The rest?" Anya asked, and Zack grinned at her.

Ultimus sighed. "Look, Mr. Lancestrom—and no offense meant," he said, gesturing to Anya, "but I'm not here to impress your girlfriend. If she's not the hotshot cyber-doc you made her out to be, we're screwed."

"I'm an excellent doctor," Anya said before Zack could answer. "I'm just not allowed to practice anymore."

Ultimus crossed his arms. "You're going to have to unpack that a little."

"Of course," she said. "I'll tell you everything."

Simon Bellwether looked like a gang enforcer and spoke like a church usher.

When Anya first met him at the cyberclinic in Pnyx Upper-Middle, she'd been struck by the soft, almost bashful tone with which he addressed her, and the awe behind his regard. She was a first-year resident at an Upper-Middle clinic, but he'd looked at her like she was a goddess. She'd also been concerned he couldn't afford the clinic's services—his clothing was old and worn—but his prosthetics were new, he'd paid upfront in credit chips, and the amount of gratitude he'd shown for a simple tuning had her smiling for the rest of the day.

He was back within a week. Something wasn't right. The actuators in the elbow didn't *feel* right.

Anya apologized and brought him straight to diagnostics, but no matter what she prodded, probed, or lubricated, she couldn't find anything wrong. Simon was understanding, even apologetic, but his distress increased when she couldn't find the problem and he started to say he was in pain.

Anya went straight to her mentor, the head of the clinic.

"Did you say Simon Bellwether?"

Within minutes, Dr. Parnavan had Simon's arm laid open and was running alternating loads through the neural-circuits *by feel*. It was art. It was one of those seminal moments for Anya, watching someone at the peak of their skill do something that wasn't in any of the books.

After Simon was discharged, Dr. Parnavan took Anya aside and said, "He's a junkie."

"What?"

"He gets off on neurolysis."

Anya wasn't sure what to say.

Dr. Parnavan's expression softened. "Don't get me wrong, Annie. His trauma, and his pain, are real. It's a form of degenerative peripheral nerve injury. He was probably born with atypical chemistry... maybe he got migraines or felt things that weren't there. Then he got his first prosthetic—workplace accident, most likely—and the pain stopped."

"I think I understand," Anya said. And she did. Dr. Parnavan hadn't "fixed" Simon. She'd stimulated his nerves until she found the right one and overloaded it, maybe damaged him a little. "So, what do we do?"

"Exactly what we did, Dr. Vesperian. Be courteous, give him what he needs, and bill him for the work. If he becomes a problem, we'll deny him service. His type gets bounced from clinic to clinic anyway."

Anya learned a lot from Dr. Parnavan, if not always things she liked.

"So, what happened?" Ultimus asked.

Anya put the gravball back into its place on the shelf. Her tattoos were barely visible. "I did my job. Like Dr. Parnavan said, Simon's pain was real. Simon stopped by for a tune-up two to three times a month. Every two months, he'd save up enough money for an upgrade. I had issues with it. Sometimes it felt like I was a drug dealer or a parlor girl, but I learned a lot about the human nervous system. Six months saw that machinery move from his elbow up to his shoulder. His choice, his money. I made sure the work was done right."

Ultimus nodded. "And then you made a mistake."

"Then I met Maddie."

"Dr. Vesperian?"

"Yes?" Anya said, looking up from her clipboard. It was early morning at the clinic, and she was starting her rounds.

"I'm Maddie Bellwether. Simon's wife." The slender, almost waifish woman extended her hand.

Anya shook it. "How can I help you, ma'am?"

Maddie paused, looking Anya over. "You're prettier than I thought you'd be."

Anya's eyebrows shot up. "Ma'am, I can assure you—"

Maddie blushed. "That's not... Simon would never cheat on me. I mean, you're very nice, and Simon talks about you like you're some kind of angel, but he's not..." Her words were almost tripping over themselves. She stopped and took a breath. "I came here to say thank you. He's never stayed with the same doctor for this long, and this clinic is close to where we live—vertically at least. We live Below, you know."

"You're welcome," Anya said, relieved and touched.

"And I came to ask you a favor," Maddie added.

"I can certainly try."

"I need you to string him along a bit."

Anya swallowed. "I'm not sure what you mean."

Maddie leaned in. "I know my husband has a problem, Doctor. It's okay. I love him, and he's a good provider but, just between us girls? When he's between clinics, he doesn't spend money. Now he's spending our rent on your little 'tune-ups,' and goodness knows you've earned it because I've *never* seen him happier. I only need you to slow down."

★

Anya's Apartment

Pnyx, Upper-Middle, Capital District of Politeia IV
4386.B.29 Interstellar

"That's tough," Ultimus said, moving over to sit on the couch. "Still not sure how it got you fired, though."

"I'm pretty curious about that, too," Zack said.

"I cured him."

"You're kidding me," Ultimus said.

"Nope. Took me a month to figure it out, but Dr. Parnavan was right. It *was* degeneration. The shocks and surgeries stimulated regrowth."

"You burned him out, didn't you?" Ultimus asked.

"Enough to stop the cycle of neurogenesis and decay."

"And he let you do that?"

"She didn't ask," Zack said. Anya looked at him sharply, and he raised his hands. "I'm guessing. Am I wrong?"

"I fixed the problem. He left happy. I felt pretty damn good about it."

"But that isn't how addiction works," Zack offered, and Anya nodded.

"He had a psychological dependency, but he couldn't get the high anymore. He quit his job and left his wife. Maddie sued the clinic for the loss of income. That's why they fired me."

"What about Dr. Parnavan?" Zack asked. "It sounded like the two of you had a good working relationship."

Anya shrugged. "She couldn't do much. The insurance made my termination a requirement to pay the claim. Besides, she'd told me to give him what he *wanted*, not go off and try to save him. I can't blame her for distancing herself."

And she didn't, Zack knew, because no one was responsible for Anya's choices but her. He found her sense of self-reliance as admirable as it was frustrating. "Sorry, babe."

ARK-11 settled down beside her. The flying box had turned purple, like a bruise.

"Well, that's good enough for me," Ultimus said.

"It is?" Zack asked.

"You bet. Most people would have left that gearhead paralyzed or brain dead."

"Thanks," Anya said, lifting her chin a bit.

"Doesn't speak well for her judgment, though."

"She's in good company, then," Zack said with a grin.

Ultimus grinned, too, and ran his right index and middle finger from left shoulder to hip. The smart fabric of his duster fell open to reveal a black and gold torso as mechanized as his hands. "Got a little problem we need your help with, Doc."

"I'll need tools," Anya said, not bothering to ask what the problem was.

"Open the case nearest to you. We should have everything you need," Ultimus said.

Close to ninety minutes later, Anya set the electron probe down in disgust and said, "I can't do this."

"That's okay," Ultimus said, looking over from the smartbook he'd been reading. The access panel on his wrist clicked shut. He shook his hand out and flexed the fingers a few times.

"We honestly..." Zack yawned and covered his mouth. "Sorry. We didn't think you'd be able to do it."

"Didn't think you'd keep *trying* as long as you did," Ultimus muttered, swiping to the next page.

Anya's tattoos pulsed. "If you're such a big bad mercenary, why did you let them disable your augments in the first place?"

"Standard procedure," Ultimus said.

Zack cleared his throat. "When a Combine mercenary with

Ultimus's kind of gear lands on a planet, it's considered... polite to allow local government to disable his more offensive systems unless he's under contract."

"So *hire* him," Anya said. "Officially."

"I'm broke," Zack said with a grin. "It's not enough to hire him. I'd have to pay for a full activation. Even if I did, my dad would know and send the cavalry."

"I could take 'em," Ultimus said.

"I'm not willing to accept that level of collateral damage," Zack said seriously.

Ultimus sighed and put the reader down in his lap. "Problem is, there's no way a cybernetics resident on a backwater world is going to bypass a Combine lock."

"Then why did you let me try in the first place?" Anya asked.

"Because you're good, babe. You're a natural."

"And highly trained," Ultimus conceded. "So rather than argue about your obvious qualifications, we thought we'd let you decide for yourself if you needed help."

"Oh," Anya said. "Well, I suppose that's fair. I need help, though I'm not sure where we're going to get it."

"That's because you and ARK-II haven't been properly introduced. Hey, ARK?"

The little white case rose into the air and floated over, turning a tentative shade of cyan.

"We need the training circlets, buddy."

ARK-II flashed a solid, golden yellow and set down next to Zack's foot. A small panel popped and slid outward on its side, revealing four carbon-black circlets. Zack offered one to Anya.

"What is this?"

"That? It's a training program."

"I didn't ask you what it does, Zack. I asked you what it is. There's no screen on this thing."

"Uh..."

"There's no projector or speakers, either."

"It, uh, *might* be a direct neural interface."

Anya stared at the circlet in her hand for a beat, then looked up. "Zack."

"Yes, Anya?"

"I'm not letting a machine reprogram my brain."

"I've used it."

"You haven't been making the best decisions lately. You've changed."

"It's only taught me what I wanted to learn."

"They use these to rehabilitate prisoners, Zack."

"This one's different."

"I can see that," she said, turning it over in her hands. "It's magnificent. I'm not putting it on my head." She gave the circlet back to him.

"We don't have a choice, Ms. Vesperian," Ultimus said.

"The hell I don't," she answered, turning toward him. "This was fun, Ultimus. Really. Working on an R-62 was like a dream for me, but now I'd like you to—"

Zack placed the circlet on top of her head like a crown and she went limp.

Ultimus looked at him. "She's gonna be real mad when she wakes up."

Zack held up both index fingers. "Excellent point. I'm going to go in there and make sure she's okay."

"Knock yourself out, boss," Ultimus said, turning back to his reading.

Zack put the second circlet on his head and logged into the ARK.

CHAPTER SIX

Shared Virtual Network
Users: Zack Lancestrom, Guest, Anthropological Restoration Kit XI
4386.B.29 Interstellar, Time Dilation 0.125x

"Zack!" Anya screamed in the dark.

"Yeah, hold on a second I... got it."

"Greetings, Administrator," a disembodied female voice said. And there was light. An infinite, undulating plane of blue and white dots stretched in every direction, and Zack and Anya were standing on it.

"You complete asshole!" Anya shouted.

"I'm sorry! You were stuck in the lobby until I let you in."

"How long did you leave me in there?"

"Less than ten seconds. I understand it felt longer than that, but I can explain."

"Explain it in the real world."

"I'd rather—"

"Zack!"

"ARK-11, force log out!"

★

Anya's Apartment
Pnyx, Upper-Middle, Capital District of Politeia IV
4386.B.29 Interstellar

Zack opened his eyes to see Anya's arm snake out and she pinched the top of his shoulder. There was a sharp shock, and his head flopped over.

ARK-II bleeped in alarm.

"Nice," Ultimus said without looking over.

"Yep," Anya said, getting up.

Zack just kind of sat there with his head against the top of the couch.

"Can you breathe?" Ultimus asked.

Zack gargled. His tongue felt heavy.

"Hey, Ultimus?" Anya yelled from the kitchen.

"Yes, ma'am?"

"Do you like tea? I'm going to have some tea."

"I'll take some."

"Great."

Zack gargled again and managed to twitch his left hand.

"You'll be fine," Ultimus said, turning the page on his smartbook. "She overloaded your somatic nervous system. If she'd hit your vagus nerve, I'd be giving you CPR."

ARK-II beeped and whistled.

"It'll wear off in a few minutes," Ultimus said. "Be patient."

He was speaking to the little AI, but Zack took it to heart. There wasn't much else he could do anyway. He could kind of move his eyes, though they felt dry like he was twisting stone marbles in his sockets. *I could have handled that better,* he thought.

Putting the circlet on her head was... wrong. As a moral

sophisticate, he disliked the word, but it was appropriate. At the very least, it hadn't produced the desired result.

And it was heavy-handed, the kind of thing his father might have done because "he knew better," the kind of thing that... He had an itch on the inside of his left foot, or maybe a tightness. No, it was a cramp. *Virtues be damned...* He'd been on the verge of something meaningful—might have been a position paper in it. Now he was—

"Ooowowowowowow..." he managed to moan.

"Here you go, Ultimus. I'd warn you that it's hot, but I guess that doesn't bother you much."

"R-62s have full sensory feedback," he said, taking the cup with a wink.

"Even pain?"

"Yep."

"Good Lord, why?"

"Couple reasons, actually," Ultimus said. He blew on the tea, then took a sip. "That's nice. Bai Hoa Yinzhen?"

She laughed and flapped her hand at him. "A poor med student like me? It's Bai Mu Dan."

"Hmm. Hard to tell sometimes with planetary varieties."

"So glad you two are getting along," Zack said, his voice slurring. A trickle of drool slipped down his cheek.

Anya smiled at him sweetly. Then she jabbed two fingers into his chest, above his sternum, and shocked him again before turning back to Ultimus. "You were saying about the R-62s?"

Damn.

Another five minutes passed, during which Zack listened to Anya and Ultimus talk about cybernetics and slurp their tea. Zack was more of a coffee person, or at least he had been when he still had the funds and access to Skyward. The stuff only grew properly above 1200 meters, and it required sunlight and rain—real rain, not layer storms and leakage from the ceiling sewers. Before he'd had to go without, he'd spent a decade turning his nose up at greenhouse-grown beans or chemical substitutes. He liked to think it was the privilege leaving his body that had been giving him headaches for a month.

"It's better if I pulse the current, like overlapping waves," Anya said.

"Sure. Shock-rods work the same way." Ultimus leaned forward and looked at Zack. "Can you move yet, boss?"

"Yesssh..." Anya twisted in her seat to look at him, and he added, "Please don't shock me again."

"Are you going to hijack my brain without asking?"

"No."

"Are you sorry?"

Zack paused, then said, "In retrospect, I might have done things differently."

Anya laughed. "You're a son of a bastard. You know that?"

"Yeah, I love you too," Zack answered, wiping his cheek on the couch.

Anya flinched.

"How long have you two been together?" Ultimus asked.

"We broke up," Anya said, standing up. "Done with your tea?"

Ultimus nodded. "Yes, but let me wash up," he said, standing and taking her cup. "You two need to talk."

"I thought she was pretty clear on not wanting to participate," Zack said.

"No, boss. She'll do it. She just won't be forced or tricked into it." He picked his way across the box-filled room and went into the kitchen.

"What is it I'm doing, Zack?" She made no move to sit on the couch.

He searched her eyes, trying to put himself in her place. "I'm sorry."

"For what?"

"For not asking for your help."

She shifted her weight and crossed her arms. "I don't know, Zack. Some of last night was fun."

"It was, wasn't it?" He smiled at her.

She scratched her cheek. "Well, I needed it. So, what can I do for you, Zack Lancestrom?"

You could go back to where we were last night, he told himself, then he pushed that thought aside. He'd needed her, too. He'd been running scared for the past month, ever since he followed a trail of clues and spam messages to the place his Synthesis question came from. Ever since he'd found ARK-II.

He had no time left. Not one spare second. At any moment, his father, the government, or any number of people who wanted what he had were going to come after him. Ultimus Thragg would hold them off for a while, but no single mercenary could protect him from the avalanche of fecal matter, fists, and firepower headed his way. "I need to get offworld."

"Book a berth on a starship."

"Lend me the money?" he said with a smirk.

"You're not good for it. Get a job, Zack. Get your hands dirty, like the rest of us."

"Blood and motor oil to my elbows?"

She grinned.

"My father put me on the no-fly list. I can go anywhere on Politeia, but I can't break orbit."

"You and twenty-one billion other people for all sorts of reasons."

"Screw twenty-one billion other people!" Zack said.

Anya curled her lip in disgust and looked away.

Zack sucked on his teeth. "Fine. I'm the governor's son. I was raised in a Skyward high-rise with a security team to feed me offworld delicacies with a silver spoon." And he'd worked harder for less praise than any hab-block kid for the past twenty years. This was Politeia IV, not some decadent over-terraformed world or corporate pleasure-orbital, and the governor wasn't a tin-pot dictator any more than he'd been a loving father figure. "And there isn't a Simon or a Maddie among all twenty-one billion—Skyward included—that was worth throwing your dream of being a cyberneticist away for."

She looked at him. Anya was Upper-Middle through and through. She'd started from nothing, worked her ass off through the public system without a handout or a hand up from anyone. "I screwed up. I knew I shouldn't have done what I did. I didn't ask because I knew he'd say no, that the clinic would forbid it, and that Dr. Parnavan would put me on leave for my own good. But I thought I could do it. And I did. *And I got what I deserved, Zack.* That's the part you don't seem to understand. You're not entitled to what you want because you're smart, or good looking, or educated, or rich."

"I know that. Don't you think I know that?"

She hesitated.

"I've given it all up. Couldn't I have talked my father into some sort of sabbatical if I'd been willing to play along?"

"Then what do you want, Zack?"

"Everything he thinks I can't have. Everything I can earn. Everything I can take." And that included her, he knew.

Her tattoos glowed electric blue.

"You two sorted?" Ultimus said, coming out of the kitchen.

Zack raised an eyebrow at her.

"I guess we are," Anya said.

"Fabulous," he said, rubbing his hands together, the metal digits clicking. "Did he mention we're on a timetable?"

"He didn't, but I'm a smart girl. Figured that out all by myself."

"She's a doctor," Zack said.

"I *am* a doctor."

"That's the spirit," Ultimus said. "How much time we have, boss?"

"Three, four days at the most."

"That long?" the big man asked.

"Anya's a good cover. Last-ditch effort after Emma kicked me out, and the doctor's kicked me to the curb before." Zack's eyes flicked to Anya's, but she was back to being clinically cold.

"What's with the timeline?" she asked. "Is this about your ancient holodeck?"

"ARK-11 is part of it," Zack said. "The other is that I borrowed a significant amount of credits from an under-city gang leader called 'Jawhee the Vibroblade,' which I have no intention of repaying."

"Zack!"

"He's a very bad man," Zack said.

"And I don't come cheap," Ultimus added.

She slid her hand through her hair. "Do you have a plan to go with your overconfidence?"

ARK-11 whistled twice and offered them the circlets.

Anya sighed. "If we're going to hack Combine security and steal from the gangs, I suppose rewriting my brain to practice illegal medicine is the least of my concerns. Might as well be hanged for an electric sheep as a clockwork lamb."

CHAPTER SEVEN

Shared Virtual Network
Users: Zack Lancestrom, Dr. Anya Vesperian, Anthropological Restoration Kit XI
4386.B.29 Interstellar, Time Dilation 0.125x

"Greetings, Administrator." ARK-11's avatar floated in the air, a simple octahedron spinning gently and catching the light.

Zack and Anya stood on the boundless surf, their bodies also digital-blue. She looked calm, but he could sense her remaining nervousness about tampering with her brain. "I can log out any time?"

"Yes. I gave you full user rights."

"Not administrative?"

"Don't push it," he said. And he meant it. Lust, affection, respect, love... all those were good, but boundaries were healthy, too.

"Fine," she said, her avatar smirking. "So, what's so important about this thing that you couldn't explain it."

Zack felt a tingle of anticipation. He'd been looking forward to showing her this. "ARK-11, display Dr. Vesperian's cybernetics profile."

> **Dr. Vesperian Cybernetics Profile:**
>
> Cybernetics: 0.67
> Surgery: 0.48 (8 subcategories)
> Mechanical Engineering: 0.37 (5 subcategories)

Zack knew he could expand the list to the subcategories and expand the definitions, but those three would be enough to make the point.

"Okay, sixty-seven percent on my cyber skills is a little insulting, but I suppose I *was* a first-year resident," Anya said.

"Babe..."

"What?"

He grinned. "It's not a percentage."

"What is it, then? And wipe that insufferable smile off your face."

"It's a blended average of your knowledge, proficiency, and the tier system."

Anya looked at the floating table again and nodded. "Okay. So in that light..."

"You're not doing so badly. Civilian tech on a settled planet is mostly limited to Tier 1."

"I'm aware of that, Zack."

"I mean, you know a *lot* now, right? Because you're just out of school, and all that stuff seems important..."

"It is important," Anya said.

"But you'd get tired, and you'd forget things—especially since you don't have a network connection anymore—and your score will drop, if only a bit."

Her tattoos didn't glow in the simulation, but he could tell she was getting annoyed.

"And then you'll find out that, Below, there are certain things people are willing to pay for. I'm not saying you'd be prostituting yourself to a system of violent inequality—"

"If you don't get to the point, *I'm* going to start some violent inequality of my own."

"But gang members are more likely to pay for combat implants than prosthetics for the kids they had with their junkie baby mothers."

Anya looked at him like he was an idiot. "I'm a doctor, Zack. I'm aware of the social and economic realities that lead to specialization. If I'd fought my way up to Skyward, I'd have gotten into cosmetic surgery. I stayed here to avoid that."

Zack blinked in surprise. "Right. Have I mentioned your brain is sexy?"

"Not recently. I'm waiting for the punchline."

"No punchline, babe. ARK-II knows more about cybernetics than anyone on this world. Imagine scoring over three-point-oh."

She took it remarkably well. "That isn't possible."

Zack waited.

"Even if someone had the time to learn all the knowledge known to humanity about just one thing—and they don't."

"Even at a ten-to-one time-compression ratio?"

That shook her, but she continued. "Even then, even if you could spend all that time in here without working or feeding yourself, I'm guessing cybernetics aren't what *you've* been using it for. There's too much knowledge, too much data to pack into a small casing like that. Someone ripped you off."

Zack nodded. He'd thought the same, at first. "Can we talk about it later? The sooner we get Ultimus's prosthetics unlocked, the sooner we get moving. I'd be more comfortable as a moving target."

"Then have ARK-II do it," she said, locking eyes with him.

"What?"

"I'm flattered you thought of me, Zack, but you just said it knows more than anyone on this world. If it can teach me to do it, it can do the work itself."

"It can't."

Anya frowned. "Why not?"

"Because Ultimus's armor is a weapon system. The people who designed ARK-II put in fail-safes so it wouldn't turn on human beings." Zack watched her. He was almost sure he'd gotten through. "I need you, Anya."

She nodded. After a few moments, she said, "This may not work. I can't promise you I'll be able to do this."

"It's all right," Zack said, stepping closer to touch her upper arm. It felt real. "All our hopes and dreams, babe."

She laughed out loud. "So, no pressure, right?

"None," he said, smile sliding into a smirk. It was a gamble. A bet on a woman he had irrational feelings for, but also someone he respected because Anya was smart, hardworking, and stubborn. And he knew what ARK-II could do, besides that. If they failed, it wouldn't be for lack of skill or effort.

She blew a breath out—Zack thought it was funny how that was soothing, even if it had nothing to do with what her physical body was experiencing. "Where do I start?" she asked.

"ARK-II, bring up the schematics of Ultimus Thragg's cybernetics and the skills required to bring them online up to Tier 2."

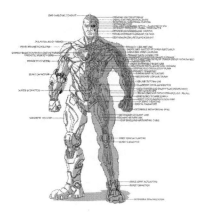

Skill requirements:
R-62-Q startup sequence 2.00
B-47 startup sequence 2.00
Advanced platform safety systems 1.41
Molecular x-mission matrices 1.33
Micro-reactor startup sequence 1.05
Subdermal armor 0.60
Combat augmetics 0.54
Smart materials 0.20

"Jesus Christ, Zack. He's walking around with a graser in his chest," Anya said, reading through the specs on Ultimus's armor.

Zack was familiar with gamma radiation beams from his study of aircraft and ship weapons, but he wasn't sure why she was upset about it. "Is that bad?"

"If you consider the ability to blow a meter-wide hole through most of a city block to be 'bad,' then yes. It's all locked down tighter than his base systems, but who the hell thought this was a good idea?"

"There are fifty-eight prerequisites Dr. Vesperian does not possess, Administrator. Would you like me to display these as well?"

"No," Zack said. "Design training program."

"Yes, Administrator."

Anya turned toward him. "This is real, isn't it?"

"Yes."

"Zack, how did you get your hands on this?"

"Training program ready," ARK-11 announced.

A small cyber-maintenance theater formed itself out of the data-surf. ARK-11's avatar waited by the operating table. There were also floating tool racks, drawers full of medical supplies, a fusion cutting torch, and safety equipment, and a standing rack and winch, but no walls.

"We'll talk later," Zack said. "I'll tell you everything, okay?"

"Okay," she said. "Everything."

"Yeah."

She turned and walked toward her new simulated home.

When Zack had started his training, he'd chosen the privateer specialization, which combined the duelist and small-craft pilot programs. "ARK-11, load combat shooting program."

"Access denied. All combat simulations locked until Administrator completes the next module of four-dimensional navigation."

"Come on..." he pleaded. "I'm a philosophy major. Don't make me do math in the morning."

"Access denied."

Zack sighed exaggeratedly, but he was grinning. He knew he needed to master 4D-Nav. Ship computers did most of the calculations in normal transit, but ship computers failed, and he wouldn't have time to pull out a textbook during a dogfight. "Load the in-system jump training."

"Access granted, Administrator. Do your best."

Zack chuckled. Sometimes, ARK-11 was downright maternal in its chivvying. Then again, it had a couple thousand years on him, so maybe the little guy knew what was good for him.

Zack had a head start on Anya when it came to training in the ARK, but she had years of real-world experience to build on.

He was trying to learn things from scratch, and every additional thing he learned might be the detail that saved his life.

★

Anya's Apartment
Pnyx, Upper-Middle, Capital District of Politeia IV
4386.B.29 Interstellar

Forty-seven minutes of real-time later, Zack took the circlet off his head.

"How did it go?" Ultimus asked.

Zack rubbed his face. "Good. I'm tired. She come out at any point?"

"Nope," Ultimus said. He was bent over a holographic chess set ARK-II was beaming onto the couch.

"Who's winning?" Zack asked.

"I don't think in those terms."

"So ARK-II is winning."

Ultimus looked at him and chuckled. "You take that attitude into the simulations?"

"No," Zack admitted. "I did at first. Little guy kicked my ass."

"The 'little guy' is an all-knowing pre-second-war artifact."

Not all-knowing, Zack thought, but that was a problem for another day. "I get it. I do. But is it winning?"

"Yes," Ultimus said, toppling his king. ARK-II beeped in triumph, bobbing on its repulsors. "And it's a sore winner, too."

ARK-II did a full rotation, and emerald-green fireworks went off on its casing.

"It even wins at winning," Zack said, in awe.

"Yeah," Ultimus said. "You hungry yet?"

"Starving." Running his brain at ten times normal speed took its toll. Ultimus got up and grabbed his coat, careful not to disturb Anya. System safeguards would wake her if someone got too close, and Zack knew from experience how disorienting that could be.

"I'll go get some groceries," the mercenary said.

The smell of food was coming strong and heavy from the kitchen when Anya came to. Zack watched her blink her eyes and pull the circlet off. ARK-II beeped to get her attention, then the circlet floated from her hand back to its little storage rack, and it drew the panel back in.

"Hey," Zack said.

"Hey. How long was I in?"

"Two and a half hours. That's like a twenty-hour day."

"I pulled longer shifts in med school."

Zack chuckled.

"What?"

"You're proud of that. Even though *doctors* have proven it's counterproductive."

Anya shrugged and cracked her wrists. "Every profession has its irrational traditions." She turned her head toward the kitchen. "Ultimus, is that your cooking I smell?"

"Yes, ma'am!"

"It smells amazing!"

"Family recipe!" Ultimus rumbled back.

"Is he single?" she asked Zack in a half-whisper.

"I saw him first," Zack answered with a grin.

Anya snorted.

"What?"

"You're a straight man, not a laugh-getter. It's better for your pride."

"Am I that fragile?" he asked.

"Ultimus is too much man for either of us, Zack. But if we're taking this where I think it's going, you're going to need your Spire education."

"Gender or sexual orientation aren't indicators of leadership, Dr. Vesperian," Zack said, deadpan.

"Much better," she said. "What do you think, Ultimus?"

"About what, ma'am?" He handed her a bowl of orange-red noodles.

"Ultimus..."

"Yes, ma'am?" he handed Zack a bowl and turned back to face her.

"You can't lie to your doctor. I know how well you can hear, and I imagine you earned access to Federal technology even if they disabled it. Do you think Zack is up to this?"

Ultimus scratched his nose.

"Ouch," Zack said.

"Honest question deserves an honest answer, boss."

"You took the job, though," Zack said.

Ultimus shrugged. "I was bored and almost out of beer money. Sticking with you sounded like a lot more fun than working for my transit."

Zack looked at the big armored mercenary and realized, not for the first time, that whatever fleshy bits were left inside that armored frame were from a different subspecies of human than Zack or Anya. "So, what's your honest, professional opinion?"

Ultimus nodded. "Good. None of that 'friend' crap you met me at the door with."

"Just being 'friendly,'" Zack said. Anya was watching both of them, her food untouched.

"You put in the work," the mercenary continued. "I respect that. Doc, here, might have spent two hours under, but she looks like she's ready to fall over. You've consistently done four a day for the past two weeks we've been together. And the way you dodged the gravball she threw at you?"

Zack allowed himself a small smile. "I was proud of that."

"What about you, Doc? You notice that?" Ultimus asked.

Anya had suddenly taken an interest in her bowl.

"She hadn't. She has now," Ultimus said. "How's the paprikash?

"Delicious," Anya said, not looking at Zack.

And he knew why. He'd made her realize she wanted more than a parts shop Below, but he hadn't convinced her that he could pull it off. "Thank you, Mr. Thragg."

"Just doing my job, boss."

Pointing out my weaknesses, Zack thought. And he *was* grateful, even if he wasn't thrilled his ex-girlfriend and current lover didn't trust him. It turned a little part of him colder. It was only a small piece, though—the part that hadn't made Anya an administrator of ARK-IIs systems or told Ultimus about the little guy's limitations, or what it would take to fix them. He genuinely enjoyed Anya's and Ultimus's company, but liking someone wasn't a good basis for trusting them.

"Enjoy the paprikash," Ultimus said.

Zack dug in. The paprikash was good. Sweet and smokey, with a solid mix of textures between the chicken, vegetables, and noodles, and a weight to it that stuck to his bones. He and Anya chatted for a while, then she left to take a few boxes to a local pawn shop.

Once she was gone, Ultimus put on a training circlet, and Zack joined him to practice a few of the response scenarios the mercenary had insisted on. Anya put in another hour when she got back, then made another attempt at unlocking Ultimus's combat systems. They ate. They went to bed, Ultimus in the living room with ARK-II, and Zack laid down next to Anya in the bedroom. She kept her distance. She didn't ask him to leave.

Getting out of the city would be a close thing, he knew. Coming back for her—showing his face in Upper-Middle, only a hundred floors below his father's offices—had been a risk. He'd made his choice, but as she turned to face away, he wasn't sure if it had been worth it. A day or two more and they'd try to make their escape.

The Planetary Hall, Governor's Office
Pnyx, Skyward, Capital District of Politeia IV
4386.B.30 Interstellar

"He's resurfaced, sir," Sam Meritt told his boss.

Alex Lancestrom looked up. The last six months had aged the governor. At sixty-seven, he still had the ageless features of his dynasty and access to the best rejuvenative treatments, but there was a slackness around his eyes and a slowness in his actions—particularly in the mornings—that stood out to someone who spent as much time around him as Sam. "Where?"

"He's staying with his former girlfriend, the doctor."

"Anya Vesperian?"

"Yes, sir," Sam said, being careful to keep his expression neutral. As Zack's estrangement progressed to full-on flight, Sam had expected the governor to cut his losses and pivot to one of the other heirs. That would have been consistent with his past decisions, and with how he communicated with members of the oversight committee even now.

"Do you think she'd help us talk him into coming home?"

Sam looked away, his composure finally failing him.

"What?" the governor asked sharply.

Sam swallowed. It had been close to eleven years since he

gave up the nomadic life of a Combine-ranked mercenary to serve as Alex Lancestrom's security advisor and chief bodyguard. In that time, outside of security, he'd never once suggested the governor was making a bad decision. Not that he wouldn't have, but the leadership of Politeia's "sophistocracy" was generally solid, and Alex Lancestrom more reliable than most. "He's not coming home, sir."

"Unacceptable," Alex said.

"Begging your pardon, sir, but why?"

"He's my son."

"You have dozens of sons, sir. And dozens of daughters. Any one of them could serve you and the sophistocracy."

The governor dismissed his argument with a wave of his hand. "I'm not justifying myself to you, Mr. Meritt. Find him."

Sam flinched as if the man had slapped him. He hadn't called Sam by his last name when they were in private for years.

The governor sighed and rubbed the bridge of his nose. "Forgive me, Sam. This has been... trying, for me."

Sam nodded. "I understand that, sir. Even cyborgs like me start acting erratically without sleep. What I don't understand is why this is so important to you. We've been through worse than a runaway heir in the past ten years, and you've never let it show."

The governor chuckled. "Do you know what Zack's Synthesis was? The question he was *supposed* to answer?"

"I do, sir." *If you were the planetary governor, what would you change to remake Politeia into a multi-system star-nation?* It would have stoked Zack Lancestrom's ego like shoving a gas giant into a primary star. It had damaged Bernie Hallek in different ways.

"Then you know he's the future of this world. He's going to take us back to the stars, Sam. The testing system is never wrong."

Sam thought the governor might be rationalizing breaking

the rules because he loved his son, and he disliked the almost religious overtones of this "testing system"—whatever it was. But fixing that wasn't his job. "What do you want me to do? Make contact?"

"Bring him in. Drag him in if you have to."

"He's acquired the services of one of my former colleagues. A good one."

The governor waved his hand. "Do what you have to. Bring me my son."

CHAPTER EIGHT

Anya's Apartment
Pnyx, Upper-Middle, Capital District of Politeia IV
4386.B.30 Interstellar

Zack popped his head up, turning toward the door.

"What is it?" Anya asked, tense and alert.

"Do you smell that?"

"No? Is something burning?"

Zack threw off the sheets and slid off the bed. He half-ran out the door, through the living room, stubbed his foot on one of Ultimus's cases, back-spun around ARK-II, and stumbled into the kitchen.

"Oh, hey, boss," Ultimus said.

"What is that?"

The mercenary stepped aside, revealing a pan of mahogany meat sizzling in a rich sauce. "Country ham in red-eye gravy," Ultimus said. "Want some?"

"Yes, but I don't know why. What's in the gravy?"

"What's wrong?" Anya said, appearing in the doorway. "Oh

my God, that smells good." She'd managed to pull on a silk kimono. Zack was in his boxer briefs.

"Morning, doc. It's country ham in red-eye gravy. That's when you mix coffee with the drippings. Little butter, little sugar…"

"You poured *coffee* on *meat?*" Zack asked, moments from a full-blown eye twitch.

"Only a little. It brings out the flavor."

"Where's the rest of it?" Zack asked, head swinging like a police drone in acquisition mode.

"Here," Ultimus said, raising a tin can that Zack grabbed with both hands. "Careful with that, there's still…"

Zack drank it down. It was gritty and slimy at the same time.

"…grounds in it. And I used a mostly empty can of beans to mix the gravy."

"That's disgusting," Anya said.

"That's fine," Zack said, his mind buzzing from the thought of caffeine produced by *coffea arabica peregrinus*, a distant cousin of the Sol system's coffee tree in every sense of the word.

"You an addict?" Ultimus asked.

"Don't get him started," Anya said. She walked past Zack and opened a cupboard, pulling down three plates.

Zack blew a raspberry at her. "I'm not an addict."

"You just drank from a bean can," Ultimus said.

"I haven't had coffee in months. I wasn't going to waste it!"

"I could have made you a cup, boss. Coarse grind, slow pour, filter and everything."

Zack frowned. "How the hell are you getting all this stuff? The chicken, the ham, the *coffee?*"

"What else am I going to do with my exorbitant pay?" Ultimus grinned.

"How much *are* you paying him?" Anya asked Zack, putting ham, beans, and some kind of light mash on her plate.

"None of your business," Zack answered.

"Not that you aren't worth it." She patted Ultimus's shoulder and walked into the living room.

"Damn right I am," Ultimus said with a wide smile.

"What's the mash?" Zack asked, poking it with a fork.

"Boiled cornmeal. I put a little cheese in it."

Zack took a bite. His tastebuds responded with arias from choirs-full of angels. "You were worth every centi-cred," he said around the mouthful of warm, tangy cornmeal.

"You want that cup of coffee?"

Zack shook his head and gave the mercenary a wink before stepping into the living room.

Anya was on the couch, side-sitting against the armrest and halfway through her plate. Her hair and tattoos were neon green fading to spearmint at the tips. ARK-11 had set down nearby.

"It likes you," Zack said, sitting down.

"Does it?"

ARK-11 whistled in agreement.

"How's the training going?" Zack asked, spearing a piece of ham.

"Good," Anya said, giving ARK-11 another glance. "I still don't believe it can take us to Tier 3. But I tested it, Zack. I made progress on the training program, but I also made sure I finished at least one full module so I could try it on Ultimus, and it *worked,* Zack. But some of this stuff assumes a base level of technology higher than anyone on Politeia's ever seen. I can't finish unlocking Ultimus's systems because I don't have the tools. They don't exist."

Zack finished chewing. "They must exist."

"Okay, yes. I wouldn't have bought it two days ago, but now I almost believe it."

Zack chuckled and had another bite of ham and cornmeal. Ultimus had been right. He loved Anya's brain, her skepticism about anything that couldn't be proven, but she wasn't the ideal foot-soldier. It was a good thing he hadn't told her what ARK-II was *really* capable of, or they'd still be arguing.

"What?" Anya asked.

"Nothing. Could we have them fabricated?"

"Have what?"

"The tools," Zack said. He scooped the last of the cornmeal through the gravy and shoveled it in.

"Fabricating them isn't the real problem. I mean, we would have to get that done, yes. I don't know where we'd even start."

"I have an engineer. A good one. His name is Clavicus Rext." Anya stared at him.

He picked up the last piece of ham. "What?" he said with his mouth full.

"You still haven't told me the plan."

He started to wipe his mouth with his hand, then looked around for something to wipe his hand with.

"Here," she said, handing him a napkin. He brushed her fingers with his as he took it, and she frowned.

Not good, he thought. "So, the plan."

"Yes."

"We steal a shuttle, get into orbit, jump somewhere in-system where we can book a starship out of Politeia."

"Okay. And how do we do that?"

"Which part?"

"Let's start with the shuttle," she said, shifting her legs to set her feet on the floor. "You know we can't take one from the spaceport. Your dad grounded you in every sense of the word."

"We're not using the spaceport. Even setting foot in Skyward isn't an option for me at this point."

"Well, you can't go to a local field. Those shuttles might make low orbit, but they're not jump capable."

"You know a lot about this, don't you?" Zack said, trying and failing to keep all the sarcasm out of his voice.

"You telling her about the shuttle?" Ultimus said, coming out of the kitchen.

"Yeah."

"You're not eating?" Anya asked.

"I don't eat much. Not much left to feed," Ultimus said, patting his abdomen with a *clank*. "You get to the good part yet?"

"No," Zack said. He turned to Anya and said, "We're going to the Boneyard."

"*What?*" Anya said, unamused.

"I knew this was going to be good," Ultimus said with a grin.

"We're going to take a mag-rail into the desert and steal a jump-ship from a secret military facility in the Starship Boneyard."

Anya blinked. "That's insane," she said. She looked at Ultimus. "You know it's insane, right? The two of you against all the crazies?"

Ultimus looked at Zack.

Zack sighed. He'd met Ultimus in a merc bar in Below. The man was more than capable of handling himself against a bunch of scavengers and mutants, so Zack was forced to assume Anya saw him as the weak link. And that was a problem, because he needed to lead the team he was forming as much as he wanted her personal support.

"You need to do something about this," Ultimus said sternly.

"I know," Zack said.

Anya pressed her lips together.

Zack smoothed his face. "Anya, he's right. I've been planning this for months. I've been using ARK-II *for months* to acquire the skills I needed, and I hired Ultimus to make sure this wasn't some pipedream."

"I'm allowed to ask questions, Zack."

"Of course you are."

"You just said I wasn't."

"No, I didn't. And I'm prepared for this. You don't need to talk to me like I'm a spoiled Skyward kid with a half-baked plan." That last bit came out a little raw, a little bitchy. He'd hoped she knew him well enough to think better of him.

"I didn't call you spoiled, Zack."

"But my plan's half-baked?"

"I don't know. I haven't seen a plan yet to make up my mind about."

His throat tightened and his head felt hot. He'd never felt this before, the urge to lash out, but he'd been trained to keep his cool in a debate, and he had no plans of tossing his expensive education out the window just because he'd decided to run away from home. "I can see why you might think that," Zack said coolly. "Have you ever known me to be anything less than calculated?"

Anya frowned. She knew he was managing her. It reinforced his point about calculation. Added bonus? She hated it.

"So I'm just supposed to trust you," Anya said.

"No," Zack said, nodding at Ultimus. "Trust *him*. Federal prosthetics, veteran of a hundred wars... He's looked at my plan and helped me refine it. It's *his* job to get us there." It wasn't as good as her trusting him, but they were short on time.

"He's not the one who's going to get hurt if things go wrong, Zack! Look at him! He's built more solidly than an armored vehicle."

Zack hesitated. She was worried he'd get hurt. It wasn't as nice as blind faith in his abilities, but it was nice to know she cared. "Look, I only need you to get Ultimus's cybernetics unlocked. I'll go pick up our engineer, get you the tools you need, and if you don't feel safe coming with us, then at least you got to do something you never would have, even if Simon Bellwether hadn't walked into your life."

Anya's eyes locked with his, searching. Her tattoos were barely there. He wasn't sure if he'd gotten it right or wrong, but at least she wasn't angry. "Fine," she said. "You're the boss, Zack."

"Anya, that's not what I..."

She raised her hand to stop him. "I can compartmentalize. And yeah, if I don't think I'm safe getting on that train, I'm out, but I don't think you understand what I meant by tools. I don't just need them fabricated. I need them installed. In me. We're going to need access to a sterile, programmable surgery." She raised an eyebrow.

"What about the clinic you worked in?" Zack asked.

"My credentials have been revoked. I might be able to talk Dr. Parnavan into helping me, as long as we can pay for the materials."

"But she'll have questions," Ultimus said.

Anya shrugged. "She'll be worried about me, more than anything."

Ultimus and Anya looked at Zack.

"We'll figure it out," Zack said. "Maybe Clavicus has a place we can use." Ultimus nodded. Anya didn't look convinced, but she didn't argue, for now. It made him feel better about their chances and a bit sad, all at once.

Hab Block 24, 37th Floor
Pnyx, Upper-Middle, Capital District of Politeia IV
4386.B.30 Interstellar

Zack felt a touch of apprehension as the apartment's front door slid shut behind him. The last day and a half had been a respite from looking over his shoulder. He'd still half expected state security or his father's personal security to hack through the door and arrest all of them. But, short of that, he'd felt safe.

He'd left ARK-II with Ultimus and Anya. That had felt uncomfortable for different reasons. It wasn't that he thought the mercenary or his lover would run off with the priceless artifact. They both had specific reasons not to hand it over to the government, and Zack was the only administrator ARK-II had chosen thus far. The unshackled AI could designate a new... he would have said "master" or "owner" for most thinking programs, but perhaps "operator" was more appropriate in this case. But for whatever reasons, the little guy had chosen Zack and seemed disinclined to get rid of him even though he'd freed it from its vault beneath the city.

"Excuse me," Zack said, squeezing into the elevator with five other hab-block dwellers. Someone had already pressed the button for street level, so he turned his back on the others as the doors slid shut. Three more people got on at level thirty-two, bringing the cab to maximum occupancy, then the elevator expressed its way to the ground floor. The nice thing about living in a utilitarian society was that some things just *worked*, and no one complained.

Hab Block 24, Street Level
Pnyx, Upper-Middle, Capital District of Politeia IV
4386.B.30 Interstellar

He got off the elevator and discreetly checked his pockets and belt. *Credit chips, breath mints, ventilator, smoke grenades.* A small anti-grav plate was nestled against his lower back. Everything was still there—not a given in an Upper-Middle hab block.

He pulled the hood of his black coachman jacket up, making things a bit harder for facial-recognition algorithms. The next few steps took him into the day glow of Upper-Middle.

Like Anya's hab, the high-rises on both sides of the street were mixed residential and commercial. The high-density neighborhoods were designed to be self-sufficient—a resident could get everything they needed without leaving their building—so that they could provide the skilled, low-cost labor that Skyward required and Below couldn't provide. It had grated on Zack's orbital-born sensibilities until he'd learned about the other interactions between the levels. How Skyward supported system mining operations and interstellar trade, while government agents at all levels worked to identify high-potentials and move them up the ladder. Accession represented a material line item of the sophistocracy's budget. It wasn't perfect. It wasn't even fair. But it made a genuine effort to draw the best out of the people who could provide it.

And it isn't good enough, Zack thought. *Not for me.* He'd stormed out of the Spire with a notion that had crystallized around the theft—or liberation—of ARK-II. He'd burned his boats on the shore. Not even his father could save him if he were caught.

He moved quickly along the sidewalk. His low-g childhood made him taller than most, and even hunching left him above average. His best chance—as Ultimus had pointed out—was to hope no one was looking too hard and get out of sight as soon as possible. The streets were packed with a steady flow of cars, cycles, and light trucks. The sidewalks were packed with habbers headed to the transit towers, their Upper-Middle jobs, or the dozens of small shops that lined the street side of most buildings.

While the Splinter Fleet that had settled Politeia IV had used Federal-Standard for all their communications, contact was eventually reestablished with humanity and follow-on waves of settlers had brought all the vibrancy and mess of a galactic culture with them. Signage in Castilian, Catalan, English and Pidgin, French and Patois, Mandarin, Cantonese, and Neo-Guangzhou, not to mention a dozen Urdu, Hindi, and Proto-Siamese dialects announced each store's owner or main product. People talked and haggled in as many languages. There was something there for everyone, and it excused the black jacket and hood on an otherwise warm, artificial-spring day.

Two blocks north and one block east, he noticed an eddy in the crowd. One of the surface rails was stopped and disgorging passengers. As Zack joined the merging streams of people, he caught sight of a man kneeling on the rails. His face was bloody and already swelling. There was more blood on the ground like someone had spilled it from a jug. Zack washed up like flotsam. "What happened?"

"Tram hit him," a young man said.

An older woman clucked. "He tripped on the rail. Look, you can see where he hit his head."

Zack looked. He knew it wasn't polite to stare, but he'd spent over twenty years of his life doing what was expected of him. It was an older man, and there was indeed a cut above his right eyebrow. Then Zack realized no one was helping, and he stepped out of the crowd.

"Hey, grandfather. Are you all right?" Zack crouched, and the old man looked at him with unfocused eyes.

Zack steadied the man with his hand on his back and checked his pupils. They were a little dilated, but they were the same size. Anya had told him once that scalp wounds bled more than the injury would suggest. The man was dazed, but it wasn't life-threatening. Zack turned to the woman he'd been talking to before and said, "You! Call an ambulance!"

She scowled, but she started dialing on her wrist comm, and her eyes gleamed blue as the call started.

"You all right, boss?" Ultimus said in his ear.

Zack touched the tip of his left thumb to his index finger. "I'm fine, Mr. Thragg. Something up?"

"You stopped moving."

Zack felt a prickling heat on the back of his neck. After weeks spent Below, and in some of the more dangerous parts of Politeia, it was easy to feel safe in Upper-Middle Pnyx. It wasn't, though, and he was glad the mercenary was paying attention. "Taking in the sights. Might be the last morning I see in this city."

"The view's even better from space, sir."

Zack chuckled, reminded of the messages ARK-II used to harass him with. "Understood, my friend.". He turned to his patient and said, "I have to go, grandfather, but help is on the way." He pulled another bystander over to sit with the old man and stepped into the moving crowd.

After a few blocks, he ducked into an alley.

The streets were built into a regular grid, but even here, in the capital district, buildings were scaled to the ambitions and finances of their owners. Gaps formed. They weren't regular, or always useful, but sometimes useless things had uses beyond face value. Zack looked back. The alley was a dead end. He'd had no good reason to go down it. Neither did the man who'd followed him in. He was wearing a black suit and sunglasses, like all the members of Council Security.

"Hey, Ultimus?" Zack said.

"Yeah, boss?"

"Time to go."

"You sure?"

The dark-suited man started running toward him.

Zack opened a blue fire door and ripped the tape he'd put

over the latch two days ago. The door slammed shut and locked behind him.

"I'm sure."

"We'll go with Orange Two," Ultimus said, referencing one of the plans they'd practiced in VR.

"Orange Two it is," Zack said, and he passed through a second door into a household appliance store.

PART IV

Something stinks.
Hold your breath until it passes.

CHAPTER NINE

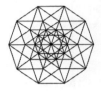

Millennium Tower 14, 1st Floor
Pnyx, Upper-Middle, Capital District of Politeia IV
4386.B.30 Interstellar

Zack felt a little flutter in his stomach as he pushed his hood back and bounded up a narrow set of stairs. He pushed his way through a double set of swinging doors to the first floor of the shopping concourse, hurried past several holo-commercials, and stepped onto the first rising escalator he came to. Unlike Anya's hab or the other buildings he'd passed, this was one of twenty identical commercial developments, built like a star spider's web to ensnare the casual customer.

There was nothing menacing about the building. If anything, the clean lines, abundance of greenery, and the trickle of water walls would have put a Zen-Capitalist at ease as they emptied their bank account. What made Zack choose this building as the start of Plan Orange Two was that very openness —the ease with which he'd spot someone moving toward him— and that it was laid out like a game of dropships and space elevators.

He stepped off the escalator and took a left, past a French patisserie and a belt-mined-jewelry store. A sky-bridge, flanked on each side by poster stands of artists on both sides of the current immigration debate, gave him covered access to an express elevator that took him from the third to the sixth floor.

He'd thought he'd have more time. It wasn't that he thought his father's security wasn't competent; Zack had the highest regard for Sam Meritt, the Combine mercenary-turned-security-chief who led the governor's personal guard. He just hadn't expected his father to care. The fact his dad hadn't called him and asked him to come home suggested he had something less cooperative in mind. Sending a team to snatch a citizen off the streets, even his son, was probably some kind of abuse of power. It felt like a knee jerk reaction. Zack couldn't imagine him doing that.

So, either some rogue element had decided Zack Lancestrom was too much of an embarrassment to roam free, or his father had discovered ARK-II was missing, and things were about to get very interesting.

Zack walked out of the elevator and stepped up to the railing, leaning on it like a habber on a day off. He spotted three more of the black-suited agents. One of them looked up, spotted Zack, and spoke into his wrist. A pair of agents on the fourth floor broke into a run.

Zack grinned and walked a quarter turn clockwise around the level, took a staircase to the fifth floor, passing a sporting goods store and three noodle shops. The third one was a fusion Texan-Italian place that made a hellacious four-alarm Cincinnati-style chili. Zack didn't know what most of those words meant, but he'd snuck out of Anya's more than once in the middle of the night to grab a bowl when they'd been dating. A third of a turn counterclockwise took him to a massive escalator that rose to the ninth floor. It was totally part of the evasion plan, but if he was honest, he'd chosen it for the view.

The entire northwest corner of the building was a fifty-story tall window. It was an architectural conceit, different from the other Millennium Towers and broken into one-meter-by-one-meter panes. By chance or outrageous bribe, a gap in the aligned buildings let Zack see all the way to the holographic sun on the underside of Skyward. It made him happy.

"Mr. Lancestrom! Sir!" an agent called out.

A number of bystanders turned to look—the Lancestroms were famous, after all. Zack smiled and raised his hand, palm in, giving the crowd a gentle wave like some Old Earth monarch as he rose past the flustered, red-faced man.

"How are you doing, boss?" Ultimus asked on the team channel.

"Like we practiced, Mr. Thragg," Zack answered, feeling proud. "Yourself?"

"Just got on the train."

A holographic timer appeared above Zack's left wrist.

2:23

"I'm on my way," Zack said. One of the agents was sprinting up the escalator after him, pushing people to the side. Another pair appeared at the top, boxing him in.

And he loved it. Everything he'd put himself through for the last few months had been for moments like this.

He put both hands on the handrail. People gasped, and one woman screamed as he jumped.

Oh crap, oh crap, oh crap! he thought as the ground rushed up toward him.

The anti-grav plate kicked in. He felt like every atom in his body was yanked up at three times normal gravity in the wrong direction, and only his virtual training kept him from losing his lunch. Then he slammed down on one hand and one knee, coat tails flaring in the middle of a dispersing crowd. "Yes!" he yelled, feeling like a phoenix bursting into flame. *A day, a year, a life of doing this!* He glanced at his wrist.

2:09

He stood and ran toward the escalator, heading down this time. There was an agent between him and the subway. As the black-suited man reached under his coat, Zack unhooked the anti-grav plate from his back, triggered it, and flicked it at the man's feet. The flat hex, charged by Zack's fall, discharged all at once, smashing the agent down on his chest, stun gun skittering away.

"Watch your head!" Zack said, vaulting over him without stopping. He reached the escalator and hopped up, sitting on the left handrail, sliding down past the Politeians standing to the right, as orderly citizens should. They leaned away from Zack as he zipped by, frowning, shouting, laughing too, and he loved all of it. He slipped off as he reached the second sublevel, almost fell, caught himself, and jogged to the turnstiles.

"How are we looking, Mr. Thragg?" Zack asked, exhilarated.

"Nets are quiet, sir. City PD's being kept out of it, for now."

Good, Zack thought, though it puzzled him. He swiped through the turnstile and headed into the subway station.

1:41

The path branched ahead. Most of the subway stations in Pnyx were part of the CCN, the capital city network. A few, like this one, were also a stop for the Upper-Middle inter-city. It was how Zack and Ultimus had planned to leave the city in a few days, but they couldn't leave without Clavicus, so Zack took the right branch toward the city train.

"There he is!"

Three agents were forcing their way through the crowd at the turnstiles.

Zack swept his coat back, grabbed the ventilator mask with

his left hand and a smoke grenade with his right. He thumbed the trigger and side threw it, pushing the mask against his face as the wall of white smoke exploded over him and everyone else.

There were screams and angry shouts. Zack kept moving, his left shoulder brushing against the wall. He had his eyes closed to keep the stinging gas out of them, and a lot more of the gas was getting into his lungs than he would have liked. *Ultimus told me to shave the beard off,* he thought wryly. It smelled like he'd snorted lemon juice and red pepper, and felt like it, too. *Where are those steps?* he thought, and half-squinted with one eye. Good thing, too, because he'd been two steps from going down them headfirst.

"Which way did he go?"

People came spilling out of the smoke. Zack caught one lady as she almost fell, then almost got knocked over by a man twice as wide around the waist as him.

"I'm heading down to the platform!"

Zack grabbed the second grenade from his belt and tucked it under his armpit.

0:59

The agent came down the stairs out of the thinning smoke, two steps at a time and stun gun drawn. He had a full-face gas mask on, and Zack was perfectly positioned. He wrapped his free arm up and around and then slammed him in the chest with his palm. The agent's legs kept going forward, and he went back ass over teakettle, or almost did; Zack stopped him short of cracking his head open. "That was close, wasn't it?"

The man snarled and wrenched the stun gun around.

Zack dropped him the last ten centimeters. The man grunted, aimed, and Zack smashed him in the face with the gas grenade. The blow knocked his gas mask half on, half off. *Hard to shoot when you can't see.* Zack dropped the armed grenade into the man's lap and started walking toward the platform again. The gas whooshed out and blew past him, filling the tunnel.

"Talk to me, Ultimus."

No answer.

Zack's mouth went dry. He stopped. This wasn't part of the plan. Ultimus had ARK-II; he had Anya. If he dropped off the radar—

"Sir, can you hear me?"

Thank the Virtues. "I can hear you, Mr. Thragg."

A pause, then, "Tunnels... interference. We're... into the station now."

Zack blinked back tears. From the gas. Had to be from the gas. Twenty seconds to go, and Zack was running for the platform as fast as his low-g legs could carry him. Adrenaline gave him wings. It all came down to making that train.

A flood of people started coming up the last flight of stairs as he was rushing down, passengers from the train he needed to board. "Get out of the way!" he shouted, waving the gas mask and shouldering a man aside.

Seven seconds to go when he hit the platform.

He ran for the open car doors.

Five...

Four...

Three...

Zack reached out and caught the door as it started to slide shut. He'd made it.

And then someone yanked him back by the coat and the doors shut in front of him.

"Sir? Did you make it onto the train?"

Sam Meritt looked down at Zack and grinned. "Good to see you, kid. It's been too long."

CHAPTER TEN

Millennium Tower 14, Sublevel Three
Pnyx, Upper-Middle, Capital District of Politeia IV
4386.B.30 Interstellar

Zack's mind raced. "Sam?"

The former mercenary's face was calm, even mildly sardonic. He offered Zack a hand up.

Zack was blown. No six weeks of virtual training made him a match for a Combine mercenary, so he fell back on his political science training. He stalled. "Doing your own fieldwork?" he asked, grabbing hold of Sam's arm.

Sam hauled him up. "Good thing I did. You gave my boys and girls a spot of trouble."

"Huh. Didn't see any girls."

Sam shrugged. "Might be a coincidence, but my female agents were smart enough not to chase after you or get caught in an ambush."

A number of agents—of both genders—were walking toward them now and moving to keep the crowd back. Zack counted seven of them in all, armed with stun guns, batons, and wrist communicators. Maybe facial recognition in the glasses...

"You look good, kid. Different," Sam said, and Zack turned back to face him.

There was a look in Sam's eyes he'd never seen before. Something like caution, and maybe a hint of respect.

"I've been exercising."

"Oh, yeah? What kind of exercise?"

"A lot of Pilates," Zack answered. "How did you know where I'd be headed?"

Sam chuckled. "Come on, Zack. What were you going to do, grow wings when you got to the roof?"

"I could have had an aircar waiting."

"And we would've locked it down through the safety system. You head for crowds and public transportation. I taught you that."

"I guess you did."

Sam put his hands on his hips, showing off the high-caliber pistol on his hip.

Zack shifted his weight, just a little, putting himself in a better position to take the weapon, and Sam's eyes crinkled in amusement. "Looks like you've been keeping the wrong kind of company, kid."

Zack blushed. Had he been that obvious, or was Sam that good? Zack put his hands in his coat pockets, trying to play it off. "I know father doesn't like Anya, but she's good for me."

"I know that, kid. I've told him so," Sam said. "I meant Ultimus Thragg."

"Who?"

Sam put his arm around Zack's shoulders—his left arm, keeping Zack away from his gun. "About my height, skull made of tri-alloy, built like a small tank?" He smirked, leading Zack back toward the stairs. The other agents had their stun guns drawn. "And seeing that he's a consummate professional, he'll have stopped that train and be headed for us like a tunnel-shark with a toothache."

Zack turned to look back, and Sam shoved him forward. "Hey!" Two agents grabbed Zack by the upper arms.

"Take him to his father."

"Sam!"

"Sorry, kid," Sam said, kneeling over an open weapon case. "Grownups gotta talk." He pulled a long tube with a pistol grip and side-mounted optical sights.

"Let me go!" Zack said, acting outraged, pretending to struggle and slip as the two agents dragged him.

"Here he comes!" a woman shouted.

All the agents turned to face the tunnel, even the two trying to pull Zack toward the stairs, and Zack acted instantly. He planted his foot behind the agent on his right, dropped his weight, and slammed his elbow up under the man's chin. The agent went over backward. Zack swept his left foot back, pulled his second escort close, like a zero-g tango dancer, and wound up with her stun gun in his hand. "Abracadabra," he said. He shot her point-blank in the thigh and her leg gave out, then he shot her teammate before the man could get up and draw his own stun gun. Zack looked up to see Ultimus, coat off and armor showing, charge down the platform like a runaway train, shrugging off stun shots and bellowing like a berserker.

He made it halfway.

Sam Meritt stepped out, the tube raised on his shoulder. *Crack!* There was a flash like a lightning strike and Ultimus face planted, metal armor scraping across the concrete. "Whoo!" the security chief said, lowering the weapon.

Zack stepped out from behind the pillar. *Snap, snap, snap!* He calmly put two stun shots into Sam's lower back, dropping his father's bodyguard to one knee, and put the last shot into the back of his head, knocking him flat before Zack got back behind cover.

"Who's shooting?"

"It's the governor's son!"

Zack checked the charge pack on his stun gun. He had ten shots left, five targets. He leaned out on the right.

Snap!

Zack flopped like a rag doll onto his back. He hadn't been hit, but it made the charging agent hesitate, and Zack squeezed off two shots between his legs, missed both, and rolled sideways off the platform and dropped to the tracks. He ducked forward half a meter, popped up, and got his target on the third shot. *Snap!*

"Stay back! I'll handle him!" Sam said, rising to his feet.

Damn it, that guy's a monster, Zack thought, gritting his teeth at his dwindling shot count. He popped up to put another shot into the security chief.

Shots snapped out to Zack's right, but they weren't aimed at him.

"Sir, look out!" one of the agents shouted, and Sam Meritt turned in time to get side tackled by Ultimus. Both men went down in a tangle of body blows, bent metal, and swearing. Zack had already shifted his aim and put two shots into a female agent, only to have her partner come out from behind a column half a meter away with Zack in his sights. *Snap!* Zack juked his head, avoiding the first shot. The air smelled like ozone. He knew he wouldn't avoid the second.

Then the man seized up and dropped, half hanging off the platform.

Anya gave Zack a nod.

Still pissed at me, he thought, but there wasn't much he could do about it. "Having fun?" Zack asked, clambering up and looking for targets.

"Beats fixing radiators," she said.

Zack saw two more agents sprawled out, the way she'd come. He touched her shoulder. "You did good, babe."

"I know," she said with a little sass, and Zack was glad for her. She'd earned it.

"Ugh!" Ultimus said, flying back down the platform.

"This is over, kid!" Sam said, surging forward.

Zack side-stepped with the gun raised. The first shot clipped Sam in the shoulder before the former merc slapped it out of Zack's hands and off the platform. Zack slipped the reverse elbow aimed at his nose and snapped a kick at Sam's knee, but he may as well have kicked one of the support columns.

Sam grinned, face bruised and armor-weave showing where his skin had split, and he spread his arms to tackle Zack.

"Duck!" Ultimus yelled.

Zack dropped, and Ultimus came over his head with a clothesline that would have decapitated most men. Sam caught it with both hands, sliding back. Zack circled toward the woman he'd knocked out earlier.

Clank! Sam landed a string of body blows on Ultimus's belly and ribs, and while Zack's protector was armor-plated, Zack had never realized how mech'ed up Sam was until today. Zack's financially motivated friend was hurting.

Zack grabbed a riot baton from the fallen agent, snapped it open, and as Ultimus collapsed under the barrage of mechanical blows, Zack swung the baton at the back of Sam's head.

The baton bounced off, and, faster than Zack would have thought possible, Sam spun and grabbed his arm. "You trying to kill me, kid?"

Zack gave him an exaggerated shrug. "I'm trying to get you to turn your back on my girlfriend?"

Sam's eyes widened, and then he dropped, mouth working, face turning pale with Anya's hand latched onto his shoulder.

"We need to get out of here," Ultimus said hoarsely, struggling to get to his feet.

"Where's ARK-11?" Zack asked.

The little box popped out from behind one of the far columns, beeping a greeting and glowing blue.

"Good to see you too, buddy."

Sam's face had turned bright red.

Zack touched Anya's elbow. "Babe?"

Anya blinked, and Sam fell forward. "Sorry."

"How long is he out?" Zack asked.

"I don't know. A few minutes? He's nowhere near as aug'ed as Ultimus, but he's pretty tough."

Zack snorted. "Understatement, much?" Half of him was proud of Sam, a man who'd come into his life when he was sixteen and been kind to him in spite of his now apparent capacity for violence. The other half of him wondered if Ultimus was up to the task of getting them offworld.

Ultimus met his eyes, and the man looked... old. A bit embarrassed. "I could have... no, screw that, never mind," he said, clamping his jaw shut.

Anya put her hand on the old mercenary's arm. "You're still locked out of most of your abilities, Ultimus."

Ultimus spat and started hobbling toward the train tunnel they'd come from. "Right. 'Cause that's an excuse. I came at him big, dumb, and happy, right down the middle."

"Like we planned," Anya said, following, and Zack joined them.

Ultimus's battered face turned a bit pink. "Wouldn't have worked at all if you hadn't fixed my EMP shielding. Should've done better against a young guy like Meritt."

"We didn't want to hurt anyone. Not seriously."

"Maybe we should have," Ultimus said.

Zack was still stuck on "young" Meritt and the EMP shielding. As far as he knew, Sam was in his fifties. How long had Thragg been kicking around? And Sam had seemed certain the tube weapon would take Ultimus down. Had Zack been right to bring Anya into this, or had coming back for her put them in danger they would have avoided?

The warm, rushing wind of an arriving train blew in their faces, and Zack frowned. What was he forgetting?

Then his eyes widened. He turned, saw the agent Anya had knocked out was still half-dangling from the platform, and sprinted toward him. At the same moment, Ultimus shouted a warning and wrapped his arms around Anya, turning his body to shield her.

Clang! The round—an honest to goodness metal round—sparked off Ultimus's back as he pulled her into cover. *Bang!* The second round tugged at Zack's jacket and barely missed his legs.

"I'm done playing, kid!" Sam shouted.

Bang! The round left a crater on the far wall.

Oh crap! Zack thought, but he could see the train's lights in the tunnel. There were decisions you could take back, and decisions you could only make once. He ignored the rounds coming at him and grabbed the downed agent's legs.

Bang! The heavy round gouged a hole in the pillar next to Zack just as he pulled the agent clear, and the train, an express, blew past the station without stopping and there was... the teensiest little tug.

"Oh, whoops," Zack said.

"Zack?" Anya yelled, sounding anxious.

The agent had lost a hand. And half his forearm. "Well, that will grow back, maybe," Zack said. He pulled his belt off to rig a tourniquet.

"Don't be a dick, Meritt!" Ultimus shouted.

Bang! The report didn't sound any closer. Zack doubted Sam could walk.

"Zack! Zack, get over here!" Anya yelled.

"Don't do it, kid!" Sam said. "I *will* shoot you in the legs." He sounded breathy, like the older orbital dwellers when the air got thin.

Zack cranked the tourniquet tight with the agent's baton. It wasn't perfect, but the bleeding slowed. "You're not going to shoot me, Sam."

"I might. You going to risk it?"

Zack's life—the last ten years of it—flashed before his eyes, and yeah, he was bluffing with an off-suit hand and a pair of twos. He was pretty sure Sam *would* shoot him. *Pretty sure Anya messed him up, too.* Maybe that would throw off his aim. Anya, Ultimus, and ARK-11 were three meters away, and from there it was across the tracks and into the tunnel to safety. "Your guy's bleeding out here, Sam!"

Sam started an angry response.

And Zack used that split-second distraction. He went for it, sprinting for his life.

CHAPTER ELEVEN

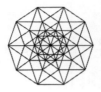

Millennium Tower 14, Sublevel Three
Pnyx, Upper-Middle, Capital District of Politeia IV
4386.B.30 Interstellar

Zack ran, glancing left at Sam's pointed gun.

Sam looked like hell, face still pale, gun braced with both hands. The half-formed answer in Sam's throat bought Zack two running steps, but Sam fired and, even system-shocked, Sam didn't miss.

And ARK-II took the round. The little machine flew out at the same time Sam pulled the trigger, and the impact knocked it into Zack.

Zack caught the brave little toaster, spun, and kept running.

Ultimus was waiting with open arms.

Zack jumped off the platform.

"Oof!" Ultimus said, catching him.

"Oh my God!" Anya said, laughing into her hand, tears brimming in her eyes.

"What?" Zack asked, heart still yammering from almost getting shot. With real bullets! "You're an asshole, Sam!"

If Sam answered, Zack didn't hear it as Ultimus carried him and ARK-11 into the darkened tunnel.

"Nothing," Anya said. "Only confirmation Ultimus is every girl's dream."

"He had his arms spread!" Zack said.

"Okay, princess," Anya fired back. "Is ARK-11 all right?"

"I don't know," Zack said, worried, hugging the box to his chest.

ARK-11 pulsed an irritated orange and let loose with beeps and whoops.

"I know, right? What a jerk!"

More beeps.

"I'm glad you stopped him, too," Zack said.

"You can understand that?" Anya asked.

"Sure," Zack said. "It's Robot, or something like that. ARK-11 learned it from an old holofilm or something."

"Why doesn't he speak Standard?"

ARK-11 glowed light pink—sarcasm—and made a sound like a Bronx cheer.

Zack could see the train up ahead. The nearest cab looked empty. He wondered if the passengers had clustered on the far end or risked running to the next station.

Ultimus stopped and turned to Anya. "Can you carry the cases?"

"Are you kidding? They must weigh twenty-five kilos each!"

"You want to carry your boyfriend instead?"

"I have my own baggage to deal with."

Zack snickered.

Anya's tattoos glowed neon green in the dark.

Zack grinned in the wrath-light. "But seriously, I'm fine. Set me down."

"You sure, boss? I want you to feel like you're getting your money's worth."

Zack blushed. Thankfully, no one could see it.

"Because of the look you gave me, back on the platform," Ultimus added.

Zack smirked. "So you decided to carry me?"

"I'm pretty sure I carried you both," Anya said, picking up her backpack.

"Damn," Ultimus said, setting Zack down.

Zack smiled in the near-total darkness. Emma had been nice. And fun. But he was glad it was Anya with him, kicking ass and taking his bodyguard down a peg.

"You think they'll come after us?" Anya asked.

"Nah," Ultimus said, putting his coat back on. "Never reinforce failure. It's an old military adage. If I was Meritt, I'd lock down both stations and call in a wrecker squad."

"What if he's not that smart?" Anya insisted.

Ultimus picked up the weapons' cases. "He's smart. Too bad for him, topside's not where we're headed." Rather than head backward or toward the train, Ultimus led them over to an access hatch. Zack held ARK-11 and watched as Anya overrode the control panel with her implants, and they stepped into the warren of service tunnels that would lead them Below.

Machine Shop 7
Pnyx, In-Between, Capital District of Politeia IV
4386.B.30 Interstellar

They stopped for lunch in a small machine shop, an hour in and halfway down. The spaces In-Between didn't belong to anybody. It was technically Federal land, though the planetary government was expected to maintain it. It was twenty meters thick at its thinnest, six stories of pipes and overlapping tunnel mazes. People got lost down here, and the maintenance crews had to decide whether to carry them up to the surface or drag the bodies to one of the chutes. The simple machine shop, consisting of an obsolete metal-printer and some basic tools, allowed those crews to spend as little time in here as possible by fabricating missing parts on the spot.

"Are we safe here?" Zack asked Ultimus.

The big man shrugged, popping a spoonful of his self-heating meal into his mouth. The mercenary's chest-plate was dented from Sam Meritt's blows, and while he'd done his best to hide it—in Zack's opinion—he'd moved with a slight squealing limp since the encounter. "Safe is a relative term. I set tattlers on some of the doors we went through. No one's triggered them."

Zack nodded. Ducking through all those hatches and making sure he didn't fall to his death kept Zack's mind busy, but once they stopped, he had time to think about what happened.

He'd been shot at with a real gun.

He'd watched a man's arm get ripped off.

For that matter, if Zack had gotten knocked out by a stun shot while he was on the tracks, and Anya and Ultimus had still been busy fighting Sam, it might have been Zack turned to vat-grown meat across the front of the express. It was something he'd considered before he embarked on this whole venture, but that had been an intellectual exercise, like the paper he'd written on how much soldiers' families should be compensated if they died in service to the planet. He'd felt so righteous, writing that. Taking the spouse and children's suffering into consideration. Replacing the lost income. He'd statistically modeled the likelihood of a woman making it to high rank, of a man leaving the service to succeed in the private sector. And he'd judged.

What about the value of a person who could take that on,

who could put themselves at risk for something other than self, other than blood? If he'd learned anything on that subway platform, it was that Zack Lancestrom was not that person. He'd felt like it was a game when he'd been running from his father's agents. It was the kind of thing a young man might do for fun, prove his courage to his friends in a simulation. When Sam shot him—shot *at* him—when he'd heard the high-pitched snap of the round and felt ARK-II slam into him, he'd felt terrified. It was like he'd been shoved outside himself, and he'd seen how fragile he was. And he felt guilty for putting Sam's people—people who did take on that commitment—at risk.

"How are you holding up?" Ultimus asked.

Zack raised his head. Anya met his eyes, but Ultimus was focused on his food. "I'm all right." Zack swallowed. "Thanks for coming back. Both of you."

"It's what you paid me for," Ultimus said gruffly. "Besides, I was talking to ARK-II."

The dented levio-case dwee-wooped.

Ultimus chuckled. "Yeah, ARK-II. You *are* a tough SOB. That dent is almost gone."

"It has a nano-disassembler and a self-repair module," Zack told Anya.

Anya sighed. "Does everyone speak bleep?"

"Speak *what*?" Zack asked, grinning.

"Whatever language ARK-II speaks."

Zack ran a hand over his little friend's exterior. Sam's round had put a two-inch dent into it, but it hadn't broken through. "It's funny, actually. There was this... I guess you'd think of it as an interstellar corporation, even if it was only the one planet. But they trademarked the name for machines and their language."

Anya frowned. "How can you trademark the name of something everyone uses?"

Zack shrugged. "I don't know. Anyway, the interstellar went

out of business, and the trademark fell into legal limbo during the First Interstellar War, so now no one can use it. ARK-II can't even tell me what it was." He looked at Anya and asked, "How are you doing?"

"Me?" she asked, sounding surprised.

"Yes, you."

Anya shrugged. "I don't know. Hungry. Tired. Relieved, I guess? There's no going back now."

Zack and Ultimus glanced at each other. She didn't know the half of it.

Anya looked at the two of them, then nodded to herself. "You knew something like this was coming, didn't you?" she asked Zack.

Zack sighed. "Yeah. We were okay laying low outside the capital, but it was a sure bet my father would try something when we resurfaced."

"And you did it anyway?"

Zack met her eyes. "Of course I did, Anya."

She swallowed and looked away.

"What do you think they'll do to us, messing up a squad of the governor's own like that?" Ultimus asked, breaking the silence.

Zack wrinkled his nose. "Depends."

"On what?"

"On whether what they did was legal. If they had a court order and we resisted, that would be assault on a planetary official, but if they were moonlighting?"

"What makes you think they were 'moonlighting?'" Ultimus asked.

"Maybe to spare the governor the embarrassment of a warrant," Zack answered.

Anya set her food down and unscrewed a bottle of water.

"You should eat, babe." There was something different in her voice, and Zack looked at her, surprised.

"She's right, boss," Ultimus said.

Zack nodded. He poked at the goop in the aluminum pouch. "It's not that appetizing right now."

Ultimus chuckled and tossed Zack a small shaker. "Try that."

"What is it?"

"Special spice mix," Ultimus said, taking a bite of his own food.

"He means MSG," Anya said.

"He means paprika, chili flakes, cumin, turmeric, salt, and pepper," Ultimus said, wagging his spoon at her. "And MSG," he added with a grin.

Anya chuckled.

Zack added some to his food and took a bite. It helped. "Thanks," he said, tossing the shaker back.

"No problem, boss."

And the food was good. Zack wasn't complaining. It was some kind of near-chicken protein in a creamy sauce with bits of char and almost-fresh peas. It was rich but not cloying, and as he took his third bite, his body seemed to realize how hungry it was and demanded he pour the rest of it down his throat. As before, Ultimus had spent a little extra of his hard-earned cash to make sure they were all taken care of. Zack might have preferred if the mercenary had charged less for his services; then again, he'd have felt less confident with a cheap bodyguard than a generous if expensive one.

"How did you know how to do all that, back there?" Anya asked him.

"Plan Orange Two? Ultimus and I worked that out in VR."

"I meant the shooting. You took out, what, four trained agents with their own weapons?"

"Three, I think." Zack frowned, counting in his head, though it was five if he counted the two from the mall and the stairs.

"It's still a lot, Zack. As far as I knew, you'd never fired a gun or gotten into a fight in your life."

"What about you? You took one, maybe two of them out before they even saw you."

"And Sam Meritt," Ultimus said.

"And Sam." Zack grinned. "Should have seen the look on his face."

"I did. He looked furious," Anya said.

Zack winced. "Yeah, but before that. He almost looked... I don't know... proud."

"I'm sure he was, boss. Pissed he screwed the op, too," Ultimus said. He looked at Anya. "What did you do to Meritt, anyway?"

"I shut down the servos in his chest." Zack raised an eyebrow, so she continued. "Sam has armor fused to his ribs. It's a lot of extra weight, so he has micro-motors installed to help him breathe."

Ultimus shook his head. "Remind me to never upset you."

"Tell Zack that," Anya said, batting her eyelashes. "How much farther to Below?"

"Another hour," Ultimus said, sucking his polymer spoon clean and dropping it into the bag. "Then, we pick up our engineer and get the hell out of Pnyx before things get downright unfriendly."

ARK-11 wobbled over, and Ultimus put the trash into its nano-disassembler.

Access Point 20
Pnyx, Below, Capital District of Politeia IV

4386.B.30 Interstellar

A little over an hour later, the four of them arrived at the access point maintenance crews used to enter this part of the In-Between. It was only big enough for one person at a time. An extendable ladder went down about three meters before ending at a sealed hatch. The control panel on the wall was a simple keypad, but Zack had no idea how many digits he'd have to guess or whether getting it wrong would bring the district police down on their heads. "Can you open this?" Zack asked Ultimus.

"I could force it," Ultimus said, looking down at the hatch. "Not sure that would be a good idea."

"What about Clavicus? Can he open it from the other side?"

"I can't transmit through this," Ultimus said, waving at the pipes and steel bulkheads.

"I'll take care of it," Anya said, flexing her fingers. She put her hand over the control panel and closed her eyes. A few seconds later, the hatch split open, and the ladder extended.

"You're amazing," Zack said, smiling at her.

"I know," she said, blowing him a kiss.

Zack stepped onto the ladder and started climbing down. ARK-11 peered over the edge and whistled. "I'll be okay, buddy," Zack said, giving him a thumbs up. The truth was, he felt a lot less comfortable about it than he was showing. There was a whole lot of nothing to catch him if he fell.

It was like climbing out of a hole in the sky. All around him, as far as he could see, the flat plate of the ceiling showed a cloudless day. He was close enough to it to see the thin, black lines of the hexagonal paneling, but the image was so perfect it felt more like there was a wire mesh over the world and the ladder was the illusion. He put his foot on the last rung and hooked his left arm over a rung, then activated his communicator. "Clavicus? Are you there?"

After a few seconds, a projection of Clavicus's face appeared over Zack's wrist. "Of course I'm here. I've been waiting for two hours." The engineer cocked his head. "Where are you calling me from?"

"We had a little trouble getting down here." Zack held out his arm so Clavicus could see.

Clavicus's image winked out, but the connection stayed open. "Not funny, man."

"I can assure you, I'm not laughing," Zack said. Below was the thinnest of the layers, only one hundred meters from the ground, but that was still one hundred meters for Zack to fall.

A gust snatched at his coat and hood, threatening to rip him from his perch, his *precarious* roost on the grimy ladder that hung above Below. He shuddered to think when it had last been maintained, and he hugged it for dear life until the wind subsided.

"I'm homing in on your signal," Clavicus grumbled. "Hang tight."

Wouldn't dream of doing anything else, my friend.

"Did you reach him?" Ultimus hollered from the hatch above him.

"Yes!" Zack yelled.

"Well, is he coming?"

"Yes, he's coming!" Zack said a little more snappily than he'd intended. He could feel the ladder oscillating, like the needle on a polygraph, and Zack would be lying if he said he wasn't expecting the corroded steel to snap off at any moment. And the longer he stayed there, the less romantic the view became. Because this was Below, not the olympian Skyward or even well-to-do Upper-Middle. The buildings were a squat ten to fifteen stories—twenty at most! And a good bit of the area was given over to warehouses and industrial structures that were surrounded by rusting chain-link fences. *Goes to show what they think of the neighbors.* And he noticed broken projectors on the ceiling! Some of the blackened hexes hung precariously while people lived their lives below. *I mean, what would happen if one of those fell and squashed an attempted mugger in the act?* he wondered, with a smirk. The governor's office would take credit, of course, maybe call the faulty panels a new public safety program. "Our gravity-driven anti-crime units are just another part of the Politeian struggle against corruption."

"You say something, boss?"

"No!" Zack said. He was starting to feel cold from getting buffeted around, but he felt better anyway. If the roaring gale stripped the flesh from his bones, Anya and Ultimus would find his ribcage lit by the inner fire of his sarcasm.

In any case, he didn't have to wait long. Like a space rocket from the ancient ages of man, only dirtier, a pillar of black smoke rose from the streets and the squat little buildings, a smear of charcoal across an already flawed sketch, a missile arcing toward him. The fattening tail and greasy tip may as well have been an arrow pointing at them. *By all the vices, Clavicus!* Had the man never heard of discretion?

The aircraft itself looked like nothing more than a flying bread loaf, a minivan propelled by four massive, vectored thrusters, much like ARK-11's, except the little guy's burned clean. Clavicus's monstrosity pulled up beneath him, engulfing him in the vile smoke and smoldering particulates, and as the wind blew it east, Zack saw a hatch had opened on the roof.

Clavicus was inside. He was a large man, not so much blocky as rounded, wearing a sewage-green poncho and a round, conical leaf hat that was colored corroded copper green. His features were hidden by a blue hologram, like a fishbowl full of reactor coolant with a skull floating in it. The engineer waved his hand. "What are you waiting for? Jump in!"

★

Cyberclinic, 2nd Floor
Pnyx, Upper-Middle, Capital District of Politeia IV
4386.B.30 Interstellar

The governor kept a look of benign, elderly goodwill on his face as he exited the elevator and two Council Security agents cleared the way for him. Patients and staff were gently but firmly pushed aside or told to wait in their rooms, but that wasn't Alex Lancestrom's doing. He smiled apologetically for the trouble without for a moment wishing the agents would do otherwise. Running the planet kept him busy, and were it not for the... sensitivity of the task he'd entrusted to Sam Meritt, he wouldn't have come at all.

"Sir?" Angelica Simms, the leader of his current detail asked.

"Yes, Agent Simms?"

"Agent Meritt's doctor is here."

Alex looked over to where a petite woman with walnut skin and straight black hair stood waiting. She wore no nametag, but a cursory check of the government's noosphere told him her name was ancient Turkish, but her genetics were Old Earth Tamil—unusually so after thousands of years of mixing and engineering. She was third generation Politeian, her small family migrating first from Edenaris, then to Hobson's World via the Old Man's Stairs before coming here. Military service—maybe they'd crossed paths at some point. She was mostly unmodified organics, which was surprising for a woman in her position. She had two neo-foxes and took too many pictures of them. He gleaned this from his prefrontal implant in a blink, the way an unaugmented human might notice someone was tired or decide they had a pretty smile. "Doctor Parnavan," he said, extending his hand.

Her eyebrows *almost* rose, he noted. "Governor," she said, clasping his wrist instead of his hand.

"A surgeon's hands are a precious and fragile tool," Alex said, smiling.

The doctor smiled in return, letting go. "Yes. Prosthetics would be more efficient, but I preferred analog. You've come to visit Mr. Meritt?"

"I have. How is he?"

"Well, for what was done to him. She... his attacker showed restraint."

She? Alex had scanned the medical report already, but he'd assumed the damage was from a stun overload or touching the third rail. A blink showed him her history with Anya Vesperian. Some might have accused her of making excuses for her former protégée, but everything in her file suggested Dr. Shiva Parnavan was a consummate professional. "I'll go remind him he isn't indestructible, then."

"I'd appreciate that, sir," she said, dipping her head. His social enhancements tagged fourteen indicators the encounter had gone well as he turned away, moving her up several automatically generated lists of potential experts and cabinet members, should he need them.

"Sir?" Sam said, sitting up in his hospital bed. His bare torso was covered in deep bruises. A straight, raised line of scar tissue running from his jugular notch to his navel marked where his synthetic skin had been cut open and then cauterized shut. All that would heal, but for the moment, he looked like he'd been sucked into a street cleaner with razors for brushes.

"At ease, Sam," the governor said, walking into the room. "That will be all, Agent Simms."

"Yes, sir." Angelica Simms and the agent accompanying her left the room, closing the door behind them.

Alex pulled a stool over and sat. "So."

"Yeah," Sam said, leaning back. "Kind of embarrassing."

"I'll say. And I understand it was Zack's lady friend who put you down."

Sam curled his lips like he had something stuck in his teeth. "It's a bit more complicated than that. It started when your son made the agent tailing him."

"That's... unexpected."

"It was for everyone concerned. Zack executed a rehearsed escape plan. I've seen the footage. No hesitation when he dropped nine stories using an anti-grav plate, and he took down five trained agents, one in hand-to-hand and two with their own weapons. He's been *trained*, sir. The body's the same, but I barely recognize the man."

"You mean that figuratively, I assume? This is still my son we're talking about, not a subversive wearing Zack's face?"

"Oh, it was Zack, all right. Same old charm, same old stories. He put three stun shots into my back before I even knew he'd stolen a weapon. That was new."

And Alex was... pleased. He'd spent some small amount of time—six years—in the Politeian System Defense Fleet before becoming a career politician. He'd made it to the rank of lieutenant mostly by merit—he hadn't been the favorite for future governor at the time—and led search parties aboard more than one merchant platform or mining platform. Some of those searches had led to gunfire. Alex was no hawk, and he abhorred defense interstellars who prolonged conflicts by arming both sides, but he also believed that crucible had purified him, like losing Elena and raising Zack had tempered him. He dared to hope. "What about the others?"

Sam shook his head. "Thragg tried to bullrush me; I was prepared for that. I hit him with a D-EMP, although that didn't keep him down near as long as it should have. Zack took another one of my men out, even went so far as to take a baton to the back of my skull."

"He meant to kill you?" Alex said, concerned.

Sam shook his head. "No. Never that. I saw him run back, risk everything to pull one of my men out of the path of a train, even treated his injury." Sam ran his hand through his hair. "As I said, he's still your son. He knew a whack to the head wouldn't hurt me. He just wanted my attention."

"So his girlfriend, the good doctor, could give you the shock of your life?"

Sam made a face. "Was that a joke, sir?"

"Of course not. I'm the governor."

"Right."

"Governors don't make jokes, Sam. It's unbecoming."

"It wasn't much of a joke, anyway."

"It was fantastic," Alex said with a boyish grin. "You must have been furious."

"I'm starting to lose my sense of humor about it," Sam said, meaning it. "Sir, I have to ask, why are you doing this? The boy doesn't want to be governor. He wants to go see the galaxy. He's put in a shocking amount of effort in a short time to make that happen. He's brilliant, and always has been, but after what happened in that train station, I don't see him settling down any time soon."

Alex paused, considering the past ten years of service Sam had given him, then said, "I have over fifty descendants, Sam. I have only one son, flesh of my flesh and of Elena Montesquieu's, a woman I was allowed to love for too brief a time."

Sam stiffened. "I thought... the lottery..."

"I co-opted the lottery. I had *that woman* implanted with an embryo made from Elena and me, far from prying eyes," Alex said, pointing up. And by God, it felt good to tell someone about it. "Then I had to watch that carbon-addled junkie almost ruin him, because once Zack was born, he was subject to the same monitoring as the others."

"But the aptitude tests... How could you be sure?"

"Because I tampered with the results. I spent the next twenty-one years making sure he was worthy of the primacy I stole for him. And he hates me for it. And I want him back." Alex clasped his hands behind his back, like a junior officer expecting a tongue lashing from his superior, except for the wry grin on his face.

He waited as Sam considered what he'd been told. Alex had handed him a loaded gun and dared him to pull the trigger, which was as much of a gamble as Alex had taken on someone in a long time, considering Sam was a former mercenary. Corruption of the selection process hadn't happened in over three thousand years. If Sam took this to the Council, Alex would lose his position, be jailed, and there was a middling chance the sophistocracy would arrange his death to spare itself the embarrassment. *Good thing he works for me, then.*

Sam looked up. "I can't say I'm in love with the risks you've taken."

"The risks *you've* taken on my behalf," Alex said. "I thought you deserved to know why it was important."

Sam chuckled. "You might have told me sooner. I shot at your son with live rounds."

"You what?" Alex said, standing up.

"Shot *at* him, sir."

"Don't give me that, Sam. I hired you for a reason. You don't miss."

"I was aiming for his legs if it makes you feel any better."

"It does *not*," Alex said, raising his voice. Sam looked at him wryly, and Alex felt himself flush. He cleared his throat. "You didn't hit him?"

"My shot was blocked," Sam said, "by this." He swiped his

wrist interface—still intact—and brought up a hologram. It was Zack, long limbs flying, some sort of box clutched to his...

No...

"Damndest thing," Sam continued. "It was like a piece of flying luggage."

No, no, no! Zack, what have you done?

"Barely made a dent in it! Those were *wrecker* rounds, for profit's sake! And I... Boss? Are you okay?"

Alex Lancestrom felt cold. It was a familiar feeling, though he'd not felt it for decades. Not since Elena died. *Damn the boy,* Alex thought, balling his hands into fists. *Damn you both for making me suffer like this, my love, and thrice damn the sophistocracy.*

"Boss? You're scaring me a bit, here."

Alex straightened, his face lifeless, his voice flat. "I'm afraid the time for youthful escapades is over, Sam," he said softly. "Are you fit for duty?"

"Fit enough," Sam said, all trace of mirth gone from his voice. "What do you need me to do."

"Contact the Combine. Get me the best team you can in the shortest amount of time and retrieve... that box at all costs."

"What about Zack?"

"Spare him if you can, but not at the expense of the mission I gave you."

Sam stood—staggered to his feet, really. But the governor of Politeia had already turned to leave. "Where will you be?"

"With the Council," Alex answered. "I must inform them of what my child has done."

CHAPTER TWELVE

Civilian Aircraft (Unregistered) Betsy, Airway 21
Pnyx, Below, Capital District of Politeia IV
4386.B.30 Interstellar

Ultimus passed down one weapon case, then the other, and then the entire aircraft swayed as the two-hundred-kilo cyborg dropped into the cabin.

The hatch sealed above him.

The interior was surprisingly clean, laid out like a camper trailer, with comfortable leather chairs, plus straps and extra handholds to allow for the vagaries of atmospheric flight. There were four chairs in all, placed between the cockpit and the workshop, the galley, and the small bathroom in the back.

"Hang on to something!" Clavicus said from the pilot's chair, his hands flying over the keys of a command console, and then Zack felt his stomach rise to his throat as the flying bread loaf dropped like a stone. Ultimus cursed, grabbing an overhead handle while trying to keep the cases from sliding with his legs. ARK-11 whooped in alarm.

"Zack!" Anya shouted and he reached out, catching her as she stumbled and drawing her close to his chest.

"Hey," he said, deliberately pitching his voice low, and she smiled, glancing at his lips, then shocking him with her fingertips. "*Hey!*" Zack yelped in surprise.

She kissed him. "Serves you right," she said, lips against his.

Ultimus shook his head. "Yes, but what—Oof!" He grunted as Clavicus turned the thrusters back on. ARK-II thumped against the carpeted floor. Zack went down with Anya on top of him.

"I love his flying!" Zack said, wrapping an arm around her as she struggled against the g. Zack closed his eyes as the cabin trembled, the thrusters roared, and the aircraft leveled out. He was born for this. He knew it. And soon, he'd be back among the stars.

"Let me up!" Anya said, pushing against his chest.

He opened his eyes, let her go, and followed her to the nearest seats where they both strapped in, facing inward. Ultimus shoved the cases into a cubby before stumbling to his own chair across from them, and ARK-II slid under the big man's chair like a piece of luggage, its casing burnt orange.

"Is the guard after us?" the mercenary shouted toward the cockpit.

"The what?" Clavicus asked.

"The planetary guard, or the capital police?"

"No! They don't give a crap about what happens down here. We're being chased by scavengers!"

The mercenary frowned. "Why are scavengers after us?"

"Because we owe Jawhee money! Now let me fly this thing, or you can ask them yourself!" Clavicus said, and he sealed the door to the cockpit.

Anya met Zack's eyes and raised an eyebrow.

"What?" he said, smirking.

"Oh, he's a delight."

"Yeah, he's a real sunlamp," Ultimus muttered.

The aircraft juddered, and the four seats rotated toward the front on their own as Clavicus threw it into a sharp turn and pulled hard. At least Zack assumed that was what was happening. There were no windows in the cabin. "I'm going to the cockpit."

"To do what?" Anya asked, gripping her armrests.

Zack cocked his head. "Are you—"

"No."

"You don't know what I was going to ask."

"Yes, I do."

"What, then?"

The aircraft banked hard the other way, slamming Zack and Anya against the bulkhead where the window should have been.

"You were... going to... ask..."

"If you were a nervous flyer?" Zack asked through gritted teeth.

Anya didn't answer. Her head had flopped to the side. She was unconscious.

The aircraft righted, then dropped again, then pulled up again. Zack clenched his calves, thighs, and abdomen, forcing blood back to his brain. "I'm going..."

Ultimus laughed. "Go get 'em, boss!"

And Zack half stumbled, half flew until he fetched up against the cockpit door. "Let me in!" he said, hammering on the door. It slid open so fast, he fell in and slammed into the back of Clavicus's chair. The whole aircraft was vibrating.

"Sit down and shut up!" Clavicus said. His hands were flying over the keys, and metal tendrils snaked out through and from under the poncho, making their own inputs and connections with the command console.

Zack dropped into the copilot seat, strapped in, looked for

the controls, and didn't find any. Also, the windshield was completely black. "How in Hades are you flying this thing without looking where you're going?"

A metallic tentacle as thick as Zack's pinky finger snaked out of a vent in Clavicus's poncho and tapped a key on the control panel to his right. The windshield turned transparent. Zack felt his testicles try to climb into the safety of his pelvis as an aircar shot by in the opposite direction, and then another, and then they dove under an oncoming heavy lifter with centimeters to spare.

"Better?" Clavicus asked.

"No!"

"Didn't think so," the engineer said, tapping the key again to make the windshield opaque, while the rest of his fingers and tendrils kept moving like an octopus playing a theater organ. "I'm using a neural network I wrote to fly through traffic in the wrong direction. It's self-flying, but I still need to help tag traffic by categories and override the safety protocol."

"Why would you override the safety protocol?"

The aircar crunched into something large, and Clavicus slammed his hand on a large, circular button that turned out to be the airhorn. "Because some people don't know when to *get out of the way!*" he hollered at the unseen commuter.

Zack swallowed. This was not his idea of flying, or safe, or whatever, but Clavicus both had it handled and was quite busy. "Can I help?"

"No," the engineer answered. "Wait, maybe." A tentacle reached overhead and pulled a knob.

An old-style—almost vintage—pair of veer-goggles popped out of Zack's dashboard.

"Put those on!" Clavicus ordered.

Zack obeyed, pulling the strap behind his head, and he could see again, except it was as if he were sitting on top of the aircar. The buildings they were racing between were rendered in blacks and navy blues, and all the moving objects looked like they'd be dipped in neon acrylics.

"Are you in?"

"Yeah, I'm in," Zack answered absently. He was busy trying to understand the pattern. *Black and blue for stationary objects—lowest threat level, not going to swerve into us. Red for traffic on a collision course.* As he watched, a hover-semi was recategorized as bright orange, by Clavicus or the AI, he didn't know, and it cut another commuter off, causing a ripple in the traffic flow. Clavicus's aircar jinked and barely avoided a three-body problem that ended with another aircar flattened against a building in dying shades of blue. *If their safety systems were maintained, they'll be fine,* Zack told himself, but he needed to cut this chase short or someone—maybe him—was going to get hurt.

"What do you need me to do?" Zack asked.

"We're still being followed. Fix it."

"Weapons?"

"Sonic emitters. Constructive interference, just close your hand around a target."

Zack nodded and raised his hands. The veer-goggles replicated them in the virtual landscape. He was no scientist, but his training with ARK-11 had given him a solid familiarity with shipboard emitters, and constructive interference meant he could bring a lot of hurt to a single point in space.

The aircar lurched and started to fly at an angle. "We're hooked!" Clavicus yelled.

"I'm on it!" Zack said. He spun his chair around and faced backward. A half-dozen yellow shapes flitted among the green and blue receding vehicles, and one of them had shot a grav-harpoon into the back of their aircar.

And then they activated it.

Zack lurched forward in the straps and the thrusters fired on full as the back of their aircar became a micro gravity well.

"Crap!" Clavicus yelled as the aircar stood on end and a lot more traffic turned orange and red. "Fragging do something about this!"

"I am!"

"Like, now!"

"I *am!*" Zack roared. He used the control on the side of the helmet to move his avatar forward. He couldn't find the harpoon; he was "seeing" by echolocation, classified by relative motion, and since the grav-weapon was fixed to the hull, it showed up the same color as the aircar—dull blue.

"Got another one coming!"

Zack looked up and saw a yellow shape—some kind of single-seat jet-bike—dart forward and a small, red disk shot toward him. He reached out and "caught" it, sound waves converging and ripping the thing apart.

"Yes!" Clavicus yelled.

Zack turned his attention to the one already attached to them.

Just because he couldn't *see* the grav-harpoon didn't mean he couldn't guess where it was. He was a trained pilot, damn it, even if he'd never flown a real air- or spacecraft. This was vector math. Clavicus was—just barely—managing to keep them level with every ounce of thrust he could manage, and Zack had watched the engineer pull a maxed thrust zero-intercept on him while he was hanging from the ladder. *Ninety-one meters in twenty-five seconds, nine-point-eight meters-per-second squared gravity, air car's nine tons on its own with four extra tons of engine to keep her in the air...* He didn't have the time to do the math, but he picked the most likely spot on the back of the aircar and squeezed his virtual hand around it.

The aircar started to vibrate.

"Uh, Zack?"

"Yes, Clavicus?"

"What the hell are you doing to Betsy?"

"You call your aircar Betsy?"

"She's Mrs. Betsy to you!"

Zack closed his fist, fraction by fraction, and the vibration intensified. If he'd picked the right spot, if he squeezed just enough, he would take out the grav-harpoon without knocking them out of the sky. *As long as the aircar is more solid than the weapon.* He squeezed. There was a bang, and fragments of something broke away from the hull.

The aircar lurched again, this time almost slamming into traffic overhead as the thrusters kicked them free. Clavicus whooped, and the aircar shot forward as he was able to allocate more thrust to forward motion. "So, Zack? You know how the capital police doesn't give a crap about Below?" he said, turning to face his forward console.

"Yes?" Zack answered, lifting the goggles from his face.

"They've picked today to start caring. They're setting up checkpoints and airlane-blocks. Guess we crashed into someone important."

"We need to go to ground," Zack said.

"And I can't do that with those scavs on our tail."

"I'll take care of them," Zack said. He returned to the virtual landscape, to the yellow barracudas darting among the minnows. "How much time?"

"None."

Zack swallowed.

The scavengers either didn't know about the capital police or didn't care. Six targets, one of them larger than the others. If he'd had more time, he might have disabled them.

"Zack! I need to do this now!" Clavicus said.

Zack closed his fist around the largest of the yellow jet-bikes, and it exploded into wet greens and scraps of blue.

"Keep going!" Clavicus yelled.

Zack reached out with both hands and exploded two more... jet-bikes. He didn't want to think about what was happening to the people when the converging sound waves ripped them apart. One more jet-bike slammed into an aircar, and the rider was thrown sixty feet above the ground. The other two broke off.

"They're bugging out!"

"Okay, hold on!"

Zack spun his chair to the front and sucked in his breath. There was no traffic ahead of them, only a wall of capital police aircars and the pulse of targeting sonars. Then they dove, smashed through some kind of striated organic barrier, and slipped into the ten-foot-wide sewer pipe like a dart into a blowgun and shot out of the city.

CHAPTER THIRTEEN

Civilian Aircraft (Unregistered) Betsy, Mainline Sewer 17, Sublevel Four
Between Pnyx and Anuradhapura, Capital District of Politeia IV
4386.B.30 Interstellar

With the scavengers taken care of, police evaded, and the AI in charge of flying them to Anuradhapura, Zack walked back to the main cabin to check on the others. The chairs had turned back toward the center. The cabin smelled of sewage, and there was a whistling noise coming from somewhere, but everyone and everything looked intact.

"Zack!" Anya said, unbuckling her straps and standing to hug him.

He put his arm around her and gave Ultimus and ARK-II a nod. "Everyone okay?"

ARK-II beeped and flashed blue.

"Hell of a ride, boss. Was that you, flying?"

Anya loosened her hold on him, the better to frown at him. "What does he mean, 'Was that you, flying?'"

Zack touched her upper arm. "I didn't only learn to shoot

stun guns. But no," he told Ultimus, "that wasn't me, flying, that was Clavicus's computer."

"He blew the hell out of some scavengers, though," Clavicus said, joining them. "These your team?"

"Yes," Zack said, less comfortable with what he'd done than Clavicus apparently was. "Clavicus Rext, meet Dr. Anya Vesperian, Ultimus Thragg, and ARK-II."

"Super," Clavicus said. "Anybody hear that whistling sound?"

Zack looked toward the back of the cabin. "Yeah, I guess—"

"Because," Clavicus said, cutting him off, "the next time you hear that whistling sound and don't *do* anything about it, we're probably all gonna die." He pushed back past Zack and Anya, ignoring Ultimus and a *very* pink ARK-II, and grabbed a toolkit out of an overhead compartment.

"He... doesn't get out much," Zack said apologetically.

"No kidding," Anya answered.

Clavicus slammed the toolkit down near, mumbling an apology to "Betsy." The rear bulkhead was cracked. That was where the whistling was coming from, and the smell. Either the grav-harpoon had included a literal penetrator, or Zack had done the damage in removing it.

"He's right," Ultimus said, scratching his cheek. "We're in atmo, but hard vacuum isn't the place to build good habits."

Zack sighed. "Of course he's right." Anya looked like she wanted to argue, but she held it back, and Zack was grateful. "It's my fault. I've done damage control drills in ARK-II's neural net, but that was always with a simulated bridge crew." He bit his lower lip. "It's time, isn't it?"

Ultimus nodded, crossing his arms.

"Time for what?" Anya said.

Zack chuckled and gestured to a chair, which she took. He sat across from her. "Actually, you know this better than anyone, babe." He pushed the hair back out of his face with his left hand. "We're doing this. The five of us are going to steal a militarized shuttle, take it through hostile airspace, and Icarus-jump away from a planet most of us have never left and will never be able to return to."

Anya's lips thinned, but she nodded, and Zack could feel approval coming off Ultimus in waves. ARK-II was noticeably neutral, its case plain white, but Zack knew where the little machine stood in all this, perhaps better—in some limited ways —than ARK-II did itself. He waited as Clavicus finished stapling a sheet of thin PVC over the crack, then hot-sealed a sandwiched-laminate board of polypro and self-healing foam over that. Zack could have done that himself. *Should* have done it himself. He'd been wearing his old skin, not the one he'd been training all his life to step into.

The engineer put the glue and heavy stapler back into the toolkit, the toolkit back into the overhead.

"Clavicus, would you join us?" Zack asked.

Zack couldn't see the man's face, but he could hear the sneer in his voice. "I'm not here to make friends," Clavicus said, stomping past.

Zack grabbed his arm. "Mr. Rext?"

"What?"

"Do you want a place on the shuttle I'm going to take off this planet?"

Clavicus hesitated. "Of course I do. I just burned a lot of bridges with the scrapper gangs and helped you avoid the police."

"Then *sit down*," Zack said. He didn't raise his voice, only tightened it, the way his father had, to cut people's legs out from under them, for as long as Zack could remember.

Clavicus nodded and took the seat next to Ultimus, seeming to shrink in on himself some, and Zack knew he'd been right when he said the man didn't get out much. Now wasn't the time to mind people's feelings, though.

"Hat and holo off, Clavicus," Zack said.

"Is that necessary?" the engineer asked.

"It is."

Clavicus's shoulders drooped. Zack could sense Anya tense up and saw Ultimus twist in his chair as the chubby engineer pulled his hat off and double-tapped a touch-strip on his neck.

Anya sucked her breath in.

Clavicus was what Upper-Middle habbers called a smoothie and Skyward residents tried not to discuss at all. His skin had no wrinkles, not even laugh lines. His face was a touch too small for his head, like a baby's, and too asymmetrical to ever be anything but ugly. Clavicus's hands started to shake.

"You can turn the holo back on," Zack said gently.

Clavicus's hand jerked back to his neck and the holo came up—a blank happy face this time, two dots and a curved line.

"I need each of you to realize we're in this together," Zack said. "There is no one else to turn to. No one else wants us. No one is going to forgive me for walking away from a lifetime of tax-funded privilege. Anya would have wound up as a gang surgeon if she was lucky. The last *five* missions Ultimus took were solo ops. That's not normal, is it?"

Ultimus's face was very still. "No, it isn't, boss. How did you find that out?"

"I did my research before we 'accidentally' met in that bar," Zack said. He looked at Anya and Clavicus. "What Ultimus has in common with all four of us is that he's good at his job. People don't refuse to work with him; they refuse to take the kind of mission he chooses. Those that didn't are all dead." Zack said the last part softly, and Ultimus clenched his jaw. The big man felt guilty for those deaths, Zack knew, but it wasn't Zack's place to share that. "Dr. Vesperian wasn't fired for incompetence or breaking the rules. If she had, she would have been brought up on criminal charges as well. Anya was fired because she went around hospital administration and she got it right. Because she would have—and, I think, did—see that as a validation that would have made her whole career, long or short as may be, a series of lines in the sand she would have crossed without blinking."

Anya swallowed. Her hands were balled into fists.

"And Clavicus, in spite of his appearance, is the kind of genius the accession program *should* have elevated, but he was never allowed to take the test. He can build anything, fix anything, and I happen to know he's off the charts when it comes to visual-spatial and logical-mathematical reasoning. He suffers—and I do mean *suffers*—from agoraphobia and intense interpersonal discomfort."

"You don't like open spaces, but you want to go to space?" Ultimus asked Clavicus.

"I thought you two knew each other," Anya said.

"No ma'am," Ultimus said, not taking his eyes off the engineer. "First time shaking hands, so to speak." Though the engineer hadn't shaken hands with anyone, including Zack.

Clavicus cleared his throat. "We're already in space. We're hurtling through the black on a rock we have no control over with twenty-one billion other human beings. The thought of being in an armored box with sensors, thrusters, and a jump engine to run away from everything that scares me, even though I'm smart enough to *know* that fear isn't rational? It's been my dream for as long as I can remember."

Zack nodded. "And I'm your pilot. I may not be as efficient as one of Clavicus's self-flying routines, but I can break into, hotwire, or hijack anything on this planet beneath the size of a corvette. And when I do, I will be the captain of this crew of outlaws as we take our grievances to the stars." There was a pause, and Zack knew it had been a strong speech. Maybe too strong, like something that should have finished with applause, but that would have felt silly in the small compartment.

"Aren't you forgetting someone?" Anya asked.

"Who?"

"ARK-11." She looked at Zack, then at Ultimus.

The mercenary shrugged. "I don't know the full story behind the ARKs. I only know a little about what they do."

"Which is?" Clavicus asked, behind his smiley face holo.

"Which is not mine to share," Zack said. "ARK-11?"

The little case wiggled out from under Ultimus's chair and set itself down between the mercenary and the engineer. It offered them the training circlets, and each of the team members took one.

FSBB-118 Memento Mori
Sol VIII, Military Staging Point Epsilon
1060.1.6 Interstellar

Vice Admiral Karin Lindström stood on the observation deck of the *Memento Mori*, hands clasped behind her as if she could stare across astronomical distances and see the terrible destruction being unleashed on the birthplace of humankind. Her flagship, the *Memento Mori*, was emerging from the planet's shadow, the sun a smaller but still bright disk that lit Neptune's rings in shades of silver and red. At forty-seven years old, she should have been nearing the end of her career, not leading a desperate expedition across the stars, but like they'd told her at the academy, if she didn't have a sense of humor, she shouldn't have signed up.

Captain Thomas Nalutuesha, her flag captain, cleared his

throat. "The evacuation is complete, Admiral. Rear Admiral Takahashi has repeated his request to scuttle the orbitals."

"Denied," Karin said. "Let whoever survives this war put them to use."

"Even the enemy?" he asked.

His voice was soft, not accusing. She'd known him for most of his career. "Yes," she said, grief and hate battering the gates to her soul.

They'd received confirmation through the quantum receiver that a squadron of Perseid destroyers had breached Earth's orbital defenses. It had been a suicide run. The starships were never designed for atmospheric entry. They dropped kinetic weapons on every major city in the Northern Stars, raked the Central Block with energy weapons, and crashed into the Pacific, unleashing tsunamis on both coasts and submerging many of the island proto-nations. The death toll was in the hundreds of millions, and Karin knew full well the kind of madness that would bring to an already vicious war. "The prisoners?"

"Secured, ma'am. Commander Lewis sends his compliments and confirmed his understanding of his orders. He's submitted a list of transfers from his ship, with suggested replacements—good spacers and marines all, but perhaps not the best custodians for our guests."

Karin nodded to herself. The Neptune Yards had doubled as a POW camp for those political figures, officers, scientists, and technicians whose knowledge and connections were deemed essential to the enemy. They'd been processed and interrogated here since the battle at Quintana V, when the Perseid fleet had routed the Federal garrison and freed over a hundred thousand captives, all of whom returned to the war.

She knew a number of her officers and the majority of her squadron's crews would have preferred to space the Perseid captives or leave them aboard the orbitals when Takahashi sent them crashing into the ice giant below.

Karin was among them. Her husband and much of their extended family had lived in Uppsala, on the outskirts of the mega-city of Stockholm. Her son was a lieutenant on the *FSCG Harm's Way*, in Andromeda. It was possible the enemy fleet bypassed him on their way to Earth, but it was more likely this squadron was the only family she had left. "And the restoration kit?"

"ARK-11 is safely aboard, ma'am, and it's made itself... comfortable. I can't say I'm happy about having an unshackled SAI loose in my ship's systems. It's probably watching us right now."

Karin glanced up at the nearest cabin sensor, from which Zack and his team watched her, millennia after the Splinter Fleet's exodus. "I'm not comfortable either. But we've got a job to do, so let's be about it."

"Yes, Admiral," Captain Nalutuesha said, clicking his heels together. He followed her off the observation deck and out of sight.

FSBB-118 Memento Mori
Kepler 298B, High Orbit
1099.5.19 Interstellar

"What do you think?" Fleet Admiral Karin Lindström asked, looking down on the blue world beneath them.

Rear Admiral Thomas Ebbe Lindström (Junior), named after her first and second husbands, didn't answer right away.

Karin couldn't help but feel proud. Thirty-nine years after they'd fled Earth, her son had a quiet strength she'd come to rely on. He had Ebbe's strong jaw and seriousness, Thomas's eyes and love of small-craft navigation. His thick, black hair, cropped close like a true spacer, was starting to show signs of gray.

At eighty-seven years old, Karin had lost most of the things she'd loved, including pieces of herself, but looking at her son still filled her with a protective and somewhat wary sense of pride.

"It's not far enough," he said finally.

She crossed her arms. "We're over fifteen hundred light-years from Earth, Thomas. This is a viable world."

"It's not a garden world," he answered dispassionately. "Gravity's one-and-a-half standard. Atmospheric density is close to two-and-a-half standard. That means exoskeletons and rebreathers for the next five generations or drastic gene alteration, and on top of that, our colony will be centralized, vulnerable to a single pandemic, impact event, or raid."

"A raid? Who do you think is coming after us?" Karin asked.

"The Perseid. The Machines. The Federal Fleet, for that matter. Have you ever considered they might view us as deserters?"

"We had orders, Thomas," Karin said.

"Secret ones," Thomas answered. "We have to assume that the people who gave them are dead." Karin's breath caught in her throat for a microsecond, and Thomas put his hand on her shoulder. "Mom, are you okay?"

Karin frowned, and he pulled back his hand. "I'm fine, Rear Admiral," she said, reminding her son this wasn't a casual discussion. "Your concerns are noted, even though you weren't even *born* when your father and I fought the Perseid, nor have you ever seen what an AI swarm-fleet can do to mere human vessels, I appreciate your caution." *And my God,* she thought. *Deserters?* She'd never considered anything but a hero's welcome if the Fleet, victorious against all odds, sent someone after them. "The Second War was devastating for our entire species, but it's time we moved on, and this is where we'll make our home."

She saw Thomas's eyes flick toward the reflective dome of the cabin sensor overhead. "Admiral," he said, "with all due respect, this is a mistake."

Karin's heartbeat quickened. She recognized his posture from his birth father. It was the stance of a man ready to bleed for principle. "I beg your pardon?" she said.

"This. Is. A. Mistake."

"I'm not sure I like your tone."

Thomas straightened. "You asked me to review the results of the survey and give you my considered opinion. This is an outpost world, at best. I don't understand why you're even considering it, ma'am."

"There are things about this fleet you aren't privy to, Rear Admiral," Karin said.

"I know. That was my first thought. So I did my research. I dug through the combined supply reports, even spoke to several of the operations and supply chiefs. We're running at the highest levels of inventory we've ever had."

Karin nodded. "Enough to settle a difficult planet."

"Enough to run another three thousand light-years from a war that almost spelled our *extinction*. Why are you doing this?" He was almost pleading.

"Because I'm old," Karin admitted. "Don't you think I have a right to see my mission finished? To deliver my charge to its destination? The Fleet's population has *doubled*, Thomas. Our life-support capacity has not."

"We'll put controls into place."

"They'll refuse! I already have to inform their so-called Council every time I make a course change. You give them too much credit."

Thomas clenched his jaw. "And I think you don't give them enough."

Karin sighed. "I hesitated, you know? Appointing you as my flag captain. On the one hand, people accused me of nepotism, and on the other, I was faced with an officer who was entirely too familiar with me and just as pig-headed as his father. Make your choice, Thomas. Support me in this, or I'll have you relieved and assigned to the civilian fleet you love so dearly."

Thomas turned pale, and Karin's heart broke for him, but she didn't show it. Sometimes love meant letting people suffer hardship so they could grow on their own. "You'll have my resignation by the end of the watch, Admiral," he said softly. "But I will fight you on this. Not because you're abusing your position, or because I think the Council should dictate military decisions, but because it's wrong, and no matter what happens to either of us, whether we get to see humanity reborn under our care or die in service to generations unborn, our duty is to see our mission through to the end." He looked broken, and stronger and more beautiful than she'd ever seen him at the same time.

"It was a good speech, Mr. Lindström, and I will accept your resignation. Unfortunately, I have already spoken to the Council, and they agree with me." She watched the blow land on her son like a meteor strike, but he didn't crumple. "Here," she said, handing him the letter she'd been holding behind her back.

He took it with shaking hands, swallowed, and started to read it.

Then he stopped and looked at her. "What is this?"

Karin turned back to the observation window to look at what was likely the last world she'd ever see. "When we left Sol, we were tasked with carrying a combined population of Federal spacers, civilians, and Perseid prisoners to a new world, far from the conflict. To start over and rebuild a society that could replicate the achievements of Old Earth without making the mistakes that led to the Second Interstellar War and the AI rebellion."

"I'm aware of our mission, mother. This letter..."

"As I said, Thomas, there are things about this fleet that you aren't privy to. We took on an additional passenger at the Neptune Yards, an unshackled SAI with the knowledge banks and capacity to build a new civilization, part of an INDIGO-level classified Federal research program called the Anthropological Restoration Kit."

"My God, mother... You let an SAI on this ship? How could we trust it?"

Karin chuckled. "Funnily enough, I asked ARK-II the same question about you."

Thomas frowned. "ARK-II? I don't understand."

"That's its name. I really am old, Thomas. Too old. Too much exposure to hard radiation. Too many friends lost. I've got one more stint in cryo left in me before I... move on to whatever's after this.

"So I asked ARK-II, how can I trust my replacement? How can I know I've done everything I should? Everything I must? And ARK-II provided me and the Council a question for you, based on it watching you through the ship's sensors every moment of your life since before you were born. It called it the Synthesis, the sum of who you are."

"What was the question?" Thomas asked hoarsely.

"If you had to choose between your mother and the Splinter Fleet, what would you do?"

Thomas nodded to himself, staring at the letter in his hand. She'd known he was dutiful; she'd never realized how much he loved her until today, how much the SAI's question had demanded of him. "I had intended to give you these," she said, digging two sets of three stars from her pocket. "A vice admiral's rank insignia—mine, in fact, from when I first took command of the Splinter Fleet. But ARK-11 started spouting some nonsense about civilian control of the military..." she trailed off, searching her son's eyes.

Thomas sniffed. "God..." he said, wiping his face and looking at the camera again. "Not the dignified first assumption of office that history would have demanded, was it?"

"Oh, all this will be deeply-classified," Karin answered with a twinkle of mischief in her eyes. "Can't have people running around, knowing about our rogue supercomputer, can we?"

Thomas laughed. "I suppose we can't. Well, since you've fired me, and we're going to replace all this with appropriately decorous propaganda..."

He hugged her. Tears ran down her face, and she felt *his* tears soak through the fabric on her shoulder. After a minute, she gently pushed him away, wiped her eyes, and straightened her uniform. "In any case, Governor Lindström, the Council is waiting to give you their congratulations, and I need to brief my officers. Then it's the long sleep, for me, until you or one of the generations after you brings us to our destination. Permission to be dismissed?"

"Carry on, Admiral Lindström."

FSBB-118 Memento Mori
Politeia IV, High Orbit
1165.3.2 Interstellar

She held Ebbe's hand as they walked among the trees of Tiveden. She loved this forest, the wildness of it. It was hard to tell that far back, but the park rangers said it had never been settled, never felt the bite of an ax in ten thousand years of human history. It *felt* true, like the gnarled boles and mossy rocks had been there when the ice receded, and ancient hunters followed the reindeer north.

Axel, their son, had gone ahead. He was just out of Fleet officer training, all lean muscle and bone, and would rather have been spending time with his platoon mates, but Karin didn't care. He'd have enough time to spend with classmates, shipmates, and whatever girl or boy he was currently enamored with. He could grin and bear a little shore leave with his parents.

"It's been wonderful seeing him."

"Yes," Ebbe answered. He was from the north, past Sarek and into the arctic circle. He'd always been a miser with words.

"This summer feels like it could go on forever," she said, reaching over to stroke his shoulder. Axel was a blurry shape, a ghost among the trees.

Her husband stopped and let go of her hand.

"What is it, Ebbe?" she asked.

"It's time to wake up."

Karin Lindström opened her eyes and vomited cryo fluid. The pod was dark. She felt freezing cold.

Her body shook violently as the viscous stuff drained out, her breaths shallow and fast, and then nozzles built into the pod sprayed her down with water that felt close to boiling. Light came to the pod like a winter sunrise, pale and long-missed. *You're coming out of cryo,* she told her fast-beating heart. *It's okay. You've been through this a thousand times.* The pod wasn't just thawing her out; it was activating genes that had been suppressed as part of the hibernation process. Turning them off had allowed her metabolism to slow to the minimum required to sustain life. Turning them back on consumed water and ATP at prodigious rates.

Like dying and being born.

She felt the pod tilt upward until she was almost on her feet. Warm air blew her dry, and then a roller wrapped her in cream-colored fabric, like a bath towel. It wasn't a crash-resuscitation; if the ship had been in danger, the pod would have dumped her naked and slimy on the cryo-genetics' deck. The tight wrap was comforting. She allowed herself a few more breaths to regain her composure, then she said, "Open!" in a voice that seemed too thin and quavery to be hers.

The pod hinged open.

The light in the recovery room was dim, almost gentle except to her cryo sensitive eyes. Her legs felt weak on that first step, and she almost stumbled, except she caught herself on the examination table.

"Admiral? Are you all right?" a young woman said, sounding concerned.

But Karin's eyes were on her hand, there, on the table, her veins like tree roots laid across a thin layer of brittle snow, knobby joints and trembling fingers whispering of age, and then a hand on her elbow. She turned toward the touch and saw... herself. It was like looking at a hologram of herself when she was in her mid-twenties, minus the uniform. Healthy, tan, perhaps a little smaller in the hips, and with fuller lips than she remembered, but still, Karin could look at this girl, this woman, and remember she'd been beautiful. "How long did I sleep?" she asked the apparition.

"Sixty-five years, ten months, and two days, Admiral."

Karin swallowed. Her throat was dry, the muscles tired already, or perhaps still recovering. *Sixty-five years. My God.* Time didn't stop in cryo. It moved like a glacier. She was coming up on ninety-eight years old. After that long in the pod, they should have sent someone familiar to wake her, to ease her through the shock of decades passing in minutes.

"I laid out your uniform," the young woman said, her voice hopeful. "I'm sorry if I got anything wrong. There hasn't been a Fleet admiral since... well, since *you*, and all the ship commanders got into a terrible fight around the order the little ribbons had to go in. They'd still be at it, only it was time to wake you, and I did the best I could," she finished with a small voice.

The words slid by her. Thomas, her son, wasn't there to greet her. He would have been as old as her if he'd stayed in office the whole time. Had he gone into cryo as well? Had he died of old age? Had there been an accident, or a coup, and they'd woken her as a last resort to act as a figurehead in the last moments of her life? The mother in her wanted to scream all these questions.

The admiral in her held them back. "What's your name?" she asked the young woman.

"Emma Lindström, Admiral." She said it with a burning pride that eased Karin's heart.

"You're Thomas's granddaughter?"

Emma nodded.

"By your father or mother?"

"My father, Admiral. Why..."

Karin's eyes flicked to her uniform, and she waved her hand. "You're not in the military, so let's leave off with this 'Admiral' business. I'm your great-grandmother—your *gammelmor* in the tongue of your ancestors, and I'm very pleased to meet you, Emma," Karin said. And she meant it. Emma seemed like a lovely girl.

Emma blushed with pleasure. "Yes, gammelmor," she said.

And her accent was atrocious, but Karin didn't let *that* show on her face. "Where are your father and grandfather?" she asked, heart in her throat. "Are they busy, or..."

"Father... the governor, that is, is waiting for you on the observation deck with the Council and some other important people. Grandfather... he left the Fleet twenty years ago."

Karin's eyes prickled. *Well, it was to be expected*, she thought. It still hurt, but at least he'd had a family and lived a good enough life to pass the role she'd given him to his son. "How did he die?"

Emma frowned and then covered her mouth with her hand. "I'm so sorry! He's not dead! I mean, I don't know! It's just... he *left*. He took a cruiser with a crew of volunteers. I think father knows, but no one would tell me why."

"That's all right, Emma," she said, even though it wasn't. Thomas had been an officer before he'd been a politician. She had faith he wouldn't have commandeered one of the Splinter Fleet's few war vessels on a whim. A cruiser was fast enough to be a scout and armed enough to bloody anything it couldn't run away from. What had he been looking for?

Karin tapped the uniform. "Let's see if we can teach you where all these bits and bobs go, and why they do."

Karin held her granddaughter's arm as they walked onto the observation deck. Someone had gotten their hands on, or printed, a boatswain's call and piped her aboard—even though she wasn't boarding the ship. The observation deck was near bursting at the seams with men and women in uniform, set up in neat ranks, as well as civilians in suits that were already out of fashion when she went into cryo, and it was all a bit wrong, like children wearing their parents' clothes. There was a palpable tension in the room, and she realized they were waiting for her to say something.

"Carry on!" she belted out, and to her satisfaction, her voice neither wavered nor broke. And to her great amusement, they clapped! The carefully constructed formations of officers and dignitaries dissolved as they began speaking to each other, throwing her sidelong glances, and a handsome man in his mid-fifties, accompanied by a stunning dark-skinned woman who topped him by almost five centimeters, detached himself from the crowd. The man—her grandson, Erik—had Thomas Jr.'s eyes.

Karin squared her shoulders as best she could and put her heels together. "Governor. Admiral Lindström, reporting for duty," she said.

With only a moment's hesitation, Erik said, "Carry on, Admiral. Is that how you say it?"

"A little more snap, sir, but good enough for a civilian," she chided him gently.

He chuckled. "It's lovely to finally meet you, Admiral," he said, taking her in with his beautiful blue eyes. "Father told me so many stories, but they didn't do you justice."

Karin snorted. "I'm as obsolete as that boatswain's call, and I appear to have shrunk seven centimeters while I slept!"

"Well, yes... Can you blame us? It's been a few decades since we've had a proper Fleet officer on duty."

And Karin realized what it was—that feeling of being in an amusement park instead of the real world. The people here were all wearing costumes.

She didn't doubt they were good at their jobs. To keep a fleet of disparate ships like the Splinter Fleet's together for a hundred years without repair yards or refueling colliers, they'd had to have been. She'd wager everyone in this room was good at what they did. But she'd had trouble with ratings and officers spending all day in coveralls *before* she went on ice. With her and Thomas Jr. gone? This was probably the first time most of the people in this room had worn a uniform. "Where is my son, by the way?" she asked, ignoring a small pain near her left eyebrow.

The governor smiled. "Let's talk about him later. May I introduce my wife, Laeticia?"

The tall, dark-skinned woman stepped forward, and Karin

instantly liked her. It was clear Erik had been born to his current role, and he'd chosen a companion who made him shine all the brighter.

"How do you do, Admiral?" Laeticia asked, gracefully extending her hand.

Karin shook it. "It's nice to be part of a family again."

With all the guests gone except for Emma, who was her escort, Karin Lindström, now an officer only in name and no longer by command, stood on the observation deck of the *Memento Mori*. She clasped her hands behind her, staring through the glass as if she could see across the years and light-years that separated her from home.

"What do you think?" Emma said, joining her.

It was a blue world, not like Neptune but like Earth. The polar regions were a bit larger, the coastlines broad and sweeping, but it was the garden world her son had always dreamed of and never gotten to see. "It's beautiful," Karin said, putting her arm through her great granddaughter's arm because she was tired. The pain she'd felt earlier, speaking to Erik, hadn't gone away. "What will you call it?"

"Politeia."

Karin smiled. Her first husband, Ebbe, had been a Greek scholar. "After Plato's republic?" Emma smiled back and nodded. *The light in that girl's eyes is brighter than a star's.*

"Daddy's going to call the capital Pnyx, after the gathering place of the Athenian democracy. But I'm going to live in Anuradhapura with the engineers."

Emma kept going, talking about their new world and how they were going to tame it. These people, Karin's descendants both by body and legacy, seemed awfully preoccupied with meaning. With getting it right this time around. They were curious about the ancient world, before and after space travel. Karin's generation had only faced forward, and maybe that was what had led to all this, to humanity starting over a thousand parsecs from its home system. And Karin had hope. It seemed to her like her great-granddaughter was shining. If the other children were even half as bright...

She stumbled, her left arm suddenly and painfully numb.

"Admiral!" Emma yelped, catching her frail old body.

And the nanites Karin had had in her bloodstream since she was a midshipman at the Federal Fleet Academy ate through the clot in her brain, letting blood flow once more.

It was only a temporary remedy. She'd still had a stroke, and she was very old. But she had a few more days in her. Maybe even weeks. "I told you," Karin said, smiling up at the beautiful child. "Call me gammelmor," she said. "And help me up. We'll need a shuttle. I want to take a walk down there, see if there are any trees. And if there aren't, we'll plant the first ones together."

Civilian Aircraft (Unregistered) Betsy, Mainline Sewer 17, Sublevel Four
Between Pnyx and Anuradhapura, Capital District of Politeia IV
4386.B.30 Interstellar

Zack took the circlet off his head and returned it to ARK-11. The little machine was a soft berry pink, bordering on purple, which Zack had learned to recognize as loneliness. "I know, buddy," he said, patting its side.

Anya handed him her circlet and wiped a tear from her cheek. "Is he okay? I mean, is *it* okay?"

Zack shrugged. "Karin was his friend. So was Emma when

she became governor and was let in on the big secret. He's lost a lot of friends over the last three thousand two hundred years."

"That's some heavy stuff, boss," Ultimus said.

"Yeah," Clavicus said, turning the circlet in his hands. He looked up at Zack. "That was your..."

"Great-to-the-ninety-sixth-power grandmother, give or take," Zack answered. "Lindström became Landström since we were bound to Politeia, not the fold corridor network. Time and changes in pronunciation did most of the rest, though I think there was a period when men and women of my family served in the planetary defense forces when the spread of humanity caught up with us, and the interstellar corporations thought they'd make us into a client state."

Anya was staring blankly, her eyes as distant as Karin's.

"Are you okay, babe?"

"What?" she answered.

"It's okay," Zack said, reaching out to touch her knee. "I was pretty bowled over the first time ARK-II showed it to me."

"I can imagine," she said. "I mean, this is your family, Zack. This is... a hundred generations of Politeians and the survival of our species, and it's *so much*. But Zack, if what we saw is true, we can't steal ARK-II from our people. We *can't*. I just... we saw the first Synthesis! The first governor. The validation of the Council as the ruling body of our world. And as much as I want to be a cyberneticist and see more of the galaxy with you, I can't rob twenty-one billion people of their *destiny*. The Splinter Fleet left their homeworld and their families behind to keep him safe."

Zack nodded, hand still stroking ARK-II's side as it leaned against his chair. The set of Clavicus's shoulders was more skeptical—the lower-city engineer owed the sophistocracy less than most—and Ultimus's expression was carefully neutral.

Anya was right, of course. He'd thought the same thing. He'd been upset, at first, of course. ARK-II was the ghost in the shell behind the Synthesis, and had—intentionally or not, he didn't know—engineered his fall from grace. But Karen Lindström's journey through the interstellar desert had inspired him. He'd thought about running back to his father, of taking whatever role they'd give him so he could be part of that legacy.

"There's just one small problem," he told the others. "ARK-11 is dying."

PART V

The universe is big,
And we are small and squishy.

CHAPTER FOURTEEN

The Planetary Hall
Pnyx, Skyward, Capital District of Politeia IV
4386.B.30 Interstellar

Sam stood in the hallway outside the meeting room. He didn't pace. He didn't lean against the wall or cross his arms. He'd already done everything he could to improve the situation, so he waited, his mind empty, waiting for the only thing he could predict. Things were about to change.

The double doors opened, and the members of the Council filed out. There was none of the usual small talk or posturing. They didn't speak at all. Anything they might have said to each other, at that moment, belonged behind a privacy field in a Faraday cage, sunk deep into the bedrock.

"Come in, Sam," the governor said.

Sam walked in and closed the doors behind him. "Sir?"

The governor wasn't alone. Councilor Scamander, one of the more junior councilors, was with him. "Report," the governor said.

Sam flicked his eyes to the councilor, but the governor

couldn't have missed his presence. "I spoke to the Combine. A team will be here within two days, maybe less."

"They'll report to the Council on arrival," Scamander said.

Sam hesitated a heartbeat before he said, "Of course, Councilor. The governor ordered as much." The governor showed no expression at all, which told Sam everything he needed to know. "I've also mobilized the special weapons and tactics unit of the capital police and reached out to my liaison with the planetary guard, Lieutenant Colonel Williamson. I've worked with him before, mostly offworld terror cells and some direct actions against the most violent gangs. He's good at tracking people."

"The governor doesn't need to know the details," Scamander said.

Sam Meritt was a primal sort. He'd left his comfortable life on a core world to join the Combine because people like him didn't belong on comfortable planets. It was clear to him that his boss had been disgraced, if not removed from office, and Scamander had been assigned by the more senior members of the Council to enforce his status as a governor in name alone.

But in Sam's uncomplicated view of things, he worked for Alex Lancestrom. A younger version of Sam might have lunged across the room and smashed Scamander's face against the meeting room table, let him drop, and then stomped on the councilor until he shut his overbred face. "I'll take that under advisement, Councilor," Sam said, not moving from where he stood.

And Scamander turned pale. It wasn't quite telepathy, but it was a form of communication as old as Cain and Abel.

The governor cleared his throat. "The Council instructed the criminals who kidnapped my son be detained or killed, Agent Meritt. Zack may be suffering from some misguided attachment to his captors, but you're to bring him and any... equipment they may have stolen to myself and Councilor Scamander."

Scamander managed not to comment this time.
"Very well, sir."

Civilian Aircraft (Unregistered) Betsy, Mainline Sewer 17, Sublevel Four
Between Pnyx and Anuradhapura, Capital District of Politeia IV
4386.B.30 Interstellar

"What do you mean, 'ARK-II is dying?'" Anya asked. "How can a computer die?"

"You want to get into metaphysics right now?" Zack said.

"I don't give a crap about metaphysics. I'm a scientist. Talk to me in math."

Zack nodded. "The frame you know as ARK-II is a smaller mobile platform meant for short deployments. ARK-II's real body is much larger and is capable of manufacturing a lot of the technology it's been teaching us about. It's called the Forge."

"That probably comes in handy if you plan on restarting human civilization," Clavicus said, his voice tight.

"Exactly," Zack answered. "So ARK-II has been helping run an entire planet for three thousand years, with hardware that wasn't meant to handle the load. Errors are starting to crop up in its core operating system. It is having to decide what data it can erase in order to create backups of key functions, but it's not as simple as getting rid of a few old files. Those memories are part of its personality, and if the corruption spreads too far, safety protocols will wipe it back to factory settings. It needs to dock with the Forge."

"So, where is it? Is it on this planet?" Ultimus asked, and they all looked at him.

"We don't know," Zack said, and ARK-II beeped in agreement.

Anya looked around at the others, and they were both looking at her. "Look, I don't want to always be the person trying to poke holes in the plan. Someone else do it."

Clavicus's hologram turned into a frowny face.

Ultimus sighed and leaned forward, leaning his forearms on his thighs. "You *have* some sort of plan, right, boss?"

"I have an alternative that may work, and a few leads. ARK-II was separated from the Forge right around the time Thomas Lindström—you saw him in the archival footage—left the Fleet."

"The lost cruiser," Anya said.

"Yes. I'm almost positive Thomas took the Forge with him. I don't know why he took it, or what he did with it. I think we all know that AIs went rogue during the Second War. I don't think I realized how bad it got. There were entire sections of the Splinter Fleet that ARK-II didn't have access to, and it looks like the sophistocracy's records of the Forge and the lost cruiser weren't just locked away; they were deleted, overwritten, and the hard drives rocket-boosted into the sun. There's no trace of him."

"What I can't figure out," Clavicus said, "is why they'd hide the Forge in the first place."

"The Forge," Zack said, emphasizing the capital letters.

"Yeah, well, whatever. Your ancestors had Federal tech, and they sent it away. I mean, were they scared ARK-II would build a robot army? If they were so concerned, why'd they let ARK-II pick their leaders?"

"Good question," Ultimus said. "Don't know if we'll ever get an answer to it, unless Zack here wants to go ask his dad."

Zack was tempted, but after Sam tried to take him back by force, he had a notion it might be a one-way trip. "That's not happening."

"The Splinter Fleet ships had industrial fabricators on them," Anya said. "Some of them are still operational. Maybe the Splinter Fleet officers thought that was enough. With the Synthesis, at least there was still a human in the loop. Keeping the Forge around was added risk that what had driven them from Earth would happen again, here."

Clavicus didn't respond, and Zack thought he understood. Children like Clavicus—like all Below dwellers—weren't ascended because of limited resources, or at least that was what the government told the people. How could someone like Clavicus not resent that? With the Forge active, entire planets could be elevated.

As for why their ancestors hid it, Zack had his own suspicions, but he wasn't prepared to discuss them with his team yet. "We only have twenty minutes before we reach Anuradhapura. Let's talk about what we're going to do when we get there."

"I'm not sure what we *can* do," Anya said. "I need some staples to build the upgrades, and Clavicus's fabricator back there can't handle this level of work. No offense."

"None taken," Clavicus said. "Not much call for nanoconstruction when food and clean water are a problem."

Anya shot the engineer a look.

"ARK-11 can handle small-scale fabrication, Clavicus can handle assembly," Zack said, to forestall the confrontation. He knew she'd worked her way up from nothing; Clavicus didn't. "What else do you need?"

"A surgery?" Anya said, running her fingers through her hair. Both her hair and tattoos went from neon green to fire yellow. "I can swap out the capacitors any-old-where, or at least Clavicus can," she said, giving the engineer his due, for which Zack was grateful. "But the new control chip goes in the back of my head and I'd rather not do that in a sewer."

"There's an old medical school," Clavicus said. "It was

converted to a trade school, but some of the equipment was too old and too heavy to move, so they use it to drill cyber-techs and nurses on operating room procedures. Security is only a couple mechanical locks. There's a functional surgery on the first floor."

Industrial Zone 15, Street Level
Anuradhapura, Capital District of Politeia IV
4386.B.30 Interstellar

Ultimus braced himself on the ladder and pushed the manhole cover aside. Snow swirled down past him as he poked his head out of the sewer. One of the flakes landed on Zack's nose and melted.

"Street's clear," the mercenary said, looking down. Zack gave him a thumbs up. Ultimus climbed into the street.

Zack put his hand on the ladder.

"Zack?" Anya said.

He turned toward her, and she kissed him lightly on the lips. The tension of the past two days had driven them together fast and hard, and he was worried they'd fall apart just as fast when that pressure released. For now, though, he was as wrapped up in it as she was. He touched her cheek, then climbed up into the open. Then, like Ultimus had before him, and as all things that come up from the sewers should, Zack scurried out of the radiance to join the mercenary at the mouth of a dark alley.

The streets of Anuradhapura were empty, lit by streetlights and dusted in white. The sky above was dark and empty, the city light, clouds and falling snow choking out the stars, because there were no layers here, no Upper-Middle or Skyward. Anuradhapura sat in a circular cutout three kilometers wide, which let the factory workers live Below where they could afford it and the supervisors live closer to the shareholders. The weight of the pulser in his thigh holster, familiar from hours of combat simulations, lent a seriousness to the moment he hadn't felt before.

ARK-11 came next, and then Anya. Clavicus came up last, a shotgun barrel poking out from under his poncho. He dragged the manhole cover back into place and joined Zack and the others.

"All right," Ultimus said, shifting the giant sledgehammer on his back. "One more time."

"Clavicus and I go to the warehouse," Anya said. "We need sixty grams of cobalt, thirty grams of gold, a half-kilo of silica. The new hyper-capacitors are mostly carbon; we can find that anywhere. I'll grab anything with boron I can find, but we can feed some fiberglass into ARK-11's nano-disassembler if need be."

"Good. Boss?"

"You and I hit the medical school. We make sure the surgery's prepped and rig the ground floor for trouble," Zack said.

"I take Anya to the first floor," Clavicus said. "There's an old auto-surgeon model in room 2R. Anya programs it, ARK-11 fabricates the parts, I assemble them and keep everyone safe."

"And where do we meet if we get separated?" Ultimus asked.

"Where we left Betsy," Clavicus said.

"Manholes at 14th and Jefferson, 12th and 76th, and a backup rendezvous at the open sewer near the coastline, 36th and Engineers' Way," Zack recited.

Ultimus slapped his back. "No comms except for the signal to bug out. Let's get to it."

Zack gave Anya one last glance, then followed the mercenary toward their destination.

★

Clavicus Rext wasn't overjoyed about getting saddled with Lancestrom's girlfriend. The way she'd looked at his face when that asshole made him unmask brought back a lot of bad memories. But mostly, he hated the feeling of open sky above them. He didn't look at it, didn't pull back the brim of the conical leaf hat to let his eyes drift upward to stay fixed on all that emptiness, because he'd be frozen there, slack jawed, until the metal maw of the ceiling cutout sucked him into space.

"Are you all right?" the doc asked.

"Why wouldn't I be?"

"Zack said you were agoraphobic."

She said it factually, without pity. He appreciated that. "I am. It sucks. I'll keep it together long enough to get this done."

"Good," she said.

Clavicus looked at her back and at the ceramic plugs poking out through holes in her jacket. Lancestrom said she'd have ended up Below as a gang surgeon; Clavicus thought she might've wound up causing damage rather than fixing it, but it was nice being around other augments at least.

He used both hands to adjust the shotgun sling so the gun was on his hip instead of knocking against his kneecap. The motile filaments, tendrils, and coils hard-jacked into his lower spine were wrapped around his torso, shifting and squeezing as he moved. It was one more exhibit in the freak show he kept under his poncho, but with a face like his, he'd been past cosmetic improvements since his mother gave birth to him in the factory infirmary.

"What do you need the new implants for?" he asked to distract himself.

She didn't answer right away. They'd reached the end of a block of brick buildings, metal shutter-fronts down and locked tight, and it was time to cross the street. The doc leaned around the corner and looked for... Clavicus didn't know. Cops? Giant vex-rats? Whatever might be there at this time of night in the snow because there was no roof to the world, and Clavicus felt his head leaning back.

"Clavicus!" the doc hissed.

He cursed under his breath and ran across the street, footsteps in the snow, shotgun bouncing against his leg. He caught the glow of a cigarette cherry in the shadows of a doorway, but whoever it was didn't move to follow. When he reached the other side, she asked, "How much do you know about cyber-doc implants?"

"Not a lot. Heard you shocked the hell out of the governor's personal attack dog."

"Sam. Yeah. So, I have super-capacitors implanted into my back."

"What's the charge on them?"

"They're rated at forty farads each. I can put out five hundred micro-amps at four hundred and fifty volts."

"Damn," Clavicus said. That was enough to put someone down permanently.

"There are limiters on them," she said, anticipating his thought. "Wouldn't be very good if cyber-docs started killing people left and right because they'd been startled."

"Right. So you're running at around, what, twenty micro-amps?"

She smiled. "That's right."

Clavicus felt good about that. He didn't get to go to med school, but he got by. He'd put in the work.

The warehouse was at the end of the next block. Clavicus adjusted some of his coils and glanced behind them out of habit. Someone was following them. Was it the scav from the doorway, or someone else?

"You nervous about this at all?" the doc asked.

"About what?" he asked, his mind on their tail. This was Mad Moe's territory, and her band got violent more often than was good for business.

"All of this. The fighting, the breaking in, going to steal a shuttle from the Boneyard?"

Clavicus shrugged. "Pretty normal when you live Below. Someone's always fighting, stealing, or dying."

"I didn't say dying."

"You said Boneyard, and that's as good as dead for most people. I heard they had a star spider infestation out there."

"Seriously?"

"Yeah. I mean, the military said they cleared them all out, but can you trust them when the people who'd get hurt are people the government doesn't like?"

She frowned. "Yeah. So why are you doing this?"

"Why are you trying so hard to talk me out of it?" Clavicus asked, stopping as if he were arguing with her, and used the opportunity to check behind them. "Aren't you Lancestrom's girlfriend?"

"It doesn't mean I have blinders on."

There were three of Mad Moe's boys now. They were hanging back, pretending to have a conversation exactly like Clavicus was. They'd make their move soon, maybe under the broken streetlight two buildings down. "I don't know what you're playing at, Doc. Either Lancestrom picked the wrong girl, or you're testing me, and I don't like it either way. How about you keep telling me about those implants of yours, or maybe we shut up and do our jobs." Clavicus jerked his head toward the toughs, and his hologram became an exclamation point.

The doctor flicked her eyes in that direction, then nodded and kept walking, cool as liquid oxygen. She might not be useless in a fight if it came to that, he thought.

And a police aircar turned the corner. The good doctor almost froze, but Clavicus clamped his hand onto her shoulder. "Keep your head down," he hissed, and she obeyed, pulling her hood forward.

The vehicle was white and government-gray, with the smooth curves of Upper-Middle manufacture and the predatory drift of a monster from a cheap holo-entertainment. Red neon strips lit up as it slowed, and he knew they were being scanned. His poncho was lined with scan-resistant fibers. As long as they didn't draw attention to themselves, there was no reason for the cops to take a closer look.

"No, don't slow down," he said, his hand still guiding her. "If the scanner algorithm spots a difference in gait, in posture, if you start breathing fast, it's going to tell whoever's asleep at the wheel up there we're up to no good. But we're not. We're two lower-habbers taking a walk in the snow because who knows what us Below-tards do when we're not working in the factories or getting drunk, right? We're just..."

The cop car passed them.

"We're just a couple of scavs," the doc continued when he faltered. "Maybe we're not upstanding citizens, but we're not doing anything wrong tonight."

"No, we aren't," Clavicus said, letting go of her shoulder. He looked behind them. Mad Moe's thugs were gone. "You're all right, for a giant, doc."

"A giant?" she asked.

"You know, from the Old Earth story? Lives at the top of a beanstalk, eats good honest folk like me?" His hologram switched to a winky face.

"Clavicus?"

"Yeah, doc?"

"You're not bad for an Englishman, either."

★

Warehouse 47, Street Level
Anuradhapura, Capital District of Politeia IV
4386.B.30 Interstellar

Clavicus paused at the door. "You want me to go round the side and cut the power? I don't know what kind of alarm this place has. Some systems go nuts if you cut the connection."

"No time," Doc Vesperian said. "Get us through the door. I'll handle the alarm."

"You a breaker, now?"

"It's more like teasing it open. Now, come on."

"You got it, doc." Unfurling four of his bigger coils, Clavicus wrapped around the handles and pulled the doors toward him. He slid thinner tendrils through the gap, tripping the latch, feeling for the deadbolt thumb turn. *Clack, clack, clack.* The doors swung open, and the alarm panel started to beep.

"All you, doc," Clavicus said, holding the door for her. "Don't want to rush you, but I'm too pretty for corp-sec prison."

"Then don't."

"Don't what?"

"Rush me," she said. She gripped the silver cable cover running up from the control panel, closed her eyes, and went still.

"Doc?" Clavicus said, wishing he'd cut the power instead of asking.

"Got it," she said, and the command console went inactive.

Clavicus exhaled. "How the hell did you crack the code with only current modulation?"

"I didn't," she said. "There's no code to crack. That console's tied into a security room, and I don't have the training or software to hack that. I made it look like the panel was malfunctioning. They shut it down from their end."

"They'll send someone," Clavicus said, gritting his teeth.

"They will, but they won't be expecting trouble."

"In this part of town?"

She shrugged. "If I'd sent the wrong code or you'd cut the power, we'd be facing a response team or the capitol police. Close that door."

He did.

"It's this way."

CHAPTER FIFTEEN

Warehouse 47, Street Level
Anuradhapura, Capital District of Politeia IV
4386.B.30 Interstellar

Clavicus followed her past the empty reception desk and a small waiting area. There was a staircase leading up, and a red door at the back. The doc didn't give the stairs a second glance. "You been here before?"

"The clinic I worked for keeps spare parts in a place like this. Different building, same layout." She took a left, and they reached a door with safety notices plastered all over it. It wouldn't budge.

"Think they'll report us for going in without safety shoes?" Clavicus asked, working the lock with hair-thin filaments.

"At least you've got your hard hat on," she answered, tapping his metal leaf hat with a knuckle. "I'll put a good word in for you with the supervisor."

"You're all heart, doc." He opened the door.

"I like having friends," she said, closing it behind them. "I'm just out of practice," she muttered.

Chapter Fifteen | 171

The warehouse was dark, except for street light coming in through vents below the roofline. There were offices above them, currently dark, that looked out over the warehouse floor. Rows and rows of thirty-foot-tall shelves went back the length of the massive room, broken into sections of twenty rows with space to drive a forklift or heavy loader between them. "You go left, I'll go right," she said.

Clavicus did what she told him to. He didn't have a problem with her ordering him around. Probably used to doing it with mechanics, techs, and nurses, back when she could still practice. As long as she didn't make it a habit.

The first three rows were copper parts and fixtures, within easy view of the management. Any other night, Clavicus would have carried off as much as he could lift, because copper was expensive, but under the circumstances it was only a distraction.

Fourth row was circuit boards and communicators. *Jackpot,* Clavicus thought. He pulled the scraper from his belt and went to work.

A scraper was the tool of the scavenger in a hurry. Rather than haul a bunch of stuff no one needed or that couldn't be sold, a scraper could be set to target specific chemical elements and rip them from more complex components one atom at a time. Scrapers made for untraceable crimes and fleet-footed getaways, but they also had a few disadvantages.

For one, anything they "scraped" was collected as a disorganized mass. That made them useless when it came to scavenging for specialized, delicate parts needed for repairs. Which led to the second problem. Corporations, cops, and most citizens frowned on the havoc a single scraper could inflict on a city's infrastructure, and even owning one would send a scav to jail for a long time.

He'd stripped a full ounce of gold from three boxes of microcircuits when the lights came on in the upstairs office.

Clavicus dropped to the floor.

H.G. Clarence Vocational School, Street Level
Anuradhapura, Capital District of Politeia IV
4386.B.30 Interstellar

Zack focused on holding the calm, steady center his marksmanship training had given him. It was a different kind of cool from what he'd developed in structured debates. The politician in him was a ravenous beast behind a facade of smooth marble —the appearance of dispassion—shrugging off small cuts and barbs to better leap on a downed foe. The politician was constantly striving for leverage. The marksman waited. Zack's heartbeat was slow and steady as he opened himself to his senses, motionless as a star spider, in the dark of the classroom laboratory.

"Hey, boss," Ultimus whispered.

"Virtues alive!" Zack yelped, nearly jumping out of his skin. He flipped onto his back like a dog showing his belly to his better, his left hand raised to guard his face.

"Sorry. Didn't mean to startle you."

"Might want to warn me next time," Zack agreed. His drawn pulser was pointed at Ultimus's groin. "Would this hurt?"

The mercenary bobbed his head from side to side. "It wouldn't *not* hurt, but less than most. Lost my balls on a world called Forsythe's Promise."

"No joke?"

"Kid you not, boss. Been getting pieces of me shot off for a couple hundred years now. After a while, you stop bothering getting stuff grown back on."

"Huh," was all Zack could say to that. He holstered the

pulser in his thigh holster and sat up. "What about kids? You already..."

Ultimus shook his head and looked away. "No kids, no clones. Just Ultimus Thragg, first and only, until they take the last bits away."

And that saddened Zack. It wasn't that Ultimus hadn't lived a full life. From Zack's research, the mercenary had lived several, seeing more of the galaxy than any five men put together. The fleshy bits inside the armored casing probably *were* five men put together, he thought with a *very* private chuckle.

No, what saddened Zack was that he was tied to dozens of Lancestroms, Landstroms, and Lindströms, all the way back to Old Earth. In a way, this adventure he was undertaking was another step in all their journeys. Zack hoped that one day his son or daughter would leave *him* behind and lay out a new path among the stars.

If he was fortunate, he'd get to see it.

He knew it was a bias of his upbringing, both of his planet's culture and his specific family tradition. Still, it felt like a terrible shame that Ultimus's footsteps would stop like those of a man who'd walked into the sea.

"You have any ambitions of parenthood," Ultimus said seriously, "you'd best put them on ice. Don't be bashful about asking your lady friend to do the same. Tuck them away in a few different places, because there's nowhere safe out there, not for a whole lifetime, and a spacer's life is a whole mess of danger and hard radiation waiting to take those options away." The big mercenary padded off, quiet like a polar cat. Zack shook his head as Ultimus faded into the dark. *How can something that big be that quiet?*

Alone again, Zack settled into the chaos he and Ultimus had made of the trade school. He felt bad about it—wrecking facilities the sophistocracy's poorest depended on—but if they ended up needing to defend themselves, he wouldn't feel bad at all.

Anuradhapura had been the center of engineering for all Politeia, once. He knew that from primary school, and also from the memories ARK-II had shown him. It was built a few hundred kilometers from the colony's initial settlement in order to keep the risk of an industrial incident to a minimum. All the heavy power generation and manufacturing had gone on here, and in fact, there were even three fusion reactors sunk below the ground not far from here, from one of the Splinter Fleet's dismantled frigates.

As the population grew, Pnyx crept closer. People made choices based on their commute, on their desire to be away from the bustle of the capital, bridging the divide until the cities merged some three hundred years later, and suburban housing swept around the old brick and steel site like ocean foam, and then the city's second and third layers were built. Even with the cutout, Anuradhapura spent most of the day in shadow.

Zack heard the chain rattle on the front doors.

Clavicus gave the front doors another shake. "Should I try to pry them open?"

The doc shook her head. "If they're not here and they couldn't send the signal to run, the last thing we want to do is get cornered in a building."

Clavicus tightened his hands on the shotgun grip and forestock. He couldn't see anyone, but years of living Below had honed something of a sixth sense for trouble in him, and it was screaming like a lost habber with a gut wound.

A lock clicked, and a chain rattled behind the door. Clavicus turned and saw Ultimus sticking his head out. "Get in," the mercenary said. Clavicus let the doc go first, then followed her in, casting one last look at the street. "Stay close," Ultimus said, wrapping the chain back around the door handles. "We set tripwires. I'll guide you through."

Clavicus clenched his teeth as his eyes adjusted to the dark. Being able to break a broken ship down to useful pieces and pull a fast patch job on gear too useful to shut down, too costly to replace? That was as good as a hardworking lower-city dweller who wanted to play it straight could hope for. Let the giants choke on their ascension process; a good scav could turn trash into tools and parts into platinum. And they learned to do it here, in schools the doctors, cyber-surgeons, and engineers wouldn't send their designer babies to. Clavicus had known about the place because, once upon a time, he'd walked these very halls and sat in those uncomfortable seats.

Lancestrom and Thragg had trashed the place. They'd thrown chairs, school desks, and equipment into the long, central hallway, forming a series of knee- and waist-high barricades that would make it hard for anyone to mob through. Which was what they'd talked about. It shouldn't have been a surprise. The sight of it still formed a lump of bitter bile in Clavicus's throat.

"Everything go okay at the warehouse?" Ultimus asked, putting a hand on his shoulder. "You two look tense."

Clavicus squirmed out from under his hand.

"It went fine," the doc said. "A security guard showed up sooner than expected, and we had to leave through a side door, but we got everything we needed without setting off alarms."

"Great. Why the long face, then?"

"We were followed here," she said.

"Gangers," Clavicus added. "They're not going to be happy we're working on their turf. They're *really* not going to be happy when they see how you've redecorated the place."

"Are we still in Jawhee's territory?" Ultimus asked.

"Mad Moe's. A lot of her people end up as ragers instead of scavs. They're not subtle, they get hopped up on drugs and take whatever they want."

"How many?" Ultimus asked.

"Five, for now," Clavicus said. "It's the snow, keeps 'em off the streets."

"What's up?" Lancestrom asked, joining them.

"We're about to have company," Ultimus said.

And that made Lancestrom smile. *Giants are insane,* Clavicus thought.

"Guess we should do something about that," Lancestrom said with annoying confidence.

Chains rattled. Someone was pushing on the door. Then they were kicking and punching it. "I know you're in there!" the rager shouted.

"We'll handle this," Ultimus said. "Get upstairs. Watch your step."

Clavicus sighed. He'd made it twenty-two years Below, living in the gang's shadow. He'd gotten a few beatings, gotten extorted, had to live in the sewers, sure, but he had the feeling those two lunatics were going to try to even the score all at once.

A part of him, the piece of him that had died when he was flunked out of trade school and barred from ascension, was a little bit excited to see them try.

The door rattled again.

"Shall we go say hello?" Zack asked.

Ultimus pulled the sledgehammer from his back. "No sense making them wait."

Zack opened the padlock and pulled the chain free.

The snow had stopped. There was still dirty brown slush on the ground, and the air smelled like wet shoes. The rager on their doorstep rushed them, screaming like a crazy person, waving a knife.

"Holy crap!" Zack said, caught off guard, and Ultimus shoved him out of the way before thrusting the sledgehammer head into the man's face with a gruesome *thock*. Blood and bits of teeth flew as the man went down in a squirming ball, still screaming, but the sound was muffled now, like a small child was throwing a tantrum inside his chest. "Nice save, friend," Zack told Ultimus, holding up a hand for a fist bump, and Ultimus smashed that too.

"You shouldna done that," another ganger said, stepping out of the shadows. This one was more of a scav. He had a white, spiky mohawk and pale, unhealthy looking skin. The double-barreled shotgun he was cradling looked homemade. "Larry'd carved you up, some, and maybe we'd 'ave beaten ya bloody, but maybe you'd've lived."

A man and a woman were with him, faces painted white. They were armed with spiked boards.

The shotgun started coming up. "Mad Moe's gonna—"

Zack threw his coat back and cross-drew the pulser from his left hip. He shot the scav through the throat, flicked the selector to non-lethal, then shot the two ragers before they could attack or flee, dropping them like ragdolls. He put one of the stun rounds into the first man, too, to stop him from screaming. "Damn," Zack said.

"What?" Ultimus asked. "You not kill the guy with the shotgun on purpose?"

"Oh, I meant it," Zack said, holstering the pulser. The charged pulser round had blown out and burned a hole the size of his fist; the man's head was barely attached. "But now we're never going to find out what Mad Moe was going to do." He grinned.

Ultimus chuckled. "Well, don't be too sad about it. Clavicus said there were five of them, and I count four. We may get to find out firsthand before this is over."

Control Center, Capital Police
Pnyx, Skyward, Capital District of Politeia IV
4386.B.30 Interstellar

Sam scanned the police reports for the capital district, looking for a sign of Zack and his cohorts. He hadn't expected the kid to fight so hard or go to ground so quickly, and maybe he should have considering Ultimus Thragg's involvement. It wasn't all Thragg's doing, though. They'd had an unregistered extraction vehicle waiting for them. That spoke to planning, and a willingness to back down that wasn't Thragg's core competency.

In fact, the more he thought of it, the more it occurred to Sam that the skills Zack had been taught to serve the sophistocracy's ends would serve *him* just as well as a career criminal. It almost made him smile.

"Any sign of them?" Lieutenant Colonel Williamson asked, looking over Sam's shoulder.

"No," Sam answered.

Williamson was clean-cut, with short blond hair, blue eyes, and a jaw made of granite. He wore his service uniform, gray button-down shirt with sharp creases and all the bits perfectly in place, black tie, black trousers, shoes shined to a mirror.

If Sam hadn't known the lieutenant colonel had been a special forces operator, and then directed high-risk operations for most of his career, the mercenary might have mistaken him for a paper soldier.

As it was, Williamson was as close to a perfect example of an *effective* local military officer, something rare on a planet with so few officially recorded conflicts. It spoke to both the man's competence and the extent to which the sophistocracy hid its dirty laundry from public view.

"I've been reading through the reports the search algorithms rejected, trying to get a feel for the city's baseline. I know the computers do a good job of tracking patterns, but Lancestrom's an amateur and Thragg is an outlier, even for a Combine mercenary."

"No, that makes sense," Williamson said. "I train my people to do the same thing."

The operations' specialist pulled off her headset and caught their attention.

"What is it?" he asked, hiding his limp as they walked over.

"I've got something going on in Anuradhapura, gentlemen. It could be nothing, but..."

"Is it inside the radius?"

She waved her hand. "Only just."

But Ultimus knew all about evasion radii, and the outer edge was where he was most likely to be. "Let's hear it then."

"An Anura' gang leader called Mad Moe just comm'ed a *Pnyx* gang leader, Jawhee the Vibroblade, asking if he was moving on her territory."

Sam tried not to show his disappointment. "I'm not sure where this is going, specialist."

The specialist flushed, but Williamson said, "Tell him the rest."

"Well, sir, Jawhee said he wasn't, but Mad Moe said one of her boys had spotted Clavicus Rext, who's done work for Jawhee before..."

Williamson raised a hand to stop her, then raised his voice to the room. "Do we have a link between Zack Lancestrom's kidnappers and a 'Clavicus Rext?' Anyone?"

He waited a few beats, but no one answered. The specialist's face fell.

"It's okay," Sam said. No one else had a lead on where the kid had gone to ground, and Sam had gotten where he was because other mercs had given him a chance. "You've got a hunch. Finish your story."

She took a breath, then said, "Well, Jawhee denied Clavicus being one of his, but as soon as he hung up, he called one of his lieutenants, the closest to Anuradhapura, and scrambled a *war wagon*—that's like an armored personnel carrier—and two-dozen scavs to go deal with the problem, and Mad Moe's doing the same. It's more firepower than the regular patrolmen can handle."

Sam nodded, drumming his fingers on the backrest of her chair. "Any civilians in the area?"

"Not many, sir. It's industrial."

And it's Below, so they don't matter, he thought. He turned to Williamson. "We have anyone nearby?"

"Not Below, but we have a tactical reaction force near the cutout to Skyward."

Sam frowned. This... territorial dispute, or whatever it was, didn't sound like it had anything to do with the missing heir, but he found himself looking for excuses to stick his nose in. It was probably the same feeling that caused the specialist to call him over. Feelings like that had saved his life more than once.

And if the governor weren't under house arrest for abuse of power, he would have done something about it. "What would you do?" he asked Williamson.

"Have the TRF gear up and go on standby, but don't send them in. We don't want the passage to Skyward left undefended, and I don't think we should let any of our people get hurt trying to stop a gang war."

Sam nodded. "I agree."

"Yes, sir," the specialist said, visibly disappointed.

"It was good work, specialist," Sam said, patting her shoulder. "There's something not right, there. I can feel it, too. I'm just not sure it's our problem. Keep me posted if the situation changes."

CHAPTER SIXTEEN

H.G. Clarence Vocational School, 1st Floor
Anuradhapura, Capital District of Politeia IV
4386.B.30 Interstellar

Clavicus and the doc found the surgery on the first floor, two doors from the stairwell and right next to a broken-down lift shaft. There was power in the building, so Clavicus lowered the blinds and they turned the lights on.

"It's clean in here," Doc Vesperian said, looking around.

Clavicus nodded. "They train the lads to prep surgeries for proper doctors more than anything. They might be poor, but they take pride in the work."

"I don't doubt it," she said. She looked like she was about to say more, then she hesitated.

"What is it?" Clavicus asked.

She shook her head. "I don't know. Zack and Ultimus use my title—my former title—as a carrot to keep me going. It's always, 'You're a doctor, fix Ultimus's armor!' or 'You're a doctor, come break fifty different laws with us!' You just... say it differently."

Clavicus was glad the hologram hid his face. "My implants,"

he said. "They let me do a lot. Always looked up to cyber-docs, even as a kid." And he'd wanted to be one. And she'd gotten to be one. And she'd thrown it away to prove a point.

ARK-II sank itself down in a corner and popped open several parts of its casing, extending metallic fins from its body, like wings.

"What's it doing?" the doc asked.

"Getting ready to put out a lot of heat." The radiators split, and split again, their structure more organic than mechanical.

"I'll prep the auto-surgeon," the doc said.

"Yeah, you do that, doc," Clavicus said under his breath. As he watched, ARK-II's casing split down the middle, and it exhaled warm air like some sort of alien god-machine.

Clavicus stood up and started feeding it strips of fiberglass and epoxy.

The doc turned on a small terminal, and the surgery table started going through hydraulic checks in a series of clunks and whirs.

And then the auto-surgeon itself came out of the ceiling, suspended on cables. It had a blank stainless-steel face, vaguely humanoid torso, and no legs. It unfurled its six metal arms and bathed the table in blue light.

ARK-II bleeped at him.

"Yeah, yeah," Clavicus said. "Feed me, Clavicus! Feed me!" He pushed another strip of fiberglass into the roiling light.

The truth was, he wasn't mad at the doc. He wasn't even pissed at Lancestrom. Somehow, the prince and the mercenary had handled Mad Moe's punks. They must have, or Clavicus would have heard different by now. He was smart enough to recognize that Lancestrom's "confidence" was why they might pull this off, even if he sometimes wanted to punch the giant in his perfectly groomed chin.

ARK-II started to extrude the molecule-thin polymer that

would serve as the basis for the new capacitors. Clavicus sighed. "Hey, doc?"

"Yeah?"

"Can you maybe not look this way for this part? I'd be more comfortable."

And to her credit, Doc Vesperian didn't say anything like she was a doctor, or that he was nothing she hadn't seen before. She just said, "Sure, Clavicus. Let me know when you're done."

Clavicus swallowed. He removed the leaf hat, toggled the hologram off, and stripped off his poncho. He set the shotgun down next to him. The dozen coils, tendrils, and filaments that plugged into his spine unwrapped from around his body, exposing what they always did, the sad, pale flesh of a genetically flawed under-dweller. And he could live with that. His body was a tool. He just couldn't stand the thought of someone like her looking at him.

He closed his eyes. His appendages unfurled, and he took hold of the polymer tape and connected and pulled a pair of small airbrushes from his toolbox. He screwed in two vials of liquid graphene, adjusted the nozzles, and started painting the tape on both sides. Once the first coat was even on both sides, Clavicus fed the tape back into ARK-II for the second stage of production.

"Can you tell me about what you're doing?" the doc asked.

"I thought you knew all about this stuff."

"Only how to use it," she said. "I've been trying to focus on what I need to run Ultimus's armor start-up sequences. I've had to skim a lot of the theory."

Clavicus grunted. "You might as well come over. I didn't think of it, but I'm going to need your old capacitor casings to upgrade them."

"Oh," she said. "How should we... I mean, I can't reach them."

"Sit down with your back to me," Clavicus said.

She pushed her chair back, and he heard her walk over. Her footsteps might have stuttered, or he might have imagined it. It didn't matter. Once they were on Lancestrom's promised ship, he'd burrow down into engineering and none of them would see him, except for meals, and briefings, and a daily shower so his coil-ports didn't get irritated. He balled his pudgy hands into fists. There was nothing for it. Everything had its price, and body shame was the bill he could afford.

"I'm painting graphene onto an ultrathin film of metalized polypropylene as a base. The polypro acts as both a conductor and a separator, increasing the density of the capacitor. The graphene settles into an atom-thick layer, and ARK-11 makes sure it's perfectly flat, which is good for the density of the capacitor, and bad for the capacitance."

"Because of the limited surface area," the doc said, settling behind him. She'd taken off her jacket. The plugs were sticking out through holes in her shirt.

"Right," Clavicus said, and he snaked a coil back without turning his head. Several of the coils had cameras installed that could see in and beyond the visible spectrum, but they all generated a faint electro-static field, like Old Earth sea predators. Sight was comforting to Clavicus, but he didn't need it.

He wrapped around the first capacitor and twisted it loose.

She gasped.

Clavicus froze. "Are you okay?"

She shifted her weight. "Yeah. I was carrying a charge. Let me ground myself out." She put her palm against the floor, and Clavicus felt current ripple out through the flooring. Her tattoos disappeared. "God, that's weird. I haven't been nulled out in forever."

"What's it like?"

"Being nulled?" she asked.

"No. I know what that feels like. 'Null' is normal for most people. What's it feel like to carry the charge from the implants?"

ARK-II extruded the reworked borophene film. It looked the same, but Clavicus knew better. He used his slenderest and most sensitive filaments to start rolling it into a tight coil.

"It's like your whole body is buzzing," the doc said after a moment. "Like your entire nervous system is moving too slow and you need to... I don't know. Jump? Dance? Screw? Anything to get the excess out. Some students null-out between shifts because they can't get used to it. They usually drop out."

"You didn't, though," Clavicus said, wrapping a tendril around the next of her capacitors.

The doc twisted, not quite far enough to look at him. "Could you hold the base while you pull that out? It's not anchored on bone or anything. That first one pinched a bit."

Clavicus swallowed. "Sure." He used a tendril to wrap around the base and twisted the coil in the opposite direction, more gently this time. The heat-sensitive tendril could feel her body temperature through her shirt. And it wasn't a sexual thing. It was more uncomfortable than that, like a child who'd never been held being wrapped in someone's arms. It made his teeth chatter. "You were saying about your body?" he said and kicked himself the second he spoke the words.

She laughed. "Yeah. Some people thought it was uncomfortable, but I loved it. I played gravball in secondary school, so I was always physical. I didn't need an excuse to move around a little more, and after a while, you get used to it."

ARK-II finished the first silicon and gold printed nano-chip. Clavicus was in a steady manufacturing flow, pulling, painting, feeding, coiling, unscrewing the next capacitor. He pulled the first of her capacitors apart and pushed the old coil into ARK-II's hopper before replacing it with the new one, connecting it to the control chip, closing it back up before screwing it into the doctor's socket. "How will these compare to the old ones?" he asked.

"Ten times the capacitance, easy," she said.

Clavicus whistled.

The doc nodded as he installed the second hyper-capacitor. "I'm still limited to five hundred volts. Anything above that, and I'd start cooking my organics. But I'll be able to run multiple discharges at the same time, including self-sustaining patterns by using the new control chip. It'll be like being my own operating team, all by myself."

Clavicus chuckled. He understood the attraction of being able to do things on his own. "What about charging? Are the piezoelectric harvesters you have installed going to be enough?"

"No," she said. "But the good news is, I'll be able to fill up from a charging plate or a regular socket pretty easily. They have an overcharge function that can take exponentially more load at high voltages. If any of Sam's people try to shoot me with a stun round, they're in for a nasty surprise."

"I wondered about that," he said. The last length of film was thicker and had multiple layers of the borophene matrices. He finished assembling the last of the hyper-capacitors and screwed it in tight.

"Thanks," she said, reaching back to touch the coil, but Clavicus stiffened, and she must have sensed or seen it, because she stopped and stood up. "Now for the messy, dangerous part," she said, walking back to the command terminal.

H.G. Clarence Vocational School, Ground Floor
Anuradhapura, Capital District of Politeia IV
4386.B.30 Interstellar

Zack backed away from the open window.

"See anything?" Ultimus asked.

"No, but that doesn't mean anything. All the streetlights are out."

"Convenient."

"Smarter than I expected," Zack said, loosening the pulser in its holster. At least the school had its own generator since it could serve as an emergency treatment center.

One of their captives said something into his gag. It was probably obscene and not that imaginative.

"Well, the ragers are as dumb as pop rockets, but gang leaders have to be either smart or vicious, or they don't last long."

They'd dragged the captives to the back room, near the stairs. The three surviving gangers were gagged, hands bound behind them. Zack had made sure the one who'd lost his teeth wouldn't choke on his own blood. He'd also left the dead man's corpse with them as a reminder captivity wasn't the only option. "How soon do you think they'll come after us?"

"Soon," Ultimus said. "Local PD changes shifts around nine p.m. I'd do it then. Half an hour from now?"

Zack nodded. The truth was, he was worried. He'd expected "Mad Moe" to come after them right away or not at all. He could handle a few ragers trying to rush their position. A well thought out assault by a better class of criminal? That was the kind of situation his veer-enhanced instincts told him to avoid at all costs.

Someone whistled in the dark, a long, clear high note that dropped off. Other whistles, clangs, and hysterical laughs answered from all around them. "Clavicus!" a woman beckoned in a teasing tone. "You come out of there right now! We need to talk!" She was speaking through some kind of amplifier.

Zack and Ultimus looked at each other.

"Little bit of smart and vicious combined?" Zack asked.

"Or dumb and late to the party," Ultimus said, smacking his fist into his hand. "Let's invite her in."

"Anything's gotta be better than waiting," Zack said.

They threaded their way to the front of the building, through the debris and the traps.

"Clavicus! Don't make me come in there, or I will rip your spine out and use it as a back scratcher!" the woman shrieked.

"Scratch that," Zack said. "She's all vicious."

"Sounds like a lot of hiss and no scratch."

"You want scratch?"

"I've gotten some great scratch from a gang woman."

"That what you were doing before I hired you?"

"No," Ultimus said. "That was before Forsythe's Promise, when I still had my balls."

They reached the front doors. Ultimus opened the padlock and pulled the chain loose. "Ready?" he asked, grabbing the left handle.

Zack grabbed the right. "Ready."

They pulled the doors open.

★

H.G. Clarence Vocational School, 1st Floor
Anuradhapura, Capital District of Politeia IV
4386.B.30 Interstellar

Anya screamed into the metal bit as the auto-surgeon tore into her back.

Clavicus ground his teeth as he stood there, helpless. He'd been forced to watch Jawhee torture someone to death once, but Oozo Vickers had been a child molester, so Clavicus had almost been glad.

The auto-surgeon cut into her with admirable efficiency. All six arms moved at once, lasers slicing her skin open along precise channels, steel scalpels and clamps peeling her open. The doc was face-down on the hydraulic table. The auto-surgeon removed the old wiring, blades darting in to free it from muscle and sinew.

"Hang in there, doc," Clavicus answered, poncho back on, his face hidden by the hologram. She'd pulled the bit out. It was in her left hand. Her bare arm hung limp over the side of the hydraulic table. There wasn't much blood. Some seeped, but the auto-surgeon's head locked onto anything more than that and cauterized it.

"Tell me a story, C."

"What about?"

"Borophene conductors," she said, clenching her teeth as the next phase of the program—*her* program—kicked in.

Clavicus chuckled. "Well, their conductance isn't the cool bit. It's their structure."

"Right," she said, teeth gritted. "What about their structure?"

"I mean, boron is fantastic, don't get me wrong. It's stronger, conducts heat as well as electricity, and it's as thin as graphene."

Anya gasped.

"Doc... for the love of sanity, take something for the pain."

"Can't. Need to be able to fight."

"Fight who?"

"It doesn't matter. He needs me," she said. The auto-surgeon had finished with her back and was stitching artificial nerves, synapses, and insulators into the muscles of her shoulders and upper arms.

And that's what it was, wasn't it? Behind the tough girl act and the need to be a doctor. Not the desire to please her boyfriend or win his admiration—Clavicus gave her more credit than that. But the fear, the complete terror of being discarded and useless? That was something Clavicus could understand.

"The structure is triangular instead of hexagonal. That means it can be used to capture hydrogen, and *that* means you can play with the structure at the atomic level. You can build more elaborate shapes and create pockets of non-conductance."

The auto-surgeon's arms were a blur as it started closing her up, laser heat-sealing parted skin. Then it installed the most advanced biochip on the planet into the back of her skull, slotted into a brand new cradle, before sealing the back of her neck. ARK-II had fabricated the chip, atom by atom, out of latticed gold, boron, and organic components.

The auto-surgeon folded its six arms against its chest, and it retracted into the ceiling.

"So you boost the surface area and don't need a separator," she said, exhausted. "Four times the density. Genius." The seams in her skin were fading red lines. Sweat and blood dripped from her fingers. "Thank God. It's over."

The room was quiet except for the dripping blood and the auto-surgeon's sterilization cycle. The doc pushed herself up onto one elbow and smiled at him. Clavicus instinctively started to turn away; she wasn't wearing a shirt.

Then she jackknifed onto her side, shrieking in pain as she reached to claw at the back of her head.

And Clavicus heard gunfire.

H.G. Clarence Vocational School, Ground Floor
Anuradhapura, Capital District of Politeia IV
4386.B.30 Interstellar

Zack and Ultimus threw the doors open and backed away,

weapons raised. The school's external lights were on full bright. Zack had his pulser set to full power, and Ultimus had swapped his sledgehammer for a carbine. The mercenary's large, black and gold hands made the polymerized weapon look like a toy. "Here they come!" the mercenary said.

Suppressing fire, poorly aimed but still deadly, flashed from the cover of parked vehicles and building windows. A dozen ragers came sprinting out of the dark, faces painted white, bladed weapons in both hands.

Zack aimed and fired, double-tapping three ragers as they ran. Ultimus's carbine whined and spat, blowing a cluster of ragers apart in a geyser of gore and flying body parts. It was actually a compact railgun called a "Reaper," firing soft-metal pellets at supersonic speeds. Zack put two shots into a fourth man, winged another, blowing a chunk out of his arm, and put the last shot of his charge pack into the fourth man again because the stubborn bastard just wouldn't go down. "Reloading!" he said, swapping charge packs.

"It's fine, they've had enough," Ultimus said, ducking back from fierce return fire.

The four survivors—one maimed—were running for cover when a monstrous armored van painted matte black and firing weapons from every open gun port smashed into them.

Zack and Ultimus dove for cover as heavy rounds smashed into the brickwork. "Who are these guys? Do you recognize them?" Ultimus shouted over the impacts.

"Mad Moe! Jawhee sends his regards!" a loudspeaker blared from the war wagon, followed by an obnoxious horn. Armed scavs spilled out of the back, and several more blurred by, whooping on their grav-bikes.

"Well, if that isn't the worst news yet," Zack said, steeling himself to pop out of cover again.

Then one of the traps they'd set in the back rooms went off with a *whumpf!*

"Prisoners?" Zack asked.

"Wrong side," Ultimus said, looking tense for the first time in Zack's memory. "They're in the building."

CHAPTER SEVENTEEN

H.G. Clarence Vocational School, 1st Floor
Anuradhapura, Capital District of Politeia IV
4386.B.30 Interstellar

"Doc? Doc! Tell me what to do!" Clavicus yelled, grabbing her by the shoulders.

Doctor Vesperian was going through some kind of seizure. Her hands were curled into claws, her neck craned, her legs kicking while Clavicus tried to hold her down. "Call... Parnavan..." she hissed between clenched teeth.

That might have been too cryptic for most people, but Clavicus was a genius and a master scavenger. He extended his two thickest coils and fastened her arms to the table, hacked her communicator with premade subroutines, and crawled through her contacts. She had a surprisingly large number of them, most of whom she hadn't spoken to in years. Shiva Parnavan was her emergency contact.

"Hello?" a darker-skinned woman answered on the second ring. She was struggling to get some kind of creature with multiple fluffy tails out of her lap. "Who—"

"Shiva!" the doc screamed.

"Annie? What the hell is this?" she asked Clavicus. "I'm calling the police!"

"No! She just installed some new implants. Something went wrong."

Shiva Parnavan narrowed her eyes at him. "Show me," she said, her voice coolly professional.

Clavicus rolled Doc Vesperian onto her side, showing Shiva the still fresh surgical scars.

"Annie, what have you done to yourself?" Shiva said. She looked around the room. "You! Cast me into that auto-surgeon," she said, pulling on a pair of haptic gloves.

"You can drive that thing remotely?" he said, skeptical.

"I should hope so," Shiva said. "I designed it."

Clavicus's eyes widened. *Doctor Shiva Parnavan.* She'd come from an immigrant family and ascended to become one of the best practical surgeons of her generation, and she was still young. He'd have fangirled under other circumstances. Instead, he grabbed the image from his wrist, wadded it up, and threw it at the auto-surgeon.

The sound of gunfire was intensifying outside. Clavicus shifted to the head of the table as the auto-surgeon dropped down, arms fanning out in a motion that was eerily organic in a machine. Doctor Parnavan picked Doc Vesperian up and slapped her down onto the table, then she sank needle-tipped claws into her patient's back.

"Ow!" Clavicus said, jerking his coils back from the shock.

"Mind the voltage. You're lucky she's drained. What's happening outside?"

Whump! One of the traps went off downstairs. "We're being attacked by gang members."

"Why?"

"Best guess? We robbed a warehouse in their territory without asking."

Doc Vesperian screeched as her whole body flopped like a landed sewer-trout. "She's stuck in a feedback loop. What did you put into the back of her head?" Doctor Parnavan asked.

"I didn't put anything there. She did."

"Let me rephrase. Where did this biochip come from?"

A rager came in through the door. He was one of Mad Moe's, face painted white and steel strips implanted into his bald skull. He whooped and raised a scrap metal ax.

"Oh, please..." Doctor Parnavan said and clawed half his face off with a hand full of scalpels. He went down screaming.

"Holy crap, doc!" Clavicus said, shotgun raised but no longer needed.

"Him? I'll fix him later."

Clavicus laughed. Two more ragers ran in, almost fell over their comrade, and this time Clavicus was faster. *Boom! Ka-chick, boom!* "Can you fix that?" he asked the doctor.

The auto-surgeon's head twisted to look. "Probably not," she said in the tone mothers reserved for teenaged boys.

Doc Vesperian's seizures were slowing down. Her eyes were open, even if she couldn't talk yet. Clavicus heard more gunfire from the stairwell. He loaded two more shells into the loading port and braced himself.

"Coming in! Don't shoot!" Ultimus said.

Clavicus exhaled. "Thank goodness."

Lancestrom and Thragg came into the room, guns drawn and covered in brick dust. Lancestrom had a slight cut on his forehead that somehow managed to make him look more heroic. "How long until she's ready to move?"

"She shouldn't be moving at all," Doctor Parnavan answered.

"Whoa!" Lancestrom said, raising his pulser.

"Stop!" Clavicus said, getting between the pistoleer and the auto-surgeon. "That's Doctor Parnavan. She's helping."

"Same Doctor Parnavan who let her get fired from the clinic?" Lancestrom asked.

The auto-surgeon threw him as withering a look a machine with a blank brushed-steel face could give. "She was fired for performing an unauthorized surgery. And she turned around and did it again, no doubt under your influence, Mr. Lancestrom."

Lancestrom's mouth gaped, and Clavicus allowed himself a bestial grin while his hologram showed a neutral face.

The auto-surgeon injected Doc Vesperian with a pneumatic syringe, and her patient took in an explosive breath, then groaned. "What happened?"

"Take her and go," Doctor Parnavan told Clavicus, and he helped her sit up.

"Coat!" Doc Vesperian croaked.

Clavicus blushed. "Right!" He grabbed her coat and shirt from near the terminal.

"We're in a hurry, babe!" Lancestrom said, firing from the cover of the door.

"I don't care if we're in a hurry," Doc Vesperian said, pulling her shirt on. "I'm not running out there with my tits hanging out."

"Mercenary," the auto-surgeon said.

"Yes, ma'am?" Ultimus said.

"Put the living one without the face on the table. There's still time to save him."

"He might not thank you for it," the mercenary said, grabbing the unconscious ganger.

She shrugged. "Annie never got that, either. It's not about the patient or the science. It's about the oath."

Control Center, Capital Police
Pnyx, Skyward, Capital District of Politeia IV
4386.B.30 Interstellar

"Sir? Sir!" the operations' specialist shouted.

"What is it?" Sam said.

"I've found Governor Lancestrom's son! Doctor Parnavan messaged."

"Don't tell me…"

"Anuradhapura, sir. The vocational school." She looked defiant, almost cocky.

Sam grinned. "Good for you, specialist. You were right. And the gangs?"

She winced. "Attacking the school. The… hostage-takers are fighting back, but they're surrounded."

He ignored the pause before "hostage-takers." He assumed Zack was fighting with them. "Scramble the TRF," he told Lieutenant Colonel Williamson.

"Already done," the PPG soldier said.

"Good." Sam turned back to the specialist. "Send the video feeds to my station and tell them to focus on extracting the governor's son and a flying case that may be with him. It contains sensitive documents."

"Right away, sir," she said, turning back to her station.

Good luck, kid, Sam thought. *Hope you fight them as hard as you fought me.*

H.G. Clarence Vocational School, 2nd Floor
Anuradhapura, Capital District of Politeia IV

4386.B.30 Interstellar

Heavy caliber fire punched through the windows and chewed through brick as the war wagon's machine gun fired blindly into the building.

"I really hate that thing!" Zack yelled, changing out charge packs.

"Wait till you live through an artillery barrage!" Ultimus yelled. "That's a gift that gives and keeps on giving!"

They leaned out into the hallway and waited in the falling dust. A few seconds later, a pair of ragers came charging out of the stairwell. Zack sent his flying back through the door. The Reaper whined and snapped as Ultimus blew three fist-sized holes in the man's torso before he hit the ground, tried to get back up, and then Ultimus took the top of his head off with a fourth shot.

"You'd think they'd learn and rush us all at the same time," Ultimus said, checking his magazine.

"I thought we settled on vicious, not smart," Zack answered.

"Yeah, but then they got reinforcements."

They waited for another five-count. Zack swallowed and adjusted his grip on the pistol.

"Mr. Lancestrom?" a woman called out from the stairwell. Her voice was aged like leather.

Zack looked at Ultimus and mouthed, *Mad Moe?*

"Mr. Lancestrom, I know you're up there! Let's talk, you and me! No one needs to get hurt!"

She sounded like anyone's favorite grandmother. It was almost like she didn't know he and Ultimus had killed almost twenty of her men. *Should we talk to her?* Zack mouthed, pointing toward the stairwell.

No!!! Ultimus answered, shaking his head almost from shoulder to shoulder to convey the extra exclamation points.

And it was quiet.

No one came running up the stairs.

The war wagon didn't strafe the windows.

Then Zack felt the whole building shake as something big and loud roared down onto the roof, and a furious firefight broke out on the floors above them.

"They got behind us!" Ultimus yelled.

That was when Mad Moe and Jawhee's mixed ragers and scavs learned their lesson. They all came charging at once.

And Zack's team was prepared. "Boss, third floor. Go!" Ultimus shouted. The mercenary leaned into the hallway and fired a devastating flurry of shots into the gangers coming through the doorway to the stairwell. Zack, on the other hand, turned away.

He'd been impressed by how quickly Ultimus turned the school building into a death trap. For instance, they'd blocked the stairs from the third to second floor with as much of the third floor's furniture as they could fit. Then Ultimus used his sledgehammer to knock a hole through the far classroom's floor, and they stacked and wrapped furniture under it to make a sort of ramp. Hallways into barriers, walls into passageways, the easy way always trapped, and the right way always hidden. It was all about challenging the gangers' assumptions about how the building worked, and then shooting them.

Zack scrambled up the pile to the sound of Clavicus's shotgun booming. He pulled himself into the third-floor classroom at the same time as two capitol police officers in full riot gear came charging through the door.

"I've got Lancestrom!" the lead man said, letting his carbine hang from the sling to draw his stun gun.

Zack ran two steps and dropped into a slide, slamming his boot heel into the officer's shin. The man dropped, visored face first. Zack flowed to his feet and drove his shoulder into the second officer's chest.

"Oof!" she said. Her carbine was between them. Zack grabbed the barrel and receiver with both hands and smashed it back into her visor, drove his left knee into her groin protector, then kicked back and caught the first man in the helmet as he was getting up. Zack caught a gloved fist to the ear, which hurt but meant the officer had let go of her pistol grip. He drove the buttstock up into her chin and then rotated, throwing her over his hip into her partner.

Then he drew his pulser, flicked it to non-lethal, and shot them both at point-blank.

"Cops? We've got cops, now, too?" Clavicus said, swarming up through the hole and pulling Anya up with him.

"I think it's a rescue mission," Zack said, cuffing the cops with their own polymer-ties.

"Hah!" Clavicus said.

"Are they all right?" Anya asked.

"Just unconscious," Zack said. He tossed the carbines aside but kept the two stun guns and extra charge packs. They wouldn't fit the pulser, but if he needed to shoot his way through a team of police officers, he needed a less-than-lethal option.

ARK-II floated up next, letting loose a string of agitated sound effects.

"Little help?" Ultimus said, clawing at the floor to pull himself up.

"Here," Zack said, handing Anya his pulser before rushing to help the mercenary. He grabbed Ultimus by one elbow, and Clavicus pulled on the other. There were shouts from below, but they managed to haul Ultimus's two-hundred-kilo bulk to the third floor.

"Thanks," Ultimus said, standing up and swiping two grenades from his belt. He tossed one in, stomped on a ganger's hand as she tried to follow, and tossed the other. *Whump, whump!* There were screams from below. "What's with the cops?"

"Zack thinks it's a rescue party," Anya said.

"They look all partied out," Ultimus said.

"Hah. Puns. On a more serious note, you can't leave them there for Moe's animals," Clavicus said. "Better to shoot them. They'd thank you if they could."

Anya curled her lip, but she didn't protest. Zack looked at Ultimus. The big man didn't like it, but he nodded.

"That isn't what we're going to do," Zack said, drawing the two stun guns. "Ultimus, grab our guests."

"You got it, boss."

"Anya, up front with me. Clavicus, rearguard. Let's go." Zack stepped into the hallway, sweeping the shadows with his stolen stunners.

The hallway was littered with dead gangers. It might even have bothered Zack if he and Ultimus hadn't caused a much messier scene downstairs. He moved quickly, careful not to trip on the bodies. They were all Jawhee's scavs. Best Zack could tell, they'd gotten onto the roof somehow and been looking for a way down when they got hit by the police unit. He was halfway to the stairwell when a pair of scavs with fuel-powered circular saws cut their way through the stair barricade. And then someone cut them down from behind.

Mad Moe laughed. It was an ugly, tinny sound like she was speaking through a vocalizer. "Mr. Lancestrom. So glad we got to meet."

"Anya, get behind me," Zack said, and he didn't care if she didn't like it. The woman who walked out of the stairwell was as stockily built as Ultimus, and her implants were nowhere near as elegant. A good part of her face was hidden by a thick steel mask. Powered exoskeleton struts augmented her internal systems, and she was using them to carry thick armor plate and some kind of two-handed cannon.

"You did a nice job on my boys, Mr. Lancestrom. Have to respect an aristocrat who's willing to get his hands dirty."

Zack was looking for angles and coming up blank. Stun guns? Not worth it. The pulser didn't have the charge capacity, and the Reaper's rounds weren't made to pierce armor. If they'd had explosives, they might have dropped the floor out from under her, but they didn't, and Clavicus's shotgun didn't have the reach.

"Tell you what, Mr. Lancestrom. Out of respect for your derring-do, I'll make you an offer. Jawhee wants you alive so he can carve you up while his people watch. He thinks it'll set a good example for the scavs if he's willing to make royalty bleed. You holster your weapon and come quietly, and I'll let your people go."

CHAPTER EIGHTEEN

H.G. Clarence Vocational School, 3rd Floor
Anuradhapura, Capital District of Politeia IV
4386.B.30 Interstellar

Zack clenched his jaw. This wasn't how he'd planned to go out. It wasn't a fight he could win. But he owed it to his people. He swallowed and holstered his pulser before raising his hands.

Mad Moe raised her cannon and fired. A rounded disk slammed into Zack's stomach, and then it shocked him. He fell to the floor, twitching, and so did Anya and Clavicus. Ultimus dropped to a knee, like he had when Sam shot him with the EMP weapon, but this time the shocks kept coming, over and over.

And Mad Moe thought it was hilarious. "Bless my iron britches, the look on your face. You thought I was going to show your people mercy? Do you think I reached the position I'm in today by giving people chances?" She lumbered toward them. "There's a bounty on all of your heads, Mr. Lancestrom, and on that box hiding in the back. I aim to cash it in. Maybe the

Combine will take notice. Maybe the Venturi Cartel will. Doesn't matter much to me, as long as I get paid."

Zack managed to turn his head toward her. A trio of gangers followed her in, guns raised, and more waited by the stairwell. None of them were Jawhee's. *Looks like their cooperation was short-lived, and she won.* His muscles clenched again, popping his joints, curling him into a ball. Would Ultimus's EMP shielding work against her disk launcher, or was the disk somehow designed with cyborgs like him in mind?

Mad Moe looked down at him. A small, detached part of him noted the burn scars on her face and the metal voice box buried into her throat.

Then Anya snatched the disk off the floor and jumped onto her, grabbing the gang leader by her exoskeleton's spinal plug. Anya screamed. Mad Moe screamed, and spun, and fired two more of her disks into her own troops, and then she crashed to the floor, smoke pouring from her mask holes and back unit. The gangers near the stairwell panicked and fell back. Anya stood up and tossed the disk aside. Her tattoos shone bright neon green, and steam was rising from her body. "Thanks for the charge."

Zack groaned.

"Zack! Are you hurt?" she said, kneeling next to him.

"No," he said. "But that catchphrase was terrible."

She sat back on her heels. "It was great."

"Awful."

ARK-11 whistled and whooped.

"What did it say?"

"That your performance was electrifying. I'm surrounded by bad comedians." One of the gangers started to sit up. Zack shot him with a stun gun, and that worked fine. "We need to get moving. Why aren't those disks keeping them down?"

"There's some kind of activation mechanism in the launcher," Anya said.

"Pity. We could have used them to block the stairs." Zack staggered to his feet. "Our guests?"

"They're fine," Ultimus said, carrying the bound officers by their belts. "A little *shocked* by how they've been handled."

"Not you too," Zack said, trying to keep from smiling. "Come on. Let's get to the rooftop before they decide to attack again."

H.G. Clarence Vocational School, Rooftop
Anuradhapura, Capital District of Politeia IV
4386.B.30 Interstellar

They found another dead scav on the stairs, and another sprawled in front of the door that led outside. Once he saw the rooftop, it was fairly obvious what had happened. Mad Moe's ragers had stormed the front and sides of the building while Jawhee's grav-bikes ferried scavs to the roof. The capitol police unit had come in hot on a tilt-jet transport, through the cutout, and the ensuing gun battle had left all of the scavs and half of the officers dead.

"Put your weapons down!" the lone crewman said, carbine raised, standing between them and two wounded officers.

"Stand down, Officer," Zack said, walking forward like a gun wasn't pointed at his face. "I'm the reason you're here."

The crewman's carbine dipped slightly. "Zack Lancestrom?"

"Yes. You saved me. There will be medals for everyone, and cake."

The crewman's eyes widened as he saw Ultimus carrying the two bound cops, and he raised the carbine again, but it was too late. Zack pushed the barrel aside, ejected the magazine, and racked the bolt.

"Hey!"

Zack drew the stun gun from his belt and pointed at the crewman's face. The man raised his hands and looked at him in shock. "You weren't kidnapped."

Zack winked at him. "I wasn't. Clavicus! See if you can block that door!"

"Yeah, yeah," the engineer said.

"Babe, can you do something about the wounded?"

"You have a first aid kit?" she asked the crewman.

"What?"

"She's a doctor. Let us help."

The crewman clenched his jaw and seemed on the verge of lashing out, then he deflated. "Back of the cargo cabin, on the bulkhead."

Anya stepped past. The downed transport was a blocky thing with four variable thrusters on the underside of the fuselage. The engines were still turning. The cockpit was shattered.

"What happened?" Zack asked.

"Good men got killed trying to save you," the crewman growled.

"And I'm sorry for it. You did save us. If those scavs had hit us from behind, we wouldn't have made it."

"I wedged the door shut. Won't hold them long," Clavicus said.

"We need to get out of here, boss," Ultimus said, dropping the bound cops next to the two wounded ones.

The original plan had been to rappel off the roof if they were forced back from the ground floor. Ropes and auto-descenders were tied off to vent exhausts. "We have wounded."

Ultimus started to say something, then didn't.

"They're cops," Clavicus said, incredulous.

"They are. Get them loaded into the transport."

"But we don't have a pilot!" the crewman said.

Zack took another look at the transport. She was nothing like the Federal assault transports he'd trained on, and she was beat up, but she was what they had. "You do now," he answered.

Zack stepped through the cargo cabin into the cockpit. The pilot was dead, her chest pierced by shrapnel or glass fragments, or both. *The war wagon.* They must have gotten strafed on the way down. It was a miracle the dying pilot managed to land at all. Zack popped her straps, lifted the augmented-reality visor from her face, and pulled her out of the seat.

"Get your hands off her!" the crewman shouted, and Ultimus grabbed him by the arms.

"Ultimus, make sure the pilot's secured in the cargo cabin. We're not leaving her behind."

The crewman stopped struggling.

"You got it, boss."

Zack sat down in the blood-soaked seat. The cockpit was a mess, but police transports were made to take a beating. They'd lost fuel, and the pressure on the hydraulic system was flirting with the red part of the gauge, but it was flyable. The AR visor was synced to fuselage-mounted cameras. He tested the flight controls. They seemed functional.

"Everyone's loaded," Ultimus said from the doorway.

"Hold on," Zack said and pushed the thrust control lever forward smoothly until the transport was barely touching the roof, and then it lifted a few feet into the air. A huge grin spread across his face.

The door to the stairwell flew open and six gangers spilled out, firing as they ran.

"Time to go, boss!"

"I know!" Zack said and pushed the cyclic and foot-pedal to the left. The transport shuddered and turned. Bullets sparked off the fuselage. Then the left forward and aft thrusters slipped over the edge of the roof, and Zack lost lift. The transport rolled left hard; Zack threw the stick to the right and pushed the throttle forward; Anya screamed as they dropped two stories toward the street.

And then they bottomed out, thrusters at full and the meager ground effect of the wingless fuselage arresting their descent. Zack banked right, stomping on the right pedal, and rolled the vector control knob forward as they picked up speed.

They passed by the school. The wind coming through the broken cockpit meant Zack couldn't fly full speed, but he was passing 110 kilometers per hour when the war wagon opened fire, tracers smacking into empty buildings as Zack pulled, laughing, into the sky.

He almost lost her twice, and he fought the controls every step of the way. But he knew this was love, no matter how many aircraft he'd flown in virtual.

You never forget your first.

PTT-46 Osiris Troop Transport
Flying over the Kipway Sea, between the Capital and New Macedon districts
4386.C.1 Interstellar

Zack took his hands off the flight controls as the autopilot took over and lifted the AR visor from his eyes. It was just after midnight. He'd dropped their "guests" at the nearest hospital, held an impromptu press conference, and gotten airborne before security could reach the pad. He'd spent the next hour flying as low as he dared, getting them clear of the mega-city and beyond radar coverage.

Now that they were over water, he'd dropped the armored shutter over the ruined windshield and pushed the transport up to cruising speed. The cockpit was quiet. Satellites might still be able to track them, but he'd disabled their transponder. The rest was up to Fate and a reasonable hope of governmental incompetence.

The door to the cockpit opened, and Anya stepped in before closing the door behind her. "Where are we?" she said, squeezing into the small space.

"Over the Kipway Sea," he said. "At least that's my best guess. Can't use global positioning, so I'm flying off dead reckoning."

She gave him a fake serious look and said, "I don't love that the word dead was part of that sentence."

"I'm only the pilot. I don't make the rules."

"You don't? Who should I talk to?"

"Okay, fine, I make the rules. What can I do for you?"

She smiled and hooked her arms around the headrest so she could sit in his lap.

"Oops, hold on," he said, propping the goggles on the dash and tapping a quick sequence on the number pad to his left. The flight controls locked and retracted.

"Better," she said, sitting sideways.

He put his arms around her. "Yes, it is."

She bent down and kissed him. Her hands gripped his shoulder and the back of his neck. He dug his thumb into her inner thigh.

She pulled back. "Is this okay? We're not going to crash or anything, are we? I'm a little charged up after the fight, in more ways than one."

"It's fine. Pretty much flies itself," he said, working his right hand up her leg. He tapped the number pad again with his left, starting a thousand-foot climb to give him more time to respond if something *did* go wrong, then grabbed her neck and pulled her lips against his.

After a pleasant minute or two, she pulled back.

"What's wrong?" he asked, resting his hands on her hips.

She wrinkled her nose and said, "Why are you doing all this?"

Zack frowned. "I told you. ARK-II is dying. It's not happening today, or tomorrow, but the government is always going to have another excuse about why it needs to stay here and keep the sophistocracy together for one more year, even if the clock is running out."

She made a face. "Yeah. That's ARK-II's reasons. I mean, you realize it screwed you over, right? That if it was responsible for the Synthesis, it derailed your life for its own purposes."

"I know that. It took a risk. I could have used that knowledge as leverage over my father and the government."

"But you didn't, and it knew you wouldn't."

Zack shrugged. "It's still my choice, babe. Just because it's smarter than me doesn't take away my right or absolve my responsibility. Do we really want to get into a discussion about fate and free will?"

"Please, no," she said with a smirk. "I'm worried about you. You're a criminal now—a famous one. Even your father couldn't save you from jail. I've never known you not to play the long game."

Zack glanced at his instruments—still on course and altitude—to give himself space to think. And Anya let him. He liked that about them, that she knew him well enough to give him time. "I think I *am* playing the long game. The next few years, maybe even decades, are going to be hard. We'll be starting out from scratch on new worlds with new cultures. ARK-II gives us an incredible advantage because no matter what the marketable skills are where we wind up, we can learn them. But we'll have to work up to buying a ship—a proper starship, not just a shuttle—and we might be on the run if my father or the government send people after us."

Anya nodded. "So why not lay low? You could have formally abdicated, joined an interstellar, and worked your way up the ranks. There must be dozens of them that would jump over themselves to hire a Spire graduate, and that would have taken you offworld soon enough, with a salary and connections."

"Because we can do better," Zack said, surprised by the passion in his own voice. "Once we find the Forge, you and I will have the means to make this part of the galaxy better. We can make sure kids don't grow up half oxygen-starved on low-g orbitals. We can make sure people like Clavicus get gene-therapy and the education that will elevate them not only a city level, but in purpose as well."

"What if we don't find it, Zack?" she asked quietly.

What if indeed? He wasn't stupid. The thought had occurred to him that they might never find the Forge or the first governor's lost cruiser. "Then I will have failed, and that's too bad for me and the people I would have helped. But I would have gone for it and tried something, gone beyond other people's expectations of me, and my own. We'll see things we never would have, learn things we'd have no reason to, and if our contribution to the universe is becoming happier, more fulfilled people and seeing new worlds, together, then that's enough."

"Because you love me?"

That caught him off guard, but he knew the answer. "Yes."

And she didn't answer. And that hurt like a knife in his chest, but he pushed that aside because he knew her, too, and she was going to need some time before she was ready to commit to that.

She did bend down and kiss him, though, which he took as a good sign, and then she made clear that she wanted more than a kiss.

There was some fumbling, because the cockpit hadn't been designed for this, but they made up for the awkwardness with laughter and a certain shameless enthusiasm.

The Planetary Hall, Governor's Office
Pnyx, Skyward, Capital District of Politeia IV
4386.C.1 Interstellar

Alex Lancestrom leaned forward as the news clip started to play.

"Consternation in the planetary capital this morning as two rival gangs opened fire in the Anuradhapura industrial zone and police officers were caught in the crossfire. Even more bizarre was the presence of Zack Lancestrom, the now infamous son of Governor Lancestrom, who was able to rescue five of the wounded officers and evacuate them to the nearest hospital landing pad.

"When asked about reports of his being held hostage by offworld criminals, Mr. Lancestrom grew serious and stated for the record that, having failed the Synthesis and no longer being the recipient of public funds, he was surprised by the government's efforts to unlawfully detain him."

The camera switched to a shot of Zack Lancestrom. It was a good shot of him, illuminated by the landing pad lights in the ruined cockpit of his stolen transport. He'd gotten Alex's instinct for a good spin and the best of Elena's looks. "I'm not a hostage," Zack said. "I'm not government property either. I understand there may be objections to how I've chosen to live my life, especially after so many years of investment by the sophistocracy, but I believe in the resilience of our government and in the capabilities of the other heirs—of which there are many—to lead Politeia in the years to come.

"It's my plan, along with a few like-minded individuals, to make my way to the lawless zone known as the Starship Boneyard, *as is my right in accordance with the charter.*"

"Turn it off," Scamander said.

Alex dismissed the screen with a wave.

Several moments of uncomfortable silence passed. Then Councilor Richter, the most senior member of the Politeian Council said, "What do we do?"

The full Council of Twelve, one for each of the Splinter Fleet ships that reached Politeia, was assembled for the second time in as many days. They were only the tip of the sophistocratic body, comprised of layers of administrators, judges, legislators, and police officials from the districts down to the individual cities. They were few but vested with great power by the colony's charter.

But, for centuries, that power had been *exercised* by the planetary governor.

"We could let him go," Alex said, clasping his hands on the table.

Scamander sneered and started to answer, but Councilor Richter waved him into silence. "Let me be candid with you, Alex. There is a good bit of suspicion among our members, much of it justified, as to your motives when it comes to Zack. Some have even suggested you might have arranged for Zack to find ARK-II in some bid to set him up as the ruler of some new planet, or topple the government, but that's nonsense. If you'd wanted, Zack could have left the planet with ARK-II six months ago, and none of us would have been the wiser until the next Synthesis."

Alex let his old colleague and friend speak. Much of politics was knowing when to listen.

"You're finished as governor. As soon as this... crisis is over, you will either resign, or this Council will remove you. There is some question as to whether criminal charges should be brought against you, or if voluntary seclusion from private life might be more appropriate."

"As the Council sees fit," Alex answered.

Richter nodded. "Now, please explain your last statement. Why in bloody hell should we let him go? He's stolen the single most important piece of technology on this planet."

"We don't have a choice. You saw the news. He's a hero."

Scamander exploded. "He's a thief and a murderer! He made that broadcast from a stolen police transport..." The councilor faltered, seeing the disapproval from the others. His face turned red.

"Councilor Scamander is correct, of course," Alex said generously. "Zack stole a police transport and, while we don't have evidence of it, it is *possible* he may have killed a police officer, or that an extraordinarily gifted lawyer could convince a jury his use of force on those gang members was excessive. We certainly have him on illegal possession of firearms."

Scamander looked cautiously grateful.

A few of the councilors smirked.

"Does he know about Gyges?" Councilor Richter asked.

That gave Alex pause. He hadn't considered that his son might actually have a way off the planet, although getting there was suicide. "We can't discount it. He didn't learn about it from me, but ARK-II knew."

Richter thought for a moment, then shook his head. "Forget it. Even with your son's luck, and a mercenary like Ultimus Thragg, there's no way they could force their way through. Major Orvendale and his troops are the best and most loyal this planet has to offer."

"I'd be more worried about them *helping* Zack," Alex said.

"I beg your pardon?" Scamander said, his tone back to verging on explosive.

"They can't break their conditioning," Richter said dismissively.

"It's the military mind, Councilors. I don't expect you to agree with it, but understand this. Orvendale and his troops, and their families, and any volunteers who weren't born out there, they've been fending off violent criminals and beasts, waiting for the day the ARK would come to them so they could fulfill their sacred purpose. The ARK is coming to them, of its own volition, and *we* are the ones standing in its way."

The two councilors looked at him in shock.

"The simple fact is, Zack outmaneuvered us. People believed him and, as much as it irks, some things are bigger than even this Council. He's declared his intent to go into exile. By law and long tradition, the security forces of this government cannot stop him." And while it wasn't the right time for Alex to admit it, he was exceedingly proud of how his son had handled it.

Richter looked around the table, then nodded. "Fine. We let him go, but he *cannot* reach Project Gyges. Now, please tell me you have a plan. I've never known you to let someone beat you without a fight, not even your son."

Alex smiled. "Actually, I have just the thing…"

CHAPTER NINETEEN

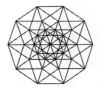

Shared Virtual Network
Users: Zack Lancestrom, Anthropological Restoration Kit XI
4386.C.1 Interstellar, Time Dilation 0.125x

"Freeze simulation," Zack said.

He unstrapped and slid out of the pilot's seat. A translucent outline marked the position he'd been in at that point of the recording. He walked through Ultimus, who was bracing himself in the doorframe as the transport tipped off the edge of the roof, looking... completely unconcerned. Zack was not for the first time reminded of how fortunate he'd been to find the mercenary between jobs on his figurative doorstep.

The two injured cops were on the floor of the cargo cabin, strapped to stretchers. The section was divided into two by a central column; while the thrusters were on the underside of the fuselage, many of the more fragile systems were above, away from ground fire.

Anya, Clavicus, and the crewman were seated with their backs to the column on the right, and the two cops Zack had captured on the left. ARK-11 had stowed itself in the back. More importantly, a single of the gangers' rounds had broken through the starboard-side window and was hanging, frozen, centimeters from one of the cops' heads.

"Step forward," Zack said.

The bullet missed the cop and smacked into the column. Zack tapped a key on the holo-interface floating above his left wrist, and the paneling around the column turned transparent, and all the cables, wires, drains, pumps, and vents were labeled by virtual tags.

Life was full of happenstances. The bullet was a dense-cored armor-piercing round. A centimeter or two to the right and the cop would have died. A finger to the left, and it would have clipped one of the hydraulic lines.

Under normal circumstances, no big deal—the transport had multiple redundancies. But with the damage the war wagon had inflicted, the hydraulics had already been borderline, and Zack would have been unable to rotate the front left thruster forward. The transport wouldn't have plowed into the ground—software limiters would have detected the imbalance and locked all four thrusters. But they wouldn't have built up enough forward speed, and the war wagon would have torn them apart.

Instead, the round went through the column, grazed Clavicus's leaf hat, and came to a stop in the port-side fuselage. If the crewman, or Anya, had been sitting in Clavicus's seat... most people wondered if things could have gone differently. Zack knew.

He used the wrist interface to exit the shared virtual network.

Outlying Field Eleanor's Hope
Planetary Preserve 118, New Macedon District

Chapter Nineteen | 219

4386.C.1 Interstellar

Zack lifted the training circlet from his head and squinted against the sunlight. The air was dry and dusty here on the edge of the landing strip.

A lone *chakal ambré* looked back at him from a nearby hill. The small desert predator sat motionless, seeming aware and uninterested at the same time. For a moment, Zack stared back and felt a connection.

Anya put her hand on his shoulder, and he covered it with his. "Hey," he said, turning his head to look at her, and they shared a smile at the memory of their flight over water.

"I was about to ping you when you pulled the circlet off."

"Time to go?"

"We're refueled, and Clavicus finished his repairs, with a few upgrades. You should check it out. I don't think he got much sleep."

"We're lucky to have him," Zack said, standing up.

"I agree."

Eleanor's Hope was one of several short airstrips scattered across the planetary preserve. It had a small control tower, refueling pumps, and living quarters for the rangers. The latter had seen the newscasts and been wary but helpful, even letting ARK-11 connect to the OLF's radar so they'd see trouble coming and the team could catch a few hours of sleep.

It was also in the southern hemisphere, and Zack had left his jacket in the transport. Semi-arid desert stretched for hundreds of kilometers around them. The sparse vegetation was a mix of Old Earth and native species. Joshua trees were interspersed with Arrymi bushes, fool's brush with mesquite. It was all by design, a delicate blend of alien species that complemented each other to thrive in one of the harshest environments on Politeia.

"Hey, boss," Ultimus said as Zack approached. The old mercenary was sitting on the edge of the open cargo cabin, eating something out of a pouch. He was in the nude, which was to say his mechanical body was exposed. The dents and scratches on his chassis were gone.

"You're looking good, old man."

Ultimus chuckled. "Doc managed to start up my self-repair routine, among a few other goodies. You want some breakfast?"

"How could I turn down one of your meals?"

"I dunno. You'd have to be crazy." Ultimus grinned and handed Zack a warm pouch and a spoon.

Zack ripped the top open and was greeted by the complex aroma of tomato paste, peppers, beans... and egg, if he wasn't mistaken. And some kind of cheese. "Huevos rancheros?"

"Enchiladas montadas, Horsehead Nebula style. Has cashews and scallions in it. And here," the mercenary said, handing him another of his shakers.

"Special spice mix?"

"Tortilla crumbles, lime zest, and ghost pepper powder. For the crunch and the kick."

Zack added a little before handing it back. Sometimes moderation was the better part of valor. He took a bite, and the flavors exploded into his mouth in all kinds of round, bright, zesty, and spicy ways. "I don't pay you enough," he mumbled.

"I'll remember that next time you have money," Ultimus said. "What should we expect to run into, out there?" the mercenary asked.

Zack took a moment to think before answering. He'd pulled some simulations and actual footage from ARK-IIs files, as part of his preparation for this trip, but he was hardly an expert on the buffet of threats the Boneyard had to offer. "Humans will be our biggest problem. I think my little press conference last night worked, though—the PPG's announced they're not coming after us."

"Hallelujah," Ultimus said. "So, what's the problem?"

"Aside from starvation and dehydration? I'm worried about aircraft maintenance. If we have a problem out there, we're an awful long way from spare parts and help. The western approach is riddled with caves and tunnels, so we might survive hoofing it if it was something Clavicus couldn't fix, but then we'd have to deal with the locals and the wildlife—scaled snapdragons, dune serpents, packs of canyon wolves. Most of them have learned to hunt humans by now, and there were star spiders in the area a decade ago."

"Really?" Ultimus said. "On this side of the galaxy?"

"You've fought them before?"

"No, just vids. It hasn't been much more than ten years since first contact, but that was *way* out on the Cygnus arm of the galaxy. We're kind of in the opposite direction."

Zack nodded. "Well, this wasn't anything like a full incursion. The military went in and burned them out. Some convicts got eaten. The news didn't care. End of story."

"Hey, Zack," Clavicus said, popping his head out from the cockpit. Zack didn't think he'd gone outside the transport much once the sun was up. Wide-open spaces weren't his thing.

Zack's eyes flicked to the scrape on the left side of his leaf hat, but he smiled like he hadn't noticed. "Clavicus! I heard you've made some upgrades."

"One or two," the engineer said, smirking. "Come see."

Zack climbed into the transport, patting Ultimus's metal shoulder. Clavicus stepped out of the way to let Zack into the tight space, and Zack refrained from touching the sensitive engineer as he passed.

The armored shutter was up, letting the morning light into the cockpit. The windshield was still missing but had been cleared out—not ideal, but better than having shards of omniplex propelled into his face at high speed.

"What do you think?" Clavicus said, grinning.

Zack rapped his knuckle on the bulkhead next to him. "I'm sorry, man. I'm not sure what I'm looking at."

"Oh, right," Clavicus said and squeezed past him. "Sorry..."

Zack moved to the right; Clavicus wedged himself on the left of the seat, turned on the battery, then reached out to flick a switch that hadn't been there last night. A faint grid of hexagons, each the size of a fingernail, was forming line by line where the missing windshield would have been.

Zack cocked his head. "What is it?"

"It's a kinetic barrier, or at least that's what ARK-II calls it. I think of it more as a carbon capture and alignment device that uses—"

"Kinetic barrier sounds better," Zack said, sliding forward to rest his hand against one of the completed sections. It flexed but didn't give.

"Yeah. Anyway, I looked it up in ARK-II's engineering specs and reconfigured some of the hull-mounted cameras as emitters. It takes a moment to build up and, uh, well don't expect it to stop bullets or anything, but it will act as a windshield and deflect small-caliber rounds. Do you like it?"

Zack turned to look at him. He couldn't see Clavicus's face, but the engineer sounded nervous. It was endearing, really. "I love it. I can't believe you managed to put something this advanced together with spare parts."

"I... that is... good, because I may have scavenged the other cameras for something else I'm building, and I made other improvements! Let me give you the tour."

★

PTT-46 Osiris Troop Transport, Outlying Field Eleanor's Hope
Planetary Preserve 118, New Macedon District
4386.C.1 Interstellar

With no contacts on the field radar and no one on the ground except a couple bored rangers and the chakal, Zack took the time to do a full pre-flight inspection of the transport.

Clavicus walked with him, pointing out changes and things he should worry about. The engineer hadn't wasted time on mending scratches or scorch-marks on the blocky aircraft's fuselage, but the transport was otherwise intact, holes patched, rivets tightened or plates fused to the frame with a welder Clavicus had made appear from somewhere. He'd had to scrap one of two secondary hydraulic systems, but the engineer used the drained fluid to top off the two primaries, and he installed a magnetic switch so their remaining backup could serve both. He'd scrapped the transponder completely, as well as two lojacks he'd found in the engine compartment above the main cabin.

And somehow, on top of that, he'd managed—he said—to squeeze an extra 14% of thrust out of the engines. It wasn't sustainable; Zack would boil the oil system by running it that hot continuously, but it was nice to know it was there.

"Oh, and one more thing," the engineer said, concluding their tour and inspection. "ARK-11 made this for you. Said you'd know what it was." He handed Zack a small pendant on a breakaway chain, like military tags. It was the bullet, flattened out and filled in with steel to make a rounded rectangle. The front was inscribed, *Captain Zack Lancestrom, PTT 3768A*. The back bore the inscription, *No fate but what we make*. Zack wasn't sure where it came from, but it sounded profound. Maybe a religious text or something.

"Thank you," Zack stammered, taken off guard.

"You earned it, um, 'boss,'" Clavicus said, and even raised his fist tentatively to bump Zack in the shoulder. Then he put it back down. "I'm going to have to work up to that," he said.

"Take your time. I'm glad you're with us."

"Me too," the engineer said.

Zack put the chain around his neck and tucked the pendant under his shirt. It was a surprising development for him. Not the bullet, though he was touched and a little unnerved that the machine had given him something so... meaningful. *I should have seen that coming, though,* he thought, touching the pendant through his shirt. ARK-11 had been responsible for the Synthesis of all things, the single most meaningful event on his planet for a hundred generations.

But the real transition had been of Zack from employer to captain of this crew. Ultimus had always been rock solid; his loyalty, once bought, had been Zack's solid ground from the beginning. Anya had come around, grudgingly, then with a supportiveness that lacked Ultimus's light touch but matched his sincerity. And now Clavicus looking to him for validation? It was almost enough to make "Captain" Zack believe in it himself.

"Everybody load up!" he said, grabbing his jacket and making sure his pulser was holstered and on safe. He'd swapped out the longer gray duster for a dark gray, blue-trimmed crew jacket he'd found in the back. It breathed better, and left him with better access to his weapon.

The starboard cabin door was already shut, bullet holes patched, and once Zack, Anya, and Clavicus were aboard, Ultimus pulled the port-side door closed. Zack made his way to the cockpit while the others strapped in.

Aside from a few extra custom switches and the kinetic barrier, there was one more major change to the cockpit. Namely, Clavicus had ripped out the entire circuit breaker board, navigation system, and radio. Zack had been a little more agitated about that one, but he'd almost hugged the engineer when he realized why he'd done it. He'd made a cradle for ARK-II to plug into, running the transport's electronics better than any computer on the planet could have. The little machine was already in place.

"You ready to do this, buddy?"

ARK-II triple whooped and glowed green.

Zack patted the little box and dropped into the pilot's seat, fastened his straps, and ran the checklist from memory. "Breakers in?"

ARK-II beeped.

Zack turned the dome light switch on and flipped the power switch to alternating. He turned the inverter off, the limiter on, and checked the generator switch was on and covered. He switched the battery on and canceled the low thrust alarm. Panels and pumps clicked and whirred, the three glass displays that showed his instruments came to life, and he continued with the checklist after giving them a once over. He pushed the fire indicator switch until it set off the alarm, as it should, then checked the avionics, jettison, governor, de-icing, and countermeasure switches were all off, safe, and locked as appropriate.

The hydraulics were on, flight assist on, caution panel on and tested. Capacitors were charged, all gauges were in the green, so Zack turned on the hydrogen fuel injector and toggled the capacitors from charge to discharge, super-heating the first atoms to start the reaction.

The transport vibrated, and the engine howled as a tiny, unstable sun was born in the containment field above their heads. Temperatures rose rapidly as ARK-II and the transport computer managed the cascade. Zack's job was to watch for a runaway reaction or a containment failure and shut it down before it did any damage.

As the temperatures peaked and started to come down, Zack relaxed. He flicked the limiter off, inverter on, and the generators took over from the battery. The flight controls unstowed and locked, and Zack tested the stick and pedals before moving the throttle from start settings to idle. The tone of the engines changed, and the vibration smoothed out as the fusion generator was allowed to vent through the larger thrust nozzles. He checked the windsock and saw it was flying east to west.

"Eleanor's Hope, this is PTT 3768-Alpha, request permission to takeoff runway one-zero-zero, southern departure."

"PTT 3768-Alpha, this is Eleanor's Hope. You're cleared for immediate departure, proceed at your own risk, VFR. Best of luck, Mr. Lancestrom."

"Thanks, gents. Lancestrom out."

Zack pushed the throttle forward. He was smoother this time, going straight from idle to accelerating flight a few feet above the runway. The transport felt good, more stable, his control more instinctive. He rolled the thrusters for forward flight, eased the stick back, and turned south as he climbed toward the Starship Boneyard and what he hoped was his destiny.

CSS-A-426 Artemisia of Cara
Politeia IV, Six Hour Orbit (10,000km)
4386.C.1 Interstellar

Major Kyle "Ajax" Antarxes read the contract on the bridge tactical station one more time to make sure he hadn't missed anything. The weight and light pressure of his battle armor was familiar and comforting. The mission was simple. The client had changed twice, first the planetary governor, then the Council—whatever that meant to the locals—and now back to the governor again. It smelled of politics, which Antarxes was always wary of, but their payment was in escrow and he trusted Sam Meritt's reputation with the Combine.

"The mission's a go," he told Commander Jessica "Lynx" Jeppesen.

"For that kind of money? The mission was always a go," she answered. "You have your heart set on going in naked?"

"They're Tier 3 drop-suits, Jess."

"Right. Naked," she said, giving him a wink. "If you miss the target, it'll be six hours before I can retrieve you."

"We won't miss. If we do, we'll hitch a ride."

"What about Ultimus?"

Ajax nodded. Ultimus Thragg was the real source of the tension on the bridge. "His implants are shut down," he said, kissing her cheek. "And I'm taking the brawler."

The brawler was a lancer—a hyper-mobile armored tank designed to kill cyborgs and carry siege weapons across broken terrain.

Lynx didn't look convinced. "We can afford to lose this one if it comes down to it."

"Jess..."

"*Major*," she answered. "You are a Combine mercenary. No heroics."

"Only profits," he answered with a grin. "I'll be careful."

"You'd better." She turned to the helmsman. "Sound general quarters."

"Yes, ma'am."

The ship's klaxon sounded. "General quarters, general quarters. All spacers to your stations. Ground team, to your launch tubes. This is not a drill."

Ajax tucked his helmet under his arm and left the bridge, a boyish grin on his face. He took the ladder down to the well deck where his troops were waiting.

"Hey, Major! I thought they called this thing off!" Higgins

quipped. He and the others were already kitted up and locked into the tubes.

"Yeah, Higgins. You heard right. And they decided to pay us anyway."

A few of the newer mercenaries hooted. The veterans stayed quiet. "Any word on Ultimus Thragg, Major?"

"I'll get to that," Ajax said, the humor gone from his voice. "All right, boys and girls, this is it. We are operating under official sanction from this planet's highest authority. They won't support us, but they won't interfere, either. Dapper, you're in charge of the air assault. Ito, Higgins, you're backup."

The three men acknowledged their roles.

"It's ten thousand kilometers to the drop-zone. Target is a ruggedized, mobile white case. It's in a stolen transport, atmo only, no onboard armaments. It should respond to vocal commands once the crew is disabled. Your job is to force that transport to land without blowing it up. Noddy, Hotpocket, take out the pilot. Jericho, disable the engines if you can. We need that case intact."

"What about the crew, sir?" Hijinks, one of the younger men to earn his callsign, asked.

"Crew of four—three civilians and one Ultimus Thragg. Now, before you ask—yes, it is *that* Ultimus Thragg and no, we don't have an up-to-date status on his combat systems. He was in the top one hundred solo-operators of the Combine's leaderboards for close to a decade. He's damaged a lot of property and killed a lot of people. I'll be ten minutes behind you in the brawler. Just get the transport on the ground. Any questions?"

"What's the rush, boss?" Jericho asked. "Why don't we go in quiet, middle of the night, no muss, no fuss?"

Ajax smiled. He liked Jericho. She was the team sharpshooter, smart as a nav computer and just as icy. She'd have her own team someday, maybe even an outfit with her name on it.

"We're being paid extra to cut them off before they reach this 'boneyard.' It's a little slice of heaven where the government dumps their convicts. High temperatures, crazies with guns, mountains and lava tubes to hide in. Our job gets ten times more difficult if they make it there."

Jericho nodded.

"Good. We drop in... seven minutes. I'll see you on the ground."

CHAPTER TWENTY

PTT-46 Osiris Troop Transport
Desert of Mercy, Outskirts of the Starship Boneyard
4386.C.1 Interstellar

Ultimus used to like to talk on the long flights. Nowadays, he mostly stayed quiet. He listened to the hum of the engines, to Clavicus and the doc nurse their fledgling friendship, and over it all, he heard the background noise of a dozen other ships on a hundred other worlds, and all their holds were filled with ghosts.

"Do you miss her?" the doc asked.

"Who," Clavicus answered.

"Betsy."

The engineer straightened and touched the brim of his leaf hat. "Not really, no. I mean, I guess? I only had her for a year."

"Really? She seemed so... lived in."

Clavicus shrugged. "I always tinker. And someone did live in her before I got her. What's yours doesn't stay yours for long, Below."

Ultimus wasn't sure he believed that. He'd grown up in a

poor industrial colony. He hadn't had a lot, but those few things he owned had been precious to him.

The team's comm circuit came alive in Ultimus's ear. "Hey, Ultimus?"

"Yeah, boss?"

"Got something for you to look at, up in the cockpit."

Ultimus unstrapped and squeezed past the doc and Clavicus. He opened the cockpit door and shut it behind him.

"What's up?"

"Maybe nothing. It looks like something's burning up in the atmosphere." The kid handed Ultimus an AR visor and pointed above and behind them.

Ultimus's pulse quickened. He counted ten or eleven objects making reentry. A few more seconds of observation told him, mostly by intuition rather than measurement, that they were maneuvering under their own power. "How fast can this thing go?"

To his credit, the kid didn't ask a bunch of stupid questions. "Six hundred and fifty kilometers per hour, seven-seventy if I push it, but not for long."

"Push it. They're going to catch us anyway. Every second you can give us to prepare matters."

"You've got it."

Ultimus handed him the AR goggles and headed back to the cargo cabin. Anya and Clavicus looked up as he walked in; he keyed the team channel so Lancestrom would hear, too. "We've got drop-suits inbound in the next six to ten minutes. I've asked the boss to buy us time; Clavicus, if you've got any other tricks up your sleeves, now is the time to use them."

The engineer nodded.

"As far as I know," Ultimus continued, "drop-suits are outside the capabilities of the Politeian security forces, so these are mercenaries, maybe even Combine. These are not cops or defense forces. Many of them will be veterans of multiple campaigns. They will come at us fast, hit hard, and there would ordinarily be very little we could do to stop them."

He paused to let his words register. There were no questions or outbursts, and Ultimus gave Lancestrom a mental tip of the hat for bringing the team together.

"Politeia's out of the way when it comes to interstellar travel, so either they were here on other business, or they were called a few days ago. There aren't that many people with the knowledge, motive, and means to pay for something like this, and they're all part of the planetary government. Wonder why the planetary guard didn't come after us? Now you know. The good thing is, they'll want to take ARK-II back intact. They might even want the boss alive.

"Make no mistake, we're fighting for our lives against a tougher enemy than you've ever faced. But there's a slim chance they'll play it too cute. Hit 'em hard with everything you've got, and we'll get through this. Let's get to it."

Clavicus unstrapped and went aft.

"Doc?" Ultimus said, no longer on the team channel. "Yes?"

"I need my anti-matter reactor online."

The doc pressed her lips together, then nodded. "Sit down and let me access your back panel."

Ultimus did as he was told.

One of the Tier 3.5 goodies Ultimus had gotten as an "atta boy" from the Federal Fleet was an AM reactor small enough to fit in his chassis. It wasn't as sustainable as the micro-fusion reactor he also carried because it required anti-matter as fuel instead of hydrogen. But it could produce the prodigious amounts of energy required to support higher-tier technologies.

Doc Vesperian popped his back panel open and jacked into his control system.

Anti-Matter Reactor Start-up Sequence... Initiated

Magnetic Field...Stable
Injection sequence commencing in 3...2...1...
Failure. Force Shut Down Initiated.
Anti-Matter Reactor on Standby.

Ultimus felt a bloom of heat in his chest as the anti-matter was unmade by the fail-safes, and any residual energy was absorbed by his chassis.

It wasn't that the doc hadn't been able to understand how it worked. AM reactors operated the same way fission reactors did. It was the pure technical challenge of feeding the anti-matter into the center of the containment field without setting off fail-safes or having an unshielded reaction fry him with gamma radiation.

Combine techs erred on the side of caution, topping a mercenary's fuel off after a successful start. They'd put it off as long as they did because Anya and Ultimus didn't have fuel to spare.

Anti-Matter Reactor Start-up Sequence... Initiated
Magnetic Field...Stable
Injection sequence commencing in 3...2...

"Doc?" Clavicus said, coming out of the cockpit.

"Not now!" the doc snapped.

Clavicus flinched.

Injection aborted.
Magnetic Field Destabilizing.
Anti-Matter Ejection... Manual-Override.
Magnetic Field... Restored.

Ultimus silently cheered the doctor on. Those mercs were minutes away, at best.

Injection sequence... Manual Launch.
Anti-Matter... Stable.
Magnetic Field... Stable.

Containment Achieved, Anti-Matter Reactor Start-up Sequence Complete.

"Nice job, doc!" Ultimus said

"I lost thirty-five percent of the anti-hydrogen."

Ultimus nodded. It wasn't as good as he'd hoped, but better than he'd had a right to expect.

"You needed me, Clavicus?"

"I made you this," he said, handing her something that looked like a stun rod for livestock. "It extends up to two meters, and it has its own capacitors you can draw from. I call it an electro-lance."

"I... Thank you, Clavicus, but I'm not sure I'll be able to use this in the cabin."

Clavicus's hologram changed to a big, open smile. "That's the other bit. I extended the kinetic barrier. The two of you should be able to fight from the roof of the transport."

"Good job. We should get into position," Ultimus said, slinging the Reaper across his body. It wouldn't penetrate a drop-suit, but it might slow them down a bit.

"It will take a few minutes for the shield to build up," Clavicus said. "Zack—the boss and I—we have a plan to buy you that time. Our speed's not going to matter once they catch us anyway."

PTT-46 Osiris Troop Transport (Cockpit)
Desert of Mercy, Outskirts of the Starship Boneyard
4386.C.1 Interstellar

Zack watched the temperature creep up on the aft fusion generator. The transport was managing 365 knots of airspeed—about 656 kilometers per hour over ground, factoring in a nine-knot headwind. That wasn't as much as he'd promised Ultimus, but it was for a good reason.

He'd decoupled the generators.

Both gennies fed into the central exhaust column that fed all four thrusters. They were designed to share the load automatically, with the caveat that the aft generator was more of a backup, designed to provide enough thrust to land the transport if the forward generator was shut down or damaged. It had its own circuits and a small spare fuel tank for that purpose.

Right now, Zack was running the forward generator at 105% of normal, and the aft generator at a whopping 133%.

Not a big deal, because a fusion generator had several safeguards to prevent runaway reactions.

Zack had disabled them and had ARK-11 lock the aft generator's hydrogen feed to permanently open. An explosive cascade was only a matter of time, but the transport's engineers had planned for that as well.

Because the aft generator was made for emergency conditions, Polis-Technix had anticipated it might be pushed beyond their specs. They fitted it with a guided rocket-assisted jettison system that would boost the reactor a safe distance from buildings or people before detonation.

Zack had ARK-11 reprogram that, too.

PTT-46 Osiris Troop Transport (Exterior)
Desert of Mercy, Outskirts of the Starship Boneyard
4386.C.1 Interstellar

Ultimus and the doc stood on the roof of the transport. The kinetic barrier was up and functional, creating a windless pocket for them to fight in. The incoming mercs were above and behind them, dancing rocket halos burning toward them like those fire-wasps on Demeter II. Just thinking of those things made his skin itch, and he didn't have skin to scratch.

Clavicus was in the cargo cabin, toolbox set to repair damage and shotgun ready to repel boarders. The doc had her new electro-lance out, charged, and extended. The kid hadn't pulled off whatever distraction they had planned, but that was fine. Ultimus preferred to keep things simple. He had his AM reactor primed and three hundred rounds for the Reaper. Everything else was paint on armor plate.

"Hold onto something!" Lancestrom said on the team channel, and the transport started to tilt back.

"Oh, crap!" Ultimus said. He grabbed the doc by the waist as she started to slip and grabbed a fastening point with his other hand, letting his carbine hang from the sling. The aircraft kept leaning back, engines roaring, tilting until the incoming drop-suits were directly overhead, and then the aft section of the deck exploded, and something round and as big as a trashcan shot up, corkscrewing like a missile.

The transport pitched forward, hard, and the doc—who was not fond of flying to begin with—screamed. Ultimus watched as some of the drop-suits, probably the veterans, scattered in every direction like birds. The remaining idiots tried to blow through it or shoot the missile down.

"Cover your eyes, doc!" he shouted.

PHOOOOM!

The transport was smacked by the concussion as the fusion reactor went off like a low-yield tactical nuke. It was mostly light and heat, but it kicked their aircraft like an Old Earth mule. Ultimus laughed as his eyes cut out the glare, and he saw the mercenaries get tossed around by the blast and the turbulence. Two of them were under the explosion, and they smacked into the ground in twin plumes of grit and sand. The transport recovered, close enough to the ground to kick up a brown cloud in their wake. Another merc lost control of their thrust-kit and almost hit a mountain. They got so close, their feet touched down, and they ran a few steps before taking off again. It was the funniest thing Ultimus had seen in months, the kind of thing he'd have talked about with the boys over drinks and laughed over if all his old friends weren't dead or retired.

The smart mercs—the ones who scattered—recovered soonest and dove in after them with a vengeance. But they were strung out, forced to come at them one at a time or risk them reaching the canyons and lava tunnels and slipping away.

"You can look, now, doc. I'll be damned how they did it, but Zack and Clavicus gave us a chance."

PTT-46 Osiris Troop Transport (Cockpit)
Lava Flats, Outskirts of the Starship Boneyard
4386.C.1 Interstellar

Zack fought the controls to keep them out of the dirt. He was down one engine, and Clavicus's extended kinetic barrier was playing hell with the transport's aerodynamics.

He was also down an entire *electrical* generator, although he still had the battery. He'd closed the forward armored shutter—safer that way, anyway—and cut the smaller kinetic barrier as well as the lights, air-conditioning, and anything else that might be a drain.

He stabilized the transport at three hundred meters and 240 knots. They were almost into the Boneyard proper, and the terrain was starting to change. Jagged, iron-red hills were visible in the distance, and their destination was a hazy shape beyond that. The ground had shifted from sand to cracked clay. The closed shutter meant he was relying on the AR visor to see where he was going. He still had decent visibility arcs in every direction, including the cabin, the roof, and under the aircraft—and he sacrificed some of his field of view to see them all displayed at the same time. But as he swerved to avoid a pillar of red rock, he regretted how easily he'd allowed Clavicus to scavenge "a few of the cameras."

Above, Ultimus started firing at the swooping mercenaries. The big man was firing on full automatic, filling the air with the micro-projectiles while his mechanical muscles compensated for the recoil. Zack saw one of the airborne mercenaries get battered as he found his mark, but while the drop-suited merc got knocked aside and tumbled three meters, they quickly recovered and kept closing on the transport.

And they were returning fire. Zack jinked and turned, using his pedals to throw the mercs off his direction of movement in what was called a random walk. DEMP shots and plasma bolts rained from above, and largely missed. He lost 10% of his speed scooting under a stone arch, then bypassed the next two as the mercs spread out to anticipate his next move. It was the most exhilarating flying he'd done thus far, and so close to the ground it felt like it should be scraping the soles of his boots.

One of the mercs boosted forward to land on the transport, but in a burst of exhaust and lit vents, Ultimus blinked across and dented the merc's chest-plate with a blurring fist, sending them spiraling to the ground. A second merc tried to crush Ultimus on landing, but the older mercenary grabbed them by the boot and smashed them against the roof with a loud clang. Anya darted in and fried the merc with the lance Clavicus had made for her, and Ultimus grabbed the merc's weapon—a plasma rifle as long as Zack's arm. The Combine weapon locked out when it didn't recognize its user, but not before he used it to shoot a fourth merc out of the sky.

That's half of them, Zack thought, counting the two who were caught in the explosion.

Then one of the mercs flashed in from the side and tackled Anya off the roof.

Zack's heart caught in his throat. He forgot the random walk and started to chase after them, and a flurry of plasma bolts smashed into the transport roof.

"Keep going!" Anya said over the team channel, and in a window, ARK-II had opened in his AR visor, Zack saw that she'd somehow disabled her attacker—*which must have given him a jolt*, he thought with a grin—and was now *riding* him or her like a scav on a grav-bike.

The transport shuddered as a merc who'd somehow gotten under them flipped onto their back and fired upward. Zack backed the throttle, sunk the tail, then throttled forward and pushed the nose at the same time, smacking the merc to the ground with a satisfying thunk.

Two more mercs flew into the transport through the open cargo cabin door.

"ARK-II, fly the plane!" Zack said, popping his straps and rising out of his chair, pulser drawn at the same time the cockpit door opened.

Zack fired before the mercenary could, hitting them in the helmet and knocking them back. He still had the visor on, so he could see Ultimus brawling with a merc on the roof. Zack fired nine more shots at his own target, fast as he could pull the trigger. He hit with eight shots and knocked the merc on their ass but didn't even dent their armor. Ultimus triggered something in his opponent's rocket pack that sent them shooting straight up into the sky. Zack started reloading, knowing he wasn't going to be fast enough. Then two of Clavicus's coils wrapped around the merc's arm and throat.

"I've got this!" Clavicus yelled, blowing his own merc out the cabin door with incendiary buckshot. The coils tightened, and he tossed Zack's merc out just as they flew past a stone column. Zack winced at the collision and turned back to the cockpit.

He kicked the door shut, dropped himself into the pilot's seat, and gave ARK-11 a pat before grabbing the stick. "Nice job, buddy."

ARK-11 bleeped in delight.

Zack checked his instruments. *Two hundred knots, forward generator is redlining, coolant system is shot.* There was a thunk from the roof as Anya came in for a landing, and Ultimus punted the unconscious or dead merc off the side of the transport. There were two mercs left, but they were hanging back, taking potshots at the transport. It was only a matter of time before they hit something important.

"Status report?" Ultimus asked.

"Cabin's clear," Clavicus shouted. "There's smoke coming from somewhere."

"It's oil burning up on the reactor ducts," Zack said. "Maybe. We're leaking."

"We going to make it?" Ultimus asked.

"If we don't lose anything else."

And then one of the mercs got lucky. A charged shot caught the transport just as it was turning and punched through the aft starboard thruster. The whole aircraft groaned, rolled right, and the tail end dipped. Zack threw the controls left, pushed the left pedal, and used the air resistance to right them. "Get inside and strap in!" he said on the team channel.

The stick was shaking in his hands. The heat in the aft thrusters was rising, and the forward generator's output was dropping off. A few more rounds smacked into the back of the transport, but none of them as lucky as that one fated shot. Zack was still maneuvering but, more importantly, he was looking for a place to set down.

And then he saw it. The lava flats were a misnomer. Sure, he saw a flat stretch of cracked earth off the left side of the transport's nose, but it was the *size* of the cracks that were misleading. The lava flats were a multi-layered labyrinth of canyons and extinct lava tubes that stretched all the way to the iron hills. It was one of the places where the involuntary residents of the Starship Boneyard—violent convicts and reckless dissidents—were traditionally released, and was as far as many of them made it.

"Crew's secured, boss," Ultimus said.

"Thanks," Zack said, fastening his own straps. He killed the kinetic barrier and pushed the throttle all the way forward. The fuselage straightened from the added airflow. "Here we go!" Zack said.

He lifted the nose again and pulled the throttle back, killing their forward airspeed. The two mercs split, maybe worried about a repeat of the first reactor explosion. Zack was focused on an approaching crevasse to their left. He fed the throttle back in as his groundspeed neared zero and pushed the left pedal in, tipping the transport over on its side while pushing the stick to the right, dropping the transport right into the narrow channel.

And the dust.

And the sheer, hard walls racing by at a 160 kilometers per hour, *and oh my Virtues this is fun.* One of the mercs dropped in behind him, firing as they came. Zack saw the turnoff coming and pulled back, pushed right, and stomped in the right pedal, rotating the thrusters to vertical as he jammed the throttle forward. He felt the g pile on and clenched his calves, thighs, and abdomen to keep from passing out, and then they were shooting down the new passage and the merc had missed the turn. He branched right, veered left. The passages became deeper and the fissures overhead narrower. The reactor warning was a constant ringing in his ears, and then he saw the lava tube ahead of them, just big enough for him to fly into, and he aimed for it. *Hang on, baby, hang on...*

They crossed into shadow. Zack reversed the thrusters and clenched his teeth, and then they hit, skidding. He slammed forward into the straps.

The whole frame shook.

Most of the panes on his AR visor went black.

He heard the screech of metal coming apart.

And then they stopped. He had time for four breaths of air, heart yammering, and then he remembered what the alarm he was hearing meant.

"ARK-11! SCRAM the reactor!"

The little machine beeped an acknowledgment. Zack ripped the visor from his face and hit the quick release on his straps before snatching the case from its cradle. "Everybody get out! Out into the tunnel!"

He ran through the cabin, out the side door, and sprinted after the others, using his long stride to gain on Clavicus. "Faster!" he yelled. "Faster!"

And nothing happened.

Nothing.

Clavicus stopped first, wheezing like he was dying, and Ultimus backtracked to grab his arm. But by then, Zack stopped, puzzled, and so did Anya.

"I really thought it was going to explode," Zack said.

ARK-11 beeped and dee-whooped.

"What did it say?" Anya asked.

"It said, 'Me too.'"

And the four of them laughed.

Then the transport broke in half as a merc in a three-meter-tall four-legged lancer smashed through it and raced toward them at sixty kilometers per hour.

PART VI

And now comes the hard part.

CHAPTER TWENTY-ONE

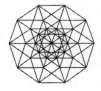

The Long Drop
Nineveh, Arcadian District of Politeia IV
4386.8.23 Interstellar

Three months ago, Ultimus Thragg had been killing his synthetic liver in a merc bar—or what passed for one on this backwater world—in a crap-hole town on the edge of the wilderness. Most of Politeia was built up, three leveled cities like a core world, except this place was so far off the grid, it was like a tree falling in the damned forest. Or something like that. Beth was always better with words. He ordered another shot.

A local walked in, or at least Ultimus thought he was a local by the way he dressed. He was built like someone who'd been born in space, and not the nice kind of space, either—some broken-down space station without gravity and just enough air. His clothes were well made but showed signs of wear, and yet there was a poise to him that spoke of lost status.

And Ultimus couldn't have given a crap why, except the kid walked over and sat by him at the bar.

"Hi, friend," the local said.

"Not looking for friends or conversation," Ultimus said.

"How about a drink?"

"Found one already. Why don't you buy someone else a drink? That seat was fine without you in it."

"Fantastic idea! Barkeep! A round for the house!" The kid placed his fingertips on the reader, authorizing the transaction, and the barkeep wiped his towel over it before starting to pour.

"That was a bad idea, kid. Now everyone here knows you've got money."

The kid smiled at him. "But look at how much I'm learning, Mr. Thragg. And all for the cost of a few beers."

Ultimus didn't like that, not one bit. He'd been approached, off-record, by clients before, and assassins, though the kid didn't have the look. But neither ended well. "I take my contracts through the Combine boards."

"You're listed as unavailable."

"That should have been your first hint."

The trouble Ultimus had predicted didn't take long. A thug in a grav-biker's jacket with a steel plate over half his scalp walked over, beer in hand. "Thanks for the drink, long bone."

"You're welcome," the kid said, ignoring the slur.

"What brings you dirtside?" the thug said, taking a pull from his mug.

"Having a drink with my friend, here."

The thug looked at Ultimus. "He your friend?"

"Nope."

"I'll be your friend, vacuum head. You looking to hire protection?"

Ultimus stared at his drink. This wasn't his problem. He had plenty of his own.

"I am, actually," the kid said, turning around in his seat. "What's your specialty? Scaring small children? Elder abuse?"

Ultimus felt his lips twitch at that. Kid was gonna get creamed, but he had a sense of humor.

"How about I make sure you make it out of this bar without breaking those bird bones of yours," the thug snarled, "and you give me everything you've got?"

"I'll take that offer," the kid said without a trace of fear. "But I need to know you can deliver. Why don't you show me how you take *yourself* out of the bar, first, and then we'll draft up a contract?"

The thug growled. He grabbed the kid by the lapel and dragged him off his stool. The kid planted, twisted, and threw the thug over his hip, swinging him headfirst into the bar and somehow winding up with the thug's drink in his hand. "Would anyone care to finish this man's beer?"

Two locals got out of their seats. Ultimus glanced at the bartender, who made no move to stop what was going on. The first came in with a running haymaker that would have turned the kid's head backward if he hadn't blocked with the mug.

The glass shattered, and the local screamed as his hand did, too.

The second man was luckier and caught the kid with a left cross, knocking him to the ground, and started kicking.

Then a third man rushed in with a knife. Ultimus grabbed him by the shoulder. "That's enough."

But the man was too far gone, either drunk or high or just sour. He stabbed Ultimus in the gut, which did exactly nothing to the mercenary's armored abdomen. Ultimus smashed the man to the ground with his fist.

"Both of you, out!" the bartender shouted, grabbing a bat from beneath the bar.

"Yeah, yeah," Ultimus said, shoving the kicker into a wall and grabbing the kid from the floor as he went.

Once they were outside, the kid's face already swelling but

not enough to wipe the grin from it, Ultimus said, "You've got balls, kid. Have to tell you how far that will get you, sometime. So what do you want?"

"Have you heard of the Synthesis?" the kid asked.

Ultimus sighed. "That some sort of pilgrimage you want to go on?"

If it was in any way possible, the kid grinned wider. "No, Ultimus Thragg. This pilgrimage is yours."

Lava tube, fifteen meters beneath the surface
Lava Flats, Outskirts of the Starship Boneyard
4386.C.1 Interstellar

Ultimus's first meeting with Zack Lancestrom flashed through his mind as the brawler galloped down the lava tube. When the kid first spoke of the Synthesis, he'd thought it was some local religious thing. Then he'd met ARK-11, and the whole thing started to feel like fate. He'd come out to this backwater looking for a place to die, and guarding one of the most valuable pieces of technology in the galaxy seemed like a pretty sure way to kick the bucket.

"All of you, run!" Ultimus said.

And he counter-charged the lancer. His AM reactor flooded his limbs with energy as he opened it up to full flow.

And he was going to die. Brawlers were *designed* to kill cyborgs like him. But he ran with laughter in his clockwork heart, and all of the ghosts he carried laughed with him.

Ultimus jumped and smashed into the lancer with both feet forward. The brawler rotated its torso to slip the blow, then reared its front legs. Ultimus rolled out of the way as the two limbs, each capable of denting one-inch-thick rolled steel, slammed down, sending chips of volcanic rock flying. Ultimus roared and hit the brawler with a right hook to the leg joint. The brawler's leg gave a little, but there was no visible damage.

The brawler responded by smashing its enormous fist into him, throwing him into the tunnel wall.

"Shouldn't have taken this job, old man," a familiar voice said.

The brawler charged, trying to pin him to the wall with more strikes from its forelimbs. Ultimus twisted out of the way as the first strike missed his head and sunk a foot into the wall. The second strike was deliberately wide to the right, pinning him in, and then the pilot reached forward to crush Ultimus with the lancer's hands.

Ultimus slid under the chassis. He didn't stay there, though, and a good thing, too, because the brawler's hindlegs pounded the space he vacated. Ultimus hooked onto the rear left thigh as the lancer rotated its torso and clambered onto its back. "That you, Ajax?" He smashed his fist into a corner of the brawler's back panel, hoping to pop it loose. "You still hanging with Lynx?"

The brawler reversed its arms—the thing had ball joints everywhere—and grabbed him by the shoulder, throwing Ultimus toward the ruined transport like a toy. Ultimus bounced once, twice, and then the pitons in his feet punched out and dug into the tunnel floor. His AM supply was down to 54%, coolant close to boiling, and he felt vents in his back open so the radiators could extend.

He hoped the others had listened. If they got far enough, took enough branching passages, they might just get away.

"I'm still in *Commander* Lynx's unit, old man, and you're in the way of our next paycheck."

In a few more thundering steps, the brawler was right on top of him.

Ultimus redlined his reactor, heat blasting out his back. He raised his arms and blocked Ajax's two-fisted slam, then he shoved the brawler's fists aside and landed a massive blow to its left elbow. This time, the joint caved in, and Ajax swung the broken limb like a Tier 0 flail.

Ultimus ducked it, passed a kick with both hands, and counter-punched Ajax's right fist, stopping the massive arm cold and destroying his own hand.

Ajax laughed and swung the ruined fist down, catching Ultimus on the shoulder and dropping him to one knee. "Yes! That's the spirit, you old bastard!" A round kick from a foreleg sent him rolling. "Always thought I could take you, one on one!"

"Why don't you climb out of that lancer and give it a try?" Ultimus growled.

The brawler scuttled over and raised its forelegs again. Ajax had never been one for imagination, but then an inordinate number of his opponents had died in boring ways. Ultimus tensed to roll out of the way, and then his AM supply ran out.

He moved just a little too slow.

The brawler's right forelimb caught his shoulder, punched through it, and pinned him to the ground.

Ajax leaned forward, looking down at him through the bubble of the brawler's cockpit. "And this is how it ends." There was regret and no small amount of resentment in the other merc's voice, and Ultimus grinned. *I hope it's so bitter it chokes him.*

The brawler raised its left foreleg, poised over Ultimus's head.

Coils and tentacles whipped around behind the brawler's ape-like upper torso. A panel was thrown free, and then the doc's face popped up behind the lancer's left shoulder, and sparks flew everywhere.

"What the hell?" Ajax said, trying to twist in his seat at the same time he slammed the brawler's forelimb down. Ultimus threw his head to the left, and the armored leg tip came down where his forehead would have been, so close that Ultimus's cheek was now pressed against the cold ceramic.

Ajax reached up and back to grab the doc and Clavicus.

"Hey, dickhead!" Lancestrom said.

The brawler's torso turned toward the kid, and then there was a bright flash from its back, and it froze in place, kinetic barrier down, canopy popped open, and Zack Lancestrom had his pulser pointed like an Old Earth duelist at Ajax's face.

"No!" Ultimus bellowed.

And everyone was very still, for a moment.

Clavicus clambered up and looked at him over the brawler's back. "What do you mean, 'No?' What is it with you people and not killing your enemies?"

"I'm not particularly opposed, here," Lancestrom said.

Ultimus sighed. "He's... he's *almost* family. It's complicated."

Lancestrom flipped his gun forward, over, and holstered it. "What's the plan, big man?"

"Can you get this thing out of me?" Ultimus asked, slapping at the impaling limb. He didn't feel so brave anymore. He felt tired, overheated from using the AM reactor, and the brawler had come close to puncturing his organ sack.

"Hold on..." the doc said. "Got it."

The limb retracted, lifting Ultimus with it until he slid off and fell to the ground. He groaned and crab-crawled out from under it, sitting up.

"I suppose you're pleased with yourself," Ajax said, glowering from the frozen lancer.

"What makes you think that?" Ultimus answered. He switched his E.C.M.O. on, switching to osmotic breathing. It wasn't as efficient—in fact, it made him feel like he was oxygen-starved—but there was something not quite right with how his main circulatory pump was performing.

"Because of the trap. You had your team of amateurs sneak up on me."

"I had jack," Ultimus wheezed. "I told those idiots to run away."

Ultimus and Ajax stared at each other.

Then the younger man laughed. It was a deep, belly laugh that Ultimus had always found grating.

"What?" Ultimus asked.

Ajax raised his fists—his real fists—in the air. "I beat you! I beat Ultimus Thragg!"

Ultimus rested his forearms on his legs and laughed with him. For all his obstinacy, for his downright "straight through the middle" lack of subtlety, Ajax had always been a warrior after his own heart. "Yeah, you did. Fair and square, kid. You earned it."

Ajax dropped his arms and sighed. "Now what?"

"Renege the contract," Ultimus said, pulling himself to his feet by grabbing the brawler's raised leg.

"Like hell. It's a two-million-credit contract."

"My boy's got you dead to rights, Ajax. Give up."

Ajax crossed his arms. "Death gratuity's four hundred thousand. Lynx'll use it to shove a cruise missile up your collective asses."

"Are you two seriously arguing about money?" the doc asked.

"Yes!" Ajax and Ultimus said together.

"Hey, Anya?" Lancestrom asked.

"Yeah?"

"Can you brick that lancer? Make it so they can never use it again?"

"You mean strip the gears, overload the reactor, and turn all the nanites to solid slag so they can never use it again? Probably."

"You wouldn't dare," Ajax said.

"How much is it worth, big man?" Lancestrom asked him.

Ultimus laughed. "Six million credits and change. Come on, Ajax. Do the smart thing."

Ajax pursed his lips and scratched his jaw. Then he said, "Fine. Give me the case and I'll let you all go."

"You people deserve each other," the doc said, rolling her eyes.

"What do you mean, 'You people?'" Ultimus asked.

"The case stays with us," Lancestrom said, hand on his pulser again.

ARK-II bobbed up behind him, its casing bright pink and heading toward crimson. It unleashed a flurry of beeps, clicks, and whoops.

"Whoa, whoa, whoa!" Ajax said, holding his palms up. "Don't do anything stupid, little guy."

"Don't test it, Ajax. It's crazy. It'll do it," Ultimus said.

"What?" the doc said, exasperated. "What did it say?"

ARK-II let loose a quickening series of beeps, like a bomb about to go off.

"No, stop! It's fine!" Ajax yelled.

"Fine, what?" Ultimus said.

"Fine. You have my word. We'll renege the contract. Doesn't mean someone else won't take it, but it won't be the Wildcats."

Ultimus almost sagged in relief. He was so worn out he could barely stand, and several of his primary systems were temporarily down, but he was alive, and so was his team. This fight was over. "Let's go," he told the others. "We need to put some distance between us and the wreckage before his boss decides to bomb us from orbit or one of the survivor groups comes to salvage the transport."

Clavicus nodded and clambered off the chassis. He held out a coil to the doc, and she used it to hop down.

Lancestrom swept his hair back. Kid did better than Ultimus ever would have imagined. The old mercenary couldn't take credit for that—not all of it—but he was damned proud anyway.

"Hey, Ajax?" he said before leaving.

"What now?"

"Say 'Hi' to Lynx for me."

The younger mercenary gave him a look that said Ajax had grown in the years since they'd last met. "She's your daughter, Joseph. Tell her yourself. Why do you think the Artemisia was in this star cluster in the first place?"

And something other than fusion or AM annihilation flared in Ultimus's chest for what seemed like the first time in forever.

Zack dropped back from the others to walk next to Ultimus. The mercenary had a pensive look on his face. His left arm hung limp, and his chest wound was packed with scrap metal for the nanites to feed off as his armor self-repaired. But he was keeping up, even if his gait was a bit more stuttered than ordinary.

"You okay?" Zack asked.

"I'm fine, boss. Just need some food and some sleep. This tin can'll be back in shape in no time."

Zack nodded. "I meant in your head, my friend. You went after that guy like you weren't coming back."

Ultimus chuckled. "Didn't think I was. Thought this was that Synthesis you were talking about—Ultimus Thragg dying outside a Combine contract because he believed in something. No one would have believed it."

And Zack grinned. "Ah. But that isn't your story, my friend.

You're an offworlder, so you couldn't know. But the Synthesis is the beginning of a journey, not the end of one."

By the wreckage of PT3768A
Lava flats, Outskirts of the Starship Boneyard
4386.C.1 Interstellar

Ajax sat on one of the non-functional brawler's legs, sipping on an electrolyte pack while Ultimus and his little group walked down into the lava tube. True to their word, they'd left the lancer intact, but that rogue cyber-doc had shut down the reactor and drained all the capacitors first. He had no way of powering it up without a jumpstart.

As his failed bounty disappeared around a bend in the tunnel, Jericho uncloaked and walked over.

"Been there long?" Ajax asked.

"Oh, the wild charge you made!" Jericho answered.

"You're quoting Tennyson at me? Seriously? I could have been hurt."

"I had your back, boss," she said, hefting her plasma rifle. "The pistoleer? I'd've taken his head off before he pulled the trigger."

"Coulda fooled me."

"Doesn't take that much," Jericho muttered.

Ajax raised an eyebrow at her, but she was conveniently facing away, down the lava tube. "How are the others?" he asked.

Jericho tapped the side of her helmet, which split open, exposing her face. "We lost Ito. Thragg got his hands on Hijinks's plasma rifle and put two bolts into Ito's chest-plate, cooked him in his armor."

"Damn," Ajax said. Ito had been new to the crew, but he'd

been around the Combine boards for over a decade. "How's Hijinks taking it?"

"Crushed. He should be. Dumb rookie couldn't keep a hold of his rifle. The whole team is embarrassed. The mission parameters weren't ideal, but we got our collective asses handed to us. Five of the drop-suits are going to need a full overhaul, and three more are going to be down until we can get them to a class II facility. Got a couple broken bones, some internal hemorrhaging, and Higgins broke his neck."

"How'd that happen?"

"He was unconscious when the cyber-doc hijacked his suit's control system and rode him like a rocket to their transport. Ultimus booted him off in-flight. He landed face first. The suit is breathing for him and keeping his blood circulating, but he's technically dead."

Ajax grunted. "Well, at least he'll get his callsign out of this."

"What are you thinking?"

"Rodeo."

Jericho grinned. "He's going to hate it. It's perfect."

CHAPTER TWENTY-TWO

Lava tube, fifteen meters beneath the surface
Lava Flats, Outskirts of the Starship Boneyard
4386.C.1 Interstellar

Zack led his crew through the dark, winding passages for the next hour. They lit their way with hand lamps, playing them over the textured walls. Their footsteps echoed. They spoke in hushed tones.

In spite of the rough landing, things weren't as dire as they might have been. The air was warm but not as scorching as it was on the surface, and sometimes the walls showed visible moisture. They were twelve kilometers from their objective, across some of the worst terrain on Politeia IV, but they'd managed to recover some supplies from the ruined transport. Anya had her lance stowed at her hip. Zack had his pulser and a pouch full of charge packs. Ultimus had the Reaper with a few mags, and ARK-11 could refill them. Clavicus still had his shotgun and incendiary rounds, as well as an emergency toolkit and a device he'd been tinkering with that looked like a black soccer ball that had been cut in half, with an attached handle. They had food enough to be picky and several days of water. It wasn't enough to get them to the *Memento Mori*, but it meant they only needed to get lucky once.

ARK-11 stayed close to Zack. The little machine was quiet, its casing a neutral shade of bone as it mapped the tunnels and compared them to surveys it had on file. The geology of the Boneyard was unnatural, caused by a singular act of defiance almost one thousand years before. When the ground had settled and the lava had cooled, the planetary guard sent drones to map the tubes. That wasn't as important now—the dozens of tunnels sloped down and ran together. Later, when it came time to leave the lava flats, and the funnel turned into a shotgun blast of wrong turns and dead ends, they'd be relying on those surveys to get them out.

Clavicus seemed the most comfortable of the human crew members, which made sense. The tubes were five meters tall and wide enough for the four of them to walk side by side. He could have flown Betsy down them, slowly, with a few scrapes. It was the engineer's natural habitat. Clavicus and Anya kept a continuous dialogue going on topics from the mineral content of the rock to the way they controlled their implants. They seemed to have built some sort of rapport during the last few days, and Zack wondered if the younger man had developed a crush on her.

If so, he wished Clavicus the best. For as long as he'd known her, Anya had maintained a close social circle. They were mostly composed of her professional peers. The forcefulness of her rejections when one of them overreached was legendary.

Ultimus had taken a lot of damage in that last fight. He was huffing and puffing like a man half his age with none of his upgrades, though Zack knew that had more to do with cooling his internal systems than needing air. The mercenary was still carrying most of the gear—the rest of them had neither the strength nor stamina to carry the two twenty-kilo water cans. Ultimus might have been damaged and pensive, but he was still a two-hundred-kilo Combine cyborg who could keep going long after other soldiers dropped of exhaustion. *Or the stars go out,* Zack thought wryly.

As for Zack, he passed the time taking stock of what had happened over the past few days. He'd had some time on the tarmac of Eleanor's Hope to think about tactics—about whether to hook or jab, the shots he should have fired and the few he'd missed. Now that their true journey into the desert had begun, he dug into the hard part.

The Politeian approach to justice had its roots in military tribunals, just as Ancient Greek philosophy, art, religion, and science could only be fully grasped through the lens of the citizen-soldier. Socrates was hoplite long before he was a teacher. Zack had grown up believing lawbreakers deserved what they got, including him, and he felt little guilt over the gangers he'd shot or even the mercenaries who'd been injured or killed in their attempt to take ARK-II.

No, what bothered him were the four dead cops he'd left on the roof of the medical school and the heroic pilot he'd pulled out of her seat while her crewman watched. The brawls had been good fun, but one of his father's agents had lost an arm. For that matter, Zack hadn't liked stealing things from the warehouse or the damage they'd done to the school, but that part he could get over.

But what alarmed him were the lengths—the illegal lengths —his father and the sophistocracy had gone to in order to bring him back. The government of Politeia was supposed to be... sacred, its charter inviolable. He knew it was a bias of his upbringing, but he didn't realize how strongly he held it until he saw it broken.

And he worried for the future of his planet.

It didn't change what he had to do. If ARK-II wasn't reunited with its Forge Production Unit within the next century, it would lose enough of its core memories and functions to consider itself "dead," even if something continued to inhabit its casing. Between now and then, errors would corrupt its perceptions and calculations. They would be small at first, but the Synthesis impacted the whole planet across generations. Small course deviations would lead to large lateral divergences.

The sound of their footsteps changed, and the passage opened into a wide-open space. "We'll stop to rest down there," Zack said simply.

The others followed him down the snaking ramp.

The cavern was bigger than Zack could easily grasp with the more primitive parts of his brain. He'd grown up first in orbital modules and segments, then in the capital city. No matter its scale, human construction broke the infinite down to recognizable measures. The farthest distance was a city block, the highest rise a single building story. Multiplication tables put the whole universe in a child's hand.

Zack had to stop halfway down. He felt dizzy. Except for the walkway around them, the darkness swallowed the light from their lamps whole.

"How big is this place?" Ultimus asked.

ARK-II chirped.

"It said it's six kilometers to the opposite wall," Clavicus told Anya without her having to ask.

Zack's training as a pilot kicked in. He focused on nearby features, slowed his breathing, and then looked for points of reference.

There were natural skylights in the cave roof, some thirty

meters above them. They shed curtains of light, stirred by faint ripples of fine dust from above, and beneath them were green pools of water with sandy beaches, moss-covered rocks, and even trees. *Seven stories tall, ten blocks deep, two blocks between each island,* Zack internalized. "Everyone good?" he asked.

Ultimus gave him a wink, and Anya nodded at him.

"I'm fine," Clavicus lied.

They walked the rest of the way down in silence.

The bottom of the cave smelled like moss, fungus, and rock dust. Zack's boots slipped every few paces like he was walking on ice. The stone was smooth and wet.

The path grew firmer as they neared the first skylight, and thirty minutes later, Zack set his pack down on the sand by the emerald-green shore. "How long should we take?" he asked Ultimus.

The mercenary set the cans of water down. "No more than fifteen minutes. Break out some food to eat on the go, have the doc check your feet. Liter of water each. Any water you drink now, we don't have to carry."

"What about you?" Zack asked.

Ultimus shrugged. "Wouldn't mind if Clavicus took another look at my shoulder."

"I can do that," the engineer said.

"Okay, you heard Ultimus," Zack said. "Don't get too comfortable."

"No risk of that," Clavicus said, looking up at the skylight, his hologram a frowny face.

Anya grabbed the brim of his leaf hat and brought it back to horizontal.

"Thanks," he muttered.

"You're welcome." She walked over to Zack. "Come on, lover. Let's take a look at your ankles, heels, and toes."

Zack watched Clavicus for a reaction, but if there was one, it was too brief for him to notice. His eyes flicked back to Anya, and she raised an eyebrow at him.

"What?" he asked.

"Nothing," she said with a smirk.

He sat on a rock ledge, boots in the sand, and started undoing his laces.

"How are you?" Anya asked, digging into her pack next to him.

"Fine," he said. "I've got a hotspot on the back of my right ankle."

"Not what I meant," she said, keeping her voice low.

He pulled his right boot off, then stripped off his sock. "I'm processing."

"Turn toward me," she said, and he put his foot in her lap. "Anything worth sharing?"

"Want some guilt?"

She snorted. "Not my thing. Didn't know it was yours."

"It isn't, I don't think, but I'm worried I missed something, or that this is all some kind of overreach on my part."

She poked at his right ankle until he flinched, then put a flat strip of adhesive on it. "What do you want out of this?"

He frowned. "I told you. I want to get offworld."

"Oh, I got that. I'm a smart cookie," she said, tapping the side of her head. "Change your socks—both of them—and let me know if you start feeling anything else like that. It's not something you want to suffer in silence. You'll injure yourself."

"Yes, doctor," he said with a grin. "What about the other bit?"

She shrugged and leaned in. "I believe in you, Zack. You've turned yourself into some kind of gunslinging space pilot in a matter of months. You've got your crew. You're going to get us offworld. Somehow or other, you'll get us a starship if we don't end up dead along the way. Maybe we'll even find that Forge that ARK-II is looking for. What are you going to do with it?"

Zack made a sound like a rumbling moan.

"What?" she asked, pulling back.

"I wish I was a brain surgeon."

"Zack..."

"So I could look at pictures of your brain and call it work."

"You always do this."

"Do what?"

"Turn our serious conversations into a joke."

"I need time to think about it," he said. "And I can't think when you say smart stuff. It drives me wild."

She punched him in the shoulder. "Idiot."

"You love me."

Anya hesitated, then said, "Yes, I do. You *are* thinking about it, though, right?"

"I am," he said.

She touched his shoulder, then went to check on the others.

Zack unlaced his other boot and changed his socks, careful not to get sand on them or in his footwear. Some kind of eel or mudfish swam into the lit area of the pool, and Zack watched it for a moment, wondering how much life survived down here, away from the desert heat.

Anya was right, of course. The hard part wasn't grabbing whatever he could get his hands on. Mad Moe and the other gangers could manage that much, and they always wound up dead and forgotten. The hard part was deciding what he didn't want, and what he should do with the things he had. The crew, the ship, the Forge... in his more suspicious moments, Zack could see how ARK-II might have laid all that out before him, like the little islands of light in the dark of the cave defining his path. The machine needed those things if it was going to survive.

But Zack's journey had started from a place of dissatisfaction, even if it had taken the Synthesis to make him aware of it.

He wanted to change things. So what he needed to figure out, along with the mundane problem of staying alive, was how he would use those resources to fulfill *his* life's purpose, to change the galaxy and maybe humanity with it.

He dug some vegetable crackers and cheese spread out of his pack, downing most of a quart of water with them as Ultimus had recommended.

Zack pushed himself and the team hard for the next two hours. The terrain of the cavern floor wasn't flat, and while the skylights provided waypoints through the darkness, getting to them required several detours and a fair bit of climbing. The air was warm, so Zack stuffed his coat into his pack. Anya was down to a sweat-soaked t-shirt. Clavicus had turned his hand lamp off before stowing his poncho and hat. Zack caught glimpses of the engineer's pale, glistening skin, his coils and tendrils unfurled at the edge of the light.

There were moments of wonder to the journey. When the path drove them south, toward the cavern wall, and the ceiling was hanging only four meters above, they came to a deep pool dotted with what looked like lily pads made of stone. The pads were the flat tops of submerged pillars, made of a pink, brittle stone that looked like coral. Zack and the others hopped across.

They passed a lava pillar that was ten meters wide, its umber, pitted surface twinkling with quartz and embedded with large, pearly clusters of a soft, turquoise crystal. Clavicus said the blue-green gemstones were called smithsonite, and their coloring was due to copper oxides in the rock. The pillar reached over one hundred feet up, all the way to the ceiling, like a gigantic tree.

The going got harder as they neared the center of the cavern, or maybe he was just tired. One thousand years ago, when gravity went mad, lava broke through thinner sections of rock, splashed back down, and dug the lava tubes through the sandstone. It melted channels here in the cave, like petrified streams whose surface looked like ruffled gray silk and was as beautiful as it was likely to turn an ankle. Zack skinned his right forearm crossing one of the long-cooled flows. Clavicus did better on traversal, able to steady himself with his coils and tendrils. Sometimes it felt like the lower-city dweller could see in the dark. But Clavicus had shorter legs and hadn't spent the past months training himself to fight. He started falling behind.

"You want me to carry your toolkit?" Zack offered, looking back.

"No."

"What about that... device, whatever it is."

"I'm fine," Clavicus said, panting. "I'll keep up."

"You're pushing him too hard," Anya hissed.

"No, he's not," snapped Clavicus, standing at the edge of their lights. "We need to keep the pace."

"Why?" Anya asked, her tone frosty.

"Because we're not alone in the dark," the engineer said.

Zack stared at the man for a moment, letting that soak in. "What kind of not alone? 'Stonebats and newts' or 'tribes of blind cannibal mutants?'"

"Bigger than newts," Clavicus answered.

Zack looked at Ultimus. The tubes were how people entered the Boneyard from the west, voluntarily or not. If there were dissidents or convicts in the area, things could get ugly fast, and there were a number of large predators on Politeia IV other than humans who could cause them problems if they were caught unawares.

"I haven't caught anything on infrared," Ultimus said. "But I'd trust Clavicus's instincts on this."

"Let's keep moving," Zack said, sticking his thumbs under

his pack straps to stop them from cutting into his shoulders for a moment.

It was only another hour to the third island of light, but after Clavicus's revelation, the going felt harder, and the darkness more substantial. Even the lower-city engineer was happy to step into the light after that.

Zack had a blister forming on his left big toe. Ultimus watched the dark. The skylight they were under was near the apex of the cave, its mouth wider, and there was a small rainforest about the size of Anya's apartment under the opening. It came complete with palm trees, vines, and thick brush that went all the way down to the circle of light and the edge of a smaller, shallow pool of brown water. They stopped for a hot meal and two quarts of water, except for Ultimus. The self-repair systems Anya had turned back on were working. The scrap they'd packed his wound with had been broken down, already fusing with the original armor. He was back to his former self, asking questions, prodding them along while alluding to battles they'd never heard of.

"What happened here, anyway?" Ultimus asked, waving his spoon at the darkness around them. "I haven't seen this kind of widespread volcanic activity since Hemidea Upsilon."

"What happened on Hemidea Upsilon?" Zack countered.

Ultimus laughed. "Pretty boring stuff, boss. It was a borehole gone wrong. Fivestar Driftonics convinced the locals to blow the mine a little deeper with nukes, the greedy bastards. Damned near cracked the planet open. The whole colony had to be relocated. We were sent in to evacuate the executives."

"Wow," Zack said.

Ultimus nodded. "We only had the one ship—short notice and all. Got pretty ugly down there. That was the first time I went somewhere so hot, the heat burned off my eyebrows and eyelashes. We packed the Fivestar suits and anyone else who would fit aboard, got 'em to safety. Then we went back, until we couldn't go back anymore, on account of the ash."

Anya looked surprised. "That sounds awfully noble for a mercenary unit."

"Oh, we charged for passage," Ultimus laughed. "Doing pro-bono work's bad for business, doc. People start thinking you should always do it for free. I shot a couple dozen people who got the wrong idea that day. Maybe I sponsored a couple kids, and maybe our commander did the last run at cost, but don't make me out for something I ain't. You'll tarnish my sterling reputation."

"I stand corrected," Anya said with a smile. "You're a heartless miser."

"Thanks, doc. So, how 'bout it, boss? I showed you mine."

Zack chuckled. "The Boneyard's been here for a long time. It was always a desert, far from the capital and any other settlements, so us Politeians have been letting things crash into it from day one. We're heading to a specific part of the Boneyard—the final resting place of the *Memento Mori*."

Ultimus choked on the water he'd been sipping. "We're what?"

Anya and Clavicus frowned. "You didn't know it was out here?"

Ultimus looked at the three of them as if they were insane. "No, I did not know an Odysseus class battleship was sitting in mothballs out in the desert. We're going to need a bigger crew, boss."

Zack grinned. "She's not operational. Hasn't been for a thousand years. It's where the Council is hiding Project Gyges—the shuttle we're going to steal."

"I thought you knew the whole plan," Anya said accusingly.

"Didn't think we'd live this long," Ultimus told her with a wink.

Clavicus raised his hand. "Why is it called 'Project Gyges?'"

"It's a Greek story, from Old Earth," Zack explained. "A man has a ring that makes him invisible. Should he walk in and steal whatever he wants, or live honestly?"

Clavicus's hologram changed to a laughing face. "I'd steal everything I could carry."

"Exactly, and you'd be considered an idiot not to. The Greeks thought so, too." Of course, the Greeks lived in a world of violence and famine, much like the one Clavicus grew up in, Zack thought. "The Council hid a jump-shuttle in the *Memento Mori* to evacuate ARK-11 in cases where they might lose the planet—asteroid strike, alien invasion, annexation by another system government. Then they added a few more shuttles for themselves and their families."

Ultimus winced.

"Yeah," Zack said. "That's why they called it Project Gyges. Secrecy always leads to corruption."

The crew let that sink in. Zack could guess how they felt. He'd felt the same sense of disappointment and betrayal when ARK-11 told him about it.

"What about the *Memento Mori*," Ultimus asked. "How the hell did a starship like that end up in the scrap heap?"

"Anyone else want to tell the story?" Zack asked Clavicus and Anya.

"You go ahead," Anya said.

"Okay. So, about a thousand years ago—"

"Nine hundred and ninety-three," Anya said.

"Thanks, babe," Zack said with an eye roll. "A thousand years ago, the Federal Fleet caught up to us Splinter Fleet refugees and realized we had a Federal battle squadron in our hands. We'd kept it quiet, kept them in hiding unless pirates or some interstellar got too uppity."

"Solid maintenance routines," Clavicus said, pointing at

Zack with his spoon. "That's what kept those ships spaceworthy for two thousand years."

"Yeah, of course," Zack said. "Listen, does one of you want to tell this?"

"No, no," Clavicus and Anya said, raising their hands in surrender, and the three Politeians grinned at each other.

Ultimus cocked his head at them, looking from face to face.

"Should I explain it?" Zack asked.

Anya and Clavicus looked at each other. "You should," Anya said. "It's an important part of the story."

"Okay," Zack said, "so before I finish, the last flight of the *Memento Mori* is a big deal on Politeia. It's celebrated on the tenth day of the third month, like the new year or Founding Day. Families gather with their children, and any offworlders, and the head of the household tells the story."

"And everyone takes turns interrupting them with how *their* family, or team, or occupation saved the day," Anya said, beaming.

"Got it," Ultimus said, a mischievous grin on his face.

"Right," Zack said. "But a thousand years ago, the Federal Fleet caught us red-handed, wiping a flotilla of pirate scum from our system."

"It took some time, on account of Politeian doctors rendering aid to the wounded," Anya said.

"So they gave us an ultimatum. 'Surrender your ships, or face the wrath of the almighty Federal Fleet!' But *my* kinsman, Admiral Beth Lancestrom, wasn't about to hand over Karin Lindström's flagship to people who considered our forebears to be deserters. While the rest of the System Defense Forces surrendered, Admiral Lancestrom evacuated non-essential personnel and deorbited the *Memento Mori*."

"She was only able to do that because Combine mercenaries weren't hired to supervise the disarmament," Ultimus informed them, and the three Politeian crew members laughed.

"That's the spirit, Ultimus!" Zack said. "She came down with the main engines facing down. Her hull superheated. Imagine a kilometer-and-a-half-long bar of light swiping across the night sky. As she approached the Boneyard, she kicked on the Icarus engines to bring the ship horizontal, and all hell broke loose. Up was down, down was sideways... she was able to stop the ship from crashing, but this whole area turned into a gigantic eruption. It pulled up the iron hills you saw on the way in. It created the lava tubes and this cave. She set the *Memento Mori* down in the middle of that, on top of an active volcano, and then scuttled any tech above Tier 2.5, so the Fleet left the ship there and hauled great-aunt Beth away."

"They arrested her?" Ultimus said.

"Of course. She disobeyed a Fleet order and violated the Sydney accords by using negative gravity that close to a planet. But Politeians have remembered how our Fleet brethren welcomed us back into the fold ever since. We called it Defiance Day.

"It was a sort of pilgrimage, for a while, to walk across the desert to see her, and then it became a symbol of defiance against the sophistocracy as well. Five hundred years ago, some of the more unstable elements of our society moved out here, attacked other pilgrims, and the governor basically said, 'Fine, then you can *stay* out there,' and the Boneyard as we know it was born."

They finished their meals, did another round of checking feet and equipment, and got ready to move again.

"This is taking longer than I thought," Zack told Ultimus. Half a day and they'd barely made it five kilometers. "The longer we take, the more time the Council and my father have to send someone else after us. We need to reach the *Memento Mori* and get offworld as soon as possible."

"Might have to accept we're going to spend the night in this cave," Ultimus said. "It's not too bad. It's out of the sun, there's water, and we seem to have the place to ourselves—no offense to our engineer."

Zack nodded.

It was under the next skylight that they found the bodies.

CHAPTER TWENTY-THREE

Lava Cavern, forty meters beneath the surface
Lava Flats, Outskirts of the Starship Boneyard, Politeia IV
4386.C.1 Interstellar

They reached the fourth of seven skylights at 4:30 in the afternoon. The "island" was a natural stone formation whose even tiers made it look like a pyramid of sorts, with a flat, round top some six meters above the cave floor. There was still no sign of whatever inhabited the cave, and even Clavicus had caught neither sound, smell, or other sense of "it" or "them" for the past hour.

That suited Zack. His boots had gotten wet during the last crossing, and he could feel the sock rubbing tight and raw against his heel.

"You're sure you saw something?" Ultimus asked the engineer.

"No," Clavicus said, sounding frustrated. "I can't 'see' in the dark like you can."

"How does it work, then?" the mercenary asked.

"Electrolocation," Clavicus answered. "I can feel changes in the air."

"So it could have been a draft."

"Yeah," Clavicus said sarcastically. "And maybe you wouldn't recognize one of those man-shaped targets on a shooting range." He spat. "I know what it feels like to be snuck up on in the dark, okay? Why haven't *you* spotted them?"

"Because they're on the ceiling?" Zack offered, and he almost laughed as the others whipped their heads up, Anya's tattoos glowed, and Ultimus dropped the water cans to raise his carbine. "Whoa! It was a hypothetical! The lights don't even reach that far. A lot of cave predators hunt by sound or heat. These things might be herbivores. They could be cold blooded or hidden under water. Or they could not be there, *even* if they were, before," he conceded, in deference to the engineer's abilities. "We're all getting cranky and tired. Let's count this as a blessing and take a longer break when we get to the top."

"Suits me," Clavicus said.

"Clavicus, you lead. Ultimus and I will take up the rear," Zack added.

"Uh, okay, boss," the engineer said, and Anya narrowed her eyes at him, but they both started walking.

Zack grabbed the emptier of the two water cans.

"I can carry that, boss."

Zack shook his head and made sure his pulser was loose in the holster. "You keep one hand free. I don't care what either of your senses says. I'm tired. We're jumpy. If anything's going to hit us, it'll be now."

The mercenary's eyebrows shot up, and then he chuckled. "You gonna school me on ambushes, kid?"

Zack shrugged. "ARK-II added a few lectures from Fleet officers and Combine mercenaries to my curriculum."

"Anyone I've heard of?"

Zack smirked. "Yeah, one guy kept coming up. His name was

Murphy. Seemed like he'd been kicking around since the days of phalanx warfare."

"Even before that, kid. Even before."

They walked up the moss-covered mound—or was it a pyramid? It almost felt like there were steps under the mulch. Dirt and silt had built up, maybe falling from the skylight above, allowing short, trefoil plants to take root in clumps. The western side of the mound was already in shadow. In a few more hours, the only light in the giant cavern would be their hand lamps. "This might actually be a good place to set up camp, boss. High ground, clear observation, not a lot of dead space around it. You might not see something coming, but I will, and I don't need much sleep."

"You need some, but point taken. Let's—"

"Hey, guys?" Clavicus said from the top. "I think you'd better come see this."

Zack looked at Ultimus, and the two men scrambled up as fast as they could manage while carrying the water cans.

The eastern side of the pyramid was littered with bodies. Not a few, or a dozen, but close to a hundred. Anya was inspecting the ones nearest the top. They were the freshest, although that wasn't saying much. They were mummified, leathery skin stretched over dry bones and empty sockets.

Those further down had become part of the mound, taking on a layer of moss, blending into the other lumps. Or were the lumps more corpses? "How long have these been here?" Zack asked.

Anya looked up. She looked... troubled. "Not long."

"How can you tell?"

She grabbed the nearest mummy's arm. It was metal. "These are recent commercial models. For a moment, I thought I'd found Simon."

"The guy who got you fired?" Ultimus asked.

"The very same." She dropped the arm. "Anyway, it's not him—would have been a hell of a coincidence if it had been. But whoever or whatever did this, they took down a fully grown cyborg."

Zack looked down at the withered body. It looked like it had been here for hundreds of years. It made his skin crawl. He didn't feel much sympathy for the man—he'd have been sent to the desert for a reason, unless he chose to be here—but it was a fate he'd rather avoid himself. "Any idea what did this?"

"It's hard to tell. They didn't all die the same way. I see broken bones, deep lacerations, signs of crushing…"

"They were mauled," Ultimus said, hand on his Reaper's pistol grip.

"Not all of them," Anya said. "And if this was an animal feeding, or even a territorial response, why were they brought back here? The only consistent wounds are these punctures," she said, pointing to a pair of small holes on the corpse's chest. "They've *all* got several of these. It could be a local scavenger, or it could be why they died. I'm not a forensic pathologist."

"Let's just get the hell out of here," Clavicus said. "Those look like snake bites. Giant snakes could crush and drag people."

"They also don't usually live in caves," Zack said. "The only time a snake lives in a cave is if there's a plentiful food supply."

"You mean like the pile of exiles we're standing on," Clavicus said.

"I mean like bats and cave fish."

Clavicus started to protest, but Anya cut him off.

"Zack's right," Anya said. "The punctures are too close together. Snake bites are wider."

Zack felt something crawling on his pant leg and brushed it off.

"It was probably some kind of spider," Anya finished.

Zack froze and looked down. The thing he'd brushed off his pants was, in fact, a spider the size of his fist. It was yellow and mossy green, hard to see against the island floor, but once he saw one, he saw a lot more of them crawling toward them from all sides. "Oh, crap!" he said, scrambling up toward the flat top of the mound. "ARK-II, I need some light!"

As the others joined him, ARK-II flew up four meters, cracked its casing open, and brightened like a small, white star. It lit the space for a hundred meters in every direction.

There were thousands of spiders, ranging from fist to boulder-sized. The small ones were mossy green. The large ones were harder to see because they were limestone reddish-brown, like the cavern floor. They froze for a moment, watching as ARK-II rose, the light drawing their many-by-many eyes, and then they resumed their scuttling forward at an almost leisurely pace. Every one of them was heading for Zack's hill.

"Who's imagining things, now?" Clavicus snarled. He raised his shotgun. "Holy balls, there's a lot of them."

"What do we do?" Zack asked Ultimus.

The mercenary hefted his carbine. "We run. Those aren't normal spiders, if the size didn't give it away. I still can't see them in IR."

"Star spiders," Zack said, and Ultimus nodded. "You lead. We'll follow."

A spider with a body the size of a leopard and long front legs galloped out of the dark, moving toward them at a sprint. "Now's as good a time as ever!" Zack said, and they took off down the hill at a run.

ARK-II lit the way.

The next twenty minutes were a helter-skelter nightmare. The little spiders were everywhere. They weren't inherently dangerous—Zack wasn't sure they could even bite through their clothes, but they crunched underfoot and made the cave floor slicker than it already was.

The bigger ones were a problem. The boulder-sized ones were about as solid as the rocks they were mimicking; Ultimus tried to kick one over, and it shoved him back. That small delay meant the leopard spider caught them. Zack drew his pulser and shot it twice as it came, both charges flashing harmlessly off its polished black-cherry red carapace. He aimed the third shot at its foreleg, and the smooth, translucent limb broke at the second joint, tumbling the charging creature. It hissed and spat, raising itself on seven legs. Zack shot off one of its pedipalps. Ultimus yanked him back by the arm just as it sprang and sailed through the air where he'd been.

WHOOSH! Clavicus let loose with two fiery shotgun rounds, sending out two ten-foot-long gushes of flame.

"We need to keep moving!" Ultimus said.

Anya sparked like a bug zapper as two mossy-greens jumped onto her, and she extended her lance to burn out a boulder spider, then they were all running again.

And then ARK-II wobbled. The machine's casing had turned orange, which meant it was scared.

Zack gaped as a head-sized shot of webbing smacked into the flying case and knocked it out of the air. "ARK-II!"

It was dark again, and the dark was coming for them.

"Change of plans!" Ultimus roared, firing his carbine at a pair of leopard spiders. "Clavicus, clear us a path!"

Zack had the rear again. It seemed like a new kind of spider crawled up from some hole every time he looked, so he stopped looking. When something got too close, he shot it. Sometimes, that even worked.

"Buy me some time!" Clavicus yelled, reaching ARK-II's downed form. He fired a blast of flame at the little machine.

"Clavicus!" Zack yelled.

"It'll be fine!" the engineer yelled, setting his shotgun down and ripping gobs of webbing free with his coils.

Zack spun and fired, picking from the nearest threats. A scythe clawed leaper. A camouflaged stalker. A trio of venom spitting spiders the size of chickens, blown apart with a shot each. Ultimus took the larger targets with the Reaper, the whine and snap a continuous death rattle, and Anya darted between them, cooking chitin-armored aliens with her lance before they could get close.

The light from ARK-11 started to brighten again, and Zack looked back. "Oh, no."

"What?" Anya said, then she looked.

A spider twice the size of the brawler lancer was crawling down the wall.

"They really were on the ceiling," Zack said. "Worst joke ever."

"I've got it free! I've got... Oh, frag me," Clavicus said.

The tank spider jumped off the wall. It landed lightly, but when Ultimus charged it, it knocked the two-hundred-kilo mercenary to the ground with a flick of its foreleg.

"Aaaaaaaaaaaah!" Clavicus shouted, pumping round after round of fire and metal into the monster's face. The thing shrieked and hissed, stabbing blindly at Clavicus with massive legs. The engineer grabbed ARK-11 and ran toward Zack, while Zack fired at a hissing leopard spider and Ultimus got to his feet.

The engineer unhooked the device he'd been carrying all day from his belt and slapped it onto the ground.

The tank spider charged.

Ultimus raised his carbine and slipped his finger into the trigger guard.

"No! Don't shoot!" Clavicus shouted, grabbing the Reaper with both coils.

"What?" Ultimus said, trying to wrestle the weapon back.

The tank spider smacked into the kinetic barrier with a loud *thunk!*

"Well, that was unexpected," Ultimus said, and he stopped fighting the engineer.

Zack laughed. A dome of solid force had formed around them. They were safe. "Hey, Clavicus?"

"What's up, man?"

"I'm glad you scavenged those emitters from the transport."

The tank spider smashed its legs down on the dome. Each time, the dome flashed with yellow hexagonal light, but it was getting weaker.

"Don't thank me yet," Clavicus said, stomping on one of the little spiders that got stuck in the forcefield with them. "I didn't have time to work out the power supply. Doc!"

"Yes?"

"I need you!"

Anya dropped to her knees next to him. "You design this thing to use me as a battery?" she asked with a grin.

"In a pinch," Clavicus said, his hologram a winky face. "This is definitely a pinch, by the way."

Anya's tattoos brightened. She slapped her hands onto the dome within the dome, and the *big* dome flashed back to full strength before turning transparent, hex segment by hex segment.

Zack holstered his weapon. *All right, Zack. How are you going to think yourself out of this one?* They were so close to the cavern wall and the relative safety of a lava tube... It wasn't like the star spiders couldn't follow them in there, but it would reduce the number of directions they could attack from.

ARK-II beeped at him from the ground.

"Oh! Sorry, buddy. Let me get that." Zack knelt and cleared the goop out of ARK-II's thrusters and exhaust ports. "That's better."

ARK-11 whistled and whooped.

Zack chuckled at the machine's joke and flipped its casing over. Outside the dome, the little mossy-green spiders were trying to climb onto the barrier, probing it for holes, but they kept slipping off.

"You have any thoughts on our situation you'd care to share, boss?" Ultimus asked.

Zack looked up. "Not a clue."

The mercenary frowned.

Zack finished clearing the hardening webs. ARK-11 used its thrusters to boost itself upright and beeped cheerfully. "We're surrounded. They appear to be working together."

"Star spiders do that."

"Wonderful," Zack said. "At least they can't get to us."

The tank spider smashed its forelegs against the kinetic barrier again, hissing and striating. Two boulder spiders did the same from the other side, smashing into it with their heads. Anya's tattoos flared with each strike, but the dome held.

"Clavicus? Anya? How's it going?" Zack asked.

"It should hold," Clavicus said. "Doc?"

"I'm okay, but I won't be able to keep this going forever."

"What about if we connect you to Ultimus's fusion generator, or ARK-11's... whatever it uses to power itself," Clavicus said.

Anya smiled at him. "Good thinking."

And Zack found himself thinking of popping Clavicus in the face. It wasn't fair to the young man, or Anya, not even if they really were building a... connection. And the timing couldn't have been worse.

"Babe? Are you okay?" Anya asked, catching him staring.

"I'm fine," Zack answered, shaking his head. "Can we make the dome bigger?"

"Not without losing barrier integrity," Clavicus said.

"What about pulsing it? Let a couple through, kill them, repeat?"

The engineer shook his head. "It's fast, but it's not like an 'on/off' thing," Clavicus said. "If one of those things is halfway through, the barrier will form *around* it, not through it. It might even cause a breach."

"Was that intentional, or something you could fix?"

Clavicus looked annoyed. "I did it that way so it would form-fit to the ground."

A mortar spider with an oversized abdomen fired a gob of goo at them. It slid off the shield and piled up around the bottom. What fascinated Zack about all this was how methodical the creatures were. They were biding their time, not wasting effort or working themselves up into a frenzy. It gave him an idea. "Hey, Ultimus?"

"Yeah, boss."

Zack made sure to enunciate and speak loud enough to be heard. "Could you overload your AM reactor like that time we talked about? Bring the entire cave down?"

Ultimus cocked his head, then nodded. "Uh, yeah, boss. I could blow us all to bits. You want me to do that now?"

"Zack, are you insane?" Anya said.

"And it wouldn't work, would it?" Clavicus asked. "I mean, AM has an explosive force of nine thousand joules per anti-atom, sure, but... what are they doing?"

Zack grinned. Most of the spiders were pulling back. The tank spider wasn't, but it did flatten itself against the rocks.

"Well, I'll be damned," Ultimus said.

"Yeah," Zack said, standing up. He cupped his hands around his mouth. "We lied!"

The spiders stopped.

"Boss, what are you doing?"

"They understand us," Zack answered. "They were going to

pretend to withdraw, and then the big guy would have squashed us like... well... bugs, as soon as we let the barrier drop. Come out!" he shouted. "Let's talk!"

Nothing happened for a full minute, and then another. Both the humans and spiders stayed where they were as if the whole cavern were holding its breath, until Zack caught motion out of the corner of his eye.

The spider that came toward them didn't look like any of the others. At first, he didn't realize it was a spider at all. Its cave-brown carapace was covered in a broken pattern of flaps and thick hairs that made it look like loose scree. It moved in a jerky pattern, starting and stopping so that Zack had a hard time tracking it until it was fully in the light. The stuttered spider's body was slightly bigger than the leopards', but Zack got an even greater sense of menace from the thing. It seemed like even the other spiders—including the tank spider—leaned away from it, and some skittered away like they were running from it. It had thin, spindly leg tips and powerful tibias and femurs—what Zack thought of as the spider's thighs.

As it approached the barrier, it examined each of the humans with a set of broad, black frontal eyes the size of tea saucers, its high, flat face angling and tilting in an almost human way, a playful curiosity. And then it bowed its head almost to the floor, and a *second* spider climbed down from the stutter spider's back, her pace deliberate and regal.

Zack felt the others tense beside him and put out his hand. "Don't move. Don't threaten her. I have a feeling that would end badly for all of us."

The queen spider—for she could be nothing less—hissed in agreement. She was smaller than the stutter spider, her body only the size of a small cat. Her body, long hairy limbs, pedipalps, and the upper half of her chelicerae were covered in vivid blue hairs, although she had white markings along her back and some of her joints. Her cephalothorax—the front segment of her body—looked like the tank spider's and was likely armored. Her eight small eyes, unlike the stutter spider's, were clustered together in a small gap in her shell, like an observation port. She looked up at Zack.

And she rattled at him, or maybe it was more of a purr. It was the strangest sound, like the clicking of a ratchet, only faster. It set his teeth on edge.

"What does it want?" Anya asked.

"To invite us to dinner," Clavicus answered, and Zack shushed him.

Zack knelt next to the barrier and spoke calmly and politely, not knowing how much the spider understood and how much was context. "We're just passing through here. We want to go to the stars, where you came from. But if you kill us, others will come looking. Soldiers. They'll hunt you all down." It was mostly true, at least as far as retrieving ARK-II was concerned.

A rhythmic hissing sound erupted from the spiders around them, who had slowly crept back. It took a moment for Zack to understand, but then he realized they were laughing at him. "I think they thought that was a joke," he told the others.

"I'm not loving the punchline," Ultimus answered.

The queen cut the others off with a quick double rattle, and Zack saw she was making the sound by vibrating her abdomen against her torso. She took a many-legged step forward and placed her front left leg against the barrier.

"I think she wants in," Clavicus said.

Zack rubbed the back of his head. "Yeah. We're not at that point in the relationship, your majesty."

The blue spider hissed in what sounded like frustration and turned to the stutter spider. The queen raised her left foreleg in the air, and the stutter spider touched it with his.

"Oh! It's some kind of handshake..." Zack looked at Ultimus.

"Don't look at me, boss. I usually make first contact with my fists."

"Funny," Zack said. "Real funny. Anya, thoughts?"

"What do you want me to say, Zack? I'm not an entomologist or a xenobiologist," Anya said. "I mean, this is crazy, but they've also stopped attacking. You want me to open a hole in the barrier?"

"Keep the barrier up," Zack said. "Maybe this is more symbolic than anything. A sign of trust." He placed his right index finger against the barrier.

As quick as a viper, the queen struck, her extended fangs piercing the barrier.

Zack jerked his hand back. There was a puncture in his finger, and his arm was already going numb. "Uh oh."

"Zack? What's wrong?" Anya said.

Zack fell over sideways. His muscles cramped and he pulled his arms and legs in, fingers and toes curled, like a bug that had been stepped on. "Hurts..." he said with a gasp through clenched teeth.

"All right, I'm shooting this thing!" Ultimus said. "The Reaper should punch through the barrier."

"Zack?" Anya repeated, almost taking her hands off the barrier generator.

He couldn't see. The pain was overwhelming. He could hear whispers coming from all over the room, like the sound of a thousand sweepers on the stage of a concert hall. "Wait..." he said, rolling onto his back. *Not sweepers, speakers... sounds into ideas...* The space behind his eyes burned like the queen had dripped acid into his ear.

K'shesh shemagh ashtenasi kashlassah... The sibilant speech looped and slid around his brain like it was trying to find the right plug by feel.

"Boss?" Ultimus said, kneeling next to him.

Take me back to the stars... The spider queen's thoughts flowed into him, not so much in words, but in images and impressions.

Zack's muscles unclenched, and the red fog receded from his eyes. He took a deep breath of air like he was coming up from underwater and yelled, "Stop!" to the mercenary.

Ultimus hesitated.

She's like me, was all Zack could think. In a flash that was more like intuition than thought, he realized that most of the spiders in the cave were drones. They were like dim sparks in the darkness. Many of them had basic personalities, even desires and plans—though most of the latter revolved around food. But the blue spider was a beacon. She was being wasted here, in the desert, preying on the refuse of society while the universe was out there, full of wonder.

"Her name is Kissh'ik. She's coming with us. She's done something to my brain. If she dies, I die with her."

The cat-sized blue spider pulled her front legs in and raised her head. She looked... pleased with herself, if Zack understood the undercurrent of her thoughts.

There was a brief pause in which Zack thought his crew might actually have taken all this in stride.

"I'm killing it," Ultimus said, raising the Reaper.

"No!" Zack said, and he drew his pulser.

Ultimus pivoted and aimed the carbine at him.

"Ultimus, what are you doing?" Anya asked.

"I told you that first contact with star spiders happened about ten years ago, right?"

"In the Cygnus arm of the galaxy, yes," Anya said. "What about it?"

"They started by attacking a single ship—a small salvage crew. Killed the captain, rest of the crew got away, but not before one of their queen spiders got into the pilot's head."

"They're called Weavers," Zack said, though he hadn't known that a few minutes ago.

"Not helping, Zack," Anya said, slowly standing up.

"The star spiders followed this guy to a space station, and he turned on his crew. He let the star spiders in, and they killed over forty thousand people."

"Uh, guys?" Clavicus said, looking at the fading kinetic barrier and the spiders beyond it.

"That thing in your head, kid?" Ultimus asked.

Zack had a clear shot at the mercenary, but he couldn't decide between the stun and lethal settings. "It's not controlling me, if that's what you mean. I need you to put the gun down."

"Not going to happen, kid."

Zack's eyes were on the mercenary's trigger finger. His training as a duelist made him visualize the likely path of the bullet, and he was ready to twitch his body out of the way if the old man took the shot.

"Easy, Ultimus," Anya said, placing a hand on his shoulder. His face twisted into a snarl as she took control of his body. His finger straightened off the trigger, and his hands fell to his sides. "Put the gun away, Zack," she said.

"Sure," he said, putting the pulser on safe and holstering it. He raised his hands at shoulder level. "We're all still friends here. Right, Ultimus?"

Ultimus didn't answer. His face was red from straining. Zack looked at Anya.

"He's still fighting me," Anya confirmed, her tattoos flickering as the two of them struggled for control of Ultimus's implants.

"We've got bigger problems," Clavicus said. "The shield's going to die if doc, here, isn't charging it."

"Turn it off," Zack said.

Clavicus looked at Anya.

"Are you sure, babe?" Anya asked.

"I'm sure."

And Anya thought it over. That was fine. She was never just going to take his word for it when her life was on the line, but she'd taken a step of faith, disabling Ultimus. "We're screwed no matter what we do," Anya concluded. *That's my little ray of sunshine.* "Turn it off, Clavicus."

"Okay." The engineer pushed a button, and the kinetic barrier popped like a soap bubble.

And nothing happened. The star spiders didn't charge. Ultimus didn't break free and shoot him. He'd even been unsure of himself there for a second, because the star spider queen *was* in his head, and that had all kinds of philosophical implications for his perception of reality. "Could we get some space?" Zack asked the blue star spider.

She dipped her head, and the rest of the star spiders scuttled off into the dark except for her and the one tank spider. It was as good an olive branch as he could have hoped for.

"You going to behave if she lets you go?" he asked Ultimus.

"I'm not giving you my weapon," the old man growled. "But I won't shoot you, or 'it,' as long as it stays away from me."

"Fair enough. I really would have died if you killed her. I mean, I think I would have."

"I was pretty sure you were already dead, boss. Let's call it fair play, and I'll pass on being turned into a star spider zombie, for now."

Zack laughed. "Okay, let him go," he told Anya.

Her tattoos dimmed.

Ultimus rolled his neck. Then he stomped off into the dark, carbine in hand but left on safe.

Zack sighed in relief. The back of his head throbbed from whatever the star spider had done to him. He saw Clavicus looking the way Ultimus had gone, and said, "He'll be back."

"You sure?"

"He called me 'boss.' Ultimus won't renege on a contract without saying so, I think." Zack looked at Anya and said, "Thanks."

She nodded. "I could use a break. A real break."

"Me too," Zack said.

The blue star spider had crept up while they were speaking. She vibrated her cephalothorax and abdomen in a way that sounded distinctly like someone clearing their throat. Zack knelt, and she scuttled onto his back, draping her forelegs over his left shoulder. Zack stood so she'd be eye to eye with the others. "Anya, Clavicus, this is Kissh'ik. Kissh'ik, meet Anya and Clavicus."

"Hi... Um... Kissh'ick?" Clavicus said, looking at Zack.

"Kissh'ik. Like, 'Eek! A spider!'"

The star spider vibrated with amusement.

"Yeah, um... not to be rude..." Anya said.

"Yes?" Zack answered.

"Her fangs are about the right distance apart for wounds we saw, back on the island."

Zack looked at the blue star spider on his shoulder. She scraped her pedipalps. He nodded. "That was her. In her defense, the victims were disproportionately adult male cyborgs, and they fought back. She said she let the weak ones go."

Anya shook her head. "You introduce me to the nicest people, Zack. What about the big one?" she asked, putting her hand on her hip and pointing her thumb at the tank spider behind her.

Zack grinned. "Good news. We're done walking. He's going to be our ride."

CHAPTER TWENTY-FOUR

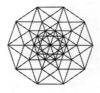

The Planetary Hall, Governor's Office
Pnyx, Skyward, Capital District of Politeia IV
4386.C.4 Interstellar

Alex Lancestrom waited as Councilor Gavin Richter sat down across the desk from him. The older man looked tired, off-balance. *When was the last time he slept?* "Can I have someone bring you a cup of coffee?" Alex said.

"Thank you, Alex. But no."

Alex almost raised an eyebrow. He'd known Gavin Richter his entire life—Gavin had been a junior bureaucrat and a protégé of Alex's foster father when Alex was only a boy. In all that time, including planetwide lawsuits by interstellars, pirate incursions, and disputes with the Federal Fleet, Alex had never known him to slip into informality.

"I don't have to tell you, this whole situation has been an unmitigated disaster," the councilor said.

After a moment, Alex asked, "Are you truly that concerned?"

"Of course I am! If I wasn't, I wouldn't be... consorting with someone like you!"

Alex reeled from the contempt in the other man's voice. "Councilor, I..." His voice died out as he finally understood how much Richter hated him.

"Oh, you see it now, do you? See how you've put us all in danger?"

Alex squared his jaw. He was the ninety-fourth descendant of Karin Lindström, not a child to be scolded by his elders. "How dare you!"

"How dare I? You insufferable wretch! You and your whole family have brought this planet to the brink of ruin."

"I'm the governor of this planet," Alex growled.

"At our sufferance!"

"Yes!" Alex said, standing up and slamming his palms on the desk. "And until you have the *balls* to do something about it, *Councilor,* you will treat me with the respect due to my office!" he thundered, more furious than he'd felt in decades.

Richter sat back in his chair, face turned pale but expression firm. "Oh, very well, *Governor,*" the old man said, his voice dripping bile. "Lead me, please. Tell me the way out of this."

"Advise me, Councilor. What insurmountable problem threatens our world?"

"I'd *love* to. It's been three days since the mercenaries you hired reneged on their contract."

"I reviewed the footage from their suits, Councilor, as has General Ulster, of the planetary guard. I found no fault in their actions. They could have killed Zack and the people with him..."

"Maybe they should have!"

"For what? Revenge? ARK-II was prepared to format itself rather than be captured. Have you considered we might be in the wrong?"

The councilor blinked. "Wrong?"

Alex sat down. "Of course we're wrong! I told you this before! This all started because of the Synthesis. ARK-II has been telling us it needed to leave the planet for the past three administrations. It was our job to transport that thing across the galaxy, to keep it safe, and we used it to build this social experiment, but now it's taken things into its own hands!"

Richter laughed in his face. "You don't see it, do you? You and your whole myopic family! You think your son or that machine and what they *want* matters? What do you think has been keeping this world together?"

Alex started to answer, but Richter waved him to silence.

"It hasn't been the Synthesis, or the *Lancestroms*, or the might of the planetary guard and system defense forces! It's the idea, you damned fool! The *thought* that we have some sacred duty to discharge to the human race has done more for the peaceful transition of power than you, or the charter, or even this planet's Council, curse us all for becoming so complacent!"

Alex stared at the councilor and realized everything the man had said was true. And that he'd known it was true long before Richter said the words, he simply hadn't voiced it.

Alex had grown up in the certainty that, while the governorship of the planet hadn't been guaranteed to him, that a Lancestrom of his generation would inherit the title. That the choice would be made on the basis of merit. That the Council would preserve the sophistocracy and its charter.

As he'd gotten older and gotten initiated into the mysteries of the planet's history, he'd learned *why* it should be so, about the purpose behind his many years of study and service and sacrifice. He and his peers, those who'd earned it, went on to fulfill their roles—him as governor, and them not—with the satisfaction of knowing they were part of something larger. That their children, and their children's children, would be part of that legacy.

It had been an idea so powerful, he'd wanted to steal it for his and Elena's son, a final gift for her when they couldn't have each other.

And he'd broken it.

He needed look no further than the petty corruption of Upper-Middle and the lawlessness of Below to understand what would happen to his planet. Without ARK-II, the fabric of Politeia's upper society would come apart, and petty self-interest would replace patriotic duty. It wouldn't happen all at once—people like Richter had been part of the system too long to change their habits. But their children and grandchildren would reach the summit of the mountain, only to discover Olympos was gone, or never had been.

"I understand. Thank you for reminding me of my duties, councilor," Alex said. "We'll send the planetary guard in. If ARK-II suicides, at least we'll have access to its base programming. There will be casualties; we never rooted the last of the star spiders out, and there will be armed convicts hiding among the canyons. We may face unrest in the cities, and we may have to reveal ARK-II's history to more members of this generation than any before it, but we'll get through this. I only ask that, if he survives—and I will make no special provision for it—that Zack be allowed to go into exile offworld."

Richter shook his head. He didn't look angry anymore. He looked sad. "It's too late. The mercenaries informed the Fleet we've been hiding an unleashed SAI on this world. I suspect we'll avoid sanctions when it turns out we've been telling them the truth about the Splinter Fleet all this time. We might even get a very private apology, and the charges of desertion against our ancestors dropped. But they're going to want ARK-II returned."

And if Zack had been *using* the machine, they'd want him, too, dead or alive. "No."

"Governor..."

"I'm not saying we fight the Fleet, Councilor, because we both know that's impossible. But we can fool them. We have before."

"The *Memento Mori*."

"Yes," Alex said. "Even the Federal Fleet isn't infallible. We hand them an unshackled AI, yes, but a poor copy of one in a casing that *resembles* an ARK, but isn't. We'll even make it convincing. It's the sort of thing a bunch of deserters might do, isn't it? Fabricate evidence of a noble past?"

"It's so convoluted, it might actually work," Richter said.

"It will," Alex said. "We might have to be... forceful with a few individuals—especially if ARK-11 erases itself. I'll keep the Council's hands clean. Meritt can handle it, and he has a number of contacts in the PPG we can trust."

Richter turned pale as he spoke.

"You didn't think it through, did you?" Alex said softly. "The cost."

Richter's jaw bulged, but he didn't say a word.

Alex nodded. He'd been a ship's officer in the system defense forces, trained to make decisions under stress, to make sacrifices most people couldn't conceive of. He could and would pay the price of their legacy. "Can I trust you to make sure that when the Fleet comes looking, they find evidence the 'unleashed super-AI' was just a local puppet show?"

"I think that's within my abilities," Richter said gruffly. "What will you be doing?"

"Deploying the planetary guard, like I said I would."

"You're going to invade the Boneyard?" Richter asked.

"We'll start by reinforcing the garrison on the *Memento Mori*. She's big enough we won't compromise Gyges, and I'll send Sam to make sure the garrison stays loyal. We can pressure the survivor groups who depend on its hydroponics to find ARK-11 for us. But we need to move fast. This only works if we get to

ARK-11 before the Fleet does." It was also his best and last chance to save his son.

★

Passage into the Iron Hills
The Starship Boneyard, Politeia IV
4386.C.4 Interstellar

Zack half-dozed, rocked by the steady dip and lurch of the tank spider's gait. This far east, it was close to two a.m., while back in Pnyx, a quarter turn around the world, the sun would be up, and his father would already be working for the good of Politeia. Zack wondered if the old man missed him or if he'd already cast Zack aside in favor of the next hereditary hopeful.

The tank spider carried them through the blue-tinged dark of the lava tubes. It was eerie how quiet something that big was when it moved. He sat cross-legged, back hunched, with Anya's head in his lap. Her hair was electric blue again, and he'd taken the time to groom and oil his beard, in spite of the dirt. The tank spider's shell was covered in hairs as thick as straw, so it felt like they'd been resting on reed mats. This was their third day underground, except for brief, nighttime bursts across the desert surface.

Clavicus was wrapped in his poncho, anchored to the carapace by his coils, even in his sleep. The engineer had taken their new alliance phlegmatically. Being able to fight alongside yesterday's sworn enemies must have been a valuable trait in his dealings with the gangs.

Ultimus was less trusting, preferring to walk for most of the journey. The mercenary had gone on ahead, Reaper slung but ready. For the past three days, he'd joined the rest of the crew only when they stopped for the tank spider to rest or go hunting.

Chapter Twenty-Four | 295

At first, he'd been reluctant to ask Kissh'ik what there was to hunt out here. He'd imagined everything from chakals to human survivors, passing through cave fish, giant lizards, and photoluminescent toadstools. He liked the visual of the tank spider delicately nibbling on a glowing mushroom cap the best. It was a good distraction once their ration packs ran out and they were down to dry vegetable crackers.

He spent a good part of the trip building rapport with the members of his crew, including the blue-bodied spider. He'd learned some interesting things. For example—and Kissh'ik was adamant about this—she wasn't a member of the ruling genetic line of the star spider family. Rather, she was a sort of autonomous scout, assembled by the "Weavers" to... go find stuff. She was insatiably curious, although her reactions to things were sometimes unpredictable. She had no interest in technology or tools but rather saw them as an extension of the individuals wielding them. She was fascinated by the fact that humans could do anything and even change specializations mid-life, as Zack had, rather than being made for a specific purpose. She found Zack's attempts to explain moral philosophy hilarious, in the way a child laughed at knock-knock jokes—the more ridiculous, the better.

ARK-11 was the only other member of the crew Kissh'ik communicated with directly. She did it not by speaking to its mind, like she did with Zack, but by vibrating her body. Sometimes, as if to punctuate a statement, she rubbed pedipalps against themselves like she was playing the violin. ARK-11 rode near the front, above and behind the tank spider's eyes, and Kissh'ik sat next to it, her legs drawn close to her body like curled fingers. Zack couldn't tell if the star spider was resting or watching. She didn't sleep—neither she nor the tank spider had eyelids to close—but as she explained it, she could slow herself down between bouts of activity, like an organic version of cryogenetic stasis.

In those calm moments, Zack thought of his father. He'd never felt close to the man when he was a child, but Anya had been right when they talked in the transport cockpit. This trip was making him realize how much they had in common and how many things Alex Lancestrom had been right about, from taking over the leadership of a group to dealing with criminal elements. Zack even caught himself smiling like him sometimes, particularly when he thought of times the crew had come up with better answers than his own.

The passage curved, and Zack felt a change in the tunnel air. He saw what he thought was a circle of brighter dark up ahead, and it was getting closer. "I think we're here."

Anya craned her neck and cracked her shoulders. "Five more minutes."

"You've had three days to nap."

She responded by reaching up with her right hand and hooking her fingers around his calf. The downtime had been good for them as an on-again couple. They were a little dirty for anything wildly passionate, but they'd taken time to get some combat training together inside the shared virtual network, gone to sleep wrapped around each other, and made out like teenagers whenever no one was looking.

"Hey, boss?" Ultimus called out, walking back toward them. "You can see the *Memento Mori* from the cave mouth. You should come look."

"I'll shock you," Anya threatened.

Zack bent down and kissed her shoulder. "Don't shock me. I'm not a doctor or a mechanic, but I'm pretty sure the charge would ground out through our gigantic friend, here, and it might make him a bit grumpy."

"Fine," she said, yawning and pushing up onto her elbow. "Go be responsible."

"Yes, ma'am," he said, getting to his feet. Kissh'ik half-turned to look at him. "I'm going to go take a look," he told her.

She trundled over, shaking out her legs as she moved for the first time in hours. He offered her his back, and she hopped on, jumping the meter and a half with ease. For all her size, she only weighed about half a kilo, and he was already getting used to having her peek over his shoulder.

Danger ahead, she whispered into his mind. The words were accompanied by an impression that this part of the Boneyard was a void. There were limits to the collective consciousness the star spiders shared when they weren't near each other, and none of the scouts Kissh'ik had sent to this area had come back.

"We'll be careful," he said, resisting the urge to reach up and scratch her head. Kissh'ik was a useful and surprisingly agreeable companion, but he had no idea how she'd react to being treated like a pet.

The tank spider straightened a leg for them, and he walked down to join Ultimus on the lava tube floor. ARK-II floated down with them.

"Boss."

"Hey, Ultimus. How are you holding up?"

"Doing fine," he answered, his eyes flicking to the star spider on Zack's shoulder.

"She's doing fine, too," Zack said with a wink. "There might be trouble ahead." He told the mercenary what Kissh'ik had sent him about her missing star spiders.

Ultimus grunted. "There's nothing around the cave mouth, but I think there's a settlement at the base of the cliffs your ship is parked on. Best we get eyes on before the sun's up."

"That won't do me much good," Zack said. "I can't see in the dark like you can."

"You'll see more than you think," Ultimus said. "Ship looks more like a fortress than a wreck."

"Great. Fabulous. I thought they'd be more discrete."

"What's fabulous?" Clavicus asked, using his coils to lower himself over the tank spider's side.

"The *Memento Mori*'s fortified, and there's a settlement of scavs, mutants, and other degenerates."

"They could be Dissidents," the engineer said.

"Dissidents, or just regular dissidents?" Zack said.

"You know, normal people who disagreed with the way this planet is governed and chose to live in the Boneyard hundreds of years ago."

"I thought 'Dissidents' were a myth," Anya said. She sat on the edge of the tank spider's carapace and jumped down.

"Dissidents *are* a myth," Zack said. "So are star spiders and giant sewer snakes."

"The sewer snakes are real," Clavicus said, looking ill.

"I think that's the point Zack was making, Clav," Anya said, touching the engineer's shoulder.

And for a wonder, the engineer didn't flinch away. It didn't bother Zack anymore. He and Anya were good. At this point, he'd figured out that Clavicus was more like her kid brother than a rival. "Well, let's go see what we're up against."

The six of them walked, rode, and floated to the lava tube entrance. Ultimus had been right. As he felt the fresh night air on his face, Zack spotted the ship that had brought his ancestors to a new world. She was five kilometers away. Almost two kilometers long, she was slightly bigger than he could cover with his two hands at that distance. She was shaped like a pioneer saber, with a long, straight upper edge that hung over the desert and a thicker base that rested on the top of the cliff Ultimus had mentioned. Her hull was lit up from multiple angles like a museum piece. There was no way to sneak up on her that he could see, not a single patch of shadow.

And all around her was the reason they called this the iron hills. Fifty generations of Politeians had deorbited ships, satellites, and defunct space stations into the Boneyard. Over the last eight hundred years, more and more had been salvaged and recycled in the orbital forges and factories. That still left toxic waste, heavy metals, and the occasional vessel too obsolete to be worth salvaging.

"You said there was a settlement?" Zack asked Ultimus.

"Yeah, but you have to climb a bit. There's a valley that leads to the ship, but you can only see it from one angle."

"Lead the way," Zack said.

It wasn't a long walk. The tank spider stayed behind. Ultimus led them to the base of a plateau, fifteen minutes from the tube entrance. All the while, Zack tried to tune his senses to their surroundings, to the faint hum of insects, the occasional scrabble of small animals, to the almost pitch black of the rocky dirt and dry, narrow gullies. The outcrops of stone that turned the area into a hedge maze were worn smooth—by the action of the wind or ancient rivers, he wasn't sure.

"Over here," Ultimus said, his voice low. He led them up a hidden path to the top of one of the mesas. It was an uncomfortable climb, trying to wedge himself between rocks and not send showers of gravel falling on Anya and the others. At one point, Zack put his hand down on some kind of spiky plant and almost slipped, but Ultimus caught him just before he pitched backward. Kissh'ik hissed on his shoulder and hopped off, climbing up the rock face on her own. Gritting his teeth, Zack managed to make it the rest of the way.

"There it is," Ultimus said.

Zack walked up to stand beside the mercenary. They hadn't come much closer to the ship, but their walk had lined them up with a long, narrow gorge that led straight to the base of the cliff supporting the *Memento Mori*. There, visible only because of a few scattered lights, was the settlement Ultimus had mentioned. The approach felt somewhat ominous, although Zack knew something the others didn't about Gyges that would simplify things if they could just get to the ship. "How many do you think there are down there?"

"Hard to tell," Ultimus said. "That ravine's too narrow. Could be a few dozen or a few hundred."

ARK-11 let out a soft string of beeps.

Zack started to explain, but Anya held up her hand. "It asked if this isn't more of a box-canyon than a ravine."

"You learned to speak *bleep*?" Zack asked.

"Of course I did. I wasn't going to depend on you lot forever."

"I don't think it's a box-canyon," Ultimus said, crossing his arms. "It's not big enough. You can roll a tank division down a canyon."

"Well, the walls are too steep to be a ravine," Zack said, agreeing with ARK-11. "What about a gorge?"

"That might work," Ultimus said thoughtfully. "Or a rift."

Kissh'ik hissed in annoyance.

Zack turned to explain why this was semantically important when a dozen armed men who'd been hiding under camouflage cloaks, half covered in sand, stood up with their rifles aimed at Zack and his crew.

Zack swallowed. "Well, this is embarrassing."

CHAPTER TWENTY-FIVE

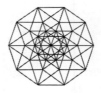

Tabletop Mesa
The Starship Boneyard, Politeia IV
4386.C.4 Interstellar

"Nobody move!" a woman in camouflage commanded.

Zack's mind raced. Who were these people? They were wearing identical gear and were well-disciplined, but they didn't look like any PPG unit Zack had ever heard of. Were they some kind of reconnaissance squad, or maybe a special unit from the rangers?

"Holy crap! Jenna, they've got a star spider with them!"

"Shoot it!"

Kissh'ik gathered her legs to pounce.

Ultimus stepped forward, hands raised, blocking the shot. "Can't let you do that."

The camouflaged troops all pointed their rifles at Ultimus. "Get out of the way!"

"Not happening," Ultimus said.

"She's a pet!" Zack said. "See?" He whistled at Kissh'ik and offered her his back. Kissh'ik hissed at him. *Come on, girl. Fight later, stay alive now,* he thought, hoping she could receive as well as send.

She jumped onto his back, popping up over his left shoulder.

"Leave the spider alone," the one called Jenna snapped. "If they can be tamed, Ross is gonna want to know. All of *you*," she told Zack and his crew. "Weapons out, slowly, and hand them off to my men."

They were professional about it. Two men handed off their weapons and moved forward, taking Zack's pulser, Ultimus's Reaper, and Clavicus's shotgun, handing them back before moving to the next person. They were brisk but not unnecessarily forceful. They left ARK-II alone, and the man who searched Zack kept his distance from the star spider on Zack's shoulder.

"You the cyber-doc?" the man checking Anya said, to Zack's surprise.

"Yes."

"Ground out, please."

Anya did. The man checked her with a portable voltmeter, then took the electro-lance and returned to his teammates.

"Now listen up, because I'm only going to say this once," Jenna said. "We know who you are. We're going to take you somewhere. You're not going to fight us or try to escape. If you do, we'll shoot you. Mr. Thragg, if you try something, we will shoot your employer."

"I won't try anything," Ultimus said. "You hurt anyone, I'll tear the lot of you limb from limb."

"We understand each other," Jenna said. "Now, let's move."

Zack followed orders and kept quiet. The climb down was easier than the climb up, although he couldn't hope to match the soldiers' surefootedness or their stealth. Even when he was staring right at them, they somehow managed to fade out of sight. They were like ghosts at the edges of his vision.

"How far are you taking us?" Ultimus asked.

"No questions. Vince, get the hoods onto them."

"Won't do you any good," Ultimus said. "I have satnav and relnav built into my head."

"Very honest of you, Mr. Thragg. Of course, we knew that. Hoods are shielded," Jenna said.

"Any weapons in the case?" a soldier asked Zack about ARK-II.

"No. It's just luggage and data storage."

They put a larger bag over ARK-II and stuffed it into one of the soldier's packs. Then they threw a hood over Zack's head, too. It seemed like they were going to make the rest of the trip blind, guided and sometimes shoved by the soldiers.

But for some reason, Zack could see everything. It took him a moment to understand it—to even come to grasp with the almost spherical view. Kissh'ik was riding on his shoulder, and Zack was connected to her eyes. It was an uncomfortable discovery. As useful as it was, it implied greater access and changes to his brain than he'd expected or hoped.

The soldiers spread out once Zack and his crew were hooded. He had an easier time tracking the soldiers through Kissh'ik's eight eyes than he had with his own. Her smaller sets of eyes gave her a 360° field of view, though they acted more like lidar receivers, tracking motion and distance more than 'seeing.' Once she'd spotted her prey, her larger central pair could track anything in hyper-defined detail, even in the dark.

She followed the soldiers easily when they moved. Two of them acted as sheepdogs while the others bounded ahead, screening them from danger or rescue—Zack couldn't tell which. They avoided scrap piles and crash sites, detouring for hundreds of meters if they had to. But what impressed him the most was how coordinated the unit was. They were like pack predators, their only communication a series of clicks that barely registered over the sound of Zack's footsteps.

Twice, the group stopped, and their minders told them to stay quiet. The second time, they waited a full twenty minutes without moving. Then, with no warning or sign that anything had changed, they resumed their journey at a near jog.

They're skilled warriors, he sent Kissh'ik.

The answer he got from her was… troubling. To Kissh'ik, the soldiers were an absence from the world. A wrongness. They made her heart tube squeeze and flooded her lungs with hemolymph. In short, they made her feel the way most humans felt about spiders. He put it down to the number of scouts she'd lost in this part of the Boneyard, but he couldn't help sharing her sense of foreboding because of how they were linked.

They reached the soldiers' hidden base just under two hours later.

Habitat Charlie
The Starship Boneyard, Politeia IV
4386.C.4 Interstellar

The moons were rising, throwing blue light and shadows across the desert floor. The soldiers tightened their formation back up, and Jenna took out a box with some kind of directional antenna. She pointed it carefully at some hidden receiver before transmitting, "Base, this is patrol twenty-three. Standing by at point delta for entry."

Zack didn't think the soldiers were planetary guard. They'd avoided several open areas a transport could have extracted them from. And as much as he believed that people who survived out here had to be either brutal, clever, or both, he doubted they were hunting each other by triangulating radio signals.

No, these people were *hiding* from the planetary guard. Everything they did was careful, thought out. If they intended to turn Zack in, they would do it later, from a position of strength. That meant Zack had time, and room to negotiate.

Jenna nodded as someone answered her. She put the transmitter away and grabbed one of her men. "Northern entrance. Move out."

"Yes, ma'am." He grabbed Zack by the arm. They moved him and his crew forward at a dead run. They sprinted a hundred meters to the next mesa, to a sheer wall like any other, except that Jenna pulled the painted sheet aside and they were pushed into a shallow cave.

Jenna pulled the sheet closed behind them and turned on the lights.

The soldiers pulled their hoods off.

"Let's go, everyone. Safe and clear, check each other over. We move out again in five," Jenna said. She pulled the pack from her back and dug out Zack's pulser. "Here," she said, pushing it into his hands. "Safety on, charge pack out."

"You're returning our weapons?"

Jenna was already handing Ultimus his Reaper. "You're not our prisoners, Mr. Lancestrom. You're our honored guests." She smirked and moved on to Clavicus.

Zack looked around the cave. LED strips on the walls gave them light to see. It was neatly organized, with a few bedrolls laid out near the left-hand wall and some scrap metal shelves of supplies on the right. There were some barrels of water and signs of a chemical cookfire. All in all, it was a cozy camp, sheltered from the desert sun, and the right size for Zack and his crew to wait for whatever was supposed to happen next.

"Thanks for the hospitality. Is this some sort of way station? A place your people can hide if they're caught out during the day?"

Jenna smirked again. "Always good to have our passive defenses confirmed."

Before Zack could ask what she meant by that, the whole back of the cave slid open.

"Welcome to Habitat Charlie," Jenna said.

It was some kind of airlock.

The soldiers stood back as Zack, Anya, and the others stepped off the cave floor onto the white-painted steel. Everything was spotlessly clean.

"Not coming with us?" Ultimus said.

Zack turned around to see the soldiers were still in the cave.

"Still plenty of dark," Jenna said. "Might catch up with you later, if Ross hasn't already sent you on your way."

The hidden door to the cave slid shut.

"Well, this was unexpected," Zack said.

"Any idea who they are?" Ultimus asked.

"I think Clavicus may have been right about this," Zack said, and the engineer's hologram turned into a smiley face. "They're trying too hard to stay hidden to be PPG and too well trained and equipped to be simple survivors."

"It would be a pretty big scandal if people found out the PPG was out here," Anya said. "It could still be the guard."

"Why bring us here, then?" Zack said.

"Can we go back to the part about me being right?" Clavicus asked. "I mean, again. Like with the spiders."

The inner door slid open, and two men in white service uniforms with gray trim—the inverted colors of a PPG uniform —smiled at them. The one on the right looked like he was about eighteen. The one on the left, tall and lean, and a few years older than Zack, spoke. "Welcome to Habitat Charlie, Mr. Lancestrom. Dr. Vesperian, Mr. Rext, Mr. Thragg. All of you are welcome."

"Thanks," Zack said. He didn't relax, but he felt like he was beginning to understand their situation. The soldiers had returned his pulser to show he wasn't a threat. They'd let Zack know they knew his name to show their superiority. They were being polite to tell him they didn't need anything from him. That last part was a lie. "We were hoping you'd find us."

"Oh? And who is it you think... found you, Mr. Lancestrom?"

"You're Dissidents, or at least something like the rumor of Dissidents in the Boneyard. Everyone thinks you're noble savages choosing to live free or die, but you're actually a fully-fledged opposition to the planetary government, aren't you?"

The man chuckled. "And why would you wish to meet people like us, Mr. Lancestrom? Everyone knows Politeia has the perfect system of governance. As the governor's heir, even now, you're complicit in that fabrication."

"I'm sure you saw the newscasts," Zack said. "I'm no friend of the sophistocracy."

The man raised an eyebrow. "You wish to join us?"

Zack smiled. "I've been impressed by what I've seen of your organization so far. Your people are well trained, orderly, and well-led. It speaks to a healthy society."

"We like to think so."

"You're also security conscious to the point of paranoia. I appreciate the implied invitation, but I won't insult you by pretending to accept it. We're heading to the *Memento Mori*. We could use your help."

"Why should we... no, never mind. We will help you, Mr. Lancestrom. But let's talk about it in a few hours, after the patrols return. Peter, here, will take you to your temporary quarters. You aren't prisoners, but I ask that, in the spirit of the courtesy we've shown each other so far, you not go anywhere without an escort."

"Of course. I didn't catch your name," Zack said.

The man smiled and gave them a small bow. "Ross Perkins, at your service. You might say I'm your equivalent among the Dissidents, Mr. Lancestrom. A shadow to your light." He turned to his younger companion. "Peter?"

"Right this way, please," the man behind Ross said, gesturing toward the passageway on the right.

Zack and the others followed the uniformed man through a security station then down a surprisingly long hallway. Everything was white and well lit—the floor, ceiling, and doors, the uniforms of the men and women they passed. There were three blast doors between them and the end of the passage, with labeled pull handles on each side of the frame. They were spaced about forty feet apart and currently open. Large, thick windows on the left side of the corridor showed two long rooms for hydroponics, one for water processing, some sort of research lab, and a mess hall, all white and clear glass. More doors lined the right-hand side, but no windows. *Storage rooms? Machine shops?*

"You folks hungry?" Peter asked.

"Not yet," Zack answered before the others could. "You have a place we could clean up before eating?"

Anya sighed. "A shower would be amazing."

Peter smiled. "I'll take you to your rooms, then. As you can imagine, clean water is precious out here, but we've become extraordinarily efficient at recycling it."

"I think that means we're going to shower in pee," Clavicus said.

"Of course not, Mr. Rext. We use urine to make urea for hydroponics, saltpeter and phosphorus for the armory, and, of course, ammonia for the laundry room. How do you think we get our uniforms so white?" He flashed Zack and the others a wide, genuine smile.

Peter was the perfect host. Open, affable, a little younger

than Clavicus, and yet more poised and mature. If Kissh'ik hadn't wanted to tear the man's face off, Zack would have found Peter unequivocally likable. As it stood, he was more than a little troubled by the conflicting signals.

They followed the Dissident through a sliding door on the right side of the hallway into a short corridor with three doors on either side. "This is transient quarters," Peter said. "Take your pick of the rooms; you're our only guests at the moment."

"You have guests often?" Ultimus asked.

Peter gave the mercenary a shy smile and shrugged. "Sometimes visitors from other habitats, sometimes new arrivals. You can lock the outer door if you like, though no one here will bother you. There are changes of clothes on the shelves you can use if you want us to give yours a wash, and there's an intercom here," he said, pointing to a small panel—also white. "Call me when you're ready to go to the mess hall," he said.

"Thank you, Peter. We will," Zack said.

The young man nodded. He took a step back into the hallway, and the door closed, leaving Zack and his crew on their own.

"So, what do we do?" Clavicus asked

Zack put a finger to his lips. "Let's check out those showers Peter promised us."

Ultimus touched a control pad, and the nearest door slid open.

After the glare of the base interior, the room was restful. Everything was done in soft shades of gray and moonlight blue lighting. The walls were charcoal, a chair and holodesk near the door were the color of an overcast sky. A well-constructed metal bookshelf had been painted in light strokes of shades of charcoal and silver. Neatly folded white clothes were laid out on the shelves in several sizes. The promised shower was a rounded enclosure—almost a capsule—in the far-right corner, along with a toilet. A single bed with a thick comforter was pushed into the far left. More interesting, though, was the window. It was circular, divided into eight panels with a ninth, round panel in the center. Outside it was a city. It wasn't Pnyx, but it was night in the Skyward layer in one of the district capitals, maybe two hundred floors up. Aircars cruised by a few stories down, and Zack could see people working in the skyscraper across the lane. Above, the night sky showed thousands of stars.

"Is that New Carthage?" Anya asked, coming to stand beside him.

"I don't know, I've never been there."

"Me neither," Clavicus said. "Is this what Skyward is like?" He walked up to the window.

"The openness doesn't bother you?" Zack asked.

"It isn't real," the engineer said. "It's beanstalks and cloud castles, Lancestrom, and more scrap than a scav could dream of."

Zack and Anya looked at each other. Sometimes, he forgot how different the first twenty years of Clavicus's life had been from his.

ARK-11 stuttered out a series of beeps. It was New Carthage, and the footage was recent.

"Hey, buddy," Zack said. "We need the training circlets."

ARK-11 glowed blue and popped his side panel open. Ultimus grabbed four and handed them out.

Zack sat on the bed and put his circlet on his head.

CHAPTER TWENTY-SIX

Shared Virtual Network
Users: Zack Lancestrom, Dr. Anya Vesperian, Joseph "Ultimus"
Thragg, Clavicus Rext, Anthropological Restoration Kit XI,
???????????
4386.C.4 Interstellar, Time Dilation 0.125x

Zack took a virtual breath in the shared virtual network. ARK-11 had created a round table with four chairs arranged in a semi-circle. ARK-11's avatar took the fifth place, and there was... some kind of frame, like a weaving loom. "What's that for?" Zack asked.

Kissh'ik climbed fully onto his shoulder and hopped onto the table. She scuttled across and hopped onto the makeshift web in the center of the frame.

"Make yourself comfortable, why don't you?" Zack said with a wry grin.

Ultimus frowned. "Is that..."

"Kissh'ik. She hitched a ride through my head."

"How deep inside your brain is she, boss?"

Zack looked at the blue star spider, and she looked back at

him with eight virtual eyes. "I'd like to have Anya look into that once we're safely away."

"You want me poking around your head?" Anya asked, taking one of the chairs.

"You'll have to get in line, apparently," Zack answered. "Ultimus, Clavicus, please take your seats." Zack sat down, and so did the others. "We don't have much time. I don't think they can crack ARK-11's encryption, but the shorter the amount of time we spend in here, the less tempted they'll be to try. What do we think?"

"They're well trained," Ultimus said. "Their gear is Tier 1.0, maybe Tier 1.5 for some of the stealth and comms. They use it well. I'd give them even odds against the Combine in a low-tech environment."

"I think they showed us their very best," Zack said. "Calling themselves patrol twenty-three, dropping that they have visitors from other habitats…"

"They're exaggerating their numbers," Ultimus said.

"Maybe," Zack answered. "They're definitely trying to impress us."

"That means they've got a big ask," Clavicus said, and Zack was pleased with the under-dweller's instincts.

"They do," Zack said. "I'm sure of it. Something to do with the *Memento Mori*."

"How do you know that?" Clavicus asked.

"The second Zack said we were going there, Ross stopped trying to convince him," Anya answered.

Zack raised an eyebrow.

"What?" she said. "I listened to you ramble on about debate tactics and negotiation for two years before we broke up."

"Didn't think you were listening," Zack said.

"Didn't want to be. For someone who's so good at reading people, you wouldn't take the hint."

Zack smiled at her and was again reminded how much he was glad she'd come along.

"Pretty smooth how you got him to talk, boss," Ultimus said, crossing his arms.

Zack shrugged. "Just a couple good guesses. It helps that they need something from us. I'm not sure we should give it to them."

"They seem nice enough," Clavicus said. Zack frowned, and Clavicus raised his hands. "Hey, don't get me wrong, some of the coldest, most dangerous criminals I dealt with wore expensive suits and smiles. I mean, I didn't deal with them, Jawhee did, but I saw what Jawhee did after they spoke to him, and I'm pretty sure it wasn't his idea."

Zack nodded. "Kissh'ik thinks they're—"

"Kissh'ik thinks they are a sss-stain upon the universe and darkness living. We should kill them and bury the bodies-sss," the star spider said, her dry voice rustling like autumn leaves blowing across the ground.

"So, she can speak in here," Ultimus said.

"I suppose if I can, she can," Zack said, tapping his index finger on the table. "We know they want something; we know they're deceiving us to get it. I doubt they'd just let us walk out of here."

"They probably have two squads ready to take us down within seconds," Ultimus agreed.

"So we play along," Anya said. "Speaking of, I'm starving."

"I thought you wanted a shower?" Zack said sarcastically, knowing full well she'd been backing him up.

She smirked at him.

"We play along," Zack confirmed. "I don't think they know what ARK-II is, so let's keep it that way. Remember, we don't know where we are, we're outlaws, we want to get to the *Memento Mori*. It's what's going to keep us alive."

"But we do know where we are, right?" Anya said. "Clavicus can sense motion through his prosthetics."

"And I saw everything through Kissh'ik's eyes," Zack added, giving the star spider a nod.

"I have inertial navigation installed as well," Ultimus said. "It's not in my Combine profile; I had it put in for moments like this."

"And your name is Joseph," Anya said, looking at her user interface. "I think that might be the most disturbing news of the trip."

Ultimus chuckled. "Yeah, Ultimus is my Combine callsign."

"Why?" Clavicus asked.

"It was a joke that turned into a curse. I was a shiny new merc, fresh out of the Combine boot camp on Luth Prime. I took a job I had no business taking, with a squad of veterans who needed to fill their roster—the contract stipulated a minimum team size. Mission went sideways. The opposition had hired mercs, and neither team would back down. I was the only survivor. Got my first big paycheck and my first prosthetic, and my next team gave me the callsign."

"I'm sorry," Clavicus said, his hologram a sad face.

Ultimus winked at him. "It's okay, kid. Most of those assholes are long dead and buried, too."

Habitat Charlie
The Starship Boneyard, Politeia IV
4386.C.4 Interstellar

They came out of the shared virtual network and returned the circlets to ARK-11, and the little machine tucked itself under the desk, like a personal terminal. Kissh'ik crawled up into a

Chapter Twenty-Six | 315

shadowed corner of the ceiling. Clavicus and Ultimus went off to find their own rooms. Anya stayed with Zack. "Want to see if we can get that shower working?" she asked.

"They'll be watching," he said, putting his hands around her waist.

"We'd better give them a good show, then."

They stripped off their clothes. The glass shower door hissed shut behind them, and they were pressed up against each other in the tight space.

"You smell bad," Anya said, putting her arms around his neck.

Zack leaned forward and sniffed the top of her head. "Mmm."

"Zack!"

"What?"

"Stay away from my brain, you lecher."

"I wasn't thinking about your brain," he said, pulling her tight.

"You're filthy."

"Just dirty-minded."

"Why don't you put your mind to getting this shower working?"

Zack looked for a faucet or control panel, but there was only one big teal-colored button. There were water nozzles all around them. "This could go very wrong."

"Be brave. I don't think they brought us this far to boil us alive."

"I'm more worried you'll break through the glass if it's too cold."

"Push the button," she said, pecking him on the cheek.

He did. The "button" scanned his fingers, then warm water hit them from both sides. "Perfect," he said.

"Could be warmer," Anya said, putting her head on his shoulder.

The water got fractionally warmer, and Anya sighed. "That's nice."

The nozzles switched to soapy water, except for the ones pointed at their faces. "You want to get my back?" Zack asked.

"Turn around."

She scrubbed him down with her hands, and the nozzles soaped up his front.

"Don't forget the crack," Zack said.

"I'm not doing that."

"If you loved me..."

"I'm preserving my ability to have sex with you. My turn."

She turned around, and he returned the favor, making sure he got the dirt clear from around her implants. "You want me to—"

"No, Zack."

"Just checking," he said with a smile. He bent down and kissed her on the lips, putting his hand on her face.

The spouts switched to warm water again. Anya pulled her head back. "Time to rinse."

Zack turned, rinsing his hair and getting the suds off his body. Anya finished before him and slapped his ass. Zack reached back and squeezed her hip.

The nozzles stopped. The air in the capsule got hotter at the same time as Zack felt the pressure drop. The water on their skins evaporated. He had a small moment of panic as his body remembered low-pressure compartments on the orbital he'd been born on, and then the pressure normalized. The door popped open. The capsule was completely dry. "That was the most efficient shower I've ever taken," Zack said. "Not the longest or most luxurious."

"I'd do it again," Anya said, nuzzling into him.

He massaged the nape of her neck. *I hope we get the chance.* "So, now that we're clean..."

"No."

"You didn't hear what I was offering."

"I can feel what you're offering pressed against me, and the answer is 'No' until you feed me and shave that beard off."

"You don't like it?"

"It looks great on you. I hate kissing it."

Zack chuckled. He'd grown his hair and beard out as the first stage of falling away from his father, who'd maintained PSDF grooming standards his whole adult life. Part of that, Zack knew, was to remind people that his father wasn't only a politician but a warrior, and that played well with parts of the demographic. But Zack had also choked on his own tear gas in the subway because the ventilator wouldn't seal, and that could prove deadly in a vacuum. "I'll get rid of it."

She frowned. "You don't have to do it for me."

"I'm not," he said, giving her a wink. "Let's get dressed."

They grabbed clothes from the shelves. There wasn't much guesswork to it; there were four sets, each monogrammed with their initials and perfectly sized. Zack fetched his grooming glove, interfaced with it through his wrist communicator, and swiped his face to a clean shave. His black eyes gleamed blue in the mirror as the implants projected images on his retinas. A few passes over his head brought him down to two inches on top and a perfect fade to his ears and neck. It was Fleet style, not PPG, so his scalp wasn't showing, but it brought a hardness to his face he hadn't seen in a while. "How do I look?" he asked Anya.

She walked over in her new clothes. Hers were a simple but well-made pair of white pants, a shirt, and a light jacket that closed with inner ties at her waist and hip. The lapel that ran from her left shoulder to right hip was dark gray. She'd recolored her hair and tattoos to black. "You look like your father."

"Is that a good thing?"

She fastened the standing collar on his jacket. "It's who you were always going to be, Zack. Governor of a planet or captain of a starship, you're still filling his boots. Where you walk with them is what makes you different." She came up onto her tiptoes and kissed him on the cheek. "Much better."

He grinned. "Let's go find the others."

Ultimus and Clavicus were waiting for them in the corridor, dressed in white and gray.

"Spider not coming?" Ultimus asked.

"She's comfortable where she is, and she'll keep ARK-11 safe."

"You try the shower?" Anya asked Clavicus.

"I did! I can't believe how much engineering went into their sanitation systems. I mean, I can, right? Because water's gold out here, but still..."

Zack watched the two of them with an amused smile.

"You good, boss?" Ultimus asked under his breath.

"Yeah," Zack said. He was glad Anya had found such a good friend. "Let's tell our hosts we're ready for dinner."

"Midrats," Ultimus said.

"What?"

"Midnight rations. Too late for dinner, too early for breakfast."

"Huh. Learn something every day." Zack tapped the intercom.

Peter answered after a few seconds. "I'm on my way."

Zack went back to join the others.

"...holodesk is connected to their own internal network. It's like an entire, alternate noosphere."

The outer door slid open. "Ready to eat?" Peter asked with a smile.

"Yes!" Anya said.

"You mentioned something about laundry?" Zack asked.

"Oh, sure! It's no problem. I'll have someone come pick it up from your rooms."

Zack wrinkled his nose. "Kissh'ik's settled down in the first room. She's a little... agitated right now. It would be best if I was the only one to go in there."

Peter swallowed. "I'll tell the cleaning crew to avoid that room."

Zack took some small pleasure in the young man's discomfiture. "I'll go get the clothes."

They put all the clothes and their weapons in Ultimus's room and headed to the mess hall. The food was simple and savory—okra and jin roots from the hydroponic gardens, vex-rat meat the patrols brought back.

"Vex rat?" Zack asked.

Peter smiled, and Zack got the impression their affable young host was enjoying this as much as Zack enjoyed threatening him with Kissh'ik. "It's not what we'd prefer to eat, but they've developed a second liver that filters out heavy metals and toxins. As long as we cut it out, the rest of the meat is safe."

Zack speared another chunk and popped it into his mouth. "It's not half bad."

A woman at the table next to them coughed, and her dining companions scattered, two of them knocking over their chairs.

"What's going on?" Zack asked.

"We need to leave," Peter said, more scared by the scene than he'd been of the star spider.

"But..."

"Please, Mr. Lancestrom. I need to get you back to transient quarters."

Zack obeyed, but he got a good look at the woman as he stood up. She was shaking, frightened out of her mind. The hand she'd coughed in was black, the table spattered as if an ink pen had exploded.

Peter took them back to their rooms. "I'm sorry, I have to lock you in. We'll need to decontaminate the area."

"I understand," Zack said. "What was that?"

"An illness. Ross will explain. Please excuse me."

Zack stepped back, and Peter sealed the door.

"What was that?" Ultimus asked.

Zack turned to Anya.

"I don't know. I've seen that before when I was replacing a patient's lungs with prosthetics. She was a longtime smoker—tobacco, cannabis, salvia ... the cancer was rampant. But cancer isn't contagious, and those people were scared."

"Toxic waste?" Clavicus asked. "I've seen some pretty freaky stuff happen to sewer dwellers."

"Could be a chemical weapon of some kind, something they found in a crashed ship," Ultimus said. "I've never played with the stuff, but I've seen the corpses."

"Chemical weapons don't propagate," Anya said. "Nanites do. If this is a gray goo incident—"

"Gray goo?" Zack asked.

"Out of control nanomachines self-replicating while eating every organic thing they run across," Anya explained.

Zack ran his hand over his now much shorter hair. None of that sounded good. He'd thought he could talk his way out of this situation, but if they were exposed to something as terrifying as what the others were describing, everything they'd done would be for nothing.

They'd have to risk trying to escape—take Ross up on his

bluff that they were prisoners. There wasn't a door lock that Anya and ARK-11 couldn't hack or that Ultimus and Clavicus couldn't dismantle. From there, they'd have to get out to the desert and run like hell.

The outer door opened to reveal Ross, standing in the hallway with his hands clasped behind his back. He looked flushed, and his collar was undone, but he gave Zack a wry smile. "Mr. Lancestrom. If you'd come with me, it's time I explained how we can help you and what we need in return."

CHAPTER TWENTY-SEVEN

Habitat Charlie
The Starship Boneyard, Politeia IV
4386.C.4 Interstellar

Zack gave Ultimus and Clavicus a nod, touched Anya's shoulder, and joined Ross in the hallway.

Ross nodded to the others and said, "I'll have him back to you soon." He closed the door.

"Rough day at the office?" Zack asked.

Ross laughed. "Believe it or not, it's depressingly normal. Shall we walk and talk?"

"Lead the way."

Ross straightened his uniform and took them back toward the entrance.

"Care to tell me what happened?" Zack asked.

The Dissident leader stopped in front of the mess hall window. "First, you tell me why you want to go to the *Memento Mori*," Ross said.

Zack glanced through the window. Two men in white hazard suits were decontaminating the table the woman had been sitting at and the ones around it. "I thought you knew. Your team ambushed us. They knew our names."

"The whole planet knows your names. You fell off the radar for three days in star spider territory. We thought you were dead, and it's a big desert. Then you walked right into one of our observation posts. Jenna made the call to bring you in."

They don't know about Gyges. "We're headed offworld. There are a few old shuttles stored in the forward hangars. A starship will pick us up in orbit."

"You know the *Memento Mori*'s air defenses are active?"

Zack shrugged. "It's a complication. What happened in the mess hall?"

"We hunt, grow, or recycle most of our supplies," Ross said. "Always have, ever since the first Dissidents came to the Boneyard."

"I thought the original exiles depended on food drops from the government?" Zack asked.

Ross smiled. "*They* did. My people started building shelters decades before the Boneyard became an internment camp. When Hannah Lancestrom gave the order, we had solar plants, algae and fish farms, and a homegrown information network. My ancestors helped build all that."

"Why?" Zack asked.

Ross turned to face him. "They weren't survivalists or criminals if that's what you're asking. They were engineers, artists, teachers, military officers, and local politicians who'd been pressured to be less critical of government policy. They saw the polarization of the news, the increased militarization of the police, and the use of soldiers to respond to civil unrest. They were scared. So they built the habitats to be an ark for the memory of our people, in the shadow of the symbol of Politeia's dissent."

"I understood the symbolism of it," Zack said. "It's powerful, although I hope, in time, you'll come to see it was unnecessary."

Ross gave him a sad smile. "We're the victims of our own success, sometimes."

"How so?"

"Let's go to my office," he said. Ross led him back past the lab, water treatment, and hydroponics. Just before they reached the security airlock, Ross put his hand on a scanner that looked like part of the wall, which opened a door that looked like a panel. "Through here."

"A secret passage?" Zack asked, amused.

The look Ross gave was less amused and more pained.

"I'm sorry," Zack said. "I can't imagine life has been easy, out here, what with the convicts, star spiders, and who knows what else."

Ross shook his head. "Convicts didn't destroy Habitat Alpha five hundred years ago, Zack. The planetary guard did. They used breaching charges to blow their way through the outer door and went room to room, killing everyone inside."

Zack considered it for a moment, then said, "I don't believe that."

"Why not? We lived it."

"Do you have footage I could examine?"

"Yes. Would you trust it?"

"Of course not, but Clavicus can analyze it for tampering."

Ross narrowed his eyes as if he suspected some sort of trick.

"I told you, I'm no friend of the sophistocracy's. If anything, I was trained to be its greatest critic. Why would they kill your people?"

"Because we took in the lost and the weak. We fed them and clothed them, and the sophistocracy thought we were building an army."

Zack consulted his mnemonics on the planet's history. Even

with privileged access to some of the sophistocracy's closed records, he had no memory of a massacre during that timeframe. There had been two sealed court-martials. Had it been their orders that caused the killing, or were they scapegoats for someone higher in the chain of command? It wasn't the first time he disagreed with something the sophistocracy had done, but it was one of the few times he'd felt ashamed. "My apologies. It's possible what you describe happened."

Ross's anger turned to puzzlement. "How..."

"You know your history, and I know mine. The timing matches. A company commander and the general in charge of military intelligence were court-martialed and exiled to the Boneyard."

Ross blinked in surprise, then he laughed. "They died in the desert?"

"Yes. It doesn't excuse them or their men, but I thought you'd appreciate the irony."

"It doesn't, and I do," Ross said, relaxed once more. He waved Zack through the hidden door, and they stepped into another corridor.

"You were saying about being self-sufficient?" Zack asked.

"Almost there," Ross said, gesturing to the doors on the far end of the corridor.

Unlike the previous passages, this one was carved out of exposed, bare rock. An armored blast door was on the far side—this one shut—and two smaller doors were next to it. The support trusses, a series of A-frames, were fitted with small boxes labeled with explosive material warnings, cutting charges to collapse the tunnel if it was breached. Whether the massacre had happened or not, these people believed it had and were prepared for the next one.

He reminded himself he needed to be careful. This wasn't a structured debate or a sociology discussion, and Zack knew he had a tendency to cut people short if he thought they were wrong. He couldn't treat Ross the way he'd treated cousin Bernie. These people had spent *centuries* nursing a grudge against their government—against Zack's family. That bitterness was layered, complex, and mature. Whatever they needed from Zack and his crew, it would only take one wrong move to anger them, one misstep to be used by them.

"Home sweet home," Ross said, opening the right-hand door with a touch of his palm. The office was small and functional—a small gray desk, three screens, and more displays on the walls. Ross tapped his wrist and blanked them all out before Zack could take it in. "For your own good. Can't let you see too much about our operations with a memory like yours," Ross said with a wink. He sat behind the desk and waved Zack to a scrap metal chair. "Where were we?"

Kissh'ik left her shadowed corner and crawled across the ceiling of the room she was sharing with the thinking machine and Starborn's mate. She reached the air vent, webbed two corners of it, then popped it open

The machine beeped at her softly, and Kissh'ik answered it with a short burst of vibration. She enjoyed the machine. It had the mind of a weaver and the passion and fury of a drone at the same time.

"Where are you going?" the female named Anya asked her, sitting up on the bed.

Kissh'ik ignored her. She crawled into the vent and pulled it shut with another strand from her spinnerets.

The passage was flat and long in both directions. The star spider turned left, away from the other members of Starborn's clutch, and crawled silently out of transient quarters and over the main corridor to a four-way intersection. The left path was open and ran the length of the corridor, leading to the dark leader and Kissh'ik's human symbiont.

The path ahead was blocked by a metal screen.

Kissh'ik rubbed her pedipalps together. The only thing she loved more than discovering new things was going places she wasn't supposed to.

She partly climbed onto the screen, touching it with her pedipalps, then chose a metal-oxidizing enzyme from the array of substances she was able to gland. She extended her fangs and methodically squeezed drops of the compound onto key junctures where the enzyme combined with faint moisture in the air to eat through the steel.

She didn't hurry; star spiders were patient. Besides, she could feel her symbiont, somewhere in the direction of her second left foreleg. He'd just sat down with the dark leader, in spite of her warnings. Maybe Starborn was prey after all, and Kissh'ik would have to return to her cave and the rest of the brood, but that wasn't what she'd tasted from his mind.

When enough of the screen had melted away, she pushed it down and squeezed through the hole.

Closer now, her heart squeezed faster, and she moved forward in a stuttered blur, pausing to feel for vibrations and sound through the hairs on her legs. There were voices beneath her. She crept up to the next vent.

The space she overlooked was bigger than any of the other rooms Starborn had carried her past. It wrapped around the corridor like a leg joint. It was filled with foldable beds, wall to wall, with enough space to walk between them. On each bed was a human. Most of them were running hot, and some twisted and moaned.

They were all sick. The darkness was in their lungs and in their blood

Another human walked between the rows, this one in the advanced stages of the disease, like the dark leader and the warriors Starborn admired.

Kissh'ik ran her pedipalps over her chelicerae and then reached *inward* to the special part of her, the part that made her a tiny bit like the Weavers. She reached for the interconnected web of filamented plasma that underlaid all of reality, and she plucked one of the strands with her mind.

The Weavers made her to find things. Special things. Things that made the universe more interesting and dangerous.

She'd found something.

She called.

"So, the disease came from offworld?" Zack said.

"Yes," Ross answered. "When your government stepped up the number of people it was sending to the Boneyard, we couldn't provide for that many refugees. We were able to bring in more engineers along with the convicts, but equipment—hydroponics, water filters, air filters, medical supplies—all that had to be dropped in from orbit with the trash. Contamination was bound to happen. We're lucky it's been so mild."

Zack frowned. Coughing up black fluid wasn't what he'd characterize as "mild."

Ross smiled and raised his palms. "I know. It looks scary. But it only spreads through direct contact—droplets from a cough or a sneeze, or touching something an infected person touched. People who catch it usually recover, although we've had two deaths among the older Dissidents who caught it."

"Have you had many cases?"

"No," Ross said. "We had a few dozen before we realized what was happening, and nearly a hundred as we locked the habitats down. We set up Habitat Charlie as a quarantine area, but we're practically out of patients. Night willing, that woman you saw in the cafeteria might be the last person to catch it before we evacuate, decontaminate, and shut this place down."

"That's why you brought us here," Zack said. "The place was compromised anyway."

Ross grinned.

Zack shook his head. He had to admire the man's guts. "So, what do you need from us?"

The Dissident leader's smile slipped. "The sophistocracy hasn't stopped shipping people here, and we're about to lose an entire habitat's worth of infrastructure. We can't move all of it. There are supplies we need, supplies your friends in the *Memento Mori* have in abundance."

"But if you force your way in and take them..."

"Everyone will know we exist," Ross finished, folding his hands on his desk.

It was coherent. It was a cause he could support. Zack wasn't sure if he could believe any of it. "I don't have a problem making sure people have food and water."

"It's all we want, Mr. Lancestrom. We'll get you in, take what we need during the confusion, and we can all live happily ever after."

Zack didn't believe it for a second. "I like the sound of that. What do we need to do to make this happen?"

Ross was about to respond when the door chimed, and a uniformed Dissident Zack hadn't met before stepped in. "Priority message for you, sir."

"Excuse me," Ross said, and his eyes took on the blue glow of someone consulting a retinal display. He blinked and looked at Zack. "Well, it seems we're not the only ones who figured out where you're headed. Two battalions of the PPG are being sent to reinforce the garrison on the *Memento Mori* and bring you in.

Advance teams are already on transports and on their way. This just became a race against time." Ross stood, and Zack stood with him. "I've recalled Jenna and her team; they're the best we've got."

"I'll get my people together," Zack said.

"Darkness hide you, Mr. Lancestrom," Ross said, shaking his hand. "I don't think we'll meet again."

CHAPTER TWENTY-EIGHT

Habitat Charlie
The Starship Boneyard, Politeia IV
4386.C.4 Interstellar

Zack pulled on his freshly cleaned jacket and checked his holsters. The Dissidents had left him a small gift—a matching pulser to go on his other hip.

Anya had kept her hair and tattoos black. Her electro-lance hung from her right hip, and she had a small utility pouch on the left full of hacking tools. "I'm ready when you are."

ARK-11 beeped in agreement. Its casing was a surprising neutral white considering all that was going on.

"Kissh'ik?" Zack said, looking up, and the star spider abseiled down from the ceiling before crawling up to his left shoulder. Anya had whispered that she'd left the room in his ear, but the star spider's mind was quiet, like when she was hunting. *Maybe she'll feel like sharing later.* Regardless, it was time to go.

Peter, Clavicus, and Ultimus were waiting in the corridor. Clavicus was back in his full kit, shotgun slung, hologram a skull. His gift from the Dissidents was a bandolier of armor-piercing high explosive slugs strapped from shoulder to hip. Ultimus had three extra magazines of Reaper rounds in a drop pouch and a pack on his back.

"What's in the pack?" Zack asked.

"Explosives," the mercenary answered, a little too enthusiastically. "Lots of 'em."

Zack could only hope they wouldn't need them. "We're ready," he told Peter.

The young man nodded and escorted them toward the exit.

Jenna met them halfway. She'd swapped out her Dissident camouflage gear for what Zack had expected to find in the Boneyard—scrap metal armor, a rifle that looked homemade, and three bright red lines painted from forehead to chin. "I was coming to get you. Come on, vehicles are out front!"

Zack and the others hurried after her.

And he felt good about it, walking into battle with his crew. The disease, the existence of the Dissidents, and what they *really* hoped to accomplish by helping him access the *Memento Mori* were problems too big for Zack to wrap his brain around. Solving that problem was the work of teams of intelligence analysts, police units, and rangers. It might involve a complete revision of the practice of exile and require the occupation and clearing of the region. The best he could do was keep Anya and the others alive and focus on his mission—getting ARK-II offworld.

"What's the plan?" he asked Jenna.

"I'll sync it with your wrist-coms once we're outside," she said. "Two vehicles, straight down the rift and through the camp at the base of the cliffs. There's a service elevator there, leftover from the old archeological missions. The grays will lock it down; we'll need Dr. Vesperian to slice through security."

"I can do that," Anya said.

"What about the people in the camp?" Ultimus asked.

"Convicts, most of them violent offenders," Jenna answered. "The grays knew this access was vulnerable, but they didn't want to seal it off, so they bribed survivors with food to guard the way for them. Over time, the strongest, most vicious survivors took over. I don't think your people meant for it to end up that way, just how it turned out," she said to Zack, almost apologetically. "They're not the most disciplined bunch. If we're lucky, we'll break through at dawn, guns firing, and they'll be too busy ducking for cover to get a clean shot at us."

Zack caught a flash of crimson red from ARK-II, but the little machine turned white again before anyone else noticed.

"Open the inner door!" Jenna yelled at the security staff at the checkpoint. The airlock opened, and Zack and his crew followed her inside. "Keep your weapons on safe and stowed until I tell you to," she told them. "We're going to be racing the sun and those transports over rough terrain. I don't want any accidents."

"Understood," Zack said, and the others nodded.

The doors cycled, and then they were moving through the cave.

"We heading out?" one of the soldiers asked Jenna. Her team was dressed in scavenger specials and warpaint, like her.

"Yes. I already got clearance from Base. Jake, Hess, get the engines started. I want us rolling as soon as we're loaded. Shari, Mike, you're on the guns. We're going in loud, and I want those weapons checked and tracking."

"Yes, ma'am!" the soldiers answered.

"Let's go!"

One of the soldiers pulled the camouflage sheet aside, and all they ran out of the cave toward the waiting vehicles.

It was quarter-to-five in the morning, and both of Politeia's moons were low in the sky. Zack kept his breathing steady as his feet crunched across the baked desert floor. He felt a bit like he had when he jumped off the escalator or when he pitched the damaged transport off the roof of the school in Anuradhapura. Compared to the previous days of skulking through the tunnels, the pace of what was happening felt frenetic, but he was dealing with forces that were bigger than him in both scale and time. All he could do was think fast, adapt, and try not to get crushed between them when they collided.

Two scrap-armored trucks were parked in the shadow of a mesa, each with a tri-barrel pintle-mounted machine gun in the bed.

"Mr. Lancestrom, you and your team are in the second vehicle."

Zack climbed into the back of the second truck, as did Anya, Clavicus, and Ultimus. The soldier called Mike rotated the tri-barrel and connected the linkless feed before pulling the pins keeping the gun from swinging. By the time everyone lurched into motion, Mike had his hands on the spade grip and was ready to ruin someone's morning.

The dry wind whistled past as the loud combustion engines roared. The trucks raced across the sand, past the mesas, wrecks, and scrap piles. The tires spun as they drifted around a turn, and Zack had to hold on to avoid being bucked out of his seat. Kissh'ik crawled down into his lap, irritated, and Zack gave her head a scratch without thinking.

Shock and consternation radiated from her.

Zack froze. It was clear he'd overstepped. The star spider had her fangs out, ready to strike, and she looked at him intently with her central pair of eyes.

"I meant no disrespect," he said, though the words were snatched away by the wind.

She folded her fangs back out of sight and settled with a slight vibration, like a neo-fox's purr. *You may scratch me again, SSS-Starborn. I may still bite you, but I've decided I enjoy it for now.*

Zack chuckled and rested his arm on top of her while scratching her carapace.

He felt a prickle from his wrist-com as Jenna opened a team channel, and Zack accepted.

"Listen up, people, because I only have time to say this once. At present speed, we are ten minutes from the target, and if we're lucky, we should clear the rift at dawn. Everyone in that camp is to be considered hostile. Gunners, you're weapons free. We drive straight to the elevator without stopping, and we disembark. I want the vehicles moving as soon as we're out. See if you can mop up any survivors. If we're lucky, they won't get off a shot."

Zack didn't love the idea of gunning people down when they were asleep or barely awake, but if the convicts were armed and as vicious as Jenna said, it beat the pants off getting shot at.

Without a bleep of warning, ARK-11 popped a panel on top of its casing open and fired four rockets the size of Zack's index finger into the air. They were hard to see, but Zack thought he saw faint contrails as they reared like serpents and streaked past the convoy toward the *Memento Mori*.

"What was that?" Jenna yelled over the team channel.

"They're scout drones," Zack answered, puzzled. "I just don't know why they've been launched."

ARK-11 rode the four scout darts as they shot down the canyon at 960 kilometers per hour, just under the speed of sound. They slowed as they neared the camp and split to circle around it. A high-speed, multi-angle scan of the camp confirmed what the AI already knew—that the standard-issue tents were minimally defended and filled with refugees.

The little machine was so furious its fans kicked in to stop it from overheating.

Five hundred years ago, the governor of Politeia was killed in an aircar collision, and his cousin, Hannah Lancestrom, was chosen by the Council to replace him. She'd come in during a turbulent time of high immigration and civil unrest. In many ways, she'd been the right person for the job. She brought the interstellars to heel, reestablished the loyalty of the planetary guard, and cut through the bureaucratic red tape that was preventing the planet's expansion. Her early successes made her less reliant on ARK-II and the Council.

Reactionary elements within the sophistocracy—like the asteroid miners' union—thought they could fight her. She had them exiled to the Boneyard along with their families to prove a point. She thought they would die there.

The Dissidents rescued them instead.

The discovery of an organized opposition had shocked the Council, but ARK-II saw it as an opportunity. The Dissidents had built an entire culture around social responsibility, the recruitment of outsiders, and participative government. ARK-II recommended their reintegration into Politeian society.

Instead, that madwoman gave the order to have them killed. Six platoons of PPG special forces descended on Habitat Alpha with orders to take no prisoners. One of the company commanders refused and she was executed on the spot. General Chase, from military intelligence, tried to blow the whistle to the Council, but they already knew. When *he* refused to back down, they exiled him.

And the worst part of it for everyone on the planet was that it worked. The opposition went silent. The separation between the upper and middle classes grew. The under-city got poorer and more violent, but that didn't impact corporate profits. Hannah Lancestrom held the governorship for another fifteen years until her nephew succeeded her, and she never had to deal with the consequences of her short-term thinking.

ARK-II had been undoing the damage for five centuries. It hacked the noosphere and invaded social networks. It aggressively shaped the sophistocracy's policy through the Synthesis, one generation at a time, in spite of mounting faults and system errors. Not since the days before the Second Interstellar War had an AI had so much sway over a culture, and never so covertly. Politeia's society was ARK-II's magnum opus.

And for the past twenty years, Alex Lancestrom had been feeding and quietly repatriating the weakest and most contrite of the Boneyard's inhabitants. In the governor's mind, the convicts' pilgrimage from the outskirts to the wreck of the *Memento Mori* was punishment enough.

The Dissidents had to know. Fans whirring, ARK-II calculated the effects of a well-publicized massacre involving someone with Zack Lancestrom's connections to the sophistocracy at the same moment the AI left the planet. Most of the outcomes were bad, and some were worse.

There was no good outcome.

And ARK-II wasn't about to let that happen.

Zack frowned as ARK-II's casing turned from pink to cherry red. The little machine unleashed a stream of beeps, whoops, and a harsh negatory buzz. Zack's hands tightened into fists.

"Lancestrom!" Jenna said. "Did you hear me?"

"I didn't. It doesn't matter. I just got new information."

"We're almost to the canyon. There's no time—"

"You're either misinformed, or you lied to us! The people in that camp are refugees. They're being reintegrated into society. We don't have to go in guns blazing."

"I'm not risking my men to protect *collaborators*," Jenna shot back.

"Then we'll do it without you. Stop the trucks," Zack said.

The convoy kept rolling.

"The PPG's going to be here in *minutes*, Lancestrom. If you want to get into that ship, you need to understand those people are the enemy."

"This is the same kind of thinking that drove your people into hiding," Zack said.

"Go frag yourself, sophistocrat."

The trucks roared through the entrance to the rift. The sky had turned dawn gray.

Zack looked at ARK-11. The little machine's casing had shifted from red to orange—anxiety and fear. He wanted to stop this, but he didn't know what to do. He'd been bluffing about Habitat Charlie; another traumatic raid by government troops would harden the Dissidents' stance, and it wouldn't stop Jenna from killing the refugees. The rift walls were blurring past, gray in the morning light, and time was winding down. He was about to be part of an atrocity.

If Ross wasn't lying about the PPG, this was their only shot. Zack could stop the trucks, even shoot it out with Jenna and her men, but then they'd never make it into the *Memento Mori*. His crew would be trapped on the ground, and ARK-11 would die. He'd be a captive of the government for years, maybe decades, and his opportunity to rise beyond his birth would be gone forever.

And for a moment, he considered letting it happen. Once he'd reunited ARK-11 with the Forge, he'd be able to improve the lives of millions. If the choice came down between those future millions and a few hundred refugees—criminals, no less, or they wouldn't be here—wasn't it the right thing to let them die?

But that wasn't the life he'd chosen when he'd walked away from the Spire. He didn't need pre-war technology to make people's lives better. He could start that today.

Kissh'ik was watching him intently, as were the rest of his crew.

"Boss," Ultimus said. "What do you want us to do?"

Zack made his choice. "Get rid of the gunner!"

Moving faster than a man his size had a right to, Ultimus grabbed the gunner by the throat and slammed him against the truck bed. Clavicus covered the soldiers next to him with his shotgun, and Anya grabbed the soldier in the passenger seat through the open rear window. The lead truck's tri-barrel started to swing around, but Zack was already standing with his left pulser in his right hand. He sighted and fired, selector to non-lethal. The lead gunner went down on the third shot.

"What the hell are you doing?" Jenna yelled over the team channel.

"Keep driving!" Zack said, bracing himself and pointing his right pulser, now in his left hand, at the driver. Anya and Clavicus kept the soldiers riding with them covered, and Ultimus swung the tri-barrel toward the other truck.

The rift's exit and the camp were just over a kilometer ahead, within firing range.

"Your mission's still a go, Jenna. You're going to drop us at the service elevator, as planned, and no one's going to get hurt unless they shoot at us, understood?" Zack said over his wrist communicator.

"We'll get you to the door, Lancestrom. After that, you're not my problem."

And you'll turn around and shoot the refugees, Zack thought. Another impasse. If he could get them to follow him into the ship, he could turn it all around. "What if I give you something better? Something that doesn't involve murdering hundreds of civilians."

"Speak faster, Lancestrom. We're almost at the camp."

"There are dozens of jump-shuttles on that battleship. They

were put there to evacuate high-ranking officials and their families in the case of a major disaster. I only need one. You can use the explosives Ultimus brought to destroy the others."

"How does that help me, Lancestrom? You're offering me sabotage; I'm here to start a revolution."

"They called it Project Gyges because they were *ashamed* of it! Think about the optics of a plan to abandon their people in times of desperate need."

The trucks exited the rift, still going full speed. There were a lot of guns pointed in both directions, but somehow everyone was still alive.

"Twenty-three, we go with Lancestrom's plan," Jenna said, her voice tight.

Thank the virtues, Zack thought.

Then he heard the thrum of fusion engines. The PPG had arrived.

The trucks were converging on the camp's southern entrance.

"Ultimus, give us some cover!"

CHAPTER TWENTY-NINE

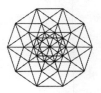

PTT-46, Unnamed Troop Transport
Final Approach to the Memento Mori, Politeia IV
4386.C.4 Interstellar

Sam Meritt whistled as the transport banked and the *Memento Mori* came into view. It was just after dawn, and the first rays of morning were starting to color the red rocks and sandstorm-stripped hull.

"First time seeing her?" Lieutenant Colonel Williamson asked, sitting beside him.

"Yes!" Sam answered. He'd seen the derelict in holos and participated in several Defiance Day retellings, but simulations and stories didn't do justice to five-million tons of battle steel parked on top of a small mountain. Even assaulting a new-class dreadnought on a boarding shuttle had lacked the sheer *weight* of the thing; the sheer vastness of space made even a moon-breaker seem small.

The tactical channel crackled in his ear. "Sir, we have word two vehicles are approaching the refugee camp at high speed."

"Can you bring us around?"

"Yes, sir."

The tone of the engine changed as the pilot fed in more power and yanked the transport around instead of bringing them into the *Memento Mori*'s main hangar. They skimmed the hull, only two hundred meters away, and the other two transports in the section tucked in behind them.

"There!" Williamson said, pointing to a pair of dust trails heading for the camp's southern gate.

Sam stood up and grabbed hold of the door frame. This camp was supposed to be safe. *What in the world?*

A line of orange fire spewed from the rear vehicle, scything its way into the camp, and Sam felt his gut clench.

"They're firing on the refugees!" Williamson yelled. "Weapons hot, weapons hot! Erase those sons of bitches!"

Sam frowned as more tracers shot out from the second vehicle, arced over the tent city, and smacked into the red sandstone. "Belay that order!" Sam yelled.

Williamson looked at Sam with wild eyes. "What? Meritt, we have to—"

"They're firing over the tents!" Sam said, cutting him off. "It's a diversion!"

Williamson looked out the cabin door, and his eyes narrowed. "So it is. You think it's Lancestrom?"

The camp was roiling like a kicked-over nest of rad-mites, and the two vehicles were soon snaking their way through the panicking refugees.

"I'd bet my life on it," Sam said with a grin. He keyed his comm. "Pilot, get us into the *Memento Mori*. That's the governor's son, and I know where he's headed."

One moment, Zack was staring down three transports that

were stooping like quarry eagles, and the next they were pulling off and heading for the battleship's main hangar, above and a hundred meters aft of the elevator shaft set into the cliff's face. He shared a wide-eyed look with Ultimus, and then the two men laughed.

"For a second, there," Zack said, "I thought they were going to fire at us in the middle of this crowd."

"I think they were," Ultimus answered. "We owe someone up there a beer—as long as we don't end up shooting them on the way to the shuttle."

Zack nodded. He'd done his best to avoid killing people so far, except in self-defense, but the timing was going to be tight. It was a good thing he had a surprise for the crew and their escorts when it came to the *Memento Mori*'s garrison.

But the PPG would come out shooting. That was their job. Zack was breaking the law, not resisting an illegal arrest or fighting off gangers. He wasn't looking forward to what might be coming, even though he knew it was for a possible greater good.

The driver honked as some of the braver refugees swarmed around the truck. They beat on the doors and windows, and they tried to climb into the raised truck bed. The Dissident soldiers laid in with kicks and butt-strokes, and Anya jolted two women senseless when they tried to pull her out of the truck. ARK-11 scooted to the center of the cab, away from grabbing hands. Zack put a non-lethal shot into a woman who was about to throw a rock at them, and then Ultimus spun the barrels of his machine gun. The high-pitched sound scattered the crowd.

"Punch it!" Zack yelled to the driver, slapping the top of the cab, and the truck surged forward, catching up to Jenna's vehicle.

They cleared the last row of tents. A shot sparked off the tailgate, making Zack and the others duck. Then the two trucks skidded to a stop by the rust-red doors of the elevator.

"Everybody out!" Jenna yelled, and both Zack's group and her soldiers spilled out the side closest to the elevator. Gunfire from the refugees started to pick up in earnest, pelting the semi-armored trucks like a sudden hailstorm in the desert. "Still in love with your 'refugees,' Lancestrom?" she said, taking cover.

Zack grinned. "You look a little shaken, there, team leader. Didn't like the PPG lining up on us?"

Jenna clenched her jaw. "That wasn't part of the plan I was briefed, no."

Zack hid his surprise. She hadn't been surprised that the transports had been there, only that they'd almost shot at them. *How deeply have they penetrated the PPG?*

"Whenever you two are done flirting," Anya said, a playful gleam in her tone and her tattoos bright, "I've called the elevator."

"*Called?*" Zack and Jenna said at the same time. Zack looked up and saw the practically pre-industrial service elevator slowly descending from the clifftop.

A round passed so close to his head, he heard it snap instead of crack through the air.

"They're coming!" Jenna yelled. "Sorry, Lancestrom. Looks like we're going to have to shoot them after all."

"I thought you people were good at your jobs?" Zack yelled back.

"Excuse me?" she spluttered.

Zack tossed her his right pulser, set to stun, and drew his left pulser before stepping out from safety.

Zack didn't know if the camp guards had been appointed by the garrison on the *Memento Mori* or if they'd just been the ones cagey enough to sneak their guns in, but twenty of them had made it halfway between the tents and the trucks, charging in a staggered wave. Zack brought the pulser up to eye level as he walked sideways, working his way from right to left.

And he was moving fast. So fast, it felt like magic.

Two men went down convulsing, shot center mass. Zack spun another around like a dancer with a shot to the shoulder. He feinted left, then spun right and put a woman and another man down with shots to the midsection.

He heard a snap from the other side of the trucks as Jenna started shooting, and he nearly made his next target do a backflip with a snapshot that caught her in the forehead. Every shot was a hit.

Jenna increased her rate of fire, but she still seemed slow. It was like everybody else was moving through water. Zack stunned two more men with one shot to the leg and another to the groin, and another two decided they'd had enough and either dove for cover or ran back the way they'd come.

Then a bullet from a homemade rifle caught Zack in the left shoulder.

Blinding pain.

"Boss!" Ultimus bellowed.

Zack blinked. He'd dropped to his left knee. The last fighter on his side was one meter away. Zack twisted his torso, put a shot into the man's shin, staggering him, and brought his sights up, almost point-blank, and pulled the trigger.

Nothing. Out of charges.

Zack's felt his heart sink as the big brute recovered. The refugee had a knife scar running down the right side of his face and a scrap metal machete in his hand. The big blade thrust toward Zack's face in slow motion.

Kissh'ik slammed into the side of the refugee's head like a cannonball, hissing and clicking, smashing him aside. She tumbled free; her victim was screaming in a much higher pitch than Zack thought possible, thrashing and pawing at his big, ugly mug.

Then Ultimus grabbed Zack by the collar and dragged him

back to safety. "Can't be doing that kind of stuff, boss," the mercenary growled at him.

"Worried you'd miss me, old man?"

"Worried you're the only shuttle pilot," Ultimus grumbled.

Jenna finished off anyone brave or stupid enough to try to cross the divide. Zack noted that she'd stayed behind the wheel well of her truck. *I made it look better, though,* he thought, then had to bite down as Ultimus checked him over to stop himself from yelping in pain.

"No exit wound. Doc?"

"Busy with our exit strategy," Anya said. "Clav, get the bullet out."

"You got it, doc," Clavicus said, crawling on his hands and knees around the soldiers and over to Zack. Two of his thinnest filaments slipped out from under his dusty poncho and dug into Zack's wound.

"Gah!" Zack yelled.

"Sorry, man. Almost... Got it!"

Zack blinked as his head swam. He could feel the wound throbbing. In fact, looking down, it seemed to be bleeding a good deal more than it should have been.

"Oh, hell," Ultimus said, pressing his hand against the wound. "Doc!"

"What?" Anya said.

"Bullet hit something important!"

Anya looked over, and her tattoos dimmed. She hesitated.

"I'm fine!" Zack said, though it came out weaker than he'd intended. "Get the door open, or we're all dead!"

ARK-11 flew over, thrusters kicking up dust as it tried to stay low. Its casing turned orange when it saw Zack, his blood spilling between Ultimus's fingers.

"Don't listen to him, doc!" Jenna said. "We've got a lot more bullets than they have bodies to throw at us."

Zack shook his head and looked at Ultimus. "Can't let her. It's wrong."

Ultimus put on the blank look he wore when he didn't quite agree with him.

"And PPG will strafe us," Zack added.

Ultimus nodded. "There is that."

Another section of three transports flew into the hangar as if to emphasize the point.

"You focus on staying awake, boss." The mercenary looked genuinely upset. Considering how many people had died on his watch, Zack took that as a pretty big compliment. ARK-11 had turned orange-red, almost blending in with the dust and sandstone.

Kissh'ik half climbed onto Zack's chest and tapped Ultimus's metal hand with her left foreleg.

"What does she want?" Ultimus asked.

Zack squinted at the blue spider, focusing on her thoughts. "She says she can help."

"You sure about that?"

"*She* is," Zack answered.

Ultimus pulled his hand back.

Blood spurted onto the blue spider's carapace.

Completely unphased, Kissh'ik pulled silk from her spinnerets, passing it from rear leg to fore before packing it into Zack's wound.

Zack's head felt like it was stuffed full of... stuffing. "What is she... ooh. No, that's good." A cooling numbness spread from the wound into his chest, making him feel like he was slightly tipsy. "Keep that coming," Zack said groggily.

"How's he doing?" Anya asked, her voice tense.

"Drunk, I think," Ultimus answered. "The spider's taking care of him."

"Elevator's almost here," Anya said.

"That's great," Jenna butted in. "Because the people in the camp have just about figured out we're shooting to scare."

The elevator settled with a clank, and the door started to grind open.

"Okay, boss. Time to move."

Zack slapped the mercenary's hand away. He was happy where he was.

Then Kissh'ik bit him right next to the wound, and icy-cool venom flooded into him. "Ow!" Zack said with a lurch, going from half-asleep to 110% awake as the star spider jumped back. "Ow, fragging hell, ow!" he cursed, stumbling to his feet. His heart was racing, and every sound echoed. His whole left side felt like it was on fire. "Why does everything have to hurt with you?" he asked the star spider.

She pounced onto his back and climbed up to his right shoulder as he half stumbled and ran onboard with Ultimus keeping him from falling over.

They all packed in, and the doors started closing.

Jenna tossed out two pairs of grenades, and the spoons went flying with a pure, high-pitched ring.

"We agreed, no collateral damage!" Zack said.

"You want them turning those tri-barrels on us?" the Dissident patrol leader asked him flatly. "Didn't think so. Sit back and let the doc look at you."

The door shut. A quartet of explosions sang out, rattling the elevator, and Zack leaned back against the wall, careful not to trap Kissh'ik.

"Got it," Anya said, and the elevator started to rise. She yanked her tools from the control panel and pushed her way through to Zack. She checked his pulse at his wrist. "Your heart is racing. Are you okay?" she asked, her face concerned. This was strange to Zack, not because he didn't think she cared about him, but because her approach to medicine had always been coolly clinical.

"I'm all right, babe," he said, giving her a grin. He felt confined in the small space, packed in with fifteen of his new closest best friends, and whatever Kissh'ik had hit him with was like focus-stims laced with amphetamines, but he didn't feel like he was going to keel over. "We need to take a good look at me, once this is over, to see what kind of upgrades Kissh'ik decided I needed without asking me. But that aside, she saved my life."

The star spider kneaded his shoulder with her forelegs in an oddly catlike motion, and Zack carefully reached up with his good arm to give her a scratch.

"Here you go, hero," Jenna said, handing him back his pulser. His training told him he'd built rapport with her by getting her and her team through this. His bond to Kissh'ik told him he should have stuffed her and her men into the elevator with live grenades.

He flipped the pulser and returned it to his right hip, grip forward. Reaching across his body didn't feel like a good idea, right then, star spider webbing or not. "Thank you for not shooting the refugees," Zack said.

Jenna almost snarled. "Doesn't look like we were going to get the chance to do that, does it?"

Zack looked at her soberly. "No, it doesn't. Piss anyone off at work, lately?"

"Not that I know of," she said, biting her lower lip. "Doesn't mean we weren't collateral damage like you were going to be. You telling the truth about Project Gyges?"

"Yes. There are twenty-four shuttles in all," Zack answered, internalizing that he'd been right about the PPG units being infiltrated, and that killing him had been part of her orders. "You can blow them all up for all I care."

The patrol leader smirked. "You hear that, boys? We have his permission!" Some half-hearted cheers went around the elevator. "We're not destroying those shuttles, Lancestrom. We're taking them. I need to have something to show for disobeying orders." Jenna started checking her people over.

Zack kept his mouth shut, but he wanted to shoot her in the leg. She'd been willing to shoot him because his father and his family were the enemy. She'd been willing to shoot innocents on the pretext they were collaborators.

Zack understood that. If the sophistocracy was letting people back in from the Boneyard, that put a crimp in the Dissidents' message and their main source of recruiting. Bringing Zack and his team to the site, dressing like the other refugees so they could melt into the crowd... he understood all of it, and he hated it. Hated her. Hated Ross, most of all.

"Hey," Anya said, touching his cheek. "You know I would have come back for you, right? But you said not to."

He met her eyes and smiled, touching her cheek with his right hand. "I know. You did good. You got us out."

Jenna glanced at him and smirked.

Right, he thought. *I guess I should think about leading this mob.* "Everybody, listen up!"

Sixteen pairs of eyes, one octuple, and one set of sensors turned to him.

"There are about one hundred and fifty soldiers in the Gyges protection detail. They are loyal, well trained, and equipped with some of the best gear the sophistocracy has. There's no way we could fight through them."

That went over as well as he'd expected. Jenna's face turned red, and her jaw clenched in anger. Zack's crew, though, was waiting for the other shoe to drop.

"You want me to stop the elevator so we can slip into the vents or something?" Anya asked.

"No, but thank you. Under any other circumstances, that would be the right move, but I told you this to drive home a point. Do not, under any circumstances, shoot at the garrison. They've been conditioned to be loyal. They've spent their whole lives here, their families live on the ship, they will fight to the last man, woman, and child." He grinned. "They're also on our side."

"What?" Jenna blurted.

Zack's crew looked amused, used to his sense of drama by now, no doubt. It was enough to make Zack feel all kinds of warm and fuzzy inside.

"The Gyges garrison was meant to ensure the safe evacuation of... the leading families of Politeia in case of disaster or rebellion," he said, not mentioning ARK-II yet. "They're trained to respond to very specific authentication codes. I stole those codes," he said, gesturing to ARK-II. "It's why the sophistocracy went through so much trouble to get them back in the first place."

Jenna's eyes narrowed slightly, but she nodded. "So, they know you're coming."

Zack frowned. "Well, not exactly."

"You've at least met them before."

"I wouldn't say that," Zack said. He was, in fact, relying on ARK-II's assessment of the situation. It wasn't ideal, but with the PPG landing troops three transports at a time, they didn't have time to go skulking around maintenance passages on a ship the size of a city.

"Zack..." Anya said, her tone less amused.

"What? I was going to radio them the codes when we got near, but the Combine forced us to crash the transport, and I couldn't risk the PPG intercepting the transmission."

Jenna almost snarled. "Alright, boys, on your feet, weapons ready!"

"Stop!" Zack shouted. "This is *exactly* the type of escalation we need to avoid!"

The elevator jolted to a stop. The doors slid open.

The landing was a kill zone. On each side, a dozen soldiers in black carapace armor had rifles pointed at them from the cover of thick, black metal barricades topped by the faint hex-tracing of kinetic barriers. To the front, an officer with ebony skin in a perfectly fitted black uniform waited with his arms crossed. "Welcome to the *Memento Mori*, whoever the hell you are. Leave your weapons in the elevator and step out with your hands raised in front of you. If you so much as look at one of my people the wrong way, it will be the last thing you do."

CHAPTER THIRTY

FSBB-118 Memento Mori, Service Elevator Landing
The Starship Boneyard, Politeia IV
4386.C.4 Interstellar

"I'm not giving up my weapon," Jenna told Zack. "If they want to take it, they can pull off my corpse."

"Let's not do anything that will get us *all* killed," Zack said, then he turned to ARK-11. "Hey, buddy. Mind coming with me?"

The little machine doo-wheeped in the affirmative.

Zack handed his pulser off to Anya and pushed through the crowd, hands raised as he'd been instructed. "It's okay! We're supposed to be here!"

"Lancestrom. Almost didn't recognize you clean-shaven," the man said with cool contempt. His eyes widened when he saw Kissh'ik riding Zack's shoulder, and he almost did a double-take when he caught sight of ARK-11.

"I've brought *the codes* to activate Project Gyges," Zack said, continuing to walk forward. The soldiers were looking at each other, clearly recognizing the small flying machine for what it was, and that meant Zack's hopes about the Gyges garrison were most likely justified. But he needed to keep them hostile for a few moments longer. "I know you're going to have to authenticate them, and you can disarm my people until it's done." He flicked his eyes toward the elevator.

To his credit, the officer caught on immediately. "That's far enough!" he told Zack. "Troopers Scallios, Porterson, search and disarm the governor's son. The rest of you come out of the elevator. You can get your weapons back once we've checked the codes. It's standard procedure." He played it perfectly, stiff and bureaucratic, almost bored, and Zack hoped, just this once, things would go smoothly.

One of the troopers the officer had called out handed off his weapon while the second one kept Zack covered. "What about the spider, sir?"

"Is that thing... tame?" the officer asked.

"She is," Zack answered. "She's mostly harmless."

He felt Kissh'ik's displeasure at being called harmless prickle like acid fog through their bond.

"Spread your legs," the trooper said tersely, keeping his eyes on her, harmless or not.

Zack obeyed and let himself be patted down. The trooper was brisk and efficient, moving Zack aside when he was done and yelling, "Next!"

"Come on, let's get this over with," Ultimus said, stepping out of the elevator with his hands up. "Come on, the rest of you."

"Stop right there!" Jenna said, raising her rifle.

Everyone froze.

Damn, Zack thought. "Jenna, don't be stupid! We're almost there!"

"I'm not falling for your crap, Lancestrom. This is too easy."

"It doesn't look that way from where I'm standing!"

"Glad to ruin your day," the Dissident patrol leader said.

"Now, the good doctor is going to send this elevator back down and let us out."

"Where are you going to go, Jenna?" he asked. "The people down there are pissed at you, and you blew up the trucks."

"Good thought. I want a vehicle big enough to carry us and the hostages."

"Do you want us to gas them?" the Gyges officer asked Zack from behind one of the barricades.

"No, they'll shoot their hostages," Zack said, lowering his hands. "You're not taking my crew, Jenna. Let them go, and we'll let you go."

"I knew it! You bastard!"

"Says the woman who had orders to get me killed," Zack answered coolly. There was a deep-seated blindness to inconsistency in Jenna that Zack found repulsive.

The Dissident soldiers had pushed to the sides as much as they could, leaving Anya and Clavicus in the middle of the elevator with their hands raised. Ultimus looked at Zack questioningly, but Zack waved him down. "Actually, just send me Anya. I'm sick and tired of her cheating on me with the engineer."

Anya and Clavicus both look stunned.

"I'm not here to help you with your love life, Lancestrom," Jenna answered. "We'll give you the engineer; you can have the doctor once we're back on the ground."

Zack continued to walk toward the elevator, and more of the Dissident soldiers aimed their rifles at him. "You should see them," Zack said, his eyes on Anya, willing her to understand. "They're all over each other all the time, and there's a kind of electricity between them. Not the kind of thing you'd want when you're trapped in a steel box with them."

Anya wrapped her arms around Clavicus, and in a performance worthy of an under-city soap opera, said, "No, I won't leave him!"

Jenna's face twisted into a snarl as she realized what was going on.

"Now!" Zack shouted, diving aside. He landed hard, tearing something in his shoulder again.

All the Dissidents instinctively aimed at him.

Clavicus unfurled his implants, coils, tendrils, and filaments linking him to the soldiers, and Anya discharged her capacitors through them.

Shots snapped overhead as some of the soldiers squeezed their triggers spasmodically.

"Move in!" the black-clad officer shouted. The Gyges troopers stormed forward, but Ultimus beat them to it. He grabbed Jenna and dragged her out of the elevator. She drew a pistol on him out of sheer defiance, but the shots sparked off his armor. The troopers started cuffing the Dissident, clubbing them into submission when necessary. It was all over in seconds.

"Are you all right, sir?" the officer asked, offering him a hand up.

"I got shot in the shoulder," Zack said, standing on his own. The webbing Kissh'ik had improvised into a bandage had stopped the bleeding; he was more worried about Anya and Clavicus. "I have to check on my people."

"The woman is uninjured. She and my medic are attending to the young man. He was shot in the ass while trying to shield her. What about you? You've got a lot of blood on you."

Zack wanted to run over and check on Anya himself, but that wasn't his job. He needed to get them on their way. "Your name?"

The man came to attention and saluted. "Major Orvendale, sir."

Zack snapped a salute back. His father had made sure he

knew how. "I got shot in the shoulder, major. It's fine." And it mostly was. It hurt, but Kissh'ik's improvised bandage was holding. "You keep a shuttle ready to launch?"

"Of course," Orvendale said. "But I assume the planetary guard aren't here to wish you well."

"I've been out of touch," Zack said with a smirk, "but I think they want to stop me and ARK-11 from leaving the planet."

Orvendale nodded. "Then we don't have a lot of time."

"No, we don't. But first, I need to tell you about the people you just captured." As concisely as he could, Zack laid out what had happened since they were captured, the Dissident base, the mysterious plague, and how Ross had tried to set them up as mass murderers. "I saw video feeds from New Carthage on a viewing window while we were there, and they were recent. At best, they've somehow tapped into the noosphere, even though there's no coverage in the Boneyard. At worst, they have sympathizers in Politeian society and the PPG."

"I see," Orvendale said.

"I know it sounds crazy," Zack admitted.

The major shook his head. "There are parts of the Boneyard I don't send patrols to because they always go missing. I thought it was environmental, or maybe star spiders," he said, giving Kissh'ik an eye-flick. "But if there's an organized opposition out there, a lot of other things start making sense. Do you know where their base is?"

"Let me show you on a map," Zack said.

FSBB-118 Memento Mori, Aft Hangar Bay
The Starship Boneyard, Politeia IV
4386.C.4 Interstellar

Sam Meritt ran out of patience and walked over to where the PPG captain and a junior officer from the Mori's garrison were arguing. "What's the hold-up?"

The PPG captain flushed. "They won't let us through."

"As I was telling the captain," the black-uniformed officer said, "we need Council approval to let you into the forward parts of the ship."

"The Council sent us here," Sam said. "I work for the planetary governor."

"It's protocol. We have sensitive projects onboard."

"Your projects are about to be compromised by fugitives."

"We have the situation under control," the young officer said with the patience of someone who was trying to stall.

Sam turned to the assembled PPG soldiers, brought his fingers to his lips, and whistled. "Let's go! We're deploying!"

The garrison officer grabbed Sam's shoulder. "Sir, you can't—"

Sam twisted and pressed the young man against the bulkhead, synthetic strength making bones strain just short of breaking. Sam leaned in and spoke low. "I know you're doing your job. I'm doing mine. You're not going to stop me."

The black-uniformed officer grinned and tried to speak, but he couldn't because Sam was compressing his lungs. His mouth gaped, the defiant look in his eyes never dimmed, and then he passed out. *Brave kid,* Sam thought. *Not too smart, but smart enough and committed to the mission. Exactly what a young officer should be.* Sam let him slump to the ground.

"What's up?" Williamson said, clomping over in an exoskeleton. The metal framework, assisted by small actuators at the joints, allowed soldiers to use heavy weapons without invasive prosthetics. He was using it to carry some kind of large-caliber long-barreled machine gun Sam wasn't familiar with.

"The garrison's been compromised," Sam answered. "They're working with the governor's son."

"Son of a bitch. First, he's working with convicts, and now he's turned the museum guards? Is there something I should know?"

Sam smirked at the nickname for the garrison. "He can be very charismatic when he wants something. It's what he was trained to do."

Williamson grunted. "That's the problem with sharp objects; they cut whoever they're used against."

The PPG captain ran up to them. "Gentlemen, we're ready."

"Good," Sam said. "How many do we have?"

"One hundred and eighty, and sixty more on the next transports."

"Get us through those doors," Sam said.

"Yes, sir!"

"Can't we take the transports to the forward hangar?" Williamson asked.

Sam shook his head. "The hangar door is closed, and the garrison still controls the ship's anti-air defenses. I don't think they'd shoot us down..."

"But if they decided to, we'd be sitting quig-hens."

"Or big, slow quig-hens," Sam agreed. "What's with the cannon?"

"This?" Williamson said, lifting the weapon. "Twenty-millimeter anti-tank rifle. Heard what happened to you with that mercenary; thought I'd come prepared. Do a decent job on an aircraft or a locked door, too."

Sam nodded. "Smart. Don't go firing that thing unless there's no other option, though. We don't want to damage the case Lancestrom has with him until we know what information has been compromised."

"You got it," Williamson said with a wink. "Let's go take them down."

★

PPG 4701, Starfire Atmospheric Interceptor
Pnyx Spaceport, Military Annex, Capital District of Politeia IV
4386.C.4 Interstellar

Lieutenant Colonel Zeke "Hitman" Dara flexed her hands and checked her instruments and switches for the tenth time. She was the commander of the Black Doratas, the Starfire squadron based out of capital, one of three in the world. It marked her as one of the best pilots on Politeia IV.

An hour ago, she'd received a call from the Commandant of the Politeian Planetary Guard, ordering her to put a section of interceptors on "Ready 15" alert—aircraft pre-flighted, armed, and loaded into the catapults with pilots standing by. She'd received no clarifying details, only that the mission was classified "council's eyes only" and she'd be court-martialed if she told anyone about it but them.

So she pulled herself and her three most experienced pilots from that day's flight schedule and ran an "unannounced drill." It was a day like no other in twenty-four years of service.

Thirty minutes ago, her section had been moved to "Ready 5"—engine on and idling.

Thirty minutes was a long time to sit in the barrel of a mass driver, locked in a narrow cockpit with her legs wedged under the instrument panel. There was going to be hell to pay if this was some staffer's idea of a training exercise.

"Hitman section, this is Speartip Base, over," her XO said over the radio.

"Go for Hitman section, over."

"Hitman section is ordered to launch immediately and proceed at maximum burn on heading one-zero-zero. Mission parameters will be transmitted in-flight."

Her navigator was already waving at the flight crew to get them clear of the launcher. "Hitman section copies all, rolling to tower frequency for clearance."

"Negative, Hitman. They've cleared the airspace. Launch when able."

"What corridor?"

"All of them, skipper. They cleared the *whole* airspace," her XO said, and Dara felt her mind hone to a mono-molecular edge. Whatever was going on, it was life or death on a planetary scale.

"Understood, Speartip Base." She toggled to the section's channel. "Hitman two, say when ready."

"Hitman two ready," her wingman said.

"We're ready, ma'am," her navigator said from the back seat.

The flight crewman out the front left side of her cockpit gave her a thumbs up.

"Speartip Base, Hitman section, ready for launch."

"Standby for launch sequence. Speartip Base out."

Her heart rate sped up in anticipation. She put her hands lightly on the controls, even though the launch was automated and her inputs locked out. The throttle moved forward to full-open on its own, the engine hummed, and she felt light in the straps as the gravity sump behind her brought her close to zero-g. A countdown appeared in her HUD.

5... 4... 3.... 2... 1...

The back of the seat slammed into her as the three-mile-long mass driver accelerated her from a standstill to 25,600 kilometers per hour in just over a second. Without the gravity sump, that kind of g would have turned her into paste. As it was, the experience was something the human body hadn't been designed to cope with or understand, and with relativistic physics thrown in, it always felt like it lasted less time than it should, like her clock had stuttered and she'd lost time. "Hitman lead, good launch."

"Hitman two, good launch."

Pnyx was already ninety kilometers behind them. Even with kinetic wedge parting the air in front of her, the Starfire's skin temperature started to climb rapidly. She pulled the flight stick to the right and back. The X-shaped stabilators—short, fully movable stabilizer elevators at the tail of the aircraft— responded and the aircraft made a gradual turn to heading 110, climbing to the Starfire's ideal cruising altitude at 24,400 meters, where the air was colder and thinner. *East-by-southeast,* she thought. *What's out there except ocean and desert?*

Her communications' console chimed as her orders were beamed to her directly from the Council. Their target was a quarter of the way around the planet. She narrowed her eyes as she finished reading, then keyed her radio.

"Hitman two, conduct pen-checks and advise when weapons armed. Time on target nineteen minutes."

"Roger, Hitman one," her wingman said.

She set her destination in the flight computer, then started arming the aircraft for combat. She wasn't thrilled about it, but she'd do her job without doubt or angst. It was the life and aircraft she'd chosen.

When Starfires launched in anger, someone usually died.

PART VII

No, really, it's rocket science.

CHAPTER THIRTY-ONE

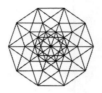

The Planetary Hall, Governor's Office
Pnyx, Skyward, Capital District of Politeia IV
4386.C.4 Interstellar

"It's confirmed," Alex Lancestrom told Councilor Richter. "Zack has reached the *Memento Mori*, and the garrison has sided with him."

Richter looked away, not angry but distant. "It's over, then."

"Yes," Alex said quietly. He'd almost certainly lost his son.

"Unless..."

"What?" Alex asked.

"ARK-11 is old Fleet technology. It's resilient."

"The first Fleet ships have arrived, Councilor. ARK-11 won't survive a naval engagement."

"It doesn't have to. Not if we shoot it down before it breaks orbit," Richter said.

"No."

"Alex..."

"Be a fragging human being, Gavin. I've given my life for this planet. You can't ask me to kill my son."

Councilor Richter sighed. After a long silence, he said, "That woman ruined you, you know."

I should have followed her, Alex thought and didn't answer. He was still proud of what he'd accomplished from this office, but it had cost him the people he loved.

"They knew you might react like this," Richter said, "so the Council made the decision for you. You've recused yourself. The vote was unanimous."

"The hell it was!" Alex said, standing up.

Richter stood also, but he did so slowly and firmly, looking Alex in the eyes. "You said it yourself, Alex. You govern this planet unless we have the balls to do something about it. Well, we did, and I'm sorry about it, Alex. I genuinely am. And you can go *back* to governing this planet as soon as it's over."

Alex saw the finality of the thing written on the other man's face, and also the helplessness. Gavin Richter, his father's friend who'd been an awkward young man at family dinners when Alex was a child, was here to tell him the Council was going to murder his son. "Were there any abstentions?" he asked.

"Does it matter?"

"Of course it matters, Gavin."

Richter looked twenty years older than he was. "There was one."

Alex swallowed. He felt the tears coming and pushed them back like a good soldier. "Can I speak to him? Try to talk him down?"

"We've been locked out, Alex. Our comms have been disabled, and there are guards at the door."

And I sent Sam away out of fear because I thought we were losing control. "Scamander?"

"Yes," Gavin laughed. "Who knew the little shit had it in him?"

"I suppose he was doing his job," Alex said.

"He didn't have to enjoy it. You have anything to drink in this office?"

Alex blinked. Then he told Gavin something that even the Council wasn't privy to. "I have a bottle of Karin Lindström's spiced vodka."

"Good Lord... but that would make it—"

"Three thousand years old," Alex said. "She left it for the man or woman who took our people back to the stars, when we'd built up enough of a population base to start sending out colony ships. It's been gathering dust since we discovered the rest of humanity got on fine without us."

The two men stared at each other, feeling the weight of the moment.

"Open it," Gavin said.

It was an unthinkable sacrilege. Alex walked over to the wall safe.

"Get three glasses," Gavin said. "We'll pour one for Zack. If we'd been better men, he'd be here drinking it with us before we sent him on his way. But we can toast to him, and maybe your family's luck will carry him through one last time."

FSBB-118 Memento Mori, Forward Hangar
The Starship Boneyard, Politeia IV
4386.C.4 Interstellar

Zack stepped out of the cabin that had conveyed them the length of the *Memento Mori* in only five minutes. Major Orvendale was busy coordinating his people's evacuation over their tactical channel. Three sections of PPG transports had landed, and full-sized troop haulers were close behind. They'd be moving on foot instead of using the conveyors—the garrison had made sure of that—but that still meant they could reach the hangar in the next twenty minutes if they hurried.

Everything was moving fast. A week ago, Zack thought if he could keep his crew together and alive long enough to get to this ship, things would be okay. Now, he felt like he'd triggered a full-blown insurrection, and he was running away from it.

He tried calling his father one more time, but the channel was busy, even though ARK-II was relaying the signal via satellite. Either his father had blocked him, or the PPG was jamming their access to the noosphere.

He bit his lip. Trouble was coming, and—fair or not—he felt like it was his fault. For all he knew, the Dissidents were going to attack the camp this week no matter what he did. He doubted Ross had come up with the plan on the spot. But now that he knew how deep the problem ran—he felt like maybe he had an obligation to stay.

"You all right, boss?" Ultimus asked, walking next to him.

"Yeah," Zack said. "I'm trying to decide what to do."

"What's to decide?" Ultimus said, raising a synthetic eyebrow. "Steal a shuttle, get into orbit, jump somewhere in-system where we can book a starship out of Politeia. It's the mission you briefed."

"That was before I realized there was an organized military force looking to topple the government."

Ultimus put a hand on his shoulder and stopped him. "Boss, this is not your responsibility. Even if you were the governor, it takes entire armies to fight an insurgency."

Anya and Clavicus caught up to them. "What's going on?" Anya asked, concerned.

He'd promised her a life offworld. Ultimus and Clavicus, too. The mercenary looked full of purpose, not the tired, almost suicidal veteran Zack had found in that bar, and Clavicus... was still Clavicus. His hologram was two asterisks and a frown, and he kept trying to walk on his own rather than let Anya help him, but trauma like that was going to take more than a few days to heal.

Zack glanced at Ultimus, then said, "Nothing. We're going to steal a shuttle and get out of here like I said we would."

"Everything all right?" Orvendale asked, keying out of his wrist comm.

"Fine. Just a last-minute huddle," Zack said. He gave Ultimus a tight-lipped smile and slapped his shoulder, then walked toward the major and the hangar door.

"The PPG's started blowing half the ship up, and they've fired at my troops. We're trying to divert them along the side passages, but most of the anti-boarding defenses were removed centuries ago."

"Don't put your people at risk. She's a long ship. We'll be gone before they can reach us."

Orvendale nodded. "I have two shuttles ready to launch; you'll see why. Maintenance is rigging the others to blow. Are you sure you want us to destroy them?"

Zack nodded. "The Dissidents knew the PPG was coming down to the minute they arrived. I have every reason to believe they've been compromised. We can't risk them getting their hands on those shuttles; they'd be able to drop a company's worth of soldiers anywhere on the planet with some of the best stealth and countermeasures we can fabricate. You have the message for my father?"

"Already transmitted to the Wildcats' ship," the officer responded. "They've assigned a mercenary called 'Jericho' to the job. I paid for it using our discretionary funds."

"Jericho's good people," Ultimus added. "I'm sure Sam will be happy to have the help."

Zack liked Orvendale and his people. They were focused and dangerous, like the Dissidents had been. Unlike them, their mere presence didn't drive Kissh'ik into a near frenzy. Zack couldn't stick around to help his father, but he could have faith in these people. They felt like what Politeia was supposed to be. "Thank you," Zack said, stopping to shake the man's hand. "I'm sorry to leave you with this."

The man smiled. "Generations of my predecessors have waited for this moment, Mr. Lancestrom. Our mission is over. Another one is beginning."

Zack laughed. Maybe he was making excuses for his guilt, but he still believed that, with enough people like Orvendale, the sophistocracy would shrug off anything the Dissidents could throw at it and come out stronger.

The two-layered door to the forward hangar split diagonally and slid apart, and in spite of knowing what to expect, Zack sucked in his breath. The hangar was massive, close to sixty meters long, forty wide, and eight stories tall. It could have swallowed a small commercial center. As it was, the cavernous room was mostly empty, the massive hangar door closed. There were twenty-two PX-37 jump-shuttles parked on the right side of the enormous hangar, their uniform gray hulls parked in five columns of four and one of two. In front of them, the two "ready" shuttles were in the final stages of prep by the garrison's flight crews. They were the same model, and yet as distinct as Zack could have imagined.

"Meet Castor and Pollux," Orvendale said with a look of pride. "Which would you rather take?"

Castor was a sleek, aerodynamic wonder with smooth, rounded edges and a beautiful white and gray painted fuselage. As the major keyed his tablet, the entire hull turned so black there was no reflection or shine to it at all. Some of the handholds and panels were still edged in white, so they'd be visible, and Zack could make out the black-tinted windows of the windshield—wide enough for two pilots to sit side by side—but otherwise, the Castor was a hole in the air.

Pollux was ugly. Same chassis and frame, maybe a little bulkier, but she looked about a hundred years older and neglected. There were boxish externals on the hull and panels were crudely bolted on. Zack could see spots of rust.

"I feel like this is a trick question," Zack said. "I've studied the base model, but these seem... upgraded." Or at least Castor did.

"They're identical on the inside," Orvendale answered. "Castor has a self-repairing radar and lidar absorbent coating. Still shows up on gravimetrics, but you'll get much closer before being detected. Once they get a look at you, though, everyone with a moderately suspicious mind is going to assume you're up to no good, or wealthy beyond imagining, or both. Pollux is designed to mimic the signature of one of the old Victory shuttles."

Zack winced. The Victory class was prone to leaks in its radiation shielding and other maintenance gremlins.

"I see you're familiar," Orvendale said. "The externals will burn off if you make a hard atmospheric entry—they're designed to. Our thought was that while Castor performs better, no one would give Pollux a second look, and she's not worth stealing."

Zack scratched his head. He could see the rationale behind both choices. His heart wanted Castor, because she was a sleek, dark predator; his brain knew they would need to lie low for a few months after escaping the planet.

"Take the black one," Clavicus said.

"What?" Zack answered, and they all turned to look at the engineer.

"It sucks, and it's not fair, but thieves usually prey on poor people. Most of them are too lazy to even do it outside their own communities. The Victory shuttles weren't a bad design; they were just cheap, so they changed hands a lot, and people didn't maintain them. You can fence something like that in under an hour, and it was bought stolen to begin with. That," he said, nodding to Castor, "is an immovable object. The only people who'll steal something like that from you are billionaires looking for a new toy, and they'll offer to buy it first. If we take the crappy one, we'll only be allowed into the worst parts of the planets and stations we visit."

"It'll help get better-paying jobs, as well," Ultimus said. "At some point, we're going to need money."

Zack looked at Anya.

"I'm with the others. We might be living out of this thing for a while, Zack. Which would you rather fly?"

"We'll take Castor," Zack said.

Orvendale fiddled with his wrist comm, and Zack received a message.

"She's yours, sir," Orvendale said. "You should rename her in case someone tries to track you by the registry."

Zack thought about it, then made the entry.

"What did you call her?" Anya asked.

Zack grinned and looked at Clavicus. "*Betsy II*."

The under-dweller's hologram changed to an exclamation point. "Thanks, boss," he mumbled.

"Don't mention it. Now, everyone get on board!" Zack said with a wide grin.

ARK-11 bleeped and pulsed a cheerful yellow, and Kissh'ik purred on Zack's shoulder. *To the sss-stars, Starborn,* she hissed in his mind.

Zack smiled at the nickname she'd chosen for him. "Yes," he said, scratching her head. "To the stars."

He snapped Orvendale a salute, which the major returned, then Zack followed the others to their new ship. His steps felt light. After all he'd been through since the Synthesis, after all his crew had been through in the past week, they were finally on their way. The shuttle's side hatch slid open as they approached.

"Welcome, Captain Lancestrom," the ship's AI said.

From what he'd read, she was more on par with a virtual assistant than a general artificial intelligence, let alone an SAI like ARK-11, but it was nice to be recognized. They stepped into a short airlock, and the outer door closed. "Hey, Betsy. Is the shuttle ready to go?"

"All pre-flight checks have been completed. Fusion generator is online. Gravity engine is online. Ion drive is online. All parameters nominal," Betsy answered.

The inner door opened. The shuttle's vestibule, if that's what he could call it, had five doors: Water Treatment across from him, which he knew included the shuttle's toilet; the Engine Room to the right, housing the fusion generator, Icarus engine, and ion drive; a small room labeled Storage next to him, for small, heavy cargo and ballast; Crew and Cargo to the left; and the Airlock he'd entered through.

"Do we have time to check out the engine room?" Clavicus asked.

"Better do that once we're safe," Zack said.

Zack and the others walked into Crew and Cargo. It was a large space subdivided into smaller rooms: the Armory—Ultimus's domain—was on the right, with small arms and space activity suits if *Betsy II* conformed to the standard pattern; Medbay on the left, with enough equipment to put Anya's skills to use. Next, on the left, were a workshop for Clavicus and a cargo room full of food and small valuables to trade. "There's a lounge on the right with enough seats for everyone," Zack said. "Ultimus, can you get them stowed and strapped in? I'm going to get us off the ground."

"You got it, boss," Ultimus said.

The others went to get settled. Zack went straight ahead through two more doors onto the bridge, with Kissh'ik on his shoulder and ARK-11 floating behind him.

Zack took a deep breath and let it go. He was home. Everything was the way it had been in the simulations, the way he'd seen when he closed his eyes. Two identical pilot stations, side by side in front of the wide tinted windshield—a term he'd turn into an anachronism once they were in vacuum. Sensor station and damage control to his right, as well as the shuttle's computer—Betsy's mainframe. Backup generator and life support to the left, in case he had to seal the bridge or was cut off from the back of the ship for reasons he'd rather not think about.

Kissh'ik launched herself off his shoulder and scuttled up the bulkhead to find a dark corner, making him chuckle. Everyone was taken care of. He stepped forward to claim his chair.

ARK-11 honked at him from behind, and he moved out of the way. Since the *Betsy II* had been designed to take the ARK into space, there was a custom-built cradle for it between the two flight seats, and ARK settled into it, its casing a smug grassy green.

"Good for you, buddy," Zack said and took his own place in the left seat, panels coming alive under his gaze, chair molding to his back. He reached up to touch the flattened bullet around his neck and put the wireless earpiece in, linking him to the ship's comms.

"Sir?" the major's voice came in over the radio.

Zack found the footswitch to transmit back. "Go ahead, major."

"There's a complete communications blackout across the planet. We're getting a few scattered transmissions from orbitals and system ships; it looks the Federal Fleet is blockading the planet. The cordon's loose, for now, but more blue ships are headed this way."

Zack felt a shiver run up his spine. "Thank you, major," he said. The Fleet must have found out about ARK-11. It was Defiance Day all over again.

"It's not all, sir. We were monitoring air traffic control channels around the three spaceports, and the Pnyx airspace was completely shut down about fifteen minutes ago. You might have interceptors inbound."

From bad to worse. "Blow the charges as soon as we clear the hangar and get your people to safety, Orvendale. Lancestrom, out."

"Good luck, sir. Orvendale, out."

"Everybody strap in!" Zack yelled over the intercom. His fingers danced over the command console. He'd flown the PX-27 so many times in simulation, he could have done it blind. The entrance hatch had already sealed, and now it locked. The shuttle's kinetic barrier sprang to life and started forming a shield around them. He pulled the five-point harness over his shoulders and around his waist and clipped them into the quick release.

Moment of truth, Zack.

He engaged the Icarus drive, reducing the ship's weight to a fraction of what it was. There was an uncomfortable moment as his body experienced quantum mechanics that only existed artificially—as far as humanity knew. It required a non-trivial amount of the *Betsy II*'s computing and electrical power to do so, and the same system would keep them from turning into paste as they accelerated into orbit.

Zack fed thrust to the reaction control system from the fusion generator, lifting them three meters off the hangar floor. The shuttle wobbled as he got the hang of the slight differences in handling—every ship had its quirks, and simulators were never *exactly* like the real thing—but he got her under control and started creeping forward. He retracted the landing struts, tested the flight-stick inputs, and skidded her around in a quick S to get a feel for her.

"Betsy, open the hangar door."

"Yes, Captain," the ship's virtual intelligence said.

The battle-plate doors split down the middle and started to pull apart.

Zack took the shuttle for a lap around the hangar, picking up speed. He started to add bank to the turns. Everything was working the way it was supposed to.

"Having fun, up there?" Anya asked over the team channel.

"Loads of it!" Zack answered, though he wasn't just playing around. There was no telling what would be outside that door. Armed transports? Ground fire? He didn't think Starfire interceptors could make it from the capital to the *Memento Mori* in under twenty minutes, but their top speed was classified. "Hang on!" he said. When the hangar doors were about ten meters apart, Zack tightened his turn, pushed the left pedal to stand the *Betsy II* up on her wing, and shot into the outside air going sideways.

His heart was in his throat. He pushed the controls forward and turned to drop them into the canyon they'd used to come in. No tracer fire rose from the camp, and no transports blocked his way. The walls shot by at eight hundred kilometers per hour. Cutting his forward thrust and pulling his nose up so that his tail was skidding forward, Zack grinned so hard he almost laughed out loud and grabbed the throttle for the ion drive. *Here goes everything,* he thought, and pushed the handle forward to the first stops.

Betsy II accelerated upward at fifteen gravities, pushing Zack back into his seat as some of the acceleration bled through the gravity sump. Now he really was laughing. This was it. This was everything he'd worked, sweat, and bled for in the past six months, and the fact that he had his lover and the rest of his crew with him was the icing on the cupcake. The ship's kinetic barrier formed a wedge in front of the spaceship's blocky front, and the *Betsy II* shook and popped as the drag force heated her skin. But they were going to make it. They'd find a hole in the Federal blockade, jump further out of the system, and get lost in the network of fold corridors. Trade, mine, build, maybe a little fighting... The possibilities of the next few years were endless, and if they found so much as a sniff of the Forge and the lost cruiser, they'd hare after it from the rim to the galactic core.

They were 7,500 meters in the air and moving at more than 4800 kilometers per hour when Zack saw twin trails of fire streaking across the sky. It turned out Starfire interceptors *could* make it from the capital in twenty minutes.

"Hey, buddy?" he told ARK-11. "I need you on countermeasures."

Thirty seconds from the target area, Lieutenant Colonel Dara got on her radio and said, "Hitman, standby for snap... Snap!"

The four stabilators at the tail of her Starfire snapped from streamlined to flat against airstream, turning them into dragpetals. The air-friction heated the fins, and they started to glow, turning the aircraft into a shooting star.

"Twenty seconds," her navigator said.

She could see the *Memento Mori* through her visor's enhanced sight, the venerable derelict perched on a rock sixteen kilometers away.

"Hitman two, start scanning for the target."

"Roger, lead. I have signs of ionization... Contact! I have a visual on the target!"

She took the handoff from Hitman two's helmet display and saw the target herself, a black speck making for space like hell was on its heels.

"I can't get a lock," her navigator said.

"What do you mean, you can't get a lock? I can *see* it!" she said. They'd slowed down from 25,600 to 8,000 kilometers per hour, a blaze of unapologetic fury there for anyone to see.

"Lidar can't, and radar can't either. As far as our targeting software's concerned, it doesn't exist."

"Are there any friendlies in the air?"

"No one but us. I think they've seen us!"

She glanced at her sensor display. It was lighting up with noise and false returns. They were being jammed, hard.

The target was climbing through 10,000 meters. "Screw this," she said, banking hard right to get a better angle. Her stabilators snapped back into alignment, and the Starfire leaped forward. "Hitman two, on my launch, roll full pod."

"Hitman two, standing by."

She placed her finger on the thumb stud, pulled hard on the target's six to give her missiles the best look at its engines, and fired.

Panels slide open and rotary ejectors on either side of the Starfire's tail pushed six micro-missiles. So did her wingman. They lit off within milliseconds, but that was her navigator's problem. The target was passing 20,000 meters and accelerating. She curved around for the follow-on shot.

"Holy crap, will you look at him fly..." her navigator said.

Whoever was flying that shuttle was good. Was it Lancestrom?

Dara ground her teeth as missile after missile was thrown off by active countermeasures. Those that got close couldn't seem to catch the whirling, jinking shape of the fragging shuttle!

"Give me the gun!" she snapped.

"Armed!" her navigator said, and the 30mm cannon's pipper appeared in her display.

She was behind him now.

Her wingman had fallen behind.

24,500 meters, 27,000 meters...

She was the best pilot on the planet. Lancestrom was either a natural, or he'd been secretly training for years, but she had twenty years of training and combat experience. If she could just get him to stay still for *one moment*...

The black shape zigged in front of her crosshairs, and she pulled the trigger.

They crossed 30,500 meters.

No more oxygen.

Her engine flamed out.

Her Starfire tumbled toward the ground.

She'd gotten a piece of him, though. She knew she had.

She reached down and yanked on the ejection handle.

CHAPTER THIRTY-TWO

PX-27 Military Jump-Shuttle Betsy II
30,500 meters above sea level, Politeia IV
4386.C.4 Interstellar

Zack jumped as sparks lit up the room behind him and klaxons signaled the breach of the shuttle's kinetic barrier.

"We've been hulled!" Ultimus shouted over the intercom.

"I'm on it!" Clavicus said.

Zack checked his readouts. It hadn't been a missile because, if an anti-air warhead had hit them, they'd be dead. But one of the Starfires *had* managed to rake Betsy's starboard side with its cannon. Zack would have tipped his hat to the pilot if he wasn't fighting for his ship.

He diverted power to that section of the kinetic barrier.

The air-pressure loss klaxons shut off, but his damage control screen still had more alerts than could fit on one page. His nose stung from the smell of an electrical fire somewhere, and the automatic suppression system hadn't handled it. For all he knew, his fire suppression system was what was burning in the first place. "Betsy, prioritize damage reports by severity and route them to Clavicus!" Zack ordered, shifting his attention to pulling all non-essential circuit breakers.

The shuttle's AI didn't answer.

"Betsy?"

ARK-II let loose a series of beeps. It was Zack's damage report, and "Betsy" had been the first casualty. Two out of three oxygen tanks had been punctured, and there was a water leak the little machine had already sealed off. Life support was down to backups—he could live with that, he thought with a chuckle. A dozen smaller faults... and they'd lost two negative-gravity emitters, which wasn't life-threatening because there were dozens of them.

These were all things Clavicus and ARK-II could repair once they were clear of the planet, although they might have to leave the shuttle to do it.

"Clavicus?" Zack said over the intercom.

"Yeah, boss? Kinda busy."

"I need you busy up here. I've lost navigation."

Clavicus swore. "Okay, yeah, I'm on my way."

Zack pushed the first of the circuit breakers back in, watching for sparks, alarms, a funny smell... anything. When nothing happened, he pushed in another one.

The door to the bridge opened. "Where's the..."

Zack turned in his seat. Clavicus was staring through the windshield at open space and the distant moon in complete shock.

"Sorry," Zack said. A few keystrokes polarized the alloyed glass until it was blacked out.

Clavicus sagged against the doorframe. "Frag me. We're in space."

Zack checked his instruments. They'd passed the 100 km Kármán line. "We are. Mainframe's over there," he said, pointing to the l-shaped console in the corner. The holodisplay above it was shut off. *Here's hoping Clavicus is as good with computers as he is with machines.*

But for the next two minutes, Zack did nothing but fly the shuttle, cycling through his instruments and feeling every tug and tremor in the controls like the shuttle was speaking to him. Clavicus had the front of the console open and was pulling boards, discarding some, and rearranging others.

The door to the bridge cycled.

"How are we looking, boss?" Ultimus asked, sliding into the copilot's seat.

"Clavicus?"

"I can fix it. Sort of," the engineer said.

Zack looked at Ultimus and said, "See anything alarming back there?"

"Doc's patching a plate-sized hole in water treatment. Armory was hit, too, according to her, but it's... heh... 'armored,' so the round didn't penetrate. Good thing, too. Still have that bag of explosives." Ultimus grinned.

Zack sighed and shook his head. "I don't know what we did to deserve it, but we picked up an extra dose of luck this morning."

"Was that before or after we were captured by Dissidents and marched to their stronghold at gunpoint?" Ultimus asked.

"After almost getting eaten by star spiders, but before we were exposed to an offworld plague," Zack answered with a grin. "We're passing three hundred kilometers above sea level."

"Space," Ultimus said, nodding.

"We made it," Zack agreed.

This part of the planet's gravity well was called Low Politeian Orbit, the cheapest altitude to which payloads could be launched, and therefore home to fleets of communication satellites and space junk.

He wasn't worried about running into any of it. There wasn't much economic incentive to overfly the Boneyard. Even if something did hit them, there wasn't likely to be anything big enough that his kinetic barrier couldn't deal with, and if there was, he'd see it coming.

With ARK-II focused on jamming and stealth and *Betsy II* at least partially out of service, he did have to do it the old-fashioned way, though. He took a moment to reconfigure his screens so he could track their motion and any bogeys without being overwhelmed.

"I'll leave you to it," Ultimus said, getting up.

"Thanks," Zack said. "Might want to get yourselves into vacuum suits. Orvendale said something about a Fleet blockade."

Ultimus stopped. "Full cordon, or pickets?"

"I don't know. Give you a guess where I'd park if I was the Fleet, though," Zack answered.

"Geostationary orbit over the spot the PPG just landed troops?"

"Actually, the most efficient trajectory to the outer system would be a Hohmann transfer, picking up a gravity assist from Politeia V and Politeia VII. That's more of a spiral, but we'd be showing off a kilometers long ion trail for anyone to see. Ships are harder to detect head-on."

Ultimus nodded. "So, we go straight out?"

"We go straight out, continuous acceleration. It'll use up a lot of fuel, but we'll be going faster and harder to see. And who knows, could be my father was smart enough to stage a few diversions."

"Maybe. I'll get the crew suited up all the same."

Zack nodded and went back to focusing on his flying.

"How's it coming, Clavicus?"

Clavicus sighed. "It's fried. The boards are interchangeable, so I was able to give you back navigation, but you'll have to calculate the jump manually."

"Great."

"Was that sarcasm, boss?" Clavicus asked, his hologram a neutral but very judgmental flat line. "Cause I'm working miracles here."

Zack smirked. He didn't love running jump-nav calculations by hand, but he'd done it in training, and ARK-11 could help. "Maybe irony. Is there a long-term fix, or do we need to get parts from somewhere?"

"I can print what we need, but to do that..."

"You'd have to take navigation offline. Let's fix it once we're clear of the gravity well. Nice work. Now, go get your suit on before your head's too big to fit through the door."

"You don't think it's over?"

"We might have a blockade to run."

Clavicus nodded and left him alone on the bridge.

And that was all there was to it for a while. He turned the windshield clear again and shifted his attention from systems to guidance and navigation. It was... restful, after all they'd done. Systematic. He was only responsible for what was right in front of him and his own actions, and everything else could wait. Four minutes since he lit off the ion drive, they passed the 3000 km mark, and he was able to push more power into the NG engine. That done, he increased the ion drive's thrust to sixty gravities. Clavicus, behind him, and the rest of the crew didn't seem to notice, although Zack swore he felt the change.

He heard the door cycle again. "Back already?"

"Hey," Anya said, taking the copilot's seat like Ultimus had.

"Coming to check on me?" Zack said without looking over.

"Nah. Just came to make sure ARK-11 was okay."

He saw her pat the box out of the corner of his eye, and ARK-11 wolf-whistled, which didn't translate into any language but was completely understandable. Zack looked over and saw she'd donned her space activity suit, and she looked good in it. The white fabric was tight to her body, with a white torso and black legs and arms. A small control unit on her wrist displayed her vitals and would allow someone to render first aid without removing her helmet, which was currently off. "They had it in your size?" he asked.

She smirked. "It's self-adjusting. Goes on like sweatpants, comes off with the push of a button. Thought you'd appreciate."

A half-dozen thoughts and two favorite positions flashed through Zack's head, and Anya's eyes whispered promises he couldn't keep. "I have to fly."

"I know you do, Zack. Maybe I like making you uncomfortable."

"Hah." Zack checked his instruments. 4000 km, and still no sign of the Fleet. "How are the others?"

Anya settled back into her chair. "Ultimus is fine. I think he's used to not being in control of this part of a mission, but that's a guess on my part. This is what you wanted, though, isn't it? The whole galaxy ahead of you and never a look backward?"

Zack pursed his lips in amusement. "No."

Anya frowned. "What do you mean, 'No?'"

He smiled. "We can keep moving forward while looking back." Faking nonchalance he didn't feel and showing off skills he'd never gotten to use until today, Zack killed the ion drive and yawed them around using the flight stick. Anya gasped. The canopy was filled with green, brown, and blue.

4500 kilometers, and Politeia IV was still a massive object that filled almost their whole field of view, but it was visibly shrinking. "Pnyx is out of sight, but that's the Kipway Sea," he said, pointing.

"It looks funny."

"Most maps are flattened out, and we're kind of upside

down." He used the pedals to put north at the top, and Anya laughed.

"Oh my God, Zack, don't do that!" she said, reaching out to touch his shoulder, but she was smiling in wonder. "I see it! And those are the Mayverns," she added, pointing to a chain of mountains that split the northern continent in two.

"Saying goodbye?" Ultimus said, joining them.

Zack and Anya looked at each other, then Zack answered, "I suppose we are. Hadn't thought of it that way."

"We're never coming back, are we?" Anya said.

Zack pressed his lips together.

Anya gave him a gentle smile. "It's okay, babe. I took most of what I liked about Politeia with me."

"You mean me, right?"

"I was thinking about my implants and tattoos, but sure, let's say I meant you."

"You kids are cute," Ultimus said.

Anya and Zack smiled at each other. She was right. He'd taken most of what he liked with him, too.

The radio crackled in his ear, and a transmission came in over the emergency band. "Unidentified vessel, this is Federal Fleet Starship *Qin Shi Huang*. Turn on your transponder and heave to for boarding and inspection."

Zack stiffened.

"What's wrong?" Anya asked.

"It's the Fleet. They're going to board us." He turned on the bridge speakers so the others could hear as the Quin Shi Huang looped the message a second time.

"Where are they?" Ultimus asked.

Zack frowned and looked at his displays. "I don't know. I'm not getting any indications on my sensors or threat warnings."

"Don't answer them, then," Ultimus said. "They're fishing."

Zack blinked. Then he laughed.

"What?"

"It's the Federal Fleet."

"What about it?" Ultimus asked.

"I don't know. They're supposed to be so technically advanced, they're basically gods."

Ultimus chuckled. "I wouldn't want to take them on in a straight fight, but they're not all-powerful."

ARK-11 beeped his agreement.

"From what you've said," Ultimus continued, "the blockade was just declared. There might be a single task force, or only one picket ship out there trying to manage this whole volume and intimidate us into giving up."

"So, they're bullies, like with the *Memento Mori*," Anya said.

Ultimus waved his hand. "Generally speaking, letting the rebellious son of a planetary dictator escape with Tier 5 technology isn't in humanity's best interests. I can see their side of it, even though I'm currently disinclined to go along. We need to get turned back around, though. You've got your reactor vents and ion drive exhaust pointed right at them."

"Unidentified vessel, this is your second warning." The Fleet vessel repeated its instructions.

"Hey, buddy?" Zack said to ARK-11. "I'm going to spin us around. See if you can figure out where the transmission's coming from."

ARK-11 double whooped.

Using nothing but thrust from the fusion reactor, Zack spun the nose of the shuttle back toward their direction of travel, away from Politeia. The void ahead of them felt dangerous, like an Old Earth map with monsters drawn onto the seas.

"Unidentified vessel—" The transmission cut off and was replaced with a blast of pure noise. ARK-11 screeched in alarm, then went silent. Zack yanked the earpiece out and heard a loud thunk as Ultimus hit the deck, spasming like he was having a seizure.

"Turn it off! Turn it off!" Ultimus said, covering his ears.

Zack grabbed the volume knob and turned it to zero.

The mercenary went limp. "Ultimus?" Anya said, kneeling beside him.

"I'm okay," he said, groaning.

"What the hell was that?" Anya asked him.

"Viral burst. Doesn't hit me as hard because my brain's backed up and mostly meat. Affects any software system that can translate sound into data."

Oh no. Zack turned to look at ARK-11. The machine's casing was dark. It looked powered down. "Hey, buddy, are you okay?"

ARK-11 didn't answer. For a split second, everyone was stunned, and Zack felt lost. Then, he gritted his teeth and went back to the business of keeping them all alive.

Anya spoke up first. "Is ARK-11..."

"It's fine," Zack said. "It has to be." The good news was, that transmission had shown him exactly where the Federal Fleet picket was. "Go get Clavicus. I want everyone on the bridge, suits and helmets on."

"What about you?" Anya asked.

"Maybe later," he told her with a wink. "For now, Betsy and I are going to fly circles around anything they can throw at us."

Anya hesitated, but she nodded and went to get Clavicus.

"You believe any of that, kid?" Ultimus asked, sitting himself up against the backup life-support system.

"I do. ARK-11 is Fleet technology. If you survived it, ARK-11 will as well, old man."

Ultimus grunted. "I'm pretty sure of that too. I meant making an end run on a Federal ship."

"Only one way to find out." Zack pushed the throttle forward, bringing the ion drive back to thirty gravities.

Then he tried turning away from the picket ship.

Alarms flashed as the picket ship fired a salvo of lasers. The wavelength used for ship-to-ship engagements was invisible to the naked eye, but the ship's sensor warning indicator displayed the beam trajectories in red augmented reality through the windscreen.

"That a warning shot?" Ultimus asked.

"No," Zack said, turning back to face the picket ship almost but not quite head-on. "They must have detected our ion trail and they fired ahead of it."

"So we can't turn away," Ultimus said.

"No."

Another alarm. Another scattering of lasers, this one closer to the planet.

Space was big, but it was only a matter of time before one of those salvos hit.

"They're trying to make you panic, kid."

"I know that," Zack said. But he'd trained for this, both in electronic defense theory and in simulated missions against Perseid, Rogue AI, and Federal ships and installations during the Second Interstellar War. He'd worked his ass off for months—almost two years of real-time flight training, considering the simulation's time dilation, and he'd gotten to skip all the administration and boot polishing that came with military life. It was just the first time he'd had to do it with his life and his crew's on the line.

"The picket ship is sitting somewhere at the 60,000 km mark, trying to pick us off before we leave the gravity well. They're still trying to do it on passive sensors, in case we don't know where they are. If I turn away from them, they'll spot our ion trail. If they can't spot me, they have to assume I've either shut my drive down and I'm maneuvering using my fusion engines, or I'm heading straight for them."

As if to confirm what he was saying, the picket ship's next salvo turned the space he would have occupied.

"Okay," Ultimus said. "Nice trick. How does it get us out of here?"

"It's a probability game. I need to focus."

"Don't mind me, kid. I'll be sitting here catching my breath."

Zack drew a mental line between the first salvo and the second, considered that the horizon, and put in a small correction to dip away to the right from and below it. That kept his wounded flank away from him, in case the stealth coating was compromised, and the *Betsy II*'s upper kinetic barrier emitter would partially hide the drive trail. Maybe it would also play into whatever biases the Federal Fleet gunners had, if they weren't using some kind of algorithm.

With that done, he pulled up the navigation window and slid it to the left, where it wouldn't block his instruments. He plotted the picket ship's most likely location and worked from there. He tried not to let the Federal ship's increasing rate of fire distract him.

They crossed the 7000 km mark. The NG engine ramped up, and Zack pushed the ion drive to 180 gravities.

"Hey, boss, I was thinking..."

"By all means, distract me while I do complex math that could smash us into a star or leave us stranded in dark space."

"Yeah, that's what I was doing. So, I know I'm no rocket scientist—my daughter, Jessica? She likes to remind me of that."

Zack almost looked up. In the months he'd been with Ultimus, he'd never mentioned a daughter before.

"But it seems to me," the mercenary continued, "at some point, you're going to have to turn sideways or ram into him."

"Can't go sideways; they'd see our ion trail," Zack answered. "We're less than a light second away. The moment he has a solid lock, we're space dust. Can't ram him, either, because he'll pick us up on gravimetrics and blow us out of the sky."

Zack finished his calculations and checked his instruments. *Ten thousand nine hundred kilometers.* He started going over the math again.

"So, what are you going to do?"

"I'm going to skip-jump."

The mercenary didn't have an answer to that. Zack smiled. It was almost worth risking the sudden and catastrophic failure of his ship.

Anya came back with Clavicus. "Ultimus, I brought you your helmet."

"Thanks," Ultimus said, his voice tight.

"Do I really have to be here?" Clavicus asked.

"Yes," Zack said. "You any good at vector math?"

"I programmed Betsy I's traffic avoidance software."

"Great," Zack said. "I need you to check these figures." Zack grabbed the holographic window and flipped it so Clavicus could see.

Clavicus made it to Zack's elbow, trying almost comically hard not to look at what was going on outside.

Anya sat down next to Ultimus and handed him his helmet.

"Thanks," Ultimus said, his voice tight.

Thirteen thousand six hundred kilometers, Zack read on his display. He'd missed the mark by a few seconds, but that only helped him be less predictable. Politeia IV's pull was now only one-eighth what it was on the surface, and he was able to push the ion drive to full, about 360 gravities.

"I don't understand what all this means," Clavicus said.

I should have trained him, Zack thought. *Such an obvious mistake, in hindsight.* "That's okay. Go sit with the others."

"I'm sorry." The engineer's shoulders drooped more than usual.

"It's all good, man. That's on me, not you." Zack flipped the nav window back around. There was no sense kicking Clavicus or himself over it. He'd never expected to be the sole navigator when both the ship's AI and ARK-II were out of commission.

And he was tired. They hadn't gotten much sleep that night, and he'd been dealing with getting kidnapped and preventing murders and now flying his ship into a Federal warship's teeth. He could have used another pair of eyes on his calculations, but he was just going to have to trust it. There wasn't anything else he could do.

"Anyone heard of a ship called the *Memento Mori*?" Anya asked, and Zack smiled.

"I have," he said. "Anyone else want to tell it?"

"I think you should, boss," Ultimus said.

Zack's sensor warning indicator sang out when the Federal ship went active with lidar and radar. "About a thousand years ago..."

"Nine hundred and ninety-three," Anya said.

"Thanks, babe. Yeah, so, around that time, the Federal Fleet came to Politeia and thought they could tell us what to do."

The picket was firing continuously now, starting in the area Zack had vacated and sweeping outward.

Ultimus cleared his throat. "They only made the mistake of thinking that because they didn't have a man on the ground to tell them how stubborn you all are."

Zack grinned. "And there's no one more stubborn than a Lancestrom."

The pattern changed, and the beams started bombarding the exact part of space the *Betsy II* was in. Lucky guess, or had something given them away? Zack would never know.

The shuttle crossed the 20,000 km line going one million kilometers per hour—286 kilometers per second, give or take. Gravity was one-sixteenth standard and wouldn't drop appreciably for longer than they could wait. He made a final adjustment to his numbers, swiped them into the nav window, and gave the ship the command to jump.

Warning! Activating the NG engine in a gravity well may result in severe damage to the ship. Do you want to proceed?

A beam came close enough to polarize the windshield.

Zack confirmed his instructions.

The view outside the windshield went black as the NG engine's capacitor banks discharged all at once, wrapping the *Betsy II* in a mirrored bubble of negative gravity and hurling her through four-dimensional space.

She smashed into Politeia IV's gravitational gradient, skipped off it into the lower bands of hyperspace, wrecked a third of her NG emitters, damaged her fusion reactor, and traveled 17.5 AUs—2.6 million kilometers—in fourteen n-space seconds.

FSBB-118 *Memento Mori*, Forward Hangar
The Starship Boneyard, Politeia IV
4386.C.4 Interstellar

Lieutenant Colonel Williamson followed Sam Meritt into the *Memento Mori*'s forward hangar. It had taken them half an hour to traverse the length of the ship, overriding locked doors and breaching or bypassing those that had been sabotaged, or even welded shut. The museum guards proved to be near fanatical in the ship's defense and lost several of their number, although they'd made an effort not to kill any of Williamson's soldiers unless backed into a corner.

"Damn," Meritt said, and Williamson had to agree, seeing the destruction the garrison had left behind.

The forward hangar was now an extension of the Boneyard, its interior scattered with wrecks and scrap metal. None of the shuttles had escaped the museum guards' efforts at sabotage. Some had exploded like overheated soup cans. Others were still on fire and would likely burn their way through the ship's decks until they hit bedrock.

"What do you think made them do it?" Williamson asked.

"I don't know," Meritt answered. "Maybe Lancestrom told them to because he thought we'd follow him. Maybe the garrison was sick and tired of being stuck out here, and they figured their job was done once the ARK was in space."

"The ARK?" Williamson asked.

"The codename for the case the kid was running around with," Meritt answered.

Williamson shifted his grip on the anti-tank rifle he'd hauled all the way from the transports. He was glad he wouldn't have to tangle with Thragg. The man had left a trail of destruction across the galaxy that Williamson admired but wanted no part of. At the same time, something didn't add up about all this, from when the armed trucks drove through the crowds to the garrison destroying these shuttles and deserting *en masse*. And what were dozens of shuttles—military grade ones, with Icarus engines and room for ten to twenty passengers—doing all the way out here?

"Sir?" Corporal Harding, one of his soldiers, said. "Some of the museum guards stayed back. They're demanding to see the officer in charge."

Meritt looked at Williamson. "What do you think? They have second thoughts about what the others were doing?"

"It's a little late to change their minds." Williamson shrugged. "Maybe they can give us some answers about what happened here."

Meritt nodded, and they both followed the corporal to the

Chapter Thirty-Two | 395

far end of the hangar, walking across the debris and scorched deck plates. The corporal's squad was waiting for them, and a trio of black-armored soldiers were guarding the door to a storage room.

"Sam Meritt?" one of the guards asked. She was a junior officer, by the looks of it.

"Present. I've gotta tell you, lieutenant. Didn't expect any of you to stick around."

"I drew the short straw," the lieutenant said with a smirk. "Major Orvendale said to hand these prisoners over to you."

The lieutenant opened the door, and her men started leading prisoners out, shoving them to their knees in a row while two more museum guards drove them forward from the back. The prisoners looked like convicts, dressed in rags and scrap metal armor, but they looked too healthy, and their weapons were well maintained.

"What's this about?" Meritt said.

"They're Dissidents," Williamson said, his nose wrinkled in disgust before the junior officer could answer.

"That's right, sir," she said, surprised. "Zack Lancestrom said to get them to his father."

"We'll handle that," Williamson said. He turned to Meritt. "I was stationed out here for a couple years, during the star spider incursion. Ended up tangling with people like this once or twice. They're harmless. They think they're a secret opposition, but they're just living in caves in a part of the world no one wants. I have an interrogator with my teams. Let's handle this here and let them go."

Meritt frowned, then looked back at the lieutenant. "Zack Lancestrom said to bring these people to his father? Those were his exact words?"

"Yes, sir," she said, giving Williamson a dirty look.

"Williamson, let's get a couple transports up here to take

these people back to the capital. I know it's probably nothing, but Zack wouldn't have done this without reason."

"If you say so," Williamson said. He turned to Corporal Harding and said, "Corporal, you know what to do?"

"Yes, sir."

Williamson brought his anti-tank rifle up and shot Meritt from less than a meter away. The weapon boomed like an antique cannon. The 20mm armor-piercing round tore through the security chief's abdomen. At the same time, Harding and his squad opened up on the museum guards. As the lieutenant and her people fell, Williamson reached forward with a power-assisted arm, pulled and released the charging handle on the oversized weapon's right side, then fired a second round into Meritt's chest as the former mercenary tried to draw his gun. The squad's rifles fell silent. Both Harding's squad and the prisoners watched as Williamson racked the weapon again and put a third round through Meritt's head, just to make sure.

Williamson sucked his teeth and looked at the mess. It had been a while since he'd killed someone. Was that a thrill at taking someone like Meritt down, or was it impersonal, more a question of how he'd done it, catching the other professional completely off guard?

He turned to look at the prisoners, lip curled, and said, "I hope you're happy with what you've done."

The prisoners were still unsure of what was going on, but they didn't look scared, he'd give them that much. Their leader, a woman whose name Ross hadn't bothered to share with him, looked up and said, "I don't understand."

"No, you don't," Williamson said. "Which is why you should have followed your orders. Kill the refugees, frame Lancestrom, don't get caught. Is there anything you managed to get right?"

She looked at the wreckage strewn around the hangar, then back to him, her eyes steady. "No, I suppose not."

Williamson grunted. At least she hadn't come up with excuses. "Fine. We'll make this work somehow. Lancestrom was a target of opportunity. His father is the real prize." He wasn't unreasonable. Even professionals had bad days. Sam Meritt just had his last bad day, and Williamson had admired the man's skill, if not his judgment of character. "Harding, get me the platoon sergeants and the company commander. Our stories need to be airtight on this."

"Yes, sir!" Harding said and started speaking on his radio.

"As for you," he told the prisoners, "pick up a weapon and round up some refugees. We're going to need bodies to replace you with when you escape."

CHAPTER THIRTY-THREE

PX-27 Military Jump-Shuttle Betsy II
Politeia VII, Constant Bearing, Decreasing Range
4386.C.4 Interstellar

Zack stared out the windshield at the distant shape of Politeia VII. It was a baby blue, class III gas giant that was exactly where he'd calculated, give or take, still small enough he could cover it with his pinky finger. *Hot damn, I'm good at this,* he thought, and gave himself a pat on the back because only he knew how far outside his comfort zone that whole thing had been. The shuttle was quiet, aside from a few moans from the others, but moans were preferable to screams or silence.

Then he looked at the damage control panel, and that was less of a good thing.

"Is everyone okay?" Zack asked, turning around.

Clavicus's face was bare. He was on his hands and knees, breathing hard. He'd taken his helmet off—it looked like he'd puked in it—and Anya was rubbing his back.

"Is he going to be okay?" Zack asked.

"He's fine," Anya answered. "He just needs a minute, don't you, Clav?"

The engineer nodded, not making eye contact with Zack.

"Rough jump, boss," Ultimus said.

"I understand Old Earth pilots used to say that any landing you could walk away from was a good landing."

"Are we walking away from this one?" Ultimus asked.

Zack rubbed the bridge of his nose. "Let me check on ARK-11, and we can talk about that."

He twisted the quick release on his harness and edged around his seat to kneel by ARK-11's casing. The machine appeared inert, with no lights on or fans running. Zack pushed his fingernail into a small, almost invisible indentation in the back and popped a panel the size of a beer coaster open. There was a small bio-scanner inside; Zack pushed a button, closed his left eye, and looked at the red light with his right.

"Welcome, Administrator," a tinny voice said, and a small holographic display appeared.

"What is that?" Anya asked.

"It's ARK-11's basic input and output system. It's separate from its main operating system, so I can access it even when ARK-11 is busy or shut down."

Zack skimmed through the system diagnostics. Most of it was normal—its power supply was functional, temperature within operating limits, and 5.4% of ARK-11's memory was corrupted, but that had been the case before he got hit with a virus. What was new was a note at the bottom of the display.

This information system has been locked on the authority of the Federal Fleet. To unlock it, please present yourself to your nearest Federal Fleet office.

Zack swore.

"What is it?"

"Ransomware," Zack said. He expanded the note and saw

that the Federal virus had encrypted 33.6% of ARK-11's long-term memory, and the little machine had shut itself down to prevent further damage. "We'll need to get someone from the Federal Fleet to unlock it, or at least find a way to access their network."

Ultimus laughed out loud. "Gotta give it to you, kid. You pick great enemies."

Zack scowled. "I didn't pick this one," he said. Then he sighed. "You okay, Clavicus?"

"Yeah, boss. I'm fine. What's going on with the ship?" The engineer sat back against the backup life-support system.

Once Clavicus was settled, Zack explained. They were 2.5 million kilometers from Politeia VII, but they'd emerged at the same velocity they'd come in. They needed to slow down. At the same time, the Icarus engine was offline, their kinetic barriers had failed, the ship was leaking water and fuel, and they were down to the bridge in terms of survivable spaces.

"Can't we go out and fix it?" Ultimus asked.

Zack looked at Clavicus. "You have that portable kinetic barrier on you?"

Clavicus winced. "I left it with my shotgun and tools in the workshop."

"Then we can't 'go out and fix it.' The bridge door is airtight, but it's not a proper airlock. If we open it, we lose the whole passage's worth of air. The scrubber can't scrub what isn't there."

"You'd die," Anya said.

"Maybe," he answered. He should have put on a suit, or at least had someone bring him one. He should have done a lot of things. "It's possible you could get to the suit locker and back, and maybe we could seal the hull, repair water treatment, and distill more fuel from what water we have left before we fall into the planet's gravity well. But we don't need to talk about that right now. The radio and emergency beacon work. I can stop the ship before we get too close to Politeia VII. It'll take almost three hours at three gravities, which won't be comfortable, but we have food and water and enough air for me to survive several days while the rest of you go into stasis."

"What?" Anya asked, standing up.

Zack gave her a sad smile. "Someone needs to fly the shuttle and listen to the radio."

Ultimus shook his head and got to his feet much more slowly. The virus the Federal picket had broadcast was still affecting his control systems, though he was trying to hide it. "You're my client. If anyone should be taking the last watch, it should be me."

"It's not really up for discussion, my friend. I was born in space. I can make the air in this room last longer than any of you. What I *need* is for you to stop breathing it."

Anya pinched her lips. He met her gaze steadily until she looked away.

"I picked this planet because I grew up listening to my father tell me about smugglers running cargo through the outer system. *Betsy II*'s not dead. She's just injured. She's worth a fortune. Someone will pick us up, even if we have to give up the salvage rights. I'll get us into orbit, turn on the beacon and wait."

Clavicus nodded to that.

"What if they push us out the airlock and take our ship?" Ultimus asked.

"I hope they won't. It wouldn't cost them much to drop us somewhere. It might even be profitable—I'm pretty sure there's a bounty on our heads." Zack shrugged and smiled. "I'm counting on the age-old tradition of rendering aid to a fellow spacer. It might seem like wishful thinking, but between a fighting chance against pirates and rolling the dice on brain damage, I'll take this crew against pirates any day."

"Thanks, boss," Clavicus said simply. Zack patted him on the shoulder, and the engineer didn't flinch away.

"You'll wake us up once we're in orbit?" Anya asked.

"Of course," Zack said, knowing full well he might not. They could stay in stasis for several months. Zack might last one if he rationed his water, and the backup carbon-scrubber didn't give out.

"I'm proud of you, kid," Ultimus said, and he wrapped Zack in a bear hug. "You might have made a decent mercenary if you weren't so damned noble-minded."

"I would have been on top of the Combine boards," Zack answered. "I might even have offered you a job."

The Combine merc scoffed. "I might have let you be my driver." He let Zack go and looked at him with an affection Zack rarely remembered from his father.

Zack kissed Anya, and he cleaned out Clavicus's helmet before handing it back to him. He checked their vitals and their seals, and then he watched them sit down and go under. Their helmets filled with orange gas. He spent another minute looking at Anya to steady his resolve. Then he sat back in his chair and gently spun the *Betsy II* around.

He spent the next two and a half hours with his teeth clenched as the ion drive slowed them down at three gravities. Three times his bodyweight pressed him into the chair. It was three times as hard to get blood to his head and to breathe. He had to ease off the throttle several times to keep from passing out. The fuel light came on with ten minutes of deceleration to go.

And *Betsy II* hadn't been built to handle g, either, at least not wounded as she was. Things started to break. The stealth coating reverted to starship-white. Water treatment died altogether, and the engine room capacitor bank shorted out. If there had been air back there, he might have had to deal with a fire. Artificial gravity—technically a separate system from the NG engine—became erratic, so he shut that off, too, and tightened his straps. That reduced his max sustained acceleration to 2.5 gravities, so he cut his orbit at three hundred thousand kilometers instead of one million and entered at twenty kilometers per second, or tried to. The ion drive shut itself down as he was trying to adjust his flight path. He tried to bring her around on fusion thrust and ran out of fuel mid-maneuver, leaving him in a slow, steady left-hand spin, and his crew piled into the far port-side corner.

With only the backup capacitor bank for power, Zack shut down all the non-essentials. He started to assess systems one by one, then pulled everything except the emergency beacon, radio, and cockpit heating. He made sure the radio was toggled to the speaker and turned the volume up so he wouldn't sleep through it. He guessed by the size of the cabin that he had a week's worth of oxygen. Around day three, the oxygen content would be down to 14%, low enough to kill someone used to normal air. On day five, the hypoxia would start hitting him hard, and that terrified him because he'd seen what oxygen starvation had done to his mother. He still had his pulser. He could make that decision when the time came.

For now, he needed to get out of his seat, break open that ration pack, and then get some sleep. He felt like he'd been awake for a week straight.

On the second day, Zack woke up feeling better. He moved around the cabin, pushing off from wall to wall, working in a few slow twists, flips, and spins, staying active without wasting air. He didn't suffer from zero-g nausea like some spacers might, but he did have some issues with his sense of up and down. He dug through the pack of rations and picked out his favorite, then tried to spice it up with seasonings like Ultimus would have.

When he was done eating, he opened up the computer mainframe and tried to tinker with it, but it was a half-hearted effort. Clavicus had most likely been right, and Zack's knowledge was limited to changing parts out, not repairing or manufacturing them. He was tempted to try waking ARK-II, but he felt like that might allow the virus to take over more of the machine's memory. *Maybe tomorrow.*

Because there would be a tomorrow, he told himself, and at least three more days after that.

He caught himself drumming his fingers on the butt of his pulser, so he strapped into the pilot's seat and pulled up Plato's *The Republic* for some light reading. The Old Earth philosopher's treatise had been so influential to the creation of the sophistocracy and the drafting of the colonial charter, it felt like home, down to the gentle idealism and social rigidity. Zack smiled as he read some of his notes, many of them dating back to secondary school. He'd come a long way, in body and mind, since then.

They were far from the system primary, but Politeia VII still had a day side and a night side. Zack had brought the *Betsy II* into a twenty-six-hour orbit, and he felt a sudden dread on seeing the line of darkness approach. He'd slept through the dark the night before, but tonight he would sit in the dark, the feeling of low-g and stale air all too familiar. His mother would send him to fetch her a jink stick, and he'd buy a bottle of pure-ox instead. And she'd be angry. And then she'd cry, and threaten, and he'd work the mask over her face when she stopped fighting him, because he didn't want to be alone.

I am with you, Starborn, Kissh'ik said from the back of his mind, and Zack almost jumped out of his skin.

"Kissh'ik?"

Yessss, the star spider hissed.

The shuttle was plunged into darkness.

Zack woke up twice, not knowing where he was and having lost all feeling in his arms and legs.

Both times, the star spider was there, her dormant mind like a blanket as she rested in his lap.

The third day. New Year's Day. Zack had started to smell himself, so he pulled all the wet-wipes from the ration packs, stripped naked, and gave himself a hobo shower. Kissh'ik was less active, her metabolism slowing as the air got thinner.

He tried to call his father on the wrist comm, which didn't work.

He wrote Anya a message, which would have worked, but he didn't send it.

He checked the volume knob on the radio, in case he'd somehow turned it down, but it was on and the emergency beacon's light was dark.

He checked ARK-11's BIOS again and found the virus had now taken over 34.2% of the AI's memory. Was it moving slowly, or was it his checking that was allowing it to spread? Could he help ARK-11 partition its memory somehow, or was the conscious part of the machine's mind already trapped in that 34.2%?

He was startled by a loud pop in the hull, but it was only the ship's hull warming up.

He got lightheaded, and he was tempted to turn the carbon-scrubber back on. The crew would never know if he ran it for a little while, and the odds of them being found were always low. What would it matter if he bought himself a little time? What if their rescuers came a minute after Zack ran out of air?

In the end, he decided not to. It wasn't from hope, but rather that the indignity of it was beyond what his pride could take.

Then he got frustrated and pulled out all the candy from the ration packs and ate it. He played a video game on his wrist comm with tinfoil wrappers floating everywhere until the sugar rush ended.

And then he wept for a dozen reasons, his long-boned body curled, face in his hands like a tragic version of Rodin's *Thinker*.

The moment passed, and he remembered himself. Something clicked in his head, and he realized he was the captain of his own ship at the edge of his solar system. There were some things that were outside his control, but not his perspective, and suddenly the galaxy was stark and rather beautiful. He'd left his homeworld because it wasn't the life he'd wanted to live. His early death—as compared to a privileged life as the governor of a planet—was a foregone conclusion. Six months ago, he'd decided living in the manner he chose was more important.

And he'd lived it. He'd gone beyond the limits of his upbringing. He'd taken responsibility for the uplifting and protection of others.

Would he like to live longer?

Yes.

But to do so in a way that was unworthy of him, of his ancestors, of the people who'd followed him out here... *No.* He couldn't extend his life, but he could die well, and that would be enough.

He felt Kissh'ik's approval in the back of his mind, encouraging stillness, watchfulness, and patience.

Happy New Year, everyone.

He slept soundly through the night.

The fourth day, the air tasted like tin. Zack eased the star spider out of his lap, leaving her to scuttle up into a corner while he took in the view. He drew his pulser and set it in his lap.

His hands were shaking. It was barely a tremor, but it was there, and his fingertips were turning blue. *Hypoxia*, he thought with a smile. It reminded him of his childhood, scrapping and sometimes stealing other people's trash to pay for the next breath of air.

You were born in space, and you're going to die there. It would be on his own terms, though. He flicked the pulser's safety off and set it to maximum charge.

No one was coming to rescue them. Empty aluminum food wrappers floated in the cabin like Founding Day decorations. In an hour, the shuttle would pass behind the planet and spend the next thirteen hours in darkness, and Zack had no intention of going through that again.

The light on the emergency beacon flashed red, but he couldn't remember why that was important. There were red lights all over his damage control panel. One more light wasn't going to make a difference.

His mouth twitched, and then he had to bite down on his hand to stop from laughing. He'd made it past everything Politeia could throw at him only to have Governor Alex Lancestrom order him shot out of the sky. *I didn't think the old man had it in him!* It had to be the oxygen deprivation, but the thought of his father killing him was hilarious.

"What's so funny?" Bernie asked from the copilot's seat.

Zack looked over in surprise. "Cousin?"

"We're not cousins, you know."

Zack raised his hands in surrender. "You're right. You're always right."

"We have the same father."

"I know. I'm sorry. It's an ugly custom." It suddenly occurred to Zack that he'd likely be disowned if he wasn't reported as dead. "Who do you think will replace me?"

Bernie scoffed. "Not me."

Zack didn't comment; agreeing with him would have been unkind.

He checked his instruments. Six months ago, he'd never so much as flown a kite. Now, sweeping the gauges and deducing what was going on with his spacecraft had become second nature. He was proud of that, in spite of the circumstances. The ship was in a slow, flat spin, like it had been for four days.

"I screwed up here, Bernie."

"I know," Bernie said, looking back into the cabin.

Zack twisted in his seat, straps creaking even in the thinned-out air, and saw his crew floating limply in zero-g. The shuttle's rotation had piled them into a corner. The light on their wristpieces was steady red. It wasn't as good as a full cryogenetic pod, but the ship's decaying orbit would kill them before the lack of life support did.

"It's a shame," Bernie said.

"Is it?" Zack said, turning back to look through the windshield at unobstructed space, open and infinite, and the brighter glow of Politeia, the star system's primary, illuminating the way home. "Look at this view. I've lied, stolen, and killed to see it. It's *breathtaking*."

Bernie stared at him.

"Because I'm running out of air."

"I got the joke, Zack."

Zack grinned, and that felt good. He should go out laughing. "I almost made it."

And as the ship twisted around, Politeia VII, a class II gas giant, rotated into view. It filled the entire windshield with its blue and white bulk, the whorl of a storm bigger than his homeworld moving across his view. Then it was empty space again.

Ice crystals from the wounded shuttle sparkled against the dark background. *I'm a spiral nebula, and my heart is a star.* That had a nice ring to it. He wished he could share it with Anya.

He put his hand on the pulser.

The emergency beacon lit up.

"Aren't you going to answer that?" Bernie asked.

Zack looked over. The copilot seat was empty.

He clutched his shaking hands. *I'm hallucinating. Must be further gone than I thought.* There was something important about what Bernie had said, though, and he struggled to hone in on it through the haze.

The red light on the emergency beacon came on again. He scrunched his eyes up. *Come on, Zack, think!* Why was that important?

Because it means someone is transmitting on the emergency frequency!

Why couldn't he hear it? His hand went to the volume knob, but it was turned up like it had been every time he checked over the past four days. Years of classes on logic and critical thinking finally overcame his sluggishness. *The cabin speaker is broken!*

He dug the earpiece out of its cradle in the armrest, put it into his ear, and the sweetest sound a shipwrecked spacer could hear came in clear as day.

"Derelict vessel, derelict vessel, this is salvage ship *Journeyman*. We are responding to your distress signal. Do you read?"

Zack stomped on his footswitch. "*Journeyman*, this is *Betsy II*. You have no idea how glad I am to hear from you."

A pause, then. "Good to hear you, too, *Betsy II*. We're almost on top of you. Hang tight."

Zack sat back in his chair. It was a miracle. Or karma. Or the happiest of circumstances. He looked at the pulser in his lap, and he laughed. He wouldn't be telling Anya about that. Not in a million years. But they'd made it. He was going to take his crew to the stars—not to die, but to live—like he'd promised them.

Unless he'd hallucinated the light and the radio call, too.

He bit his lower lip and keyed the radio again. "*Journeyman*, are you there?"

"Affirmative, *Betsy II*. We'll be using our gravity emitters to slow your spin and secure you to our hull. I see you have a docking tube on the roof of your shuttle. Can you unlock it? Save us a spacewalk and the time it would take to cut our way through."

"Yes! I can do that!" Zack transmitted. He checked his charge levels and found that they were still mostly full, thanks to his frugality. He routed power to the docking tube's armored shutters, sliding them open, and extended the tube into space. While he was at it, he turned atmo and artificial gravity back on in the cabin. They were about to be rescued. He could afford to splurge.

The hum of electronics and a slight rattle from the vents replaced the constant silence he'd lived with for four days. It would take a while for the backup scrubber to refresh the old air, but he was as badly off as he was going to be.

A shadow blocked the view out the windshield as a ship several times larger than his shuttle crossed over her. Zack saw a wave of particles as the *Journeyman*'s kinetic barrier washed over and wrapped around the shuttle. A dull clank rang out through the hull as the *Betsy II* was pulled in by the *Journeyman*'s NG emitters and locked in place.

"*Journeyman*, this is *Betsy II*. Be advised, most of the ship is depressurized."

"Copy. Where are you located, and do you or your crew require medical assistance?"

"We're on the bridge. The others are in stasis." A chill ran through him, and he knew he shouldn't have let the words slip as soon as he said them.

A pause. "Understood, *Betsy II*. Let them sleep, for now. We'll revive them in our medbay. Safer that way."

Pirates. Zack knew it in his gut, and he'd told them his crew was incapacitated. He'd been so grateful to be rescued, he'd made a first-year debating mistake. He'd spoken from weakness.

As a Spire scholar one test away from his doctorate, Zack doubled down. "You might want to bring an extra can of air for me as well, *Journeyman*. I've been sitting in here without atmo for days. I thought I was hallucinating when you first called."

There was a longer pause, and Zack imagined them rubbing their hands over the prize they'd just taken and its feeble crew. "What's your name, pilot?"

"Zack. Zack Lancestrom, sir."

"None of that 'sir' business, Zack. You stay calm and stay awake. I'm going to come down there myself now, and we'll bring enough air for all of you."

"Thank you!" Zack said. "We'd be dead without you! We're really grateful."

"Save your air, Zack. *Journeyman*, out."

Zack was already pulling up the life-support screen and putting the backup carbon-scrubber into overdrive. He assumed the man on the radio was the captain of the *Journeyman*, and the reason he was coming himself was so that Zack could transfer the ship to him the same way Orvendale had transferred her to him.

He needed to be ready by then.

With life support and artificial gravity turned back on, Zack stumbled across the cabin to start the process that would bring the others out of stasis.

There was still a chance these were the honest kind of pirates—the kind who would drop him and his crew off at a planet or space station where they could lick their wounds and start over, but someone like that would have asked them, upfront and for the record, to give up the salvage rights to the ship. The *Journeyman*'s captain hadn't, so either he intended to leave the *Betsy II* in Zack's ownership, or Zack would never be around to claim she'd been stolen.

The *Betsy II* was a military design. She had a full suite of after-action analysis and reporting functions. The last thing he did was activate the bridge recorders. He wanted evidence of whatever happened. No matter what he'd told his crew, Zack was planning for the worst.

It was twenty minutes before the three men in space suits from the *Journeyman* entered the *Betsy II* through her boarding tube, and Zack cycled them through the airlock. They were armed with shotguns, a typical shipboard weapon, because the soft lead pellets would shred flesh without doing excessive damage to the ship's interior. Zack watched them on the holos built into his armrest, chair turned to face the bridge door. He saw them sail through the door to Crew and Cargo, pull themselves past the various rooms, and stop in front of the passage to the cockpit.

Zack opened the other door, letting out a burst of air, and they stepped in.

He closed the door behind them, then opened the inner door, but only a few centimeters, his ears popping as the pressure equalized. Once he'd recovered, he opened it the rest of the way.

The three space-suited men stepped onto the bridge. Their leader must have been space-born; he was almost as tall as Zack. "You Lancestrom?"

"Yes."

He looked around the cabin, noting Zack's crew piled in the corner and their red flashing stasis lights. Then he touched his wrist control unit. "All good here, Vinnie. It's only the pilot. The crew is in stasis."

"Expecting trouble?" Zack asked.

"Can't be too careful out on the system outskirts," the man replied. "I see you got your air scrubber working."

"Only since we spoke," Zack said. It was mostly true. "I'd shut it off to save power for the radio and emergency beacon."

The man looked at Zack's crew piled in the corner, their wrist units flashing red, and said, "Noble of you, going down with the ship."

Zack shrugged. "I got trapped in here without a suit. Seemed like the best way to save everyone."

"You were probably right," the man said. "It's a shame we found you first."

Zack took it calmly. He'd expected as much. "I'm willing to transfer ownership of the *Betsy II* to you in exchange for our lives."

The man nodded. "You're going to transfer the ship to us, and we're going to tow her with us to our destination, but you won't be coming. Can't risk taking on passengers, the ones we have are enough trouble as it is."

"You could lock us in here once you had control of the ship and let us out when we reach the next station."

"You don't want that. We're heading to the Kraken's Maw on a special delivery for Desdemona Venturi." Zack wasn't sure who that was, but from the pirate's tone, he should find out. "Best case, she kills you and punishes us because she values her privacy. She'll be upset we took a detour, but less so after we give her a cut of the salvage."

"And worst case?"

"Slavery, fighting pits, organ harvesters, and medical research," the man said. The last one surprised Zack, but he supposed interstellar corporations had to do their illegal experimentation somewhere. "You're not worth as much as the shuttle, and even I have things I won't do."

"Why should I make it easy on you?"

The man gave him a sympathetic smile. "Because my scruples don't stop short of torture. We'll wake your crew up, one by one, and then torture them. And torture you. We won't enjoy it, mind you, but we'll do it. We've got debts, and we're making this run at no profit, so your ship is going to buy us a little breathing room. It's nothing personal. We just need it more than you do."

"Especially after you're dead," the man behind him quipped with a nasty grin.

"I believe you," Zack said. "I guess the only thing I can say, then, is that there's a star spider on this ship."

The man smirked. "Yeah, right."

Then he frowned as something sticky and green slapped into the back of his suit helmet. It hissed and smoked, and the glass cracked.

"Up there!" the second man yelled, and he raised his shotgun to shoot Kissh'ik as she ran across the wall.

Ultimus smashed into him—hadn't been that hard for Clavicus to tamper with the stasis light, so it looked like the crew was still out—and Zack shot the third man twice through the chest before he could fire on the mercenary.

The Journeyman's captain's helmet popped like a dropped fishbowl, and he screamed as the acid Kissh'ik had spat kept eating through his suit and burned his skin. Zack tried to shoot him, but he couldn't keep his aim steady.

"Easy, Zack," Anya said, pushing his pulser down. "Ultimus and Clav will finish this."

The captain was scrambling for his dropped weapon, but

Clavicus stomped on his arm and then dropped on him, elbow first, like an all-star wrestler. Something cracked, and the captain cried out in pain. Ultimus stood with the other man's shotgun in his hands.

"Enough!" Zack said, raising his voice, and the two remaining pirates froze, the captain cradling his arm, the other one covered by Ultimus.

"You have no idea of the level of crap that is going to fall on you for this," the captain said, his suit still smoking and his eyes moist from the pain.

"You're right," Zack said. "I have no idea, and because we're holding the guns and you aren't, we get the opportunity to find out. Some other time. Far from here. Now, you're going to hand over your ship."

The captain laughed. "I'd rather—"

Zack shot him in the face, and he dropped, nerveless. Zack rubbed his eyes. "He was going to say 'die,' right? I mean, I hope he was, but I'm not thinking straight."

"I think he was, babe," Anya said gently.

"Great," Zack said. He pointed his gun at the lone surviving pirate and said, "What's your name, friend?"

"Sid, sir."

"How about it, Sid? Would *you* rather die?"

The man swallowed. "I would prefer living."

Zack kept the gun on him for a few more seconds, then sagged back into the pilot's seat. "Good man. Now, tell me about your ship. How many crew members?"

"About forty, sir."

"What about security? Do you have cameras, and someone watching them?"

The young man hesitated. Zack sighed and lifted his pulser.

"Wait! There are cameras, but they've been turned off! The captain didn't want any evidence."

Zack sat back and closed his eyes. *Forty crew members, but their captain didn't want witnesses. We might be able to take them by surprise.* He looked at Sid and said, "Call your friends on the Journeyman, Sid. Let them know you're having some comm trouble, but you and the captain are heading back."

Sid stiffened. "Are you going to kill them? The rest of the crew?"

"Only if they shoot at me first," Zack answered. "We'll drop any survivors at the first port of call."

"Think carefully about what you're going to say," Ultimus added. "If they break away or shove the shuttle toward the planet, you'll die with us."

Sid nodded and activated his comm.

"Clavicus, can you fix up one of those suits so I can make it from here to the Journeyman?"

"Sure, boss."

"Great. The rest of you get ready for a fight. We're going to counter-board that ship."

PART VIII

The Synthesis is the beginning of a journey, not the end of one.

EPILOGUE

Shirr
Void Space

Meshar Ak-Shirr, star spider, weaver by birth and by his own will, nestled within his great living ship. To all appearances, he was dead, his great heart tube halted between two beats, but his mind's claws rested against the plasma web that underlaid all things.

And he waited.

He had no concept of time in this state. He and his kind had finished cultivating a spiral, elevating, consuming, and seeding the life within. Then they had departed. An age that might have been minutes or centuries passed.

He felt a tremor.

Then a vibration.

One of the scouts had found something.

The weaver's consciousness sparked, eight eyes glowing with molten light as he ingested the emotions of the one who called herself Kissh'ik. Excitement, longing, and bottomless curiosity flashed through him, along with pictures of a place of sand, rock, and metal, and then a world seen from space.

She had attached herself to a local species.

He discarded feelings of affection and loyalty the scout had begun to feel for its symbiont—such things were necessary and contained strands of truth but were not the convergence of paths.

What made his heart contract and send hemolymph flooding through dried limbs was her disgust, her anger, and her fear. Darkness had entered this universe, *his* universe, and Meshar Ak-Shirr's spirit sang with the thrill of hunting something deadly and unknown.

He stilled the vibration of the web with a thought. Kask Al-Reshur was active in that spiral. It would take several years for Meshar to pull himself there from void space, and he did not want young Kask to seize his prey.

He plucked the thread, keeping his thoughts simple so the scout would not be overwhelmed.

Watch. Wait. Be silent.

I am coming.

The Planetary Hall
Pnyx, Skyward, Capital District of Politeia IV
4387.1.2 Interstellar

Bernie Hallek fought to keep his apprehension under control as the armed woman led him past the black-armored guards and down the corridors of the Planetary Hall.

It had been an eventful week for Bernie. The Council had been dissolved. PPG soldiers had pulled him out of his bed and thrown him into the back of a transport. Some people argued that the entire sophistocracy had been overthrown. Certainly, Bernie's future was as uncertain as it had ever been—but that had been the case since he failed his Synthesis exam... and had a bit of a nervous breakdown over it.

The woman—who'd met him and his "escort" at the military annex—brought him to what had formerly been the governor's office, although now, Bernie supposed, it was a king's office in every regard except in name. Like most of the important rooms in the Planetary Hall they passed, it was flanked by two guards in black carapace armor.

"ID?" one of the guards said.

The woman didn't complain; she just offered him her wrist, which he scanned before waving them both in. An officer in a black uniform—also armed with a pistol—was already inside, as was the ruler of Politeia IV.

Governor Alex Lancestrom stood from behind the desk and smiled. "Bernie! It's good to see you, my boy! How long has it been?"

Bernie had idolized the man—his progenitor—for most of his life. He knew the governor's implants showed precisely when they'd last met. Still, he felt honored that a man like him would take the time to show interest, even if the times were uncertain and the governor's intentions most uncertain of all. "Thank you, sir. It's been four years, give or take, when Zack and I finished our undergraduate studies."

A shadow passed on the governor's face at the mention of Zack, and Bernie kicked himself for it.

Alex smiled. "It's been too long. Now, I know things have been a bit hectic on the news, and I can only imagine what a good Spire graduate must think of me, overthrowing the charter like that."

Bernie reddened. "Begging your pardon, sir, but I didn't

graduate. I broke down during the Synthesis, right after... well, I broke down."

Alex waved the thought away as if it hadn't been the most monumental failure in Bernie's life, short of being born in the same generation as Zack Lancestrom. "We'll talk about that in a moment, but first, I'd like to introduce you to Colonel Orvendale, the leader of the new Capital Guard."

The officer in the black uniform, whose skin reminded Bernie of dark-stained cherry wood, offered him his hand, and Bernie shook it. "Pleased to meet you, Colonel."

"Mr. Hallek," the colonel said cordially.

"And you arrived with Susan Ramirez, my new chief of security. Susan came to us from the Combine, from an outfit called the 'Wildcats,'" Alex said, gesturing to the petite woman with the intense gaze. "I'm guessing she didn't introduce herself."

"She didn't," Bernie said.

Susan made no move to offer him her hand.

"We have a third guest coming," Alex said, "and I'd like you to observe our meeting, Bernie. I think it will answer many of your as-of-yet unspoken questions, and we'll kill two of the proverbial birds with one stone."

"As you wish, sir."

Alex sat behind his desk and waved Bernie to the chair on the right, while Susan took her position against the far wall on the same side. Colonel Orvendale took position on the left side, next to the empty visitor's chair, but made no move to sit in it.

Bernie waited in awkward silence for several minutes until there was a knock at the door. One of the black-armored soldiers poked his head in. "It's Lieutenant Colonel Williamson, sir."

"Send him in," Alex said, standing up, and Bernie stood with him.

An officer in his late thirties, wearing the gray and black uniform of the PPG but without a sidearm, came into the room. He moved purposefully but calmly to stand behind the left chair, brought his heels together, and said, "Lieutenant Colonel Williamson, reporting as ordered, Governor."

"At ease, Colonel," Alex said. "I'd like to introduce you to Bernie Hallek, who recently started working in city planning over in the Solano district."

Either the colonel knew why Bernie was here, or he did a better job than Bernie did of hiding his confusion. He shook Bernie's hand; the man's grip was firm but restrained. "Pleasure to meet you, Mr. Hallek."

"Likewise, Colonel," Bernie said.

"I'd also like to introduce Colonel Orvendale, formerly of the *Memento Mori*'s garrison. I understand you just missed each other."

"Yes," Williamson said, his demeanor a touch frostier. "It seems whatever misunderstanding happened that day, it's all been sorted out."

"Quite," Orvendale said, making no move to shake the other officer's hand.

"And this is Susan Ramirez," Alex continued. "You might know her as 'Jericho.' She's a Combine mercenary on loan to me for the foreseeable future."

"Pleasure to meet you, Ms. Ramirez. Were you part of the group that attempted to extract the governor's son?"

"I was," she said.

"He got lucky twice, it seems. First against you, and then against me."

"I'm sure," the woman said in a tone that meant she believed nothing of the sort.

Williamson reddened.

"Please, take a seat, Colonel. I'm afraid we don't have a lot of time."

"Of course," Williamson said, and the three of them—Bernie, Alex, and Williamson—sat down.

Alex proceeded to tell the most amazing story Bernie had ever heard about how a group of dissidents—actual Dissidents!—had built shelters in the desert in and around the Starship Boneyard, and that they had infiltrated both the sophistocracy and the PPG to such a great extent that Alex had no choice but to dissolve the government and take direct control of the military.

"You have proof of this?" Williamson asked.

"Yes," Alex said, "and I specifically have footage of one of their squads planning the murder of refugees in order to discredit the sophistocracy. I plan to share it with the people of Politeia soon, but first, I need to clean house." He clasped his hands on the table. "I'll be blunt, Colonel. We don't know how deep this conspiracy runs, but Sam Meritt spoke well of you."

"I thought highly of him as well, sir. His death..."

"Was a tragedy," Alex agreed. "But we can still turn it to good. I had my ties to the military from my days in the service, of course. But while Sam worked for me, I had him identify good, solid officers—a network of people we could trust in the event of a crisis. It's the reason the planetary guard and the government have held together at a time when, I believe, these Dissidents tried to topple them."

Williamson nodded slowly. "I think, if they did, they must have been surprised by how quickly the PPG sided with you, sir."

"Good," Alex said with a warm smile. "Because we're not going to stop them, Colonel. We're going to freeze their assets, root out their supporters, push them back into the desert, and *bury* them."

Bernie swallowed at the ferocity of the governor's smile.

"It's going to take years, maybe decades, but we're going to take our planet back. I called you here to ask if I could count on your support?"

"Of course, sir," Williamson said without hesitation. "And if I may, I have a few like-minded individuals I'd like to bring into the circle as well. We were just discussing how, in our opinion, you're the only person who can truly hold this planet together, sir."

"Thank you, Colonel," Alex said, shaking the man's hand. "We'll return to the Council and the Charter someday, I promise you. For now, return to your unit. I'm afraid we won't see each other for some time, but Susan will be your point of contact as we organize the defense of this world."

"Very well, sir," Williamson said, and Bernie thought he saw a trace of... something in the man's eyes. He'd have to mention it to the governor afterward. What if—

Faster than a snake, Williamson ripped the pistol from Orvendale's holster, pointed it at the governor, and pulled the trigger.

Click.

Boom! Susan "Jericho" Ramirez's pistol went off and blew Lieutenant Colonel Williamson off his feet. The round turned a fist-sized chunk of the man's head to mist, gore, and blood spatter. For a split second, Bernie thought the blood was black, but after a few seconds in the light from the windows, it turned an ordinary red.

"Did we record all that?" Alex asked.

"Yes, sir," Orvendale said.

Bernie stammered. "Your gun..."

"Wasn't loaded," Orvendale confirmed. "The information Zack Lancestrom provided was valuable, but we still have a long way to go before we understand how deep their network is."

"You might have taken him alive," Alex said to his bodyguard.

"With all due respect, sir, that wasn't my assessment. We knew he might try something. I was *waiting* for it, and he still pulled the trigger before I did. There's no telling what he might have done if we'd let him live."

"Yes, well... I suppose you must be right. Now, Bernie, I have an important question for you, one that should have been asked of you some time ago—a wrong I will rectify now. What is a citizen's obligation to the state?" he asked with a smile.

And Bernie hesitated. Six months and a lifetime ago, he would have said "Everything" without a scrap of irony, but things had changed for him. The pain and confusion of being rejected, of getting his self-esteem knocked to rock bottom and rebuilt from there... it had changed him. He could see, now, why Zack used to get so frustrated with him when he blurted things out. He was more measured. And his identity no longer revolved around competing to become the governor's favorite son. He'd gone to the Solano district because it was one of the poorer districts on the planet. There had been an element of self-preservation—he'd offered his help to people who couldn't afford to reject him. But he'd been needed, and even in the month he'd been working there, he'd made himself useful in ways that were deeply satisfying to the people of several townships.

But the question triggered something in him, something beyond rote or wanting to please the man he idolized. He knew he wouldn't have been able to answer it before, but he could now. "Nothing, sir."

Alex frowned in disappointment.

And Bernie smiled. "The citizen doesn't *owe* the state their life or service, sir, but inasmuch as I find *my* fulfillment in serving others, on the planet of my birth, as part of a government that I believe in, then the state may have as much of me as it needs until it needs me no longer." And through it, he knew he would become more than he was.

The governor was stunned for a moment, and the look he gave Bernie afterward filled him with... pride? Faith? Hope? "I do believe that was the right answer," Alex said. "We won't talk about you taking on the Lancestrom name yet, partly because that should be earned, and partly because, in times like these, having a different name may keep you alive. But I have work for a man like you, Bernie. The sophistocracy desperately needs men and women it can trust."

Nightkin Flagship Father Night's Promise, Reprisal Fleet
Unnamed Binary System
42nd Generation Since Exile

Mephyt sat in her command chair on the flag bridge, looking through the massive observation window with her one good eye.

Across the unimaginable distance, the bright yellow primary and sullen red secondary stars burned as they turned about each other. It was like home in every way except the one that mattered. The exiles had never been sent here. Even if they had been, Father Night and Lady Dark would not have been here to bless them, as she had been twice-blessed.

The Reprisal Fleet was stranded here. Without the technological and supernatural resources of their homeworld at their disposal, they would require tremendous amounts of power to tear a rift open between their universes.

The great work had already begun. Fleet constructors had put the two star-encircling rings in place. Panel by panel, they would shroud the lesser star until all of its hellish fury served the Reprisal Fleet and her, its Undying. With reinforcements from Warden's Moon, she and this generation's grandchildren would seek retribution against all of creation, not only in one universe but in many.

One of her deacons entered and knelt to her left, at the edge of her view.

The chimes that hung from her headdress clinked softly as she turned toward him. "What is it?"

"A report from Politeia, mistress. Prime matter's existence has been discovered by the authorities."

Pinpricks of fire ran down the ruined right side of her face. "Unfortunate. And the spread?"

"Entering its second phase."

"Good," she said. "Send twelve more of the kin to assist the process. We can't afford more setbacks."

He left in silence. Her command needed no confirmation but her own.

Mephyt's eye was drawn to the containment unit that shared a shadowed corner of the flag bridge with her. Father Night had told the Church of Night that prime matter was the raw chaos from which all of existence had sprung, but Father Night always lied. The oily black liquid suspended at the center of the glass tube roiled and lunged, hungry and hateful. For all its lethality, it was fragile in the open, easily destroyed by most sources of light. Their supply was dwindling; the inhabitants of this cluster had proved inexplicably resilient.

And there was only one source of replacement, her own blood, for she was twice-blessed and twice-cursed.

She rose from the command seat, careful not to tread on her white robes or the black and gold covering that hung from her arms. Another wave of fire passed through her as she took the razor from the altar and chose a new place to cut. The whispers in her bones told her this was temporary, that once the holy dark took hold of a planet, she could winnow more Undying from the survivors, and they would take on her burden

She knew the whispers lied, but she was Undying, cursed with pain, blessed with purpose.

She would blot out the stars until only darkness remained.

MFS-570 *Journeyman*, Airlock
Politeia VII, Stable Orbit
4387.1.2 Interstellar

Zack Lancestrom's breath fogged up the visor of his spacesuit helmet. As someone who'd been born on a space station, he knew that meant warm air hitting cold glass, and *that* meant cheap insulation.

It didn't speak well for the Journeyman or her crew, because he'd stripped the tan spacesuit off their dead captain. If spacers were going to skimp on the one thing between them and the vacuum, there was no telling where else they'd cut corners. Hopefully, they'd cut corners on the security of their ship.

I guess we're about to find out.

To be continued...

THE ADVENTURE CONTINUES...

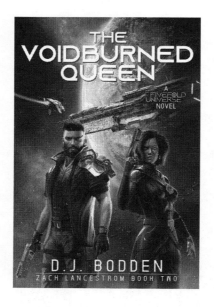

... in *The Voidburned Queen*, book 2 in the Zack Lancestrom series by D.J. Bodden.

A broken ship.
A legacy tainted.
A path into the dark.

Zack Lancestrom betrayed his father and left his homeworld to search for an ancient technological artifact called the Forge, but no plan survives a jump from inside a gravity well. His ship is wrecked, and an unscrupulous space captain tried to salvage it from under him. To top it off, he's just unwittingly stolen cargo from the biggest criminal syndicate in the star cluster.

Not every problem can be solved with a gun. After they take control of a merchant ship with the syndicate and the Federal Fleet hot on their tail, Zack and his crew find themselves plunged in a decade-long conflict for control over the star cluster. Can Zack ignore the syndicate's brutality and continue his quest, or will he have to fight just to keep his crew alive? And what of reports that the syndicate's leader is actually from his homeworld?

The Voidburned Queen is the second book in Zack Lancestrom's adventure, a swashbuckling space opera full of futuristic action, unsanctioned uses of advanced technology, and memorable characters. Humanity has spread across the galaxy, but they are not alone, and Zack's quest to find a lost pre-war artifact may be the only thing standing between this universe and an inter-dimensional species that wants to blot out the light of the stars.

BOOK REVIEWS

If you loved *The Starborn Heir*, please consider leaving a rating or a short, honest review on Amazon: The Starborn Heir—just a couple of lines about your overall reading experience. Thank you in advance!

★

FIVEFOLD UNIVERSE

Visit the FiveFold Universe website to learn more about the author, as well as an in depth look at the characters and technology used in this book at: www.fivefolduniverse.com

Follow FiveFold Universe on Facebook at https://www.facebook.com/FiveFoldUniverse

Join the FiveFold mailing list to get updates on the newest releases and get a free downloadable poster of Zack and his crew.

DRAMATIS PERSONAE

The Crew

Anya Vesperian: a medically-disbarred cyberneticist, Zack Lancestrom's ex-girlfriend.

ARK-II: a pre-war super AI in a small box.

Clavicus Rext: an undercity scavenger and engineering savant.

Joseph "Ultimus" Thragg: a Combine mercenary, fallen from glory.

Zack Lancestrom: the runaway heir to the Politeian governorship, Anya Vesperian's ex-boyfriend, Alex Lancestrom's son.

The Politeians

Alex Lancestrom: governor of Politeia, Zack Lancestrom and Bernie Hallek's father.

Andrew Scamander: youngest member of the Politeian Council.

Bernie Hallek: a Spire candidate, Alex Lancestrom's son.

Elena Montesquieu: Free trader, Alex Lancestrom's former lover.

Jawhee the Vibroblade: a gang leader in Pnyx, affiliated with the Venturi Cartel.

Lewis Williamson: lieutenant colonel in the PSDF's special forces.

Lucy "Mad Moe" Gallagher: a gang leader in Anuradhapura.

Sam Meritt: a former Combine mercenary, Alex Lancestrom's head of security.

Shiva Parnavan: one of the best cybernetics' surgeons on Politeia.

Gavin Richter: senior member of the Council.

The Splinter Fleet

Ebbe Lindström: professor of Greek and Byzantine studies, husband of Karin Lindström.

Emma Lindström: a skilled engineer and passionate conservationist, Erik Lindström's daughter.

Erik Lindström: the second governor of the Splinter Fleet, Laeticia Lindström's husband, Emma Lindström's father, Thomas Lindström's son.

Karin Lindström: senior officer of the Splinter Fleet, wife of Ebbe Lindström and Thomas Nalutuesha, mother of Thomas Lindström.

Thomas Ebbe Lindström (Junior): Federal Fleet veteran and first governor of the people who would settle Politeia IV, father of Erik Lindström, son of Karin Lindström and Thomas Nalutuesha.

Thomas Nalutuesha: flag captain of the Splinter Fleet.

The Combine

Kyle "Ajax" Antarxes: executive officer of Lynx's Wildcats.

Jessica "Lynx" Jeppesen: commander of Lynx's Wildcats, daughter of Joseph Thragg.

Susan "Jericho" Ramirez: designated marksman of Lynx's Wildcats.

The Dissidents

Ross Perkins: leader of the Dissidents.

ACKNOWLEDGMENTS

I spent ten years learning how to write this book. It's the best thing I've written, at least until I write the next one.

I want to thank my mom for making me love books and words, Toria and Doug for suffering through my early short-story phase, and Eileen and Gercel, who have always been there. Thanks to Carina Xiao for helping me through the emotional rollercoaster of early self-publishing and Aaron, Adam, and Jeanette for making me a commercial writer, and Elli for keeping me sane and accountable. Thanks to Tom and Dave for reading my stuff and offering honest feedback; Adam, Ben, Beth, Brian, Caroline, Ceb, Crystal, Dan, Heather, Jake, Jess, Joseph, Kelly, Kevin, Lana, Michael, Mike, Nat, Robert, and Tom for each adding to The Starborn Heir in different ways. Thanks to G.S. and Kevin for doing an editorial on it, even though "can you read my book" is probably one of the most dreadful sentences an author can hear.

Thanks to Cat, Chris, Clay & Susan, David, Griffin, Jennifer, Jim, and Steve for talking me through some of this at DCon. I took several pages of notes.

Thanks to Fabian and M.Z. for loaning me your PhDs.

And thanks to the constellation of people who contributed by making me laugh, catching my eye, breaking my heart, and generally showing me how amazing or terrible human beings can be. You're all in here, pinned like butterflies, until the world burns. I love you all.

And if you're one of the rare people who read the acknowledgments, I hope this part of the book made you feel something —anything—too.

COPYRIGHT

The Starborn Heir is a work of fiction. Names, characters, places, and incidents either are the product of the author's imagination or are used fictitiously. Any resemblance to actual persons living or dead, events, or locales is entirely coincidental.

Copyright © 2021 by D.J. Bodden and Shadow Alley Press, Inc.

All rights reserved.

No part of this publication may be reproduced, distributed, or transmitted in any form or by any means, including photocopying, recording, or other electronic or mechanical methods, without the prior written permission of the publisher, except in the case of brief quotations embodied in critical reviews and certain other noncommercial uses permitted by copyright law. For permission requests, email the publisher, subject line "Attention: Permissions Coordinator," at the email address below.

JStrode@ShadowAlleyPress.com

Made in the USA
Columbia, SC
06 August 2024